Fall of the House of Ramesses, A Novel of Ancient Egypt
Book 3: Tausret

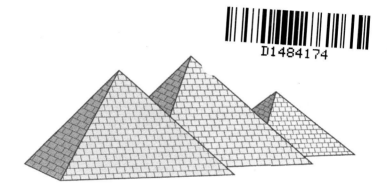

By Max Overton

Writers Exchange E-Publishing

http://www.writers-exchange.com

Fall of the House of Ramesses, A Novel of Ancient Egypt: Book 3: Tausret
Copyright 2015 Max Overton
Writers Exchange E-Publishing
PO Box 372
ATHERTON QLD 4883

Cover Art by: Julie Napier

Published by Writers Exchange E-Publishing
http://www.writers-exchange.com

ISBN **ebook**: 978-1-925191-17-2
Print: 978-1-925191-91-2 (WEE Assigned)

First Thoughts

A work of historical fiction comes from the mind of the writer, but it is dependent on historical facts. When I write about relatively modern times I have not only the bare bones of history to hang my story on, but also the personal writings of the characters and their contemporaries, and a host of relevant facts and opinions to flesh out the story. The further back you go in time, the less is available to draw upon, and by the time you reach Ancient Egypt, even the facts are disputed. Egyptologists have pored through the ruins of a past civilisation, examined the colourful walls of rock tombs and their contents, studied temple hieroglyphics and self-serving inscriptions of the kings, and deciphered fragments of papyrus to paint us a picture of what society was like three thousand years ago and more. It is necessarily incomplete, for much has been lost and what has not been lost is not always understood. The history of Ancient Egypt is a work in progress.

When I, as a writer of historical fiction, attempt to tell a tale from the distant past, I work with what is given me by serious researchers. But what am I to do with an almost unknown king like Siptah? He occurs in the record as Ramesses-Siptah and Merenptah-Siptah, and researchers are unsure whether they are the same person or even if they are king Siptah. Some people consider them to be sons of Ramesses the Great. Nobody knows for certain whom Siptah's parents are either. He has been called a son of Merenptah, and of Seti II, but is perhaps more likely a son of Amenmesse, and his mother is thought to be a foreigner, possibly a Syrian called Suterere. There was another Syrian who rose to prominence at about this time--Bay. He rose to become Chancellor (Treasurer) of Egypt and styled himself as a kingmaker who put Siptah on the throne 'of his father'. If Bay (a Syrian) was brother to Suterere (a Syrian), then that might make Bay the uncle of Siptah and give him a reason for making him king.

It is known that Seti II left behind an infant son Seti-Merenptah, yet Siptah, also a child, became king instead. Chancellor Bay supported him, but probably few other people did. The kingdoms had just come through a long civil war that ended with Amenmesse's defeat, yet only a year later, Seti II died and Amenmesse's son was on the throne. Tausret ruled as regent, but why did she favour her nephew over her son? Then a few years later three deaths occurred that changed everything. Were the three deaths coincidence or were they connected?

FLong hours were spent disentangling the blood lines and making reasoned assumptions of relationships and motives. Some of my decisions can be seen at a glance in the *Simplified Family Tree of Fall of the House of Ramesses* (below), and others appear in the pages of this book.

And so it goes on. The bones of history make the framework of my story and I must decide which opinions will clothe the bones in flesh and skin. If I choose well, my story takes on a life of its own.

I have researched this period extensively, and while I cannot claim to have read everything, I believe I have weighed up sufficient evidence to make an informed decision.

My main sources have been:

Anglim, Simon et al, 2002, *Fighting Techniques of the Ancient World*, Thomas Dunne Books

Budge, EA Wallis, 1959, *Egyptian Religion: Ideas of the Afterlife in Ancient Egypt*, University Books

Budge, EA Wallis, 1967, *The Egyptian Book of the Dead*, Dover Publications

Dodson, Aidan, 2000, *Monarchs of the Nile*, The American University in Cairo Press

Dodson, Aidan, 2010, *Poisoned Legacy: The Fall of the Nineteenth Egyptian Dynasty*, The American University in Cairo Press

Dodson, Aidan & Hilton, Dyan, 2004, *The Complete Royal Families of Ancient Egypt,* Thames & Hudson

Frood, Elizabeth, 2007, *Biographical Texts from Ramessid Egypt*, Society of Biblical Literature

Petrie, William Matthew Flinders, 2005, *A History of Egypt: Vol III. From the XIXth to the XXXth Dynasties*, Adamant Media Corporation

Romer, John, 1984, *Ancient Lives: The Story of the Pharaoh's Tombmakers*, Guild Publishing

Shaw, Garry J, 2012, *The Pharaoh: Life at Court and on Campaign*, Thames & Hudson

Tyldesley, Joyce, 2000, *Ramesses: Egypt's Greatest Pharaoh*, Viking

Wilkinson, Richard H, 2000, *The Complete Temples of Ancient Egypt*, Thames & Hudson

Wilkinson, Richard H, editor, 2012, *Tausret: Forgotten Queen and Pharaoh of Egypt*, Oxford University Press

I would like to acknowledge Jim Ashton, an Egyptologist, and expert on the Ramesside dynasties, who kindly read through my manuscript, pointing out any errors and inconsistencies. Similarly, Sara Waldheim, an enthusiastic and knowledgeable reader of all things Egyptian, gave my manuscript her careful attention.

Julie Napier was, as always, my 'First Reader' and I am indebted to her constant attention to my storytelling. She pulls no punches and once told me, over 100,000 words into a previous manuscript, that the story lacked credibility. On re-reading it, I agreed, so I scrapped several months' worth of work and started again. Excellent reviews for the finished product have proven her right. I am truly grateful for her forthrightness and honesty.

Julie Napier also comes in for thanks as my cover artist. A skilled photographer and experienced artist, she has created all of my book covers.

I would like to thank my many readers too. Some of them wrote to me when they reached the end of my Amarnan Kings series, asking if I would write another Egyptian series. At the time, I was writing another book in a completely different genre, but I started doing some reading and eventually put my other work aside and started *Fall of the House of Ramesses*. I am hoping they will write to me again and tell me what they would like me to write next.

Some notes on Fall of the House of Ramesses

In any novel about ancient cultures and races, some of the hardest things to get used to are the names of people and places. Often these names are unfamiliar in spelling and pronunciation. It does not help that for reasons dealt with below, the spelling, and hence the pronunciation is sometimes arbitrary. To help readers keep track of the characters in this book I have included some notes on names in the ancient Egyptian language. I hope they will be useful.

In Ancient Egypt a person's name was much more than just an identifying label. A name meant something, it was descriptive, and a part of a person's being. For instance, Merenptah means 'Beloved of Ptah', and Tausret means 'Mighty Lady'. Knowledge of the true name of something gave one power over it, and in primitive societies a person's real name is not revealed to any save the chief or immediate family. A myth tells of the creator god Atum speaking the name of a thing and it would spring fully formed into existence. Another myth says the god Re had a secret name and went to extraordinary lengths to keep it secret.

The Egyptian language, like written Arabic and Hebrew, was without vowels. This produces some confusion when ancient Egyptian words are transliterated. The god of Waset in Egyptian reads *mn*, but in English this can be represented as Amen, Amon, Ammon or Amun. The form one chooses for proper names is largely arbitrary, but I have tried to keep to accepted forms where possible. King Amenmesse's birth name was possibly Messuwy, though this royal name can have various spellings depending on the author's choice. It is also sometimes seen as Amenmesses, Amenmose, Amunmesse and Amunmose. I have used the first of these spellings (Amenmesse) in *Fall of the House of Ramesses*, and most names that include that of the same god is spelled Amen-. The god himself I have chosen to call Amun.

Similarly, the king known in *Fall of the House of Ramesses* as Merenptah is often known as Merneptah. Either spelling is acceptable.

The names of the kings have been simplified. Egyptian pharaohs had five names, known as the Horus name, the Nebti name, the Golden Falcon name, the Prenomen and the Nomen. Only the Nomen was given at birth, the other names being coronation names. The Horus name dates from pre-dynastic times and was given to a king upon his coronation. All kings had a

Horus name, but by the eighteenth dynasty it was seldom used. The Nebti name dates from the time of the unification of Egypt and shows the special relationship the king had to the vulture-goddess Nekhbet of Upper Egypt and the cobra-goddess Wadjet of Lower Egypt. The Golden Falcon name conveys the idea of eternity, as gold neither rusts nor tarnishes, and dates from the Old Kingdom. It perhaps symbolises the reconciliation of Horus and Set, rather than the victory of Horus over Set as the titles are usually non-aggressive in nature.

By the time of the eighteenth dynasty, the prenomen, or throne name, had become the most important coronation name, replacing the Horus name in many inscriptions. Since the eleventh dynasty, the prenomen has always contained the name of Re or Ra.

The nomen was the birth name, and this is the name by which the kings in this book are commonly known. The birth names most common in the nineteenth and twentieth dynasty were Ramesses and Seti. Successive kings with the same birth name did not use the method we use to distinguish between them--namely numbers (Ramesses I and Ramesses II). In fact, the birth name often ceased to be used once they became king and the coronation prenomen distinguished them. Ramesses I became Menpehtyre, and Ramesses II became Usermaatre, while Merenptah became Baenre, and Seti II became Userkheperure. Birth names were still used by family members on informal occasions and I have often used prenomen and nomen together, just so the reader is absolutely sure of the person's identity.

Another simplification has occurred with place names and titles. In the thirteenth and twelfth century B.C.E., Egypt as a name for the country did not exist. The land around the Nile Valley and Delta was called Kemet or The Black Land by its inhabitants, and the desert Deshret or The Red Land. Much later, Greeks called it Aigyptos from which we get Egypt. Other common terms for the country were The Two Lands (Upper and Lower Kemet), and the Land of Nine Bows (the nine traditional enemies). Likewise Lower Egypt (to the north) was known as Ta Mehu, and Upper Egypt (to the south) was known as Ta Shemau. The name 'Nile' is also from the Greek, so I have used the usual designation of the time--Great River, or Iteru.

Similarly, the king of Egypt or Kemet was later known as 'Pharaoh', but this term derives from the phrase Per-aa which originally meant the Great House or royal palace. Over the years the meaning changed to encompass the idea of the central government, and later the person of the king himself. The Greeks changed Per-Aa to Pharaoh. I have decided to remain with the ubiquitous title of 'king'.

During the eighteenth dynasty, the kings ruled from a city known variously as Apet, No-Amun or Waset in the Fourth province or sepat of Ta Shemau, which itself was also called Waset; or just 'niwt' which meant 'city'. This capital city the Greeks called Thebes. The worship of Amun was centred here and the city was sometimes referred to as the City of Amun. I have called this great city by its old name of Waset.

Ramesses II built a new capital city in the eastern delta and called it Per-Ramesses, meaning literally 'House of Ramesses'. Merenptah moved the capital to the ancient city of Men-nefer, known to the Greeks as Memphis, as this city belonged to the god Ptah and Merenptah was literally 'Beloved of Ptah'.

The gods of Egypt are largely known to modern readers by their Greek names; for instance, Osiris, Thoth and Horus. I have decided to keep the names as they were originally known to the inhabitants of Kemet--Asar, Djehuti and Heru. The Greek names for unfamiliar gods can be found in the section Places, People, Gods & Things in the *Fall of the House of Ramesses* at the end of this book.

Mention should be made of the incidence of writing amongst the characters in this book. It is generally accepted that no more than 1% of ancient Egyptians were literate and that knowledge of the complex hieroglyphic writing was the purview of the scribes and priests. Hieroglyphics are commonly seen in the formal inscriptions on temple and tomb walls. However, there was also another form of writing in ancient Egypt. This is called hieratic writing and is a form of cursive script used for writing administrative documents, accounts, legal texts, and letters, as well as medical, literary, and religious texts. This form of writing is commonly found on papyrus scraps, painted on wood or stone, or scratched onto pottery ostraca (shards). Thousands of these have been found, often closely associated with the lower strata of society, and it is believed that many more people were at least marginally literate than is commonly accepted. There is every reason to believe that people for whom some form of notation was essential to their everyday lives were capable of some level of writing.

When I refer to a person writing in *Fall of the House of Ramesses,* it should not be assumed that the person is fully literate, but instead has knowledge of writing consistent with their place in Egyptian society.

Simplified Family Tree of
Fall of the House of Ramesses (III)

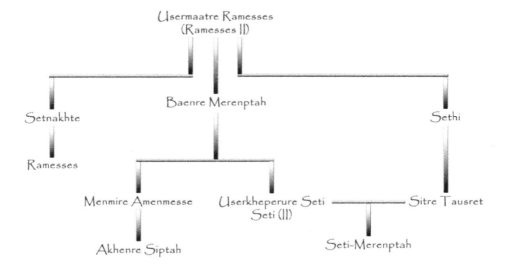

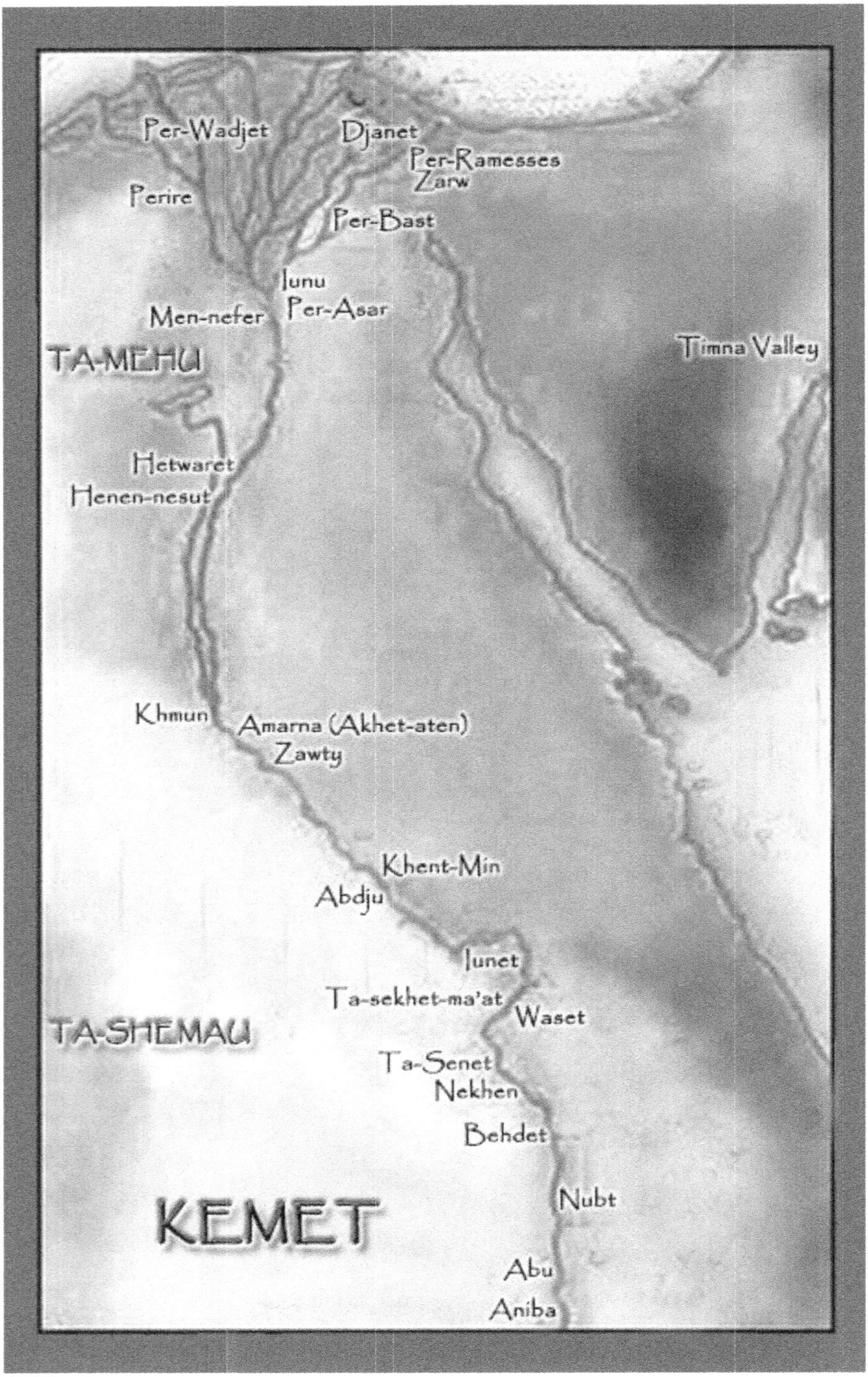
Per-Wadjet
Djanet
Per-Ramesses
Zarw
Perire
Per-Bast
Iunu
Per-Asar
Men-nefer
TA-MEHU
Timna Valley
Hetwaret
Henen-nesut
Khmun
Amarna (Akhet-aten)
Zawty
Khent-Min
Abdju
Iunet
Ta-sekhet-ma'at
Waset
TA-SHEMAU
Ta-Senet
Nekhen
Behdet
Nubt
KEMET
Abu
Aniba

Chapter 1
Interregnum

The rescue attempt took place in the darkness before the dawn on the last day of the last month of Akhet, when the palace guards dozed at their posts and the servants were just rising from their sleep. A small party of armed men slipped ashore at the Waset docks and crept silently through deserted streets, rushing the sleepy guards at the kitchen entrance and invading the palace. They encountered a few yawning servants who barely had time to widen their eyes or open their mouths in surprise before they were cut down. Torches guttered low in the passages and hallways of the great building, scarcely lighting the Kushite soldiers as they rushed toward the inner chamber where King Menmire Amenmesse was housed.

The guards outside the prison suite were tired but still alert when the Kushite warriors hurled themselves out of the shadows with bronze spear heads glinting in the torchlight. Two men died immediately, but the others stood back-to-back and fought with spear, sword and axe. Shouts and screams aroused the palace, but the last guard died before help could arrive. The Kushites broke down the door and found a naked middle-aged man facing them, clutching a chair as if to defend himself.

One of the Kushites dropped to his knees on the cold tiles and stretched out his arms to the naked man. "Greetings, Menmire, Lord of the Two Lands. We have come to release you from the bonds of the enemy."

"Who...who are you?"

The Kushite rose to his feet, towering over his king. He grinned, white teeth gleaming in the fitful light. "I am Qenna, Son of Re. Lord Sethi sent me. We must hurry for already the palace guards are on their way."

Menmire nodded. He dropped the chair and grabbed a kilt from a nearby table, fastening it about his waist and slipping on a pair of sandals. "You have a weapon for me?"

Qenna handed him a sword from a fallen guard. "This way, Son of Re. Come quickly."

Shouts and the stamp of many sandaled feet could be heard outside the chamber and the Kushite warriors called urgently to their leader. Qenna strode to the main passage and saw the glint of metal as guards hurried toward them. He turned and ran back into the suite and pointed toward the window.

"Quickly, into the garden. Perhaps we can lose them if we head past the menagerie."

The warriors vaulted through the window into the shrubbery beneath and helped their king to clamber through. Surrounding Amenmesse with a thin cordon of bronze, they set off across the gardens toward the cages and pits that housed a small collection of wild and exotic animals, while behind them the calm of the night was shattered by the clamour of armed men.

Brightly coloured birds screeched and monkeys screamed as Qenna led his men at a run past the enclosures, and a lion coughed and rushed the bars, snarling at the men just out of reach. Torches flared in the doorways and windows behind them, and soldiers poured out in pursuit.

"There," Qenna panted, pointing to the narrow strip of land that lay between the palace outhouses and the crumbling brick wall of the palace estate. "Once we're in the streets we can lose them."

"How do we leave the city?"

"By boat, Son of Re. I have other men waiting at the docks."

They ran through the gap between building and wall and emerged into a small open space. In the first grey light of dawn they saw the way forward was blocked by a detachment of soldiers led by General Setnakhte. Qenna looked behind them and saw other soldiers cutting off their escape. He grinned, and flexed his spear arm.

"We shall protect you to the end, Son of Re."

"It will not come to that," Amenmesse replied, pointing to where the colours of the opposing soldiers could now be seen in the early light. "They are of the Amun legion and are loyal to me."

Amenmesse strode forward and lifted his arm, calling out, "Stand aside, soldiers of Amun, for it is I, Menmire Amenmesse, who stand before you. Take that traitor Setnakhte into custody or strike him down, and then join me in freeing Amun's City of my brother's yoke."

Setnakhte laughed. "It won't work, Messuwy. These are loyal Amuns, not the weak-livered lot you commanded. They obey me and the rightful king."

"I know not this Messuwy. I am Menmire Amenmesse, rightful king of Ta Shemau, and I order you to stand aside."

"You may have been once, but now you are just plain Messuwy again, traitorous brother of the true king Userkheperure."

Amenmesse cursed, but tried again, appealing to the soldiers now clearly seen in the dawn light. He promised them gold, but none of them responded, standing firm with their weapons at the ready.

"Surrender, Messuwy, and I will let you live--you and your men. Or you can die, here and now--your choice."

"You would not dare," Amenmesse shouted back. "I am an anointed king of Kemet and my body is sacred."

"So was your brother, yet it did not stop you seeking to kill him."

"That was war, and besides, he guaranteed me my life. He made you promise to honour his wish. You dare not kill me."

"Perhaps, but I made no such promise concerning your men. Surrender now or they die." Setnakhte murmured an order and a dozen archers stepped through the ranks and drew their bows, aiming them at the Kushites. "Leave Messuwy unharmed, but cut down every other man on my command."

Amenmesse lowered his head in defeat. "Put down your weapons," he instructed his men.

Qenna threw down his spear and with a quick movement ducked behind his king and then raced for the crumbling wall of the palace estate. A fig tree had loosened the mud brick as its roots slowly tore it apart and the Kushite warrior scrambled up and over even as the first archers loosed their arrows at him.

The other Kushite warriors gripped their weapons and hurled themselves at their enemy, yelling out the war cries of their tribes, but they had barely started forward before arrows cut them down. Only Amenmesse was left standing as his men died around him.

"After that man," Setnakhte cried, pointing to where Qenna had disappeared. "Bring me his head." Soldiers rushed to obey him, some scrambling over the wall and others running to cut him off in the temple grounds that lay beyond.

Meanwhile, Setnakhte sauntered across to where Amenmesse stood dejectedly among the bodies of his Kushite warriors. "You will not get another opportunity to escape," he told him.

Amenmesse shrugged. "That is with the gods."

"Come." Setnakhte led Amenmesse back to his outer chamber and doubled the guards on the door, and adding more outside the window. He left him inside the room and went to speak with the Captain of the Guard.

"There are to be at least ten men awake and alert at all times, Ahhotep. Any man sleeping on duty will be executed, so make sure you change them around often. Any command to the contrary is to be refused and reported directly to me. Understand?"

Setnakhte walked back into the room and crossed to where Amenmesse now sat on a chair. "The king is dead," he said without preamble.

"What?" Amenmesse leapt to his feet and stared at his captor. "My brother is dead? Then...then I am Kemet's only king."

"His son Seti-Merenptah is the natural heir, and in case you think you can best an infant, I dare say Queen Tausret will rule for him, backed by the loyal legions."

"Why are you telling me this?"

Setnakhte smiled. "Not to give you any hope, but rather the contrary. Imagine how much the Queen must hate you, and now that the king has ascended to Re it is only a matter of time before she orders your execution. Make your peace with the gods if you can."

Menmire Amenmesse drew himself up and looked down his nose at the other man. "I do not need to make my peace; I have only done what was right. The gods will not desert me." He turned and walked into his bed chamber, paying no further attention to General Setnakhte.

Chapter 2
Interregnum

Userkheperure Seti ascended to his father Re at the end of the season of Inundation, just as the cycle of seasons turned to Peret, the time of Emergence. The soil on the banks of Iteru, the Great River, was still damp from the annual flood and the fields were in perfect condition for the planting of crops. Few people availed themselves of this opportunity, however, for the Kingdoms were stunned by the sudden death of their young king. Coming as it did less than a year from the end of the civil war that had racked the kingdoms, when brother warred with brother; it seemed as if the Ma'at of Kemet was to be shattered anew.

The powers within the kingdoms were aware of the unsettling effect of the king's death too, and were working to settle things down, though they had different ideas about how to accomplish it. The problem was that the young king had left only an infant son to succeed him, and his traitorous brother a son only a few years older. Whichever boy eventually mounted the throne of Kemet, he would face many years of minority rule under the guidance of a regent.

This regent would almost certainly be Queen Tausret, the widow of the dead king, and mother of the king's infant son. There was no doubt in her mind as to the identity of the next king, but anger tightened her features as she stared at men standing in the throne room of the palace in Men-nefer--men who dared oppose her, who dared suggest the son of the traitor.

"There can be no debate," Tausret said. "The king's son Seti-Merenptah must succeed him on the throne of his father."

"With respect, Great Wife, that has not yet been decided."

"You forget your place, Tjaty Hori," the Queen said, glowering at Ta Mehu's Chief Minister. "I have decided, and I need no other opinion."

"Please, Beloved Queen, listen to your ministers," pleaded Chancellor Bay, "for we have the good of Kemet in our hearts."

"Of course you would say that, Bay, for the only other choice is your nephew Siptah."

"Your nephew too, Majesty."

"Do not remind me of my relationship."

"Userkheperure accepted him, Majesty."

"Only as an innocent son of his father. Never as king."

"We cannot be certain of that, Great Wife," Hori interposed.

"I am certain of it," Tausret said flatly, slashing with her hand to cut off further argument.

"So we are to accept an infant on the throne of Kemet?" General Iurudef asked. "That way lies unrest and chaos."

"Seti-Merenptah is the only son of Userkheperure," Besenmut, Commander of the Ptah legion, pointed out. "As such, he is the natural heir."

"And a baby," Commander Emsaf said. "We need a strong king; someone who can defend Kemet against the Nine Bows."

"That's what we're for," Ament growled. "Strong generals and strong commanders--though I have my doubts about some commanders."

"I am as loyal as the next man," Emsaf protested. "I know my duty. I was just pointing out..."

"Emsaf is right in one respect though," General Iurudef said. "The men will fight better for a strong leader than for an infant."

"They will fight for Seti-Merenptah because he is the son of Userkheperure," Besenmut declared. "And if that's not enough, then we have Queen Tausret. Have you forgotten how she held the city of Perire for four days until the army of Baenre could arrive, or destroyed the nobles who sought to rebel against Userkheperure? The men would follow her anywhere."

"Yet she is a woman," Hori pointed out. "Forgive me, Great Lady, I state that not to lessen you but only to point out that a man must lead Kemet. It is custom."

"Yes, it is custom," the other Hori said--the one who was Hem-netjer of Ptah and father to Tjaty Hori. "Yet no matter which boy sits on the throne of his father--and both have royal fathers--it is likely that Queen Tausret will act as regent."

"That is my intention."

"And as a woman regent you will need strong men about you-- experienced men who can advise you and act for you."

"Loyal men," Tausret added.

"Of course loyal men," Hori the Elder said. He looked around at the men in the throne room. "Every man here is loyal to Kemet and seeks what is best for the Ma'at of the Two Lands."

"Then there is no argument. My son Seti-Merenptah ascends the throne and I rule as regent until he comes of age."

Tjaty Hori cleared his throat and looked down at the tiled floor. "I regret, Great Lady, that there is still disagreement on that point."

Tausret's jaw clenched and her hands gripped the arms of the throne. "I am the Queen of the Two Kingdoms. I rule, Hori, not you."

"Undoubtedly, Great Lady, yet..." The Tjaty shrugged his shoulders.

Tausret glared at her chief minister in the north. "Yet?"

"I am sure no man would openly oppose you, Great Wife, but the rule of an infant is a recipe for disaster, even with a regent in place. The people..."

"The people love me."

"Indeed, Great Lady, but they love peace more. We have just come through a war that set kingdom against kingdom, brother against brother, and the prospect of a return to those times would lead to great unrest, a lack of confidence, a rise in crime."

"And the alternative is to put Siptah on the throne instead of the rightful heir? How is that restoring Ma'at?" Tausret cast a hostile glare at the gathered men. "Are you all against me in this? Speak, for I would hear it from your own lips--each of you."

"Never against you, my lady," Ament murmured.

"Faithful Ament." Tausret bestowed a brief smile on the commander. "And the rest of you?"

"General Setnakhte also supports you, my lady," Ament said. "He told me of his thoughts before I left Waset."

"He is biased," Iurudef declared. "A child is preferable to an infant, no matter his parentage. I am loyal to you, Great Wife, but I say Siptah should be king."

"As do I, Great Lady."

"Of course you do, Chancellor Bay. I would expect nothing else. Tjaty Hori, you have already argued against my son, so I know your thoughts. What about you, Hem-netjer Hori? Will you turn against me too?"

"The grandfather of both boys was 'beloved of Ptah'. The god has not made his preference known."

"Commander Besenmut?"

"For your son, Great Lady."

"Commander Disebek?"

"Your son."

"Commander Emsaf?"

"I must stress my loyalty to you personally, Majesty, but I believe Kemet is best served by the older child."

"Commander Samut?"

"The Amun legion declares for Seti-Merenptah, as does Tjaty Parae-mheb. I was instructed to pass on his support, Majesty."

"Commander Panhesy? You too are from Waset. Is your loyalty also to the rightful heir?"

Panhesy of the Mut legion licked his lips and glanced about him nervously. "Majesty, there is another candidate. An anointed king already exists, ready to sit once more on the throne. I speak of Menmire Amenmesse..."

"Traitor!" yelled Besenmut and Samut together. Even Iurudef and Tjaty Hori, who openly supported Siptah, shook their heads and muttered.

"You cannot countenance handing the throne to that man," Ament shouted. "Why did we all fight him if we are now to bend our knees to him?"

"Unheard of," Emsaf murmured.

"And it is not going to happen," Tausret stated. "Not while I live."

"Majesty, it is not without precedent for brother to succeed brother," Chief Scribe Anapepy said. "I hasten to add that I support only the will of your Majesty, but it would be a solution."

"And he is a grown man," Panhesy added. "He has already ruled as king in the south and as King's Son of Kush before that. He is the eldest son of Baenre Merenptah and brother to Userkheperure Seti. What better antecedents could he have?"

"Except that he rebelled against my husband the king and sought to take his life," Tausret said. "Some even say that the black rot that killed him came from the hand of that man. I will not allow him to triumph."

"And yet Userkheperure allowed him to live," Panhesy persevered. "Perhaps he foresaw just such a need as now arises."

"Nobody else supports him, Majesty," Iurudef declared. "Dismiss him from your mind."

"I have. So, five of you support me and three oppose--four if you count Panhesy and his traitorous utterance..."

"We do not oppose you, Great Lady," Tjaty Hori said. "Only your choice of king...and not necessarily even that."

"What do you mean?"

"Circumstances change, Great Lady. We need a credible king on the throne of Kemet to restore Ma'at after the recent troubles, and Siptah is nine years old--almost as old as Nebkheperure Tutankhamen when he became king. But in eight or nine years, what then? Your son Seti-Merenptah is old enough to succeed, and Siptah is a sickly child with a withered leg. Who can say what the future holds?"

"What are you saying?" Ament demanded. "That Siptah would only hold the throne for Seti-Merenptah? How would that work?"

"It could not," Hori the Elder declared. "A man is raised to the godhead by the coronation process and he remains god-on-earth until he ascends to join his father Re. He cannot step down and relinquish his divinity."

Anapepy cleared his throat. "Again, there is precedent. The Heretic stepped down..."

"And look at the horror that was visited on the land for that impious act," Besenmut said.

"But there is also a co-regency," the Chief Scribe continued. "There is a lot of precedence for a king to elevate another man to share the burden of rulership. Perhaps Siptah could rule alone until Seti-Merenptah comes of age and then they can rule as kings together?"

"That might work," Tjaty Hori said.

"And what if Siptah has a son before then and decides he wants him to succeed rather than his father's brother's son?"

"Queen Tausret would still be Regent," Iurudef mused. "For another five years at least. Siptah could not act alone while she rules."

"It might be the answer," Disebek said.

"Clarify your thoughts," Tausret demanded. "What are they saying, Ament?"

"If I understand correctly, they propose that Siptah be made king and that Seti-Merenptah be made co-regent with him when he comes of age, or at such time as you choose, my lady."

"Is that what you mean, Hori? Iurudef? You are keeping very quiet, Bay."

"Yes, Majesty," Bay replied. "It might perhaps be wiser for me to stay out of this argument. I will serve you and the new king faithfully, no matter what the outcome."

"That applies to us all," Iurudef growled. "We may have differing opinions, but we all know our duty." He faced the Queen once more. "Yes, Majesty, that is in essence what Hori and I propose. Siptah is made king, with you as regent, and then when Seti-Merenptah comes of age, he is elevated to the throne alongside Siptah."

"Who inherits?" Emsaf asked. "Say both kings have sons--which one inherits the throne?"

"The eldest," Hori said.

"The son of Siptah would be logical," Iurudef added.

"Then we have a problem," Tausret concluded. "I will not see my son's as-yet-unborn son dispossessed of his inheritance."

"Can we not leave that to the gods?" Bay murmured.

"That would be best," the elder Hori said.

"There is something we could do." Ament spoke into the silence that followed the Chancellor's question and the priest's opinion. "Make Siptah king under Queen Tausret's regency, but have Siptah sign an irrevocable declaration that Seti-Merenptah is his heir even if sons are born of his body. Seti-Merenptah can still be made co-regent when he comes of age, and he will always be the next king."

"Is that fair to Siptah?" Emsaf asked. "He will be king now, but will know that he cannot hand it on."

Iurudef nodded, frowning. "Ament is right; it is the answer. The whole argument for having Siptah as king instead of Seti-Merenptah is so we have an older boy instead of a baby on the throne, not that he is inherently better. This way, he is a temporary measure until the rightful heir can take his place."

"I could perhaps accept that," Tausret admitted.

"Well, if we are looking for a temporary king only, then why not go with my suggestion?" Panhesy asked. "Make Menmire Amenmesse king until Seti-Merenptah is old enough to rule alone."

"No," Tausret said flatly. "Do not suggest it again."

"Forgive me, Majesty," Hori the priest said, "but the father would be better than the son to hold the throne open for your child. Menmire has already ruled as king, and he is a son of Baenre."

Ament snorted derisively. "And what would be his first act after being placed on the throne once more? He would kill the queen and her son, reinstate Siptah as heir, and do away with anyone who had ever opposed him. It is a ridiculous suggestion."

"And I tell you it is not going to happen," Tausret said quietly. "I will accept Siptah as sole king under my regency until such time as Seti-Merenptah can rule alongside him, and as long as my son is made official heir immediately."

"Then we are in agreement, are we not, gentlemen?" Ament said. "Are any opposed?" he stared at Panhesy as he asked the latter question.

Panhesy flushed and looked away. The officials and other commanders looked at one another. Some shrugged, others nodded, and Tjaty Hori said, "If it be the will of Queen Tausret, then let it be so."

"It is," Tausret stated.

Chapter 3
Interregnum

Deputy Commander Ament hurried from the throne room when the Queen dismissed her advisers and commanders, and made straight for the docks of Men-nefer, where the fast boat he had come north on waited for him. He showed his identification to the dock officials, and his orders signed by General Setnakhte and countersigned by Tjaty of the South Paraemheb.

"I obeyed the Queen's summons, and now I return to my station in Waset."

The Overseer of the Docks instructed his scribe to make a suitable notation in the scrolls and dismissed Ament.

The sun had scarce moved in the heavens before the boat slipped its moorings and made its way out into the river's current. A north-easterly breeze blew and the little sail caught the wind, heeling the boat over as the master pointed his craft upriver. Ament felt on edge, the recent arguments running through his mind continually, with the conclusions plucking at his heart. There was not enough room on the boat to pace, so Ament settled himself in the bow and tried to lose himself in the beauty of the river.

Although he had made the trip between Men-nefer and Waset many times, his mind drifted back to the first time. Years before, when the dead king had been a boy, Ament had been blackmailed into taking him and his sister Tausret to Waset, in direct opposition to the wishes of King Baenre. The voyage had been free of major incident and in fact had been the first step on his staircase of advancement, but Ament sometimes wished for the simple life of a soldier he had enjoyed before the royal children happened along, or even as a fisherman before that, plying his trade in his father's boat on the Great River.

He had forgotten just how beautiful the river was. A great expanse of dark green water spread out before him, reflecting back the dome of the blue sky and silver shimmers of sunlight. The sail above and behind him snapped in the vagaries of the breeze from the northeast, pushing the boat against the slow current close to the western shore. Now that they had left the city and surrounding farms behind, the land and waters displayed fewer signs of mankind. Reed beds abounded and in the quieter backwaters, water lilies dotted the surface, and the lotus stems crowded the margin between water and land. Herons and egrets stalked the muddy margins, hunting for frogs and small fish, while ducks squabbled and dabbled in large flocks near the reeds.

Away from the water's edge, grass grew thickly, though much of it was matted and bedraggled where the silt from the recent flood still blanketed the low-lying areas. Further inland, tall palms broke up the skyline, and beyond that he could catch glimpses of red desert and the yellow western cliffs.

Balance, he thought. *That is what Kemet has--balance between water and land, between the black soil of the river valley and the red sand of the desert. Life and death, gods and man...man and woman, for that matter.* That started his mind off on another path, as he remembered the young girl Tausret had been when he first met her and the powerful Queen she had become. *I desired her then, and but for the difference in our stations...and now?* Ament considered the present situation. *I still love her, but she is even further out of my reach.*

He looked up at the clear blue sky and noted that the day was further advanced than he thought. They would scarcely be out of sight of Mennefer by sunset, and they would have to stop for the night. That was no great imposition as Ament carried a writ that enabled him to claim food and lodging at any village or town along the way. If worst came to worst, then he could camp on the riverbank--he had done it before.

They found a village that night, a tiny collection of mud and straw huts. The village elder greeted the visitors and stared blankly at the writ Ament carried, unable to decipher any of the cursive writing on the papyrus, but he was seemingly impressed by the demeanour of the military man and ordered that the meagre wealth of the village be put at the visitors' disposal. Ament thanked him warmly, and in the morning gifted a copper bangle to the headman, worth far more than the food they had eaten.

Another twelve days and thirteen nights were eaten up as the little boat forged its way south against the current. Sometimes the wind blew strongly, other times it died away or backed to the south and on those days they made little headway. At last they reached the great bend in the river and caught sight of the great walls of Amun's City, just after dawn. The walls glowed warmly in the rich morning light and the smell of freshly baked bread carried to them across the water. The boat master guided his little craft through the fishing boats and ferries already plying the river near Waset, and into the docks, where slaves grabbed the ropes and tied them to the wooden mooring posts.

Ament found soldiers of the Amun and Mut legions on the docks and dispatched one at a run to notify General Setnakhte of his arrival, taking some of the others as an honour guard as he made his way up to the old eastern palace where the Tjaty and General resided. He was met on the palace steps by a messenger from Setnakhte bidding him bathe and take refreshment before he met with him in the lesser audience chamber. Ament was grateful for the consideration shown and repaired to his own residence near the City Barracks, where he bathed and took a light meal of freshly baked bread and fatty beef. Then, dressed in clean clothing and wearing the emblems of his office, he reported to the audience chamber.

Setnakhte eliminated the pleasantries of welcome and got straight down to business. "Well, what happened?" he demanded.

Ament greeted the only other man in the chamber--Tjaty Paraemheb--and then his General. "Fairly straightforward, sir. The Council was divided between Seti-Merenptah and Siptah as the next king, either with Tausret as regent. There is little doubt the king's son would have been accepted without question had it not been for his age, but that was the deciding factor." He shook his head. "Siptah is to be king, but..."

"Siptah?" Setnakhte interrupted. "That limping cripple? That mewling brat spawned of a traitor and an Amorite serving wench? Have they all taken leave of their senses? I hope you spoke out for the royal son on my behalf."

"I did sir, but it's not as bad as you might imagine..."

"How can it not be? Do you imagine I'm going to bend my knee to him? The next thing that will happen is his traitor father will be invited to court and he'll become the power behind the throne. What are they thinking?" Setnakhte rounded on the Tjaty. "What do you say, Paraemheb? Am I mistaken?"

"I think you have grasped the danger nicely, General, but I think Ament has more news to impart."

"So, speak, Ament. Don't hold back. Pour the foul decisions of the Queen's Council into our ears."

"Yes, sir. Siptah is to be king with the Queen acting as regent, but Seti-Merenptah is to be made official heir immediately, and co-regent alongside Siptah as soon as he comes of age. Userkheperure's son has not been ousted from the succession, nor Messuwy's insinuated into it."

Setnakhte snorted. "And what happens when Siptah father's a brat of his own? He'll want it to succeed him rather than Seti-Merenptah."

"Can't happen, sir. Siptah must vow on the gods to honour the agreement before he is crowned."

"He'll be king. You imagine he won't break even a sacred vow to ensure his family on the throne? I know I would."

"With respect, sir, I don't believe you would. And besides, the Queen will remain as regent to enforce the king's obedience."

"Until such time as the king decides he can do without the restraints of the regency. Ten years at the most, maybe even less." Setnakhte scowled and started pacing the chamber, his sandals slapping the tiled floor and echoing back from the pillars and walls. "Who spoke out for Siptah?"

"Chancellor Bay, as might be expected. Tjaty Hori also, General Iu-rudef, and Commander Emsaf."

"Those names surprise me. Samut now--I would expect it of him. How did he speak?"

"For Seti-Merenptah, sir. Quite forcefully. If he was ever in support of Messuwy he has changed his heart."

"And everyone else was for Seti-Merenptah?"

"The other Hori, the Hem-netjer of Ptah, and the Chief Scribe Anapepy took no side. They advised, but supported the Queen in all her decisions." Ament hesitated. "Panhesy..."

"The Commander of Mut," Paraemheb asked. "What about him? Don't tell me he refused to take sides."

"Not exactly, sir. He spoke for Messuwy."

"What?"

"He called him Menmire Amenmesse and suggested that, as an anointed king, he was the most suitable person to mount the throne."

"Set's bollocks, I did not take him for a follower of the traitor. The rot spreads deeper than I thought."

"What will you do with him?"

"Panhesy? Nothing. He's a good soldier and an able commander."

"You know your own men best."

"Exactly. You were aware we had a rescue attempt recently?"

Ament stared. "What happened?"

"You know Sethi's deputy, Qenna? Well, Qenna and some men gained entry to the palace, slew the guards and took Messuwy out of his room. They nearly made it to the streets before they were stopped."

"That is not good news, sir. I take it Messuwy is still in custody?"

"I did say it was a rescue attempt."

"So you did, sir. Sorry. Is he...was he harmed in your er...recapture?"

"No, but in light of Panhesy's defection, I rather wish I had 'harmed' him. That man will ever be a centre of disaffection. Evidently, there are still men out there who would see him restored to the throne."

"There is a solution," Paraemheb said. "You cannot restore a dead king."

Ament raised an eyebrow in surprise. "A bit bloodthirsty, Paraemheb."

"Not really, Ament. Have you forgotten he killed my uncle Neferronpet, for no greater crime than loyalty to his king?"

"I'm sorry...yes, of course you wish him dead."

"Regrettably, it is my duty to guard him and protect him," Setnakhte said.

"Even if it endangers the kingdoms?" Ament asked.

"Do you even have to ask? I swore an oath to Userkheperure, though it went against everything I knew to be just and sensible. If I was released from that vow I would kill him without a moment's hesitation. While he remains alive he endangers the Ma'at of Kemet."

"Then look the other way and I will kill him," Paraemheb said. "You agree with me don't you, Ament?"

Ament grimaced. "I dislike the thought of slaughtering a helpless captive, but sometimes it must be done. I think our beloved Userkheperure would have changed his mind about keeping him alive had he lived."

"Had he lived, we would not be beset by the problems of succession," Setnakhte pointed out.

"One could argue that your vow died with the death of the king," Paraemheb went on.

Setnakhte grunted. "Would the gods see it that way?"

"I believe they would," the Tjaty replied. "Ever since my uncle's death I have prayed to the gods for the death of that man. I asked them to send me a sign if I should forget my thoughts of vengeance." Paraemheb bared his teeth in a mirthless grin. "I received no such sign."

"What more do you need?" Ament asked dryly. "Even the gods have withdrawn their support from him."

Setnakhte considered their words. "It would certainly ease my burden if I could lay him in his tomb, but a vow is a vow."

"On the other hand, Userkheperure is a god now that he has ascended to his father Re. If he desired you to stay your hand, would he not have sent a sign to Paraemheb?"

"I could lay this burden on the Queen. Let her decide."

"She will shortly be regent to King Siptah, who is the son of this man," Ament pointed out. "It may be difficult for her to order the death of the king's father." He waited to let the weightiness of his words sink in before adding, "If the decision was taken out of her hands, however, she might well be grateful."

"But if I misread her wishes, she may order my execution."

"There is always that," Ament admitted. "However, we must weigh up the costs and benefits of removing this man. We have seen already that his followers have tried to release him, and now Panhesy of the Mut legion speaks for him. Are we to wait until a rescue attempt is successful before acting? What will the judgment of the gods be if we tip the Two Lands into another bitter war?"

"Siptah will never forgive the killers of his father."

"Do you care? He is a child, and under the control of the regent. Who knows what will happen in the years between now and him becoming sole ruler?"

"Say...just say I decide to remove this man. How is it to be done? I risk unrest in the city if I openly execute him."

"It seems to me that Qenna has provided you with the answer, General," Ament said after a few moments thought. "He tried to rescue the man a little while ago. Surely he will try again."

"I doubt it," Setnakhte said. "He gave my men the slip and is probably in Kush by now."

"The man Qenna is not actually necessary," Ament said patiently. "Only the idea of Qenna. If someone broke into the palace and tried to rescue Messuwy, but oh so sadly Messuwy was killed while trying to escape, who would grieve for him? And if they grieved, what could they do about it. They would perhaps even blame Qenna."

"Ah, I see, but who would play the part of Qenna and actually kill Messuwy?" Setnakhte asked.

"I would," Paraemheb said. "Gladly."

"There is no better person," Ament said. "No blame attaches to you, and Paraemheb secures vengeance for his uncle's death."

"I will need one thing from you though, General."

"What's that?"

"Access to Messuwy. I am known and I cannot just walk into his room with a knife. Your guards are alert after Qenna's attempt."

Setnakhte thought about this and nodded slowly. "I gave them instructions to be cautious."

"So how will you remedy the situation?" Ament asked. "We are agreed Messuwy cannot be allowed to live, and if he is to die it must be before Tausret brings Siptah to Waset for the coronation."

"Or we wait until he goes north again. There is no great urgency."

"With respect, General, there is. What if Siptah demands his father attend his coronation, or even accompany him back north? He might even insist that Messuwy becomes the regent in place of Tausret. What then?"

"It must be soon," Paraemheb agreed. "Every day we delay gives Messuwy another opportunity to escape, or for someone to persuade the Queen to release him."

"All right, I can see that," Setnakhte said. "But I cannot be seen to be responsible for his death. It must come by a seeming mischance."

"When?"

"If I leave the same guards in place, there is always the chance that Messuwy will suborn one--and one may be all it takes to effect an escape. To ward against this, I should rotate the guards regularly, and if by chance some inexperienced men should be on duty...well, these things happen."

"Where are the guards placed now?" Ament asked.

"Four outside the chambers, another two inside, and four more outside the window. They have instructions to raise the alarm as well as repel any attempts to get to Messuwy."

Ament thought for a few minutes. "Have the men inside join the others outside..."

"Won't that look suspicious?"

"Not if you say that you don't want men too close to the prisoner. Hint that he might offer a bribe. Also, move the men back from under his window. Have them guard the entrances to the gardens, and increase their numbers. It will look as if you have heard there might be a rescue and are guarding against it."

Setnakhte nodded. "That can be done. When would you act?"

"Better you don't know, General."

Setnakhte made the necessary changes to the guards the next day and two nights later, Ament and Paraemheb exited from their hiding place in the palace menagerie and looked toward the darkened palace.

"Everything's quiet," Ament muttered. "No guards are in sight."

Paraemheb brushed his clothing down, grumbling. "Did you have to put us in with the animal feed? I'm covered in hay and there were mice in there, I swear."

Ament grinned. "Come now, what are a few mice when the good of the kingdoms is in our hands. I've faced much worse in the field."

"I'm sure you have but you're a soldier and I'm not," said the Tjaty. "My duties are governing this southern kingdom."

"Well now you have a chance to strike a real blow. Are you ready?"

Paraemheb nodded, and loosened the dagger in the sheath at his belt. "Let's do this."

The two men moved quietly through the darkened gardens toward the palace, slipping from the cover of trees to shrubbery while keeping their eyes open for any hint of the soldiers guarding the prisoner. They saw no one and only moments passed before they were outside the low window of Messuwy's suite. Ament peered over the edge, scanning the room swiftly and then ducking back down again.

"The room's deserted," he whispered. "A single torch to give us some light. I'll go first and make sure there's nobody hiding." Ament hauled himself up and over the sill, and disappeared into the room.

Silence followed, and Paraemheb crouched below the window waiting. He rose slowly and looked over the sill and almost cried out as Ament's head appeared before him.

"Come on," Ament said. He helped Paraemheb into the room and pointed toward the darkened doorway to the bedchamber. "He's in there, fast asleep. No guards or servants."

Paraemheb took out his dagger and strode into the bedchamber, Ament on his heels. A simple bed lay at the far end of the room and a man lay on it, half covered by a linen sheet, breathing heavily. There was little other furniture in the room and as their eyes became accustomed to the gloom, the two men made their way over to the bed. They stood and looked down at the sleeping man and Paraemheb shuffled his feet, changing his grip on the dagger, but making no other move.

"Strike," Ament whispered.

"He's asleep."

"Well, of course he is." Ament stared at the young Tjaty incredulously. "You want to wake him up before you kill him?"

"It...it doesn't seem right to send him to the gods without a chance to make his peace with them."

"I can see you're not a soldier," Ament muttered. "All right, I'll wake him up, but you must be ready to kill him swiftly, before he can raise the alarm."

"Would it matter?" Paraemheb asked. "The guards are on our side."

"Of course it would. They'd have to intervene as their orders are to protect him. Now, give me a moment, and when he wakes, strike swiftly for his heart." Ament moved to the head of the bed and took up a position where he could grasp Messuwy firmly, and clap a hand over his mouth to prevent him crying out. "Ready?"

Paraemheb nodded and Ament took hold of the sleeping man. Messuwy awakened and immediately began struggling, issuing muffled cries for help.

"Strike," Ament said. "Quickly."

Paraemheb hesitated, and then instead of stabbing his victim, spoke. "Messuwy, you executed my uncle Neferronpet, though his only crime was obeying his king. For this you must die..."

"Get on with it," Ament rasped, fighting to hold the struggling man on the bed.

"...and I will carry out this sentence of death as my uncle's nearest relative." The Tjaty thrust forward with the dagger, piercing Messuwy's chest.

Messuwy heaved violently as the blade went in, and Ament lost his grip. The wounded man struggled to sit up, but the only sounds that escaped his lips were strangled gasps and whimpers.

Ament threw himself onto the bed and wrestled Messuwy down. "Again, Paraemheb, before he can raise the alarm."

Paraemheb stabbed tentatively, the blade barely breaking skin, and Ament swore softly, released his hold on Messuwy's mouth, reached across to the Tjaty's hand and rammed the blade home.

Messuwy convulsed, and uttered a croak as he fell back, his fingers fluttering weakly on the blood-soaked sheets. "Eh...pl...please..." he whispered. "Don't..."

"What is he trying to say?" Paraemheb gasped, dropping the dagger with a clatter to the tiles.

"He's just trying to stop us," Ament said. "Now pick up the knife and finish him off."

"N...no. Please don't...don't hurt...my son...innocent..."

Ament groaned and, stepping around the bed, he scooped the knife off the floor and bent over Messuwy. Pressing the blade to the man's throat, he started to thrust and then stopped, looking into Messuwy's eyes only a hand span from his own. "Rest easy, Messuwy. They've just made your son king."

Messuwy's fingers ceased their fluttering and gripped Ament's tunic. "T...truly?"

"I swear on all the gods, Messuwy. Siptah will be crowned king."

A bubble of blood formed on Messuwy's lips as he tried to smile. "Th...then I have...have won."

"No, Messuwy, you lose," Ament whispered. He leaned forward and thrust the knife blade deep into the man's throat.

Chapter 4

Tausret speaks:

I have in my hands a report from Paraemheb, Tjaty of Ta Shemau, in which he says that an unknown person broke into the old eastern palace of Waset and murdered the man Messuwy, sometimes known as Menmire Amenmesse, who once claimed to be Lord of the Two Lands.

According to the report, the murderer broke in through the window, stabbed Messuwy to death and vanished. None of the guards saw anything, and the death was not reported until the next morning when a servant came to wash and dress him. It is the opinion of General Setnakhte, the report says, that the murderer was a person who had a grudge against the man who was lately king of Ta Shemau, and he says there are many of those. Setnakhte says that a search for the murderer has been made, but he has vanished without trace.

I read it in the presence of my northern Tjaty, Hori, as we were conducting business in the Hall of Audiences, and of course I sent everyone except Hori away so I could digest the news in private. I read the words again, my lips silently sounding out the syllables, and when I finished I rolled it up and handed it to my Tjaty.

"I'm going to have to tell Siptah, I suppose."

"He should know his father is dead."

"But how will he take it?"

"He will grieve, but does he need to know he was murdered?" Hori asked. "All he really needs to know is that his father has died."

"He'll find out eventually."

"There will be rumours, but once he is buried in his rock-cut tomb that is all there will be."

"I suppose he must be buried? He was responsible for the death of my Seti."

"Whatever else he was, the man was anointed king and is, moreover, the father of the new king. You must give him the honours due to his station.

We can make the actual burial a quiet ceremony with only the immediate family present."

Hori was right, of course. A rock-cut tomb could be found to house his remains, though I would make sure that his name was erased from monuments throughout the kingdoms. He was responsible for the death of my beloved Seti, and I was determined to have his name chiselled out and re-carved to the memory and honour of Userkheperure Seti. I expect Siptah will take exception to my actions, but there is little he can do. He will be king, but a king lacking all power--that will reside in my hands--the hands of the regent.

It is nearly time to accompany the body of my husband south to the Great Field and there inter him with all due ceremony. His tomb is unfinished and unready to take the body of a king--another act to be laid at the door of his brother. When Messuwy claimed the throne in the south he had all work on my Seti's tomb abandoned, but through an oversight, work continued on mine. Consequently, my tomb is nearly finished and I shall let my husband lie within my tomb until his is ready.

I had thought to put off the crowning of the new king for a time, while I gathered the reins of power into my own hands, but Hori and Bay argued most strenuously against it. They have said that the Two Lands are in turmoil since the war of the brothers and the subsequent death of the king. It would calm the kingdoms, they said, to have a king on the throne once more. Confidence in the continuation of the House of Ramesses must be fostered, and in truth the foundations of that House are presently built on sand. Forgetting the multitude of lesser descendants of Usermaatre, there are only three surviving members of the central royal family--me, my son and my nephew.

I will never marry again, and Siptah is weak and crippled, hardly kingly material, so everything rests on the tiny shoulders of my darling Seti-Merenptah. It is a great burden for one so young, but I will make sure he survives, marries, and brings forth a quiverful of sons. In the meantime, I suppose I must allow Siptah to play at being king.

Shortly, we take the Royal Barge to Waset, there to lay my husband in his temporary tomb. Siptah will perform the Ceremony of the Opening of the Mouth, under my supervision, and then I will see him crowned king in Waset. I have had to think up a suitable throne name for him--something that honours the main gods of his house, but not Set. I will not have him bearing the name of my beloved Seti. A name that honours Re and Ptah, of course, and Amun, for we must get the enthusiastic support of Waset behind his reign.

Sekhaienre Meryamun Ramesses-Siptah--'He whom Re causes to appear, Beloved of Amun, Re fashioned him, son of Ptah'. What grand names for a little boy who still has his side-lock and plays with toy chariots. And what blasphemy is inherent in his names--to accuse the great god Re of fashioning such a crippled king. Still, there is little I can do about it--for now, at least. It will not always be so, for in a few years--eight or nine--Seti-Merenptah will be old enough to be crowned king, and then we shall see. The son of my traitorous brother-in-law will disappear from the throne and from memory, along with all his supporters, and my own son will reign as the worthy successor to the great Userkheperure Seti. The House of Ramesses will build itself anew and rise to greater heights than ever it was in the days of my grandfather Usermaatre Ramesses.

Chapter 5
Year 1 of Sekhaienre Ramesses-Siptah

With a great effort of will, Queen Tausret set aside her personal feelings and put in train the arrangements for the coronation. The preserved and richly wrapped body of Userkheperure was loaded onto the royal barge with priests and an accompanying honour guard of senior army officers. The funeral barge would make its slow progression to Waset and thence to the king's funerary temple on the west bank, where it would lie in state until the new king and regent arrived.

Another barge was outfitted with the luxuries necessary for conveying living royalty and, accompanied by Chancellor Bay, Tjaty Hori, General Iurudef and Commander Ament, Tausret and Siptah went on board. Tausret insisted on taking her infant Seti-Merenptah with her, despite the exhausting schedule planned, for the young boy was the Crown Prince, and the populace needed to see him as well as their next king.

The citizens and slaves of Men-nefer turned out to see them off, crowded together within sight of the wharves, lining the riverbank, and a not inconsiderable number standing and cheering from the unstable platforms of small boats up and down the river. Priests of every god gathered, uttering loud prayers for the safety and well-being of the regent, king and heir, and bright banners flew from every vantage point. Tausret fostered the good will of the populace by ordering many cattle slaughtered and roasted, and released grain from the city granaries to make enough bread and beer to satisfy everyone.

And so, amid an aura of celebration, the royal barge set out on its progress throughout the kingdoms. The captain shouted his commands, slaves slipped the mooring ropes, and the oarsmen dug deep into the cool green waters, easing the barge out into the current. No sail was raised to catch the light northerly wind, for the first part of the voyage lay within the delta, where the Great River divided and branched out, holding the rich farmlands of Ta Mehu within its encompassing arms.

The sun shone warmly from the lapis vault of the heavens, a cool wind blew, and high above a circling hawk screamed. Members of the royal party, appreciative of the tensions that pulled at the unity of the coming reign, eagerly sought out any omen in their surroundings that could be interpreted as approval by the many gods of Kemet. The disc of Re was unblemished; Heru in the form of a hawk circled overhead and then dipped to the north, pointing the direction, and Hapi as god of the Great River ran smoothly, assisting them on their way. A ripple from a crocodile in the shallows spoke of Sobek's approval, and a flight of sacred ibis flying from west to east brought forth a murmur of joy from the watchers on board. Viewed correctly, almost any natural feature of land, sky or river could be viewed as an expression of the gods, and when the gods' approval was so desperately sought, those expressions were interpreted in a favourable way.

Siptah sat in the bows, rejoicing as the barge, propelled by the sweep of oars, carved its way through the wide waters. He pointed and exclaimed as a fish broke the surface or a bird took flight, looking back to where his Uncle Bay sat, eager to share the wonders. For all that he was the new King of all Kemet; he was also a young boy of ten years and fidgeted with excitement.

"I wish my father was here," Siptah said wistfully. "How did he die?"

Bay frowned, debating how much information to offer his young nephew, how much sense the boy could make of recent events.

"All men die," he replied quietly, "and your father, while not as old as Baenre or Usermaatre, was still older than many men. He is with the gods now."

"He has ascended to Re? He was king after all, wasn't he?"

Bay nodded. "He was king in the south."

"But I will be king over all Kemet, won't I?" Siptah rubbed his hand over his shaved head, hesitating over the smooth surface where his side lock had been only days before.

"You will indeed, Majesty. Queen Tausret will act as regent until you come of age, but you will be king."

"I wish you'd be regent, Uncle. The Queen frightens me." Siptah shivered, despite the warmth of the sun, and looked back down the length of the boat to where Tausret sat with her baby in her arms. "Sometimes she looks at me as if...as if...I don't know...as if she wanted me dead. Is that silly, Uncle?"

"Yes it is, Majesty. All the officials of the court and all the army commanders got together and persuaded the Queen that you should be king, and that her baby should be Crown Prince. She accepted our advice, so you should not worry about anything."

Siptah thought about this for a time. "If little Seti is Crown Prince, then what happens when I get married and have a son of my own? Won't he then become Crown Prince?"

"Again, Majesty, this is not something for you to worry about. That is why you have a regent and many advisers who love you. They have only your best interests at heart."

"I suppose...oh, look, Uncle...did you see that fish? It leapt up and turned a somersault in the air. What do you suppose it means?"

Bay smiled. "It might mean that a crocodile was chasing it, or it might just mean the fish was very happy and wanted to see the young boy who was its new king."

Siptah laughed and stood up, stumbling a bit on his withered left leg. He gripped the prow of the boat and looked out over the river, letting loose a cry of pure joy.

Heads turned as the laughter rang out and despite her worries, Tausret smiled. She restrained her child who had hauled himself to his feet and was attempting a shaky walk across the planking of the deck.

"Someone's enjoying themselves, aren't they, dear Seti?" Tausret said.

"Why shouldn't he?"

Tausret looked round in surprise. "I did not see you there, Ament. I forget how small these boats are."

"Your pardon if I intrude, Great Lady, but I couldn't help but overhear and I don't think little Seti is ready to give you an answer."

Tausret smiled again. "Well, Siptah will find out all too soon what it means to be king. I don't begrudge him a little longer to play the child. I remember my own sense of wonder on the river when I wasn't much older than him."

"I remember, Great Lady. You and..." Ament hesitated a moment, and then ploughed on. "When you and the king made the trip to Waset all those years ago. You might have been having fun but I certainly was not."

"Poor Ament. Still you came out of it well enough."

"Perhaps, though sometimes I wish for the simple life of the common soldier. None of the decisions and all I had to worry about was where my next pot of beer was coming from."

"You wouldn't have Jerem and Ephrim in your life. How are they? I presume they're on your sister's estate?"

Ament nodded. "Acting the uncles to her swarming brats, and loving every day."

"How many now?"

"Six, and she's expecting again."

"The Kaftor are evidently a fertile breed." The smile on her face slipped and she hugged Seti close. "I wish he had brothers and sisters."

Ament said nothing. He watched the Queen closely until it appeared as if the mood had lifted, and said, "Have you identified all your enemies, Great Lady?"

"I'm not sure I have enemies now that Messuwy is dead. I have you to thank for that, I know. You carried word to Setnakhte, and he made it happen. I could not have gone against my husband's wishes, though I begged him to do it, so the act is not unwelcome."

"I merely did what I thought was best, and with respect, Great Lady, you are wrong. You still have enemies and one of them is up at the front of the boat, no doubt planning your downfall."

"What? Siptah? He's but a boy."

"I meant Chancellor Bay."

Tausret looked troubled. "Bay has always been loyal."

"Bay was always good at playing both sides. He was loyal to you while he advanced in your court, but I believe he fed information to Messuwy at the same time. Thus, whoever won the war, he could expect their gratitude."

"Can you prove that?"

Ament shook his head. "Rumours and hearsay. He's very careful."

"And very powerful. Don't accuse him without proof, Ament. If you do, I may not be able to save you."

Ament smiled. "I always thought of you as the most powerful person in Kemet after the king."

"Oh, I'm the most powerful woman, but the laden table that is Kemet has been overturned, and while we are all picking up the pieces, none can yet say who will end up with the choicest dishes."

"I have faith in you, Great Lady."

"Thank you, Ament. Let us hope I have other loyal men who remember who their king was and who is his son."

Ament looked across to where Tjaty Hori stood conversing with General Iurudef and Commander Besenmut of the Ptah legion. "You have some loyal men, Great Lady, and some who have yet to learn where their loyalty lies."

Tjaty Hori looked up as if he felt Ament's gaze upon him. He glanced over to where the Commander stood near the Queen, and a slight frown wrinkled his brow. Iurudef had continued talking, but Hori had now lost the thread of the conversation.

"I'm sorry," he muttered. "What did you say?"

Iurudef shook his head. "Evidently nothing of great interest. I was merely talking about the preparedness of the northern legions. It is only a matter of time before the Sea Peoples test our resolve again. A change of kings is ever an unsettling time."

"The changeover is going to be a smooth transition," Hori said. "The old king is dead and we have a new one ready to be crowned. Nothing unsettling about it."

"You can't possibly imagine it will be as simple as that," Besenmut said. "The boy's father ripped the kingdoms apart. People will remember that and look for the son to repeat his actions."

"There is no reason for him to do so," Hori replied. "Siptah will be king of both kingdoms, so who will oppose him? You? You spoke against him in Council."

"I spoke for the son of the true king," Besenmut said with some heat. "But the Council decided and I will abide by the decision."

"Good. It gladdens me that some Commanders, at least, know where their duty lies. That one..." Hori glanced toward Ament and the others turned to look. "That one took it upon himself to have Menmire...Messuwy killed. Do you think he will be any less hostile to his son?"

"He's a good man and an able commander," Iurudef said. "Also, he's a confidant of the Queen. She has agreed to Siptah's accession, so he'll follow along, I'm sure."

"Meanwhile, she rules as regent," Hori went on. "And what happens if the unthinkable happens and Siptah dies? The only other choice is her son Seti-Merenptah. In effect, she becomes king."

"A woman as king?" Besenmut asked. He looked uneasy. "That couldn't happen, could it?"

"It is not unheard of. Maatkare Hatshepsut most recently, but Merneith and Sobek-kare Sobekneferu before her."

"I've never heard of those others."

"It doesn't matter," Hori said. "The point is that women have been king before, and I think Tausret would grasp the throne with both hands if the opportunity presented itself."

"Or maybe create the opportunity," Iurudef murmured.

"Precisely."

"I think you tread a dangerous path, Tjaty Hori," Besenmut said. "You put yourself in opposition to Queen Tausret, who as regent holds the power of the kingdoms in her hands. It would be a small matter for her to strip you of your office and consign you to a prison cell or worse."

"I am completely loyal to king and regent," Hori declared. "Do not confuse my musings with actions, Besenmut. Your position is a lot more precarious."

"The position of Legion Commander is within my purview," Iurudef noted. "I make and break commanders."

Besenmut bowed stiffly. "Then you must do as you see fit, General, and no doubt you will break Ament and other loyal commanders at the same time." He made as if to leave and then turned back to face the senior officer. "It seems that troubled times have returned to us already, and the king not even crowned yet."

Hori glanced at Iurudef. "Calm down, Besenmut," he said. "Nobody said anything about replacing you or any other commander. I know you are loyal and would have you by my side under any circumstance."

Besenmut bowed again, but made no further move to leave.

"I would replace Ament," Iurudef said. "He has shown himself dangerous already and will no doubt act in the Queen's interest again."

"Is that necessarily a bad thing?" Besenmut asked. "She is the queen after all."

"As long as she does not covet a higher office. If she stretches out her hand for the throne, then she will set her dog on it."

"Then remove him, General, if commanders are yours to make or break."

"Ament is perhaps an exception. He rises and falls on the whim of the king and queen."

"Then you need a more permanent solution," Hori said quietly. "One that can't be countermanded."

"And there you have it," Besenmut observed. "The times of trouble are upon us once more, when men are struck down on a whim and no one is safe. Is there no answer that does not involve murder and violence?"

"As long as there are two contenders for the throne, there will be dissension," Hori said. "We had Userkheperure and Menmire, now we have Seti-Merenptah and Siptah."

"And the queen presiding over it all."

"There must be another solution," Besenmut muttered. He was prevented from exploring the possibilities by a cry from one of the helmsmen on the great steering oars.

"There lies Iunu, Captain."

The barge captain hurried to the side to watch as the sacred temples slowly swam into view, where Queen Tausret joined him, holding little Seti-Merenptah in her arms. The oarsmen redoubled their efforts now that their first destination was in sight, and within a hand span of time, the craft was nosing into the city docks.

Crowds had gathered to welcome their young king, and priests from every temple of the Nine were on hand, dressed according to the precepts of each god and goddess, and a host of acolytes blew rams' horns, shook sistra, blew on flutes, plucked on harps, and clashed cymbals. The eruption of noise disturbed flocks of wildfowl on the river and nearby farm animals brayed and bellowed as if taking part in the welcome.

Loud as the temple music was, the cries of the populace drowned them out when they caught sight of the young king in the bow of the barge. The cheering faltered a little as he limped down the deck toward the gangplank, and some murmuring started, quickly quashed as the temple guards laid about them with staves. Tausret led the royal party to greet the high priests and the Governor of the Heq-At sepat. The latter gave the official welcome, waxing lyrical as he offered up a host of honorifics in praise of Queen, King and Crown Prince, before finishing on a more intimate note.

"You will, of course, be my guests in my Residence here in the Place of Pillars. I, and the Hem-netjer of Atum, have arranged the details for the coronation tomorrow."

"Thank you, Governor Puyemra, Hem-netjer Nefertem," Tausret said. "It is fitting that the Nine of Iunu are the first to acclaim the new king."

The coronation at Waset would be the main one, it had been decided, as Siptah derived from a southern family, and the support of Amun would be needed if the Two Kingdoms were to be fully united once more. Ceremonies in the other cities of Ta Mehu and Ta Shemau would be considerable less elaborate and would consist mainly of showing the king to his subjects and having the priests endorse him. Tausret was determined that this would also be an opportunity to let the people see Seti-Merenptah--the true successor to Userkheperure Seti.

The next morning, Siptah stood at the start of the spiral road of temples dedicated to the Nine, clad only in a short, white kilt and plain reed sandals. His withered left leg was hitched up, his toes the only part touching the ground. He looked lost and afraid, a ten year old boy lately just a palace child and now thrust mercilessly into kingship. His fear was not even private, as a host of onlookers watched to see how he would behave.

A horn sounded and Siptah looked across to where Tausret and Bay smiled encouragingly, before limping slowly up the spiral road. As he came to each temple, the priests emerged and greeted him, sprinkling him with sacred water and blowing heavy smoke of incense over him. The priestesses of Nebt-Het passed him on to those of Auset, and those to the priests of Heru, of Set, of Asar, and so up the spiral past the temples of Nut, Geb, Tefnut and Shu, where each high priest offered up blessings from their own god or goddess.

At the culmination of the spiral, at the highest point of the low sacred mound, he came to the Great Temple of Atum, the Creator God. Here Nefertem greeted him, but instead of sprinkling him with sacred water or blowing smoke over him, the Hem-netjer led him inside the shadowy temple, passing through the columned forecourts and halls into the dimly lit precinct of the god himself. They stopped at a small inner chamber into which the only light fell was from the open cedar doors. Siptah peered inside, afraid but curious, but could see nothing.

"Are you prepared to meet the god, Sekhaienre?"

"In...in there?" Siptah stared into the darkened room.

"The god dwells in the sacred mound, the ben-ben. In the beginning were just Nu, the primordial waters, and then Atum the Creator caused the ben-ben to rise from the waters to provide a place for the god to rest. Inside that room is the original ben-ben, and the god resides within it."

"Must I go in there?" Siptah quavered.

"If you want to be king, you must. Before the gods can welcome a new king as god-on-earth, they must meet him." Nefertem smiled and put a hand on the boy's shoulder. "Enter, Sekhaienre. The god will look kindly on the pure of heart."

The Hem-netjer pushed him gently toward the entrance and Siptah lurched forward, across the threshold, his shadow preceding him into the gloom. The door swung shut and Siptah cried out in fright as blackness rushed over him. Then silence. Siptah stood shivering, staring wildly into the darkness, imagining all sorts of gods, demons or beasts creeping up on him, but after a little while, when nothing happened, he grew calmer.

"It's just a test," he whispered. "Locking me in a dark room. They'll come a let me out in a bit and ask me if I've seen the god."

The silence and darkness dragged on, and Siptah wondered what he ought to say when they let him out. "Does the priest know if the god visits me? If I say he has, he might know I'm lying, but if I say he hasn't, they might not let me be king."

The silence grew and with it a feeling of oppression, as if a great weight was settling on the temple roof. Siptah gulped, wondering if this was the presence of the god. A glimmer of light appeared in the darkness, faint and flickering so as to make the boy doubt it was really there. A gentle susurration whispered about him, a faint breeze that stirred the fabric of his kilt for a moment before dying away.

The light grew stronger and illuminated the tip of a steep-sided pyramid of dark granite. Within the glow, Siptah saw the figure of a seated man and trembled, for this was surely the god himself. Kingly he appeared, crowned with Pasekhemty, the combined red and white crowns of the Two Kingdoms. The heka and nekhakha of his authority were held in hands crossed on the figure's chest, and Siptah saw the nekhakha tremble slightly. This faint movement was the only sign that this was a living man rather than a statue or a perfect god.

"Welcome, Sekhaienre Siptah." A voice, deep but hollow as if issuing from a tomb rather than flesh and blood lungs and throat, shivered in the still air.

"I...I hear you, m...mighty king, lord of creation," Siptah stuttered, bowing and making a sign of obeisance.

"Rule wisely in the time you are given, Sekhaienre Siptah."

The glow at the top of the pyramid started to fade and within the space of ten breaths, the chamber was once more in darkness, the only sound being the rasping breath of a small boy. Shortly thereafter, the cedar doors behind him creaked open, letting in a shaft of light, and Nefertem appeared.

"Did the god appear to you, Sekhaienre?"

Siptah wondered if the priest had played the part of the god, but could not detect any similarity between Nefertem's rather ordinary voice and the sepulchral tones of the god. "Yes, he did. He told me to rule wisely."

"Then the god has accepted you, King Sekhaienre. Come out now from the precinct of the god and show yourself to the people."

The sunlight dazzled Siptah as he came out into the forecourt of the temple and he stood with a hand shading his eyes as the people of Iunu, commoners and nobles alike, applauded and cheered their new king. Tausret and Bay guided him back down the spiral road and into the Governor's residence, where he was offered refreshment--milk and honey cakes.

"I'm king now, aren't I?" he asked.

"Not yet," Tausret said. "First you must open the old king's mouth and then be formally crowned in Waset."

Bay saw the look of disappointment on the boy's face and put his arm around his nephew. "If the god accepted you, then yes, you are king," he said. "The rest is just formality."

Chapter 6
Year 1 of Sekhaienre Ramesses-Siptah

The royal progress continued on through the lush farmlands of Ta Mehu. From Iunu, the barge made its way down to Per-Ramesses, where the coronation ceremonies and presentation to the common people was played out again, though here the Temple of Re was the main host. Upriver the barge went, moving between the branches of the Great River and delivering the players of the kingly drama to the cities of Per-Bast, Khem, Imu, Sau, Per-Wadjet, Djedu and Perire, before making a brief stopover back at the capital city of Men-nefer.

"Is it over?" Siptah asked. "I'm tired of going from city to city and temple to temple. I want my own bed and my toys."

"You are no longer a child," Tausret snapped. "Behave like the king you hope to become. Show yourself to your people and stop complaining." She relented as his eyes filled with tears. "Go and play now, Siptah. We leave for the south in two days where we will bury King Userkheperure and make you king in his place. You'll like that, won't you?"

"Then nobody will be able to tell me what to do," Siptah muttered as he slouched off.

Two days later, the royal barge set off again, this time forging upriver with the northerly winds filling their sail. The oarsmen had less to occupy them most days, only manning the oars when the wind fell, or the barge was eased into city docks along the way. Henen-nesut, Khmun and Zawty praised their new young king and lifted their voices in joyous cries, but the cities of Tjenu, Abdju, Iunet and Gebtu murmured when Siptah appeared staring sullenly at Tausret and the soldiers of the northern legions.

Khent-min was where Siptah had spent his early years and many people knew of him or had known Messuwy when he had retired there between being relieved of his position of King's Son of Kush, and grasping the reins of power as Menmire Amenmesse. The populace turned out to stare with curiosity at the child now elevated to the throne of his father, and at the widow of the king who had brought such ruin down on Ta Shemau--for that is how many people understood the recent internecine conflict that had ravaged the kingdoms.

The barge passed Waset by to visit the southern cities of Ta-senet, Behdet, and Nekhen City of Hawks. People crowded the walls of Amun's City as the barge thrashed its way upriver, the wind having failed half a day before. The banks of the river were also thronged with peasants and farmers, the inhabitants of any village or town within a day's travel making their way to the water's edge to see their young king.

A few days later, the barge returned to Waset and disgorged the royal party. The northern Tjaty, Hori, had been left behind in Men-nefer to govern Ta Mehu, and Tjaty Paraemheb joined them now. They stayed in the old eastern palace in the main city, resting until that evening when the burial ceremonies would commence.

The body of the dead king had been brought to Waset ten days before and lay in the Mansion of Millions of Years dedicated to King Userkheperure Seti on the west bank. Now, as the royal party boarded the barge once more and cast off, being carried swiftly across the river in the twilight, the body of the king in its heavy gilded sarcophagus was loaded onto the funerary sledge, and teams of oxen hitched to it. Chariots brought the Queen and boy-king to the funerary temple, but here they dismounted and would walk beside the sledge all the way to the tomb and back. The dust and discomfort was part of their sacrifice to the memory of the king.

The funeral party set off, along the road that lead to the Place of Truth, where some of the tomb workers joined the procession, and on through the sand and loose rubble into Ta-sekhet-ma'at and the waiting tomb. Howls of wolves shattered the silence of the night as they entered the valley, their wailing cries calling to Anapa, the wolf-headed god of death. The procession became slower as they moved deeper into the dry valleys, the runners of the heavy sledge grinding the rubble beneath its weight, while the chill of the desert night sucked the sun's heat from the rocks.

Priests of Amun led the funeral party, wearing their ceremonial white robes with leopard-skin capes draped over their shoulders. They carried pottery lamps with twisted flax fibres in pools of fine oil casting a reddish flickering light over the proceedings. Acolytes trudged beside the priests, carrying spare oil in jars, replacement wicks, and a host of other paraphernalia that would be required within the tomb. Behind the priests walked Tausret and Siptah, holding hands, and with them were Chancellor Bay, Tjaty Paraemheb, General Setnakhte, Commander Samut, Commander Panhesy, and numerous minor officials of the Waset court.

Bringing up the rear of the burial party, treading in the dust and ground rubble of the sledge, were the Servants of the Place of Truth and a number of slaves to take care of the lifting of the heavy sarcophagus and carrying it into the rock-cut tomb. Guards followed, loyal soldiers of the Amun and Mut legions mostly, but also aides from the northern legions acting as witnesses to the entombment of the dead king.

Other eyes watched the funeral procession. Above, on the top of the cliffs surrounding the burial valleys, men watched whose hearts were filled with avarice, and minds with the thirst for the gold that was soon to be sealed within the rock tomb. When the funeral party had left, and the fervour of the guards had faded into boredom, they would descend to the valley floor and see if there was a way to break into the tomb and rob the dead. The penalties for robbing tombs were horrific, but some judged the rewards worth the risk.

The procession arrived at the tomb--three tombs in fact. One was the one excavated for Userkheperure Seti, another for Queen Tausret, and the third for Chancellor Bay. Only Tausret's tomb was even approaching completion, and it was from its rock-cut depths that golden light spilled out into the valley. The body of Userkheperure would be buried here until his own tomb was ready to receive him. Soldiers spread out to guard the surroundings, while the slaves wrestled the heavy sarcophagus off the sledge. The Servants of the Place of Truth hurried underground to make sure everything was in readiness for the burial. Priests of Amun blessed the sarcophagus, uttering the first of hundreds of prayers that would din the ears of the gods, while the acolytes set up the Ka statue of the dead king, even as the sarcophagus was slowly lowered into the first corridor of the tomb.

"Are you ready to perform the Opening of the Mouth, Siptah?" Tausret asked.

Siptah nodded, his eyes wide as he stared at everything that was going on. "Wh...what do I do?"

"I will tell you."

Hem-netjer of Amun, Mahuhy, who had formerly been Royal Secretary, took up his position in front of the Ka statue. He washed the statue with purified water and then with sanctified oil, while the other priests chanted the sacred phrases that would centre the attention of the spirit of the dead king on the statue. Mahuhy finished the lustrations and wiped his hands on a clean linen cloth before accepting a spooned blade of rose quartz from an acolyte. He held the Pesheskef out to Siptah who, prompted by Tausret, took it.

"Hold the tip to the lips of the statue," Tausret murmured.

Siptah had to reach up to do it and Tausret whispered the ancient prayers for the boy to repeat. "Your mouth was closed, but I have set in order for you, your mouth and your teeth. I open for you your mouth; I open for you your two eyes. I have opened for you your mouth with the instrument of Anapa. I have opened your mouth with the instrument of Anapa, with the implement with which the mouths of the gods were opened."

One of the priests took the Pesheskef, and Mahuhy handed Siptah an adze made of 'that which falls from heaven', the Seb Ur sceptre, which gleamed coldly in the light of the oil lamps. Again Siptah reached up and touched the statue's lips, and once more Tausret whispered the required phrases.

"Heru, open the mouth! Heru, open the mouth! Heru has opened the mouth of the dead, as he in times of old opened the mouth of Asar, with the iron which came forth from Set, with the iron instrument with which he opened the mouths of the gods. He has opened your mouth with it. You shall walk and shall speak, and your body shall be with the great company of the gods in the Great House of the Atum, and you shall receive there the ureret crown from Heru, the lord of mankind."

Finally, the Ur Hekau sceptre was passed to the boy-king. This was a strangely sinuous piece of polished carved wood with a ram's head at one end, surmounted by the royal uraeus. Siptah touched the tip to the Ka statue's lips and eyes four times, while reciting the words Tausret whispered to him.

"I declare that I have secured for you all the benefits which accrued to the god Asar from the actions of Nut, Heru, and Set, when he was in a similar state. It has been said that every dead man hopes to be provided with the Hekau, or words of power, which are necessary for him in the next world, but without a mouth it is impossible for him to utter them. Now that the use of the mouth, has been restored to you, I must give him not only the words of power, but also the ability to utter them correctly and in such wise that the gods and other beings will hearken to them and obey them; I touch the Ur Hekau instrument four times on the lips and eyes and these four touches of the Ur Hekau instrument endow you with the faculty of uttering the proper words in the proper manner in each of the four quarters of the world."

The Ka statue, its eyes and mouth opened so the spirit of the dead king could once more enjoy the good things of the world, and also utter the protections necessary for its continued existence, was carried into the depths of the tomb and set about with offerings of food and drink. Beer and wine, baskets of grain, baked bread and roasted meats, piles of fruit and vegetables waited for the dead king's feasts in the afterlife, and ushabtiu set up in readiness. These tiny figurines represented the servants that would wait upon the king should he be called on for any work to be performed. Spells written on the figurines would magically awaken them when their services were required.

Tausret left Siptah in the care of his uncle Bay and walked deep into the tomb, to the chamber where lay the sarcophagus. Ignoring the priests still in attendance she put her arms out, pressing close to the cold granite, her tears now falling freely.

"Wait for me, my beloved Seti. Wait for me in Sekhet Hetepet, the Field of Peace. Wait for me in Sekhet Iaru, the Field of Reeds, wherein lie all manner of good things prepared by the gods for those they love. It may be many years before I join you, but join you I will, O my beloved Seti."

She turned away and passed back through the long corridors and chambers to the outside world. Behind her the masons closed up the tomb and the priests of Amun tied the doors closed with sacred linen cords, washing them with purified water and fastening them with holy knots. Finally, on the outermost brickwork, the masons applied a layer of plaster and Remaktef, the Scribe of the Place of Truth affixed his seal. Slaves moved in to fill the entranceway with rubble, packing it in tightly and sweeping the sand to obscure any sign that a tomb lay in the rock beneath the valley floor. Now it was only the presence of guards that hinted at a hidden tomb, but soon they too would disappear, leaving only the guards at the valley entrance to watch over the sleep of dead kings.

The stars wheeled in the darkened body of Nut and now, with dawn approaching, the royal party stumbled back down the valley, past the workmen's village to where chariots waited to carry them to the river and the ferry. A day would pass between the burial of the old king and the coronation ceremonies, and already Siptah was asleep in the arms of his uncle Bay.

The day of the coronation dawned with young King Siptah in place before the Great temple of Amun. Crowds had gathered to watch the public aspects of the ceremony, but most displayed a reluctance to become too involved. Men had been born, lived and died between the coronation of Usermaatre Ramesses and his death and then in the space of twelve years, three more kings had ascended the throne of the Two Kingdoms. Now a fourth one presented himself before the god and many men wondered how long this one would last. It seemed as if the gods of Kemet could not make up their minds as to who would join them.

Siptah shivered with the chill of the early morning as he waited for the ceremony to begin. He was clad in a simple white kilt, barefoot and without adornment, and hungry. The young boy had eaten his last meal the previous night and would not eat again until he became god-on-earth. Tausret and Bay stood off to one side and Siptah stole glances at them, looking for signs of encouragement. All he received was a small nod from his uncle. He had been thoroughly coached in what he must say and do, but there were gaps in his knowledge, lacunae where the secrets of the temple allowed no foreknowledge.

A single ram's horn sounded within the temple, a mournful cry calling a boy to his destiny. Siptah started forward and almost fell as his withered left leg buckled under him. He swiftly recovered but as he limped through the gateway of the pylon into the courtyard, a murmur ran through the crowd of onlookers, and many muttered about the ill omen at the start of the king's reign.

Priests of every god awaited Siptah in the courtyard, but it was Mahuhy, the Hem-netjer of Amun who led him to the Lake of Cleansing. Here four men dressed as gods with golden masks over their faces, took charge of the boy. They stripped him of his kilt and ritually cleansed him, pouring water over him from golden vessels. Other priests dried him with clean linen and dressed him, and then men representing Atum and Heru guided him forward into the Hall of Jubilation. Siptah gaped in awe at the dazzling displays of silver and gold and at the carved columns marching in serried ranks into the shadowed interior of the temple.

Despite the warnings he had received, Siptah was unprepared for the presence of Wadjet, the cobra protector of the kings of Kemet. When she emerged from her shrine, her black length rasping against the tiles, her black eyes expressionless and her flickering tongue tasting his fear, he could not help himself. He screamed and drew back, and the snake struck at him with fangless jaws. Priests muttered in the shadows at the terrible omen and one hurried forward to comfort the crying child as another carried the cobra back to its shrine.

A priest hurried to fetch the Iunmutef and apprised him of the situation. "What do we do, holy one?"

"You continue the ceremony," the Iunmutef said. "What else?"

"But Wadjet has rejected him. The boy cried out in fear."

"Is the child dead? Did Wadjet strike with her fangs?"

"No, of course not, holy one, but..."

"But nothing. Admittedly, the omens are not good but do you want to be the one who tells the Regent she must choose another king? Besides, he may still be accepted as king. Bring him through and let the ceremony continue."

Iunmutef the Pillar, as a representative of Heru, took the child in hand and set the crowns of Kemet upon Siptah's head--the white Hedjet crown, the red Deshret crown, Padsekhemty crown, the Ibes crown, the Nemes headdress and Seshed headband, finally setting the blue leather Khepresh crown on the boy's head. With each new crown, the priests uttered cries of exultation, forcing away the horrors of the bad omen and praying that the gods would accept the new king.

Atum and Heru of the Horizon led Siptah into the Holy of Holies deep within the temple and there, in the dim red light of the innermost sanctuary, presented the king to the god Amun. While Siptah knelt in shivering awe, the man playing the part of the god lifted the crown and replaced it.

"Accept this crown from your father Amun."

The god had now accepted him and all that remained was for the assembled people to see him placed on the throne and given his names. Priests of all the gods thronged around the little boy and guided him, limping, to the raised throne in the open temple courtyard. Five priests came to the fore and each addressed Siptah in turn, intoning the royal names by which the boy-king would now be known.

"Let Heru empower you," cried the first priest. "Your name in Heru shall be Kanakht Meryhapi Sankhtanebemkafraneb, Strong Bull, Beloved of Hapi, who causes the whole land to live by means of his Ka every day."

"Nekhabet and Wadjet name you also," the second priest said. "Your name of Nebty shall be Saaiunu--Made Great in Iunu."

"The gods recognise you as their son on earth," said the third. "Heru Nebu names you Aami Itefre--Great like his father Re."

"Nesut-byt--King of Ta Mehu and Ta Shemau, North and South," cried the fourth priest. "Sekhaienre Meryamun--He whom Re causes to appear, beloved of Amun."

"Sa-Re--Son of Re," the fifth priest said. "Ramesses-Siptah--Re fashioned him, son of Ptah."

A sigh of relief swept through the people in the forecourt. At last they had a king again who was consecrated to Amun and through their god to the city of Waset. They could see before them a Kemet united again. Userkheperure and Menmire had fought to the death and destroyed the Ma'at of the Two Kingdoms, but now, under the reign of Sekhaienre Siptah, they could look forward to a restoration of all the good things--a time of peace and prosperity.

Chapter 7

Chancellor Bay speaks:

I am exhilarated. I am in Waset and I have just seen my nephew raised to become god-on-earth. I am now uncle to the King of Kemet. My star edges closer to the central point about which the body of the goddess Nut revolves. A thousand years ago--so the priests tell us--a star within the body of the Snake stood at the centre of the night sky and all other stars danced in attendance. This star represented the King of Kemet, receiving the submission of the kings of the Nations. Now another star takes its place, a star which can only be that of my sister's son Siptah. My own star is close by and who knows, maybe the gods will select it to follow upon my nephew's reign?

It is not beyond the bounds of possibility for already the seemingly impossible has come to pass. I thought that when I threw in my lot with Userkheperure against my sister's husband King Menmire, that all I could reasonably hope for was a position of power within the court of Men-nefer. That came to pass when I was elevated to the high station of Chancellor of All of the Lands of Kemet. But then Userkheperure died and I saw my influence shredding and falling away. I thought to transfer my allegiance back to Menmire, but he was captured and soon died in captivity. To whom could I now look for preferment and position? Tausret was only Queen and her son an infant, while Menmire's son was a child.

I do not doubt that Menmire was executed, despite the story being put about that first a rescue was attempted, and then someone broke into the royal apartments and killed him. It can never be proved--and I dare say no longer matters. Queen Tausret has taken control of Kemet and is king in all but name.

I spoke to as many people of influence as I could in the dark days following Userkheperure's death and managed to convince a handful--Tjaty Hori, Legion Commanders Emsaf and Panhesy, and even General Iurudef--that there was an alternative to raising an infant to the throne. Only Panhesy displayed a natural sympathy for the line of Menmire, but I was able to play upon the fears and expectations of the others and at length convince them that Siptah was the logical choice to bring peace to the Kingdoms.

It was a calculated risk, for I knew that Queen Tausret would never give up her son's claim to the throne, and to be seen to openly oppose her was to gain her enmity. It was accomplished though, and Siptah is king, while Tausret maintains her position of strength as Regent. Tausret's baby son is made heir, but so many things can change. Only the gods know what the future holds. When the time comes, and after Siptah is settled on the throne, then we shall see what can be changed. I must find Siptah a wife and get him to produce a son. Every man wants his son to succeed him and Siptah will be no different. The strength of the House of Ramesses will flow through the line of Menmire Amenmesse rather than through the line of Userkheperure Seti. They were both the sons of Baenre Merenptah after all.

Meanwhile, Siptah's position is by no means secure. If anything was to happen to him, Tausret would rule as regent until Seti-Merenptah came of age. He is king, but a king with little power, and few friends. In fact, the only person Siptah can truly rely on is me. Thus, I must ensure that I am there to protect him, and the only way I can do that is to become powerful. I am already Chancellor and Treasurer; I have the status of being Uncle to the King; I must become regent.

I do not fool myself that Tausret will allow that, but as Siptah grows in maturity and power, he will be able to effect change, and as a first step I can become co-regent with the Queen. I am responsible for bringing him to the throne after all, so I shall play on my role as Kingmaker--'he who establishes the king on the throne of his father'. The stronger Siptah becomes, the stronger I become and the weaker Tausret grows.

So what must I do now? I feel that these days in Waset with Siptah still bemused by his elevation to the throne are my best opportunity to strengthen my position. I shall approach him in the guise of the kindly uncle and talk to him of his father, of his childhood, and of his mother. At the moment he is alone, but soon will come the sycophants, those seeking to advance through false friendship, and I must be there to protect him. He will foster my own advancement if I ask it, and if I can show myself as a true friend and support, I will gain much.

I must, of course, temper my thirst for power with caution, for Queen Tausret still holds the reins of government tightly in her fists. So I will dissemble, putting myself forward for the arduous task of guiding the young king, and prove myself indispensable. When Tausret is convinced that I seek only what is good and true for Kemet, then I will be able to turn the king's head and secure for myself the position of Regent in her place.

Chapter 8
Year 2 of Sekhaienre Ramesses-Siptah

"Tell me another story, Uncle Bay."

Bay regarded the small boy fidgeting on the ground beside him with affection. They sat beneath the deep shade of a tamarind tree in the grounds of the western palace, alone except for the brace of Kushite guards waiting just out of earshot. After the coronation, Tausret had made the decision to spend some time in Waset before returning to the north as she appreciated the need to settle the southern city down after the recent troubles. She and Tjaty Paraemheb strove to dispense justice, while the presence of the young king placated the many people who still looked fondly on the recent reign of the king's father.

The Chancellor had been the one to point out that the eastern palace, within the city itself, held painful associations for Siptah, as it was where his father had been held prisoner and later killed. He suggested that the western palace, though long disused, could be easily refurbished. It was close by moreover, and the king could swiftly be brought into the city for any official functions. Bay volunteered to act as a mentor and tutor for the young boy, and Tausret, distracted by her many duties, saw no harm in it.

Bay organised tutors to school the young king in mathematics, writing, history, and the proper study of the gods, while he guided Siptah in matters of law and personal history himself. Siptah took to his lessons avidly, but his favourite classes were the informal ones with his uncle where he found out who he was and where he fitted into the grand scheme of things. Stories were a good way of imparting this knowledge, and if not everything he heard was the complete truth, at least it served to bolster the young king's confidence.

"What would you like to hear about?" Bay asked. "Another tale of your grandfather Baenre Merenptah fighting the Ribu at Perire? Or perhaps of your great-grandfather Usermaatre Ramesses at the Battle of Kadesh?"

46

"I've heard all those." Siptah dug into the dark earth beneath the tamarind tree with a short stick. "Tell me about my mother. How did she meet my father?"

"Ah, now that was a love story. Your mother Suterere was my younger sister, and we were brought into Kemet by Usermaatre when he captured our parents during one of his campaigns. We all served in the palace at Per-Ramesses and later..."

"They were slaves?" Siptah frowned. "I am descended from slaves?"

"Not in the least," Bay assured him. "Our father was descended from the kings of Amurri, so you could say your mother was a princess of sorts. I mean, she was captured by Usermaatre and brought into Kemet to serve him as a servant, but she was still royal."

"Why didn't he take her to wife then? He married other foreign women."

"Your mother had not yet been born, otherwise he assuredly would have. She was a real beauty, but as a humble palace servant she escaped the notice of anyone important until she and I came to serve in the palace in Kush. There, your father caught sight of her and fell in love."

"And he married her? Instead of just taking her as one of his women?"

"Indeed. As I said, he was in love. And you were a product of that love."

"Born of love, but not loved by the gods, else they would not have given me a crippled leg."

"Yet here you are as Lord of the Two Lands. How can you say the gods do not love you?"

"My father was king."

"Yes, Menmire Amenmesse."

"But only king of Ta Shemau, not of the Two Lands."

Bay hesitated. "Strictly, that is true, Majesty, yet he was crowned as King of both kingdoms. It was only because his brother--his younger brother--disputed his sovereignty that he ruled only in the south."

"But I rule both kingdoms?"

"Truly, Majesty. In this you are greater than your father or his brother. It makes you more like Usermaatre or Baenre, both of whom ruled all of Kemet."

"They were warrior kings, Uncle. With my withered leg I am unlikely to be able to fight the Nine Bows."

"Do you imagine they fought on foot with axe or spear? They led their armies from their war chariot, fighting with the bow and slaying hundreds. You can ride a chariot already."

"If somebody drives for me."

"A king does not have to drive his own chariot--that is why there is a royal charioteer."

"I'm not very good with a bow," Siptah confessed. "I only hit a target five times out of ten...maybe six. And then only if I'm on foot. A chariot sways around too much."

"That is easily remedied. I shall instruct the local commander to give you practice in riding chariots and shooting from them. You'll soon be proficient, but even if you weren't, you can still command your army. The men are heartened by seeing their king and fight all the harder."

Bay was as good as his word and talked to Commander Panhesy of the Mut legion. Panhesy arranged for skilled charioteers to offer instruction in all aspects of driving a chariot and caring for its horses, and for his best archers to guide the young king. By the time he left Waset to assume his duties in the north, he could brace himself within a swaying chariot and at least hold a bow and arrow, even if he was not yet capable of releasing the arrows accurately.

Three months after the coronation, Tausret called Bay to her and told him of her decision to move back to Men-nefer.

"I commend you on your attention to your duties, Chancellor Bay. I have been kept busy setting up the foundations of good government here in the south, with Tjaty Paraemheb, and have not had the time to worry about the boy. I hear he is doing well in his studies."

Bay bowed. "Indeed he is, Majesty. The king has a fine mind and applies himself to all his lessons."

"He is versed in knowledge of the gods and of the law?"

"He is, Majesty."

"Good. He is scarcely what Kemet needs as a king, but even he will need to know what is happening about him."

"Siptah is not as useless as you believe, Majesty," Bay said. "He has the makings of a good king."

"A king needs to be more than just a priest and a judge, Bay. Once upon a time, the kings would run around the city to prove they were fit to lead the army into battle. Even today, a king is expected to carry the holy paraphernalia in front of the barque of the god on holy days. I cannot see Siptah ever doing that. A crippled king is no king."

"He is young yet, Majesty, and his withered leg can often be overlooked."

Tausret shook her head. "He limps wherever he goes and has to hold onto someone or wield a stick to stop himself falling over."

"Not when he sits in judgment, Majesty."

"When he what? What nonsense is this? Paraemheb conducts judicial business."

"I have had him sitting in judgment on certain minor matters regarding disputes between the Servants in the Place of Truth. They were happy to have the king sit in judgment upon them."

"That was not well done, Chancellor Bay. Siptah may only be holding the office of king open until Seti-Merenptah can ascend the throne, but he will make the throne a laughing stock. He is a child and a cripple and that is why I am regent--so he can remain unseen, in the background."

"He is still the king, Majesty, and his actions by no means bring the throne into disrepute. If you could but see him yourself, you would surely agree."

Tausret scowled. "Very well. I shall come over to the west bank tomorrow and watch him as he plays the king. But be warned, Chancellor Bay, I shall shut his little court down at the least sign of impropriety."

Queen Tausret had herself ferried across to the west bank the next morning, and arrived at the Place of Truth without fanfare and with only a single chariot and a single guard for protection. Bay greeted her at the village gate and guided her through to the house of the Scribe of the Great Field where the unofficial court convened.

"Thank you for attending so informally, Majesty," Bay said. "I feared that a large entourage would disrupt proceedings."

"It would also serve to offer legitimacy to his actions," Tausret replied. "I will decide that after I have watched him."

Bay escorted the Regent into the scribe's hall where Siptah sat on a small raised chair, clad in long flowing robes and wearing a small version of the Double Crown upon his head. Their entrance turned heads and stimulated a rush of mutterings as people recognised the Queen. She nodded casually and seated herself at the rear of the room while her guard hovered near the doorway. Bay sat beside her and together they watched the little law court at work.

Siptah looked up from the case he was hearing, and saw the Queen at the back of the room. His eyes widened slightly before glancing at Bay and then back to the men kneeling before him.

"I find for the mason Neb," Siptah said. "Scribe Remaktef, let it be recorded thus."

"As you command, Son of Re," Remaktef said. He made some notations on the scroll in front of him. "The next case is brought by the woman Hoya against her husband Antep. She charges that he hit her in a public place and caused her shame and embarrassment."

"Can the elders of the village not deal with this?" Siptah asked.

"They found for the husband," the scribe said. "So she now appeals to the king."

"And she will accept my decision as final?"

"Yes, Son of Re."

"Then let her put her case."

Hoya stood and offered up her version of events in a straightforward manner, and then sat down again.

"Does the husband dispute her account?"

"No, Son of Re, but he asks that you listen to his explanation." Siptah nodded and the man stood, bowed, and started talking.

"Majesty, a man has the right to discipline his wife when she errs. On this particular day, I came home after a hard day in the Great Field to find that my supper had not been prepared, and that my wife was not even in the house. I found her in the main street gossiping with other women, so I chastised her with a single blow to the face and ordered her home."

"Was a blow really necessary?"

"Yes, Majesty, for she was wilfully neglecting her duty to her husband."

"And what of a man's duty to his wife?" Siptah asked. "Do you not love your wife?"

"Of course, Majesty, but..." Antep flushed and stammered. "With...with respect, Majesty, what has love got to do with it?"

"Does a man who truly loves his wife then hit her? Does he subject her to ridicule and shame in front of her neighbours?" Siptah turned to Remaktef. "Has Hoya offered up an explanation for why the meal was uncooked and she was found gossiping in the street?"

Hoya bounded to her feet, and shot an angry look at her husband and the elders seated nearby. "Majesty, I have already made a defence to the elders and they have found against me, unjustly."

"So make your defence to me, Hoya."

"The fire in my home had gone out, Majesty, so I could not cook the evening meal. I went to my neighbours to beg fire and a little fuel, but as I was pleading with them, my husband rushed up and struck me."

"Antep, did you know of this?"

Antep flushed again and looked down at the dirt floor of the room. "Later, Majesty," he muttered. "I admitted my fault to her privately but she would not be appeased. She insists on accusing me publicly before my neighbours and the village elders. She now tells others of my behaviour in the bedchamber and I am laughed at and held up to ridicule."

"Hoya, you are not willing to forgive your husband?"

"Yes, Majesty, but what of my injury? He shamed me without cause."

"And you, Antep? Are you willing to forgive your wife?"

Antep shrugged and muttered beneath his breath.

Siptah turned to Remaktef again, his youthful face screwed up into a perplexed frown. "What am I to do?" he whispered. "I would award damages to the wife, but the husband's assets belong to her too."

"I do not know, Son of Re, but whatever you decide will be accepted."

Siptah thought about it for a few minutes. "I am ready to render my judgment," he said at length. "A husband and wife should love each other and neither should seek to shame the other. Antep has erred grievously by striking his wife and Hoya has erred in turn by sharing the secret things of a marriage. I cannot fine one without hurting the other, so you will do this instead. You will both stand in front of the whole village and ask forgiveness of the other for the injury caused and then will swear your undying love for the other. A husband and wife should live only in love and harmony. Do you agree? Hoya? Antep?"

The man and woman looked at each other. Antep grimaced and nodded, while Hoya nodded and smiled.

"Let it be recorded thus, Remaktef," Siptah said.

"He handles himself well for a young boy, doesn't he?" Bay asked Tausret quietly.

Tausret nodded. "You have schooled him well, but these cases are trifling, and no doubt you have instructed the villagers to accept his decisions without question."

"What else would you expect, Majesty? This is the king who sits in judgment upon them. Of course they are going to accept his decisions. Would you have it any other way?"

Tausret was silent for a few moments. "No, you are right, Chancellor Bay. We must all act our parts."

"And sitting there he is king in every aspect, wouldn't you agree?"

"Yes. I thought that his withered leg and posture would detract from his demeanour, but you have disguised it well in his flowing robes--and even that small crown upon his head. He even looks kingly, I suppose."

"As he should," Bay said. "He is the anointed king."

Tausret scowled and got up, walking swiftly outside and into the hot morning sun outside the scribe's house. Bay followed.

"Remember he only plays the part of king," Tausret said. "Seti-Merenptah is the true successor of Userkheperure and Siptah merely holds the throne for him until he is of age."

"Not exactly, Regent. Sekhaienre Siptah is truly king, anointed and accepted by the gods. Your infant son will join him on the throne and succeed him, but that does not make that boy in there..." Bay gestured toward the scribe's house, "...any less royal. They are both grandsons of Baenre and descended from the great Usermaatre."

"I dare say I will never be allowed to forget that," Tausret commented. She looked around for her charioteer and beckoned him closer. "I will return to the city. Bay; prepare the young king for the journey north. We leave in three days."

Bay watched the queen leave the Place of Truth before turning back to the house with a contented smile on his face. Inside, he found the meeting breaking up and the elders shepherding the villagers out of another door. Siptah looked up as Bay entered and he beamed as his uncle approached.

"I did well, didn't I, Uncle?"

"Indeed you did, Majesty. You learned your lines so well, even I was fooled."

Bay took a leather purse from his belt and handed it to Remaktef. "Distribute that as you see fit, Scribe. The villagers learned their lines well."

Remaktef bowed and accepted the purse. "Thank you, Chancellor. The Servants in the Place of Truth are ever at your disposal." He bowed again, and again to Siptah before withdrawing and leaving uncle and nephew alone.

"She doesn't like me, does she?" Siptah said.

"The Queen? She doesn't know you like I do, Majesty. She will come to accept you, I promise."

"What did she say?"

"She said you behaved in a kingly manner and that she was pleased. Did I not say that I would act for you and seat you firmly on the throne of your father?"

"I wish you were regent instead of her."

"One day, Majesty, if you wish it, but for now we must work to show you as a real king and one worthy of the support of peasants and nobles alike. Once we have the army supporting you we can supplant the queen and you can do as you like."

"But you'll always be there to look after me, won't you, Uncle?"

"Of course, for as long as you need me. You are my whole family."

"Can we go back to the palace now? I'm tired and these robes chafe me."

Bay led the way outside and sent for the king's chariot which was waiting outside the village gates. They rode back along the dusty roads between the Mansions of Millions of Years of former kings, farms and villages, fields and orchards, and came at last to the western palace.

"Be ready for a river voyage," Bay said as the king alighted within the courtyard. "The Queen returns to Men-nefer in three days and you are to go with her."

"I don't want to go, and if I want I'll stay here. I'm the king, aren't I? I like it here in Waset where people knew my father. Nobody liked him in Men-nefer."

"Remember what I said, Majesty. One day you will be able to do as you please, but for now you must obey the regent. I will look after you and everything will be as it should."

Chapter 9
Year 2 of Sekhaienre Siptah

The voyage downriver to Men-nefer was uneventful to start with, but pleasant. Siptah had not been looking forward to it, having been dragged away from the city he identified as being his father's, but his status had changed since his last voyage and now everyone was deferential and sought to please him. The only irritation stemmed from the presence of Queen Tausret, who still treated him as if he was a boy rather than king, and grew impatient if he expressed a desire to go ashore or indulge in a little hunting in the reed beds. At these times, Chancellor Bay would intervene, sometimes persuading Siptah to forego transient pleasures and other times using those very surrenders to extract a short delay.

Siptah had discovered the delights of hunting wildfowl in the reed beds along the margins of the river. The royal barge would put in to a nearby village and commandeer several reed boats or shallow drafted punts. Villagers would fall over themselves in their keenness to serve the young king, poling the boats out into the still waters between the reeds and allowing the king to shoot at the birds with his bow. The king had a withered leg, but that did not affect his arms and, with practice, he had become quite skilled with the bow and the throwing stick.

Dusk was the best time for the hunt when the ducks that had spent the day foraging amongst the fields and irrigation canals, returned to the security of the reed beds. The punts would lie, hidden by reeds on the edges of open water, the occupants sitting quietly and scanning the sky for the return of the flocks.

"There, Majesty." The villager poling the king's punt pointed to the north, where a skein of ducks dropped through the evening air toward the water. Siptah half stood, rocking the little boat, and then thought better of it, seating himself again.

"We wait," he whispered.

The flight of ducks passed overhead, wheeling and returning with honking cries as they scanned the reed beds for signs of danger. Finally, they dropped lower and landed, spraying water. They immediately started preening and flapping as they paddled around in the open water. A dozen pairs of eyes watched them, unseen from the fringe of vegetation, and soon their patience was rewarded. Flocks of ducks appeared, and taking heart from the few already on the water, started their descent.

As the front of the flock passed overhead, Siptah stood and in a fluid motion, drew his bow and released his first shaft into the mass of birds. At that range it could scarcely miss and a duck fell with a splash. Around the king, other men stood, balancing in their rocking craft, and shot their own arrows or hurled throwing sticks. More birds plummeted to their deaths as missiles slashed through the flock, and cries of alarm rose from a thousand throats. With a thunder of wings, sounding like the storm wind when it rattles the fronds of the palms, the flock wheeled and rose again, passing back over the reed beds, even as more arrows flew.

By the time the ducks had fled that particular patch of water, dead and wounded birds lay scattered over the surface and the exultant cries of the archers rose in a paean of victory. Siptah grinned and pointed out ducks that he had brought down and several small boys, following their fathers out on the hunt, jumped into the water and swam out to the stricken birds. Most held single dead ducks in their teeth and swam back, but one enterprising youth took a small fishing net with him and stuffed it full of birds before dragging it back. Siptah applauded his efforts and slipped a copper bracelet from his arm, pressing it into the boy's hand. Some ducks had merely been wounded and either swam in circles, transfixed by an arrow, or fled for the cover of the reeds. The boys hunted them down and broke their necks before returning to the boats.

The hunters returned to the village and barge and laid out their catch on the riverbank for others to admire. Bay whispered a suggestion in Siptah's ear and the young king received much praise when he declared that the proceeds of the hunt should be shared amongst the villagers as well as the crew of the barge. This act of sharing greatly lessened the amount of flesh available to each person but the village elders brought out vegetables, bread and even some thin beer to add to the festivities.

"You see how the people love you, Majesty?" Bay whispered.

"Just by giving them a few ducks?"

"More than that. They see they have a king who cares about them; who regards them not just as a resource to be used but as men and women in need of the same things as kings. Repeat this act of generosity up and down the kingdoms and the common people will throw their support behind you."

The villagers turned out to cheer their king the next morning as the oarsmen propelled the barge out into the current once more, but the praise soon fell into silence as the land slipped past. They entered a stretch of river with few villages and where the cliffs on either side approached the life-giving water, constricting the belt of farmland and field to scarcely more than a stone's throw in width. Siptah sat with Bay under an awning and watched the swirl of waters and the white birds fleeing from the passage of the barge, while Tausret sat with her court officials and army commanders further back and dealt with the everyday business of the kingdoms.

A cry from an oarsman caught their attention--a cry filled with dread and apprehension. Other men looked round and took up the cry, pointing at the sky.

"Set is attacking Re!" one man called, and others fell to their knees, stretching out their arms toward the sun, wailing their fear and grief.

"What's happening?" Siptah asked. He sprang to his feet and limped to where crew members were gathered.

"The sun's face," Bay muttered. "There is something wrong with it."

Siptah squinted, peering up at the sun through slitted eyelids. "I can't see...what is that? Is something eating the sun?"

Tausret turned to the priests and scribes in her party and demanded an explanation. "What is happening?"

The priests, who had been muttering and praying to their various gods, looked from one to another, not wanting to voice their concerns to the regent. Eventually, a senior priest of Re cleared his throat and turned his face from the heavens.

"Re will overcome," he stated, though his voice shook with emotion.

"Is the god being attacked?" Tausret asked. "By Set, as those sailors think?"

"That is a vile calumny," declared a junior priest of Set. "Set would not attack a fellow god."

"Why not? He has before," a priest of Asar said. "Set seeks disorder."

Tausret motioned the priests to silence and bade the barge captain turn the craft in to shore. "We will offer up prayers and sacrifices to all the gods."

It was difficult to watch the battle between the sun god and his unknown adversary as the light from Re's face blinded them, causing them to squint and look away blinking. Even so, it became apparent that Re was losing the battle as more and more of the disc of the sun was overcome by shadow.

"What else can we do?" Tausret demanded. "We cannot just stand idle and watch the light of Re being eaten up."

Siptah clung to Bay's robe and turned his face away. He was close to tears, but Bay exhorted him not to show fear.

"Remember you are the king and a god. Re is your father, and you must stay strong in the face of his distress."

"Majesties, I believe there is no great cause for concern."

"Who speaks?" Tausret asked. "Stand forth and explain your words."

One of the scribes pushed his way through the knot of priests. "I am Pepy, son of Anapepy, Chief Scribe to the Court at Men-nefer. Majesties, this thing has happened before, and therefore we need not be concerned that the sun will suffer lasting injury."

"I have never heard of such a thing," Tausret responded.

"Nor I," Commander Ament added. "Have you actually seen it before, Pepy?"

"No," admitted the scribe. "Nor have few living men, I think, but the records speak of such a thing happening early on in the reign of Usermaa-tre--around year twenty-two I think--and before, in the time of the Heretic and his successor Nebkheperure Tutankhamen."

"If it has happened that often, why do we know nothing about it?"

Pepy shrugged. "If only peasants saw it, they could only speak of it to those they met. There would be no written record."

"But there is a written record," Ament said. "For you say you have read it. Where was the attack on the sun seen?"

"The vision that appeared to the Heretic was seen in Akhet-Aten, while that of Nebkheperure was in Aniba of Kush, and that of Usermaatre in Waset. It may be that it has happened more often, in places where only peasants saw it."

"But what does it mean?" Tausret asked. "If this has happened before, then Re is able to fight off his attacker, but what causes it? Who or what is attacking the sun?"

"That is only known to the gods," said a priest piously.

"We can only offer up prayers that the gods will come to the assistance of Re."

A moan of fear went up from the sailors as the light visibly dimmed. A large shadow now lay across most of the sun's disc and the birds in the palm trees and scrub started twittering loudly. The shadow seemed to move more swiftly now, as if certain of victory. A chill swept over the watchers as the last of Re's light was extinguished. The sailors grovelled on the ground in awe and fear, and Siptah wept softly. It was all the rest of them could do to not cry aloud, but Pepy stood with face upraised, a rapt expression on his face.

"Oh, look," he cried out. "A wash of pearly light sweeps out from the vanished sun and the stars in the body of the goddess Nut shine forth as if it was night time."

As they watched, a flash of light appeared, slowly growing as the shadow withdrew. The stars paled and disappeared and light washed over the land once more.

"Re conquers his enemy," cried a priest of the sun god. "Rejoice, for Re is powerful."

"The Akh of Re is abroad in the kingdoms once more," said another priest. "See how the shadow flees."

As they continued to watch, the sun grew stronger and before long it was apparent that the sun had suffered no harm. The barge captain drove his men back to their stations, and Tausret gathered her officials, the priests and scribes together.

"I accept that we cannot know what this shadow is or what makes it attack the sun, but there is another question that must be answered," Tausret said. "Why has it occurred now, in the second year of Sekhaienre Siptah?"

Heads turned to look at the scribe Pepy, son of Anapepy. He frowned and hesitated before answering. "It might be better to enquire of the priests, Majesty. Knowledge of the gods is their purview."

"Do any of you priests know why this has occurred now?"

None of the priests was prepared to offer up an explanation so Tausret gestured for Pepy to reply.

"I cannot be certain," the scribe said, "but it would appear that such things happen at a time of crisis for Kemet. That it happened in the time of the Heretic is no great surprise as that man raised up the sun's disc to the exclusion of the other gods. Again, in the days of Nebkheperure Tutankhamen, Kemet faced warfare between brothers."

"And in the days of Usermaatre Ramesses?" Ament asked. "Kemet was at peace."

"The treaty with Hatti had just been signed," Pepy said. "Perhaps that had something to do with it."

"There have been plenty of other crises," General Iurudef said. "Even as in the days of Nebkheperure. Why did nothing like this occur when brother fought against brother in the last few years?"

"Perhaps it did, but nobody of note saw it or recorded it."

"Then what is the point of it? Gods battle in the heavens for us all to see. It must mean something."

"And what does it mean for us, today?" Tausret asked. "The gods made sure we saw it, so it must pertain to those of us here."

"They would not bother for ordinary men," Ament said. "There are only two people it could relate to--Queen Tausret as Regent and King Sekhaienre Siptah."

"More likely the king," Bay murmured. "Re overcame the shadow and the king is Son of Re. A son supports his father and I am certain that on the spirit level the Son of Re aided his heavenly father in his struggle. Sekhaienre is the living Akh of Re."

"He whom Re causes to appear has become the living spirit of Re," breathed the senior priest of the sun god.

Tausret shook her head in annoyance. "He is still just a young boy guided by my experience. I think we should resume our voyage as we have wasted enough time here."

The barge sailed on, but the people on board were very much quieter after the great event that had taken place in the skies. Small groups of people huddled together and talked, discussing what it all meant. The priests were content to leave it all in the gods' hands and Pepy occupied himself with paper and ink, busily recording every detail while the events were clear in his mind. Tausret was advised by the senior priest of Re to get the opinion of the Hem-netjer of Atum at Iunu, as Atum-Re was the principal incarnation of the sun god. Bay, meanwhile, talked quietly to Siptah, discussing the wonders they had seen and what it meant for the future of his reign.

"Something like this divides our lives in two--what went before and what comes after, as I'm sure the gods meant it to. I don't know how many people saw the sun god conquer the shadow, or even realise that you as Son of Re played a part in that struggle. I think that we must impress on the rest of Kemet just how important you are to the continued Ma'at of the Two Lands."

"How, Uncle?"

"I don't know. Let me think on it."

Chapter 10
Year 2 of Sekhaienre Siptah

Back in the capital city of Men-nefer, Siptah resumed his studies. Tutors schooled him in every aspect of the law and such learning as a king would need, and Bay oversaw everything. Nothing the king did, from rising from his bed just prior to dawn, until retiring for the night, escaped Bay's notice. He insisted the young king learn the prayers of the dawn services for Khepri, the light of the rising sun; the morning services for Heru of the ascending light; the worship of Re of the noonday sun; and the evening ceremonies dedicated to Atum the unified light as he dipped below the western horizon.

"You are the Son of Re," Bay reminded him. "Especially now that you, as god-on-earth have aided your heavenly father in his struggle against the shadow."

Siptah's other duties were not neglected. He had sat in judgment over the Servants of the Place of Truth when he was in Waset, and even though the men and women there had recited their lines as if play-acting, he faced the real thing in the law courts of Men-nefer. Tjaty Hori ruled here, sitting in judgment over the disputes of noble and peasant alike whenever the regent was busy elsewhere, and the young king was required to sit and listen, and even comment if called upon to do so. Siptah much preferred sitting in on Hori's court than that of Tausret. The Queen Regent made him feel like a boy--a naughty boy--whereas the Tjaty treated him with at least a modicum of respect, instructing him as to why each decision was made, and making a show of asking his advice.

The other duty of the young king was in the training in arms. His father, at his age, though only a prince with no likelihood of becoming a king, was expected to become proficient in at least some aspect of warfare. The nobility would lead the army in times of war, and had to learn how to command men. While a Commander or General was not required to excel in all weapons, he was expected to be good in some. An army commander would likely fight from a chariot and so had to know everything about the vehicle and the team of horses that drew it. Not only did he drive a chariot, but he must expect to fight from it, to engage the enemy hand to hand, and the commonest form of attack was the bow. Siptah was handicapped by his withered leg, but his instructors found ways by which he could be strapped into the chariot unobtrusively, and without having the worry of keeping his footing, both drive a chariot and fight from one. The young king developed great strength in chest and arms to compensate for his weaker lower limbs.

He took part in regular army manoeuvres, racing his chariot against others, leading mock charges, and loosing arrow after arrow at targets while bouncing and rolling across sand and soil at great speed. Siptah may have been still technically a boy of eleven, but he was also a king and showed great determination to prove himself a warrior and leader of men. Bay lost no opportunity to build up his confidence and warn him of his enemies.

"Do not imagine Queen Tausret will let you just cast her aside in a few years' time. Her son Seti-Merenptah is your heir, but you may be sure she will want him to take his place beside you on the throne--or even supplant you. Your only chance of ruling as sole king is through strength. You must become a skilled warrior and a popular leader of men."

"How can I do that when I am under the hand of instructors, Uncle? I need to lead men against the Nine Bows."

"Kemet is at peace."

"Then how can I become a leader of men?"

"The hunt is an acceptable alternative to war, and is good training besides."

"I have been on hunts. Ducks are not the same as men, and skewering a hundred wildfowl is no training for war."

"Perhaps I could organise a hunt for...for gazelle."

"Find me a lion, uncle."

Bay frowned. "The Regent will not allow such a dangerous hunt. Perhaps some other beast?"

"The Regent is not here. She has gone downriver to see about some temples."

"But when she finds out..."

"By then it will be too late. I am the king, and I command it. Find me a lion."

It may have been Siptah's understanding that Tausret had gone downriver to 'see about some temples', but that had been only an aspect of her absence. The governing of the kingdoms was in the hands of Tjaty Hori and Tjaty Paraemheb and Siptah was being trained in Men-nefer, so she took herself off to attend to other matters.

When her husband Seti had been alive, he saw to it that the gods were honoured throughout the Two Lands, and that his own name and deeds were inscribed on every available surface. The king was dead, however, and a new king reigned in his place. Tausret, as Regent, must now assume those duties. It was her intention to travel up and down the river, visiting all the major cities and temples to make sure Siptah's name was added to the holy places. The boy-king had, as yet, no exploits worth boasting about on stelae or pylons, but simple inscriptions bearing witness to his existence would do for now. If nothing came of his reign, then there would be less to chisel out when her own son assumed the throne.

One other thing was in the forefront of the Queen Regent's mind--the recent attack on the face of the sun. She needed advice on what this meant for Kemet, and the place to find this advice was in the city of Iunu, at the temple of Atum-Re.

The Hem-netjer of Atum, Nefertem, bowed to Tausret when she arrived at the temple at the end of the holy spiral dedicated to the Nine of Iunu. He brought her in to a room not far from the shrine and offered her food and drink. She accepted only a little wine and plain barley bread and Nefertem smiled to see her exercise such restraint.

"How may I be of service, Majesty?" he asked, when she set aside her cup and plate.

"You saw the marvellous thing that happened in the heavens a month ago? When either Re hid his face in the middle of the day, or something attacked him?"

"I did not see it, nor did any priest of Re, but I have heard reports of it."

"How is it that no priest of Re saw this attack upon their god?"

Nefertem hesitated for a few moments. "There are some revelations from the god that I cannot reveal even to you, Majesty, but it is likely that the...incident...was seen by few besides the royal party. It is ever that way.

Some may have seen part of the sun's disc obscured, but in this case, only you and the king were granted the full manifestation."

"So what does it mean?"

Nefertem shrugged.

"You do not know, or you will not say?"

"The god has not spoken of the meaning to me."

Tausret started to rise. "Then I will take up no more of your time, Hem-netjer. It seems this was a wasted journey."

"The god does not always speak directly, Majesty. Sometimes his revelations occur silently, or through other aspects of his creation."

Tausret stared at the priest before slowly sitting back down. "What do you mean?"

"The king is styled 'Son of Re' and he was present when Re struggled against the shadow and overcame it. If there is meaning in the actions of the gods, we can assume that they have a message for the king."

"What message?"

"The king was crowned Sekhaienre--he whom Re causes to appear. Now Re is telling him he is more than that. He aided the god in his struggle and he now represents the god."

"Represents him how?"

"He is the living spirit of Re."

Tausret stared at the high priest, trying to work out what it was that the chosen one of Atum-Re was saying. "The king is no longer Sekhaienre, but is now...Akhenre?"

"It is not without precedent, Majesty."

"I am aware of that."

"And there is something else."

"What?"

"The king must throw off the shackles of the south and embrace the north. No longer Meryamun--beloved of Amun, but rather Setepenre--the chosen one of Re."

"That could cause unrest in Waset."

"Yet it must be done. And there is more."

"Why do I think you want me to do something I don't want to do?"

"Not me, Majesty. The gods require it of you."

Tausret sighed. "Tell me."

"All of Kemet knows that you dislike the boy whom you believe has supplanted your son on the throne."

"That is not true, priest."

"No? Then tell me the truth, Regent of Kemet."

"It is true that my son Seti-Merenptah should be on the throne of his father, but he is too young, whereas the son of my husband's brother is old enough to at least be a figurehead until my son is old enough. I act as Regent to both boys, and if I favour my son, well...that is natural. And Siptah has not supplanted my son. Seti-Merenptah will be king one day."

"If the gods will it. But the gods demand something else, Majesty. They require you to act toward Siptah as if he was your true son."

Tausret made a moue of distaste. "I cannot do that."

"You must. The gods require it of you."

"I knew I should not have come to you for advice."

"But you did. The gods guided you here."

"And if I refuse? Will the gods punish me?"

"The gods will do as they see fit, but a man...or a woman...disobeys them at their peril."

"I do not appreciate being threatened, priest."

"Not threatened, Majesty, only warned. And really, is it any hardship? Love an orphaned boy as if he was your own. Do good by him and your heart will weigh less than the feather of Truth."

"You would have me favour Menmire Amenmesse's son over that of Userkheperure Seti?"

"Favour them equally, Majesty. Siptah is a motherless boy--be a mother to him and help him be king. Seti-Merenptah is a baby--be a mother to him also, and raise him to be a future king."

Tausret sighed. "I suppose I could try."

"The gods will bless you. And if it will help you, change his given name from Ramesses-Siptah which was the gift of his father Menmire, and..."

"I am not calling him Seti-Siptah."

Nefertem smiled. "I was going to suggest that you strengthened his ties to the great Baenre Merenptah who was the grandfather of both boys, and call him Merenptah-Siptah. Then both boys will bear the name Merenptah and will be brothers."

"Being brothers does not prevent enmity," Tausret observed.

"Indeed, Majesty, but they are both children and amenable to instruction. Raise them to love their brother and they will."

"This is what the gods want?"

"Yes. The struggle in the heavens reflects what could happen on earth. Re overcame the shadow and Ma'at was restored, and so will the Ma'at of the kingdoms if Siptah can rule wisely and in peace. You, as Regent, influence the king."

"Then I shall do what I can," Tausret said.

Tausret cut short her travels and returned to Men-nefer, where she announced that henceforth the king would be known as Akhenre Setepenre Merenptah-Siptah. Eyebrows were raised at the studied insult to Amun inherent in the god's removal from the king's coronation name, but as the population of Men-nefer favoured the gods Re and Ptah, no objections were raised. Siptah accepted the change without comment, and Bay, after some cogitation, pronounced himself in favour, as if his approval was necessary for the change.

"I will join with my king on this auspicious day and change my name also," he announced. "I am known to you all as Bay the Amorite, yet I was born in Kemet and feel myself to be fully Kemetu, even as I am uncle to Akhenre Siptah, Lord of the Two Lands. I will take for myself Kemetu names that reflect the god Re, but also Amun, for my parents served in Ta Shemau. Henceforth, I will be known as Ramesse Kha'amen-teru Bay--Re fashioned him, spirit of the god Amun, Bay."

Bay's announcement caused a stir. A number of people objected to this Amorite taking holy Kemetu names, but others were uneasy about the man identifying himself with the spirit of Amun. It was one thing for a king to claim such close kinship with a god, but for a commoner--and a foreigner too--to do so, smacked of arrogance. These objections were voiced, but came to nothing when it was seen that the king supported his uncle's decision. Tausret said nothing then, but later she spoke to Ament in private.

"I knew I should not have raised up Bay."

"He takes much upon himself," Ament admitted, "but his position is exalted, and not just because you and Userkheperure raised him up. Like it or not, he is uncle to the king, so perhaps he feels it is his due."

"He is a commoner and a foreigner and the post of Chancellor is as high as he could reasonably look. The king is his sister's child, not his, so he has no royal blood. Yet he takes on a name that would suit a king. What does that suggest to you?"

"You think he aims that high?"

"It has happened before. The commoner Ay was uncle to King Neb-kheperure and when that young king died untimely, he grasped the throne for himself."

Ament frowned. "Those were troubled times."

"And these are not? How long will it be before Bay demands to be made regent alongside me?"

"He can ask, but you don't have to agree."

"Even if the king asks? He will, you know, and it will be hard to refuse him."

Ament smiled. "I'm sure you'll find a way, Majesty."

"Perhaps. You know what Nefertem told me? He said I had to act like a mother to the king, to put him in equal place to my own son."

"You think Bay put him up to it?"

"I had not thought so until this moment."

"On the other hand it could cut Bay's feet out from under him."

"How so?"

"If you became a mother to him, it might lessen Siptah's dependence on Bay."

"And what of my own son?"

"Why should that change? He is still your natural son and must take precedence--in your heart, if not upon your lips and in your actions."

"Thank you, Ament. Why is it that all manner of men are willing to give me advice, but only you get right to the heart of matters?"

"Perhaps because I have known you longer than most."

Tausret nodded. "Perhaps. So advise me, old friend. What do I do about Bay?"

Ament grunted. "The safest course would be to remove him perma-nently, but you cannot do that if you mean to treat Siptah as your son. He is close to his uncle and you will be estranged if you do away with Bay without good cause. Failing that, you must hold him close so he finds it difficult to plot against you. Know what he is doing at all times. Subtly re-move men who support him; insert trusted men into his household; create trusted companions for the king."

"Is that all?"

Ament's grin flashed chipped but still strong, white teeth. "I'll probably think of other things."

"And what of this plea from Siptah that he be allowed to hunt lions and go to war?"

"What parent does not want their son to grow up strong?"

67

"Meaning?"

"He is king, and a king must lead the army in times of war. The hunt is good preparation for war."

"Hunting lions is dangerous."

"Your concern as a mother is understandable, but you must allow your boy-child to grow up. He will be guarded, but..." Ament shrugged his shoulders and looked away.

"But?"

"As you say, hunting lions is dangerous. At least you have another son if the unthinkable should happen."

Tausret paled. "I could never...no, that truly is unthinkable."

"As I said, Majesty. Unthinkable."

Chapter 11

Setnakhte speaks:

I am proud to be a son of Usermaatre Ramesses, arguably Kemet's greatest king, and though I am far removed from the succession, I am loyal to him and his successors unto death. The succession of the House of Ramesses is clear--Baenre Merenptah was the legitimate heir of Usermaatre, and Userkheperure Seti was the legitimate heir of Baenre. I never supported the pretender Messuwy and neither can I support his son Siptah, despite him sitting on the Double Throne. Seti-Merenptah may only be a baby, but he is the legitimate heir of Userkheperure Seti and rightful king.

My own son Ramesses asked me why I allow Siptah to remain on the throne if he is illegitimate, insisting that as General of the South I have the military might at my disposal to remove Siptah and install Seti-Merenptah. I thought to disregard his question, but he is a grown man and a grandson of Usermaatre, so he has a right to know my thoughts.

"It is like this," I said. "I swore an oath of allegiance to Usermaatre, to Baenre, and to Userkheperure in turn, and when Seti-Merenptah takes his place upon the throne of Kemet, I will swear allegiance to him also. Each king has been legitimate and is ordained by the gods to rule the Two Kingdoms. I opposed Messuwy, the man who made himself Menmire Amenmesse, as a pretender to the throne, and thus his son Siptah, now styled Akhenre, is also an imposter and no true king of Kemet."

"But father," Ramesses said. "Why do you not oust Siptah from the throne and set the rightful heir in his place? You have the Southern Army at your disposal."

"You would have me plunge Kemet back into civil war? And to what end? To put a baby on the throne?"

"For the rightful king."

"I would lose, and Siptah would be more secure than ever."

"You would not lose, father. You are Kemet's best general."

I smiled fondly to hear his praise, but disabused him of my capabilities. "Even the best general needs men to fight for him and I only have two southern legions to oppose at least five northern ones. I would lose, and all my efforts would come to naught."

"There must be men in the north who feel as you...as we...do?"

"Very likely, my son, but none prepared to risk all at this time."

"So we do nothing?"

"On the contrary, we trust in Queen Tausret. She is Queen Regent and mother of the true heir. She will not allow his birthright to be snatched from him by a pretender. Siptah will not reign forever, and as soon as Seti-Merenptah attains his majority, he will claim what is rightfully his. Then we will support him with the military might of the south. In the meantime, we strengthen our position and put spies in the north to report on those who support the pretender--Tjaty Hori and Chancellor Bay."

My son Ramesses is a good man, but lacks experience in war. He served as my aide during the years of 'brotherly conflict' and should have gained much knowledge in military matters had it not been for his health. Early on, he succumbed to a fever which laid him low, and by the time he recovered, the main fighting was over. I will have to rectify his lack of experience, for if I am to use him to the full, he must know how to command men. Perhaps I will send him on a punitive expedition into Kush--those men are ever in need of a firm hand. Ramesses is already a Troop Commander within Amun, and I intend to raise him further to command the Amun Legion. I need men I can trust in the top positions.

Tjaty Paraemheb feels as I do, and together we can turn Ta Shemau into a bastion of support for the heir. There will have to be changes made. Samut of Amun must go to make way for Ramesses, but I have never liked having that traitor in such a position. A man who betrays one master will betray another. Panhesy of Mut might have to go too--he supports Siptah-- but then again, he is a good commander and I think I can win him round. I intend to start raising other legions, from Kush and hopefully elsewhere. Kushites are fierce fighters but unruly and I infinitely prefer disciplined men I can trust.

Then there is the court at Men-nefer. I must get good men into positions of trust within the palace; men that I can rely on to spy on Bay and his supporters and report back to me. Waset is ten to fifteen days from Men-nefer, and I cannot rely on the slow spread of gossip or even the official royal messengers to give me the news. I want my own sources reporting to me swiftly and I shall set up a small fleet of fast boats to ply the waters between North and South.

Siptah is king for now. I have to accept this unpalatable truth as Queen Tausret desires it so. She has her reasons for not putting her son forward at this time, and I must obey, but it will not always be thus. One day, Prince Seti-Merenptah will rise up and claim the throne for his own and I intend to be there with my Army of the South, ready to aid him in his struggle for the throne.

There is one other thing I should mention. News filtered down to me of a wonder in the heavens. Peasants who live and work north of Waset reported seeing the sun devoured by a monster and then regurgitated, the sun apparently continuing on its course unharmed. Arrant nonsense, I thought, and then an official came from the court, saying that the sun had fought a great battle but that the Son of Re had come to his heavenly father's assistance and overcome the Enemy. Well, it did not seem any more believable, so I enquired of the priests, but they were not very helpful. They muttered about the gods' ways being obscure, and unknowable by men, and then one young man, a priest of Nut, told me of his studies.

It seems that he, and a few other priests had, over the course of several lifetimes, studied the body of the goddess, counting the stars that are strewn across her body, noting their position relative to one another, their brightness and colour. Especially note was made of the 'wanderers'--those stars without a fixed position in the heavens but which still follow fixed paths. Other moveable stars are those that fall from the heavens and the occasional one that creeps like a snail relative to its neighbours. I asked to see one of these 'snails' and had it pointed out to me. I could detect no motion, but the priest told me if I came back in twenty years I might just discern its movement. What a waste of time their lives must be if that is all they do.

Then he told me of the full moon becoming blood red at times, and that this phenomenon can be predicted. He did not say how, and offered no evidence, but he also said that some within his sect also say it is possible to predict when the sun will be attacked and eaten. I had to laugh, because this is nonsense. If it was possible to predict an attack, then the sun god would surely be at pains to avoid his enemy. I came away feeling as if my head was full of wool, my thoughts fuzzy and confused, and thanked the gods that they made me a military man rather than a priest. Whatever the reason for the attack on the sun, there has been no lasting damage done. As for what it means--well, I can guess. The sun god hid his face from Siptah, showing his displeasure at the boy being made king. That we are not all now dwelling in darkness only shows the love Re has for Kemet. The god has shown his displeasure and is now prepared to wait until men remove the offence.

I think he will not have long to wait.

Chapter 12
Year 2 of Akhenre Siptah

The palace echoed with Siptah's cries of excitement when Bay brought him the regent's permission to go hunting. He only calmed down when it was pointed out that permission had not been given to hunt lions in the desert, but only 'those animals that are to be found in the cultivated land beside the Great River.'

"That means wildfowl, gazelles, and maybe a feral bull if there are any," Bay explained.

"What about a crocodile?"

"It would be better to leave them alone. They are hard to kill unless an arrow strikes them in the right place."

"I am skilled with the bow," Siptah boasted. "Every creature shall feel my wrath."

"I look forward to viewing my king's prowess."

Bay organised the hunt, calling on the royal huntsmen to scour the river lands for suitable game and to prepare short expeditions lasting no more than a day or two to give the young king a taste of hunting without inconveniencing him. Hunting did not interest Bay, and he was not looking forward to the heat and dust that was an almost inevitable part of outdoor pursuits, and certainly had no intention of foregoing a comfortable bed every night.

Three days later, Overseer of the Hunt Senefer reported to the king as he sat in an open room looking out over the palace gardens. The day had been hot, but the evening breezes off the river cooled the room enough for roasted meats and fresh-baked bread hot from the ovens to be palatable. Senefer entered the room and dropped to his knees, extending his arms toward the seated boy.

"Son of Re, I have found gazelle for the hunt."

Siptah picked up a slice of beef and bit off a piece, chewing it as he looked at the huntsman. "Only gazelle? Can't you find anything more manly for me to hunt?"

Senefer licked his lips and cleared his throat. "I...er, what did you want to hunt, Son of Re?"

"Lion. Failing that, perhaps crocodiles or wild bulls."

"I know where there are ostriches..."

"I have no interest in birds," Siptah interrupted. "Find me something worth hunting, or find yourself another king to serve, for you will no longer please me."

Senefer broke out in a sweat, despite the cool breeze off the river. "I can find you a bull, Son of Re. Perhaps a day from here, or two."

"That will do for now, but I also want a lion, so have your men search for one."

"I hear and I obey." Senefer got to his feet and bowed, before exiting the room. Outside, he hurried in search of his assistants, ordering them to bring him the latest information of the wild bull north of the city and to find him a lion.

His principal assistant Menka frowned. "Wild bull? There isn't one. Only that one that was injured and escaped near the village of Benetu. Is that the one you mean, or..."

"That's the one," Senefer said. "By all the gods, do you expect me to send our crippled king against a proper wild bull? I'd have him pit his skill against a cow if I thought he wouldn't spot the difference."

The Overseer of the Hunt issued his orders, bringing together the equipment necessary for the hunt, including luxurious tented accommodation for the king, lesser tents for the necessary servants, food and wine, cooks, grooms and personal attendants. All of this was packed into ox-drawn wagons, while huntsmen brought hounds on leashes and a small detachment of soldiers came along to guard the royal person. Siptah himself rode in a light hunting chariot pulled by a single stallion, while Bay rode in a heavier two-horse chariot, as did the commander of the guard.

All this took some time to organise, so it was late the next morning when the expedition finally set out from Men-nefer. Their route lay north, bordering the river for half a day before turning westward. Close to the life-giving river, the pastures were luxurious, the sweet grass being cropped by herds of the royal cattle with young boys no older than the king to tend them. They stood and stared in amazement as the procession wound its way past, and their charges barely lifted their heads from cropping the grass. Verdant fields lined the river also, the rich dark earth supporting a variety of plants, and peasants worked bent-backed, clad only in a short kilt, hoeing and weeding the crops or letting in more water from irrigation ditches. The farmers ceased their work as the king passed by, kneeling in the dust with heads bowed.

The land dried out as they moved further from the river, and the red sandy soil of Deshret showed through the black river silt. Only an exceptional flood brought silt this far from the river, and the water soaked away quickly, so the vegetation became sparse. Fewer people travelled the road out there and the hard-packed soil became obscured by wind-blown sand. Soon, the chariots and wagons were trundling over a broken surface as the hunting expedition skirted the cultivated lands.

Siptah became impatient with the slow progress dictated by the supply wagons and marching men, and urged the chariots onward. Bay stayed with the wagons, content to go over a sheaf of accounts that required his attention, but commanded Senefer to keep up with the king.

"I hardly need tell you that the king believes he is capable of more than his stricken body allows. Take the captain of the guard with you and keep the king safe from harm. Let no ill befall him or you will suffer for it."

By mid-afternoon the chariots were out of sight of the wagons and Siptah revelled in the freedom he experienced. His charioteer drove, while he braced himself against the chariot's framework and ran his fingers over the bow in its rack beside him, and the sheath of arrows. He looked all around, hoping for some game to appear so he could start hunting, but nothing moved in the sun-rippled heat of the day. A hawk hung above him, lazily circling in the pale blue bowl of the sky and Siptah took it as a sign of the god's favour--one hunter to another.

The vague dirt road led down into a steep-sided gully and Siptah reined in his stallion and studied the descent carefully. Senefer took the opportunity to close with the king and addressed him quietly.

"Son of Re, we would do well to wait for the wagons."

"Why?" Siptah asked, his eyes never ceasing to scan the gully.

Senefer glanced across to where Ahtep, the guard commander stood in his chariot. "You should not be so far from the guards. Chancellor Bay told me..."

"There is nobody out here that would seek to harm me," Siptah replied. "Besides, I have my bow." He pointed into the gully. "See there, that is out way down, then to the right and up there." Siptah looked at his charioteer. "You can manage that?"

"Yes, my lord."

"Then do so. Come along, Senefer. It's getting late and I want to find that bull today."

The king's charioteer guided them down into the gully and they bounced and shuddered along its bed for a short time before he urged the stallion up the far side. Senefer and Ahtep followed in their heavier chariots and by the time they crested the far lip of the gully, the king's chariot was some distance away. They followed at as great a pace as they could manage and gradually overhauled the royal chariot.

Siptah turned and grinned at Senefer as they drew level. "I let you catch up," he said.

"I do not doubt it, Son of Re. May I suggest we wait for the wagons at..." he looked ahead, "...that patch of trees? The wagons will be held up by the gully and if we do not wait, we could lose them."

The king grimaced petulantly. "How far ahead is this bull supposed to be?"

"My huntsmen have not reported back to me yet. It could be only a sun span ahead or a full day." Senefer hesitated. "It would be better to meet it fresh, rather than after an arduous day."

"I feel quite strong enough to face a bull."

"Of course, Son of Re, for your heavenly father sustains you, but I meant your horse. It will need to be rested before it meets a fierce foe."

Siptah scowled. "At least find me something to hunt today--while we are waiting for the wagons."

"I believe I can do that, Son of Re."

Senefer led the three chariots to the clump of trees near the gully, where they all dismounted and stretched their limbs, slapping the dust from their clothes. The charioteers stayed behind to tend to the horses, while Senefer led Siptah and Ahtep down into the gully again.

"The gully is dry, as you can see, Son of Re, but the beasts have scraped a waterhole with their hooves and if we approach quietly, we should surprise some antelope."

Senefer led the way. Siptah followed with his bow strung and three arrows clutched in one hand, while Ahtep brought up the rear with his long spear. They made little noise, though Siptah's left foot often dragged in the sand and occasionally small rocks clicked together. He scowled and made an effort to lift his withered leg clear with each step.

Senefer gestured for complete silence and pointed to some large boulders that had fallen from the lip of the gully, indicating by signs that the waterhole lay beyond it. Siptah nodded and limped forward, moving between two boulders and kneeling to peer over a lower one. He saw a stretch of sand ploughed and churned by many feet, and a small expanse of muddy water. On the far side, three antelope stood ready to drink. Two had already lowered their heads to the water, front feet slightly splayed, while the buck, with slender horns lifted, stared across the water and mud toward the boulders.

As Siptah watched, the buck stamped its foot and he could plainly hear the snuff of its breath as it sought out the scent of danger. The king felt a puff of breeze on his face and knew that the wind carried his scent away from the antelope. Silent and unmoving, he watched the buck deciding whether to drink or flee, until suddenly it dropped its head and moved forward to join its does at the water's edge.

Siptah rose in a fluid movement, drawing and releasing an arrow. The buck saw the movement and reared in alarm, turning, its hind legs bunching and releasing as it sprang back, but the arrow took it in the chest, just behind its foreleg. Both does turned and raced back along the gully, leaving the buck kneeling in the sand, blood-flecked foam drooling from its lips and its eyes rolling in their sockets. Senefer ran forward with a bronze knife and slit the animal's throat, tipping it on its side as its legs kicked out in its death throes.

"Magnificent, Son of Re," Ahtep said. "There is not one of my guards who could better that."

Siptah grinned and limped forward to stand and stare down at the fallen beast. Senefer looked up and met his monarch's gaze. "Truly a mighty hunter," he said. "We'll find you a bull tomorrow."

By the time the wagons caught up, Senefer and Ahtep had built a small fire near a stand of trees and had skinned and prepared some of the meat for the evening meal. The cooks immediately set about producing a suitable field dinner for the king, and everyone praised Siptah for his prowess in the field.

Bay offered his praise too, but also offered caution. "An antelope is a timid creature, but a bull is a very different one. He is just as likely to attack. You must hunt him from a chariot rather than on foot, for you will need mobility."

Siptah scowled, annoyed that his uncle seemed to be belittling his efforts. "Are you telling your king that he is incapable? Even with the infirmity that the gods have seen fit to thrust upon me, I am a match for an insensate bull."

"I do not doubt it, but Kemet needs its king and I implore you not to endanger yourself unnecessarily. We would be lost without you."

"Then I will hunt from my chariot, Uncle. I would not want to see you bereft."

The next day, Senefer reported to the king that his hunters had found the bull they sought on the edge of the cultivated land. He grazed alone in a field that had been allowed to degenerate almost to scrubland. The chariots were made ready, and then Siptah announced that he would be driving his own chariot. When Bay remonstrated, Siptah drew him aside.

"I told you that I would hunt from the safety of my chariot, Uncle. You cannot expect me to make it too easy with a charioteer to control the horse while I kill the beast. Therefore I will do both."

The king would hear no counter-argument and limped off to his chariot. Bay looked at Senefer and the Overseer of the Hunt nodded, his face grim. Senefer took over the control of his own chariot and ordered two of his huntsmen to join him, while sending others running ahead to find the bull. Ahtep followed in the third chariot, with an extra archer beside him.

The hunters on foot led the way, trotting through the light scrub in a direction that took them back toward the river and the cultivated lands. Scrub gave way to lank grass and one of the hunters slowed, pointing ahead. Siptah shaded his eyes against the morning light and stared at what looked like a large brown boulder. As he looked, he saw a head rise up, wide-spreading horns black against the pale blue of the sky.

"It is a big one," he murmured.

Senefer, in his own chariot alongside the king's nodded. "Let my hunters go in and soften him for the kill, Son of Re."

Siptah shook his head. "First blood is mine, Senefer. Make sure your men understand that." The young wrapped the reins carefully around his waist, bracing his right foot against the wickerwork frame of the chariot, and his withered left foot he slipped into a special supporting brace. His stallion caught Siptah's excitement and tossed his head, stamping his feet, eager to start but mindful of the master's touch on the reins.

The king pulled an arrow from the sheath and examined it closely, running a finger along its length, seeking out imperfections. He tossed it aside and picked out another, examining it in its turn, nodding with satisfaction as the sharp bronze head caught the sunlight. Siptah fitted it loosely to his bow and tested the string and the supple strength of the bow by drawing it back and then easing the pressure. With a click of his tongue, he started the stallion moving forward toward the bull.

As he approached the bull it stood and shook itself, and Siptah saw it was even bigger than he had thought, a brown mountain of muscle that fixed the intruder with a belligerent stare. It pawed the ground as the king's chariot neared and then lumbered forward with a bellow. At the same instant, Siptah leaned right and the motion of his body, transmitted through the reins wound around his waist, guided his horse to that side. The stallion broke into a gallop and moved in a wide circle, drawing the bull after it. Siptah looked back over his shoulder and yelled with excitement, changing his course into a left hand circle as the lumbering bull tried to turn inside his circle and meet them.

The scrubland was pitted with holes and indentations and these, together with scattered stones and gnarled shrubs, made the chariot bounce and slew, forcing the king to steady himself with one hand. Already the bull was tiring, slowing to a trot, apparently under the impression it had chased away the intruder. Siptah immediately hauled on the reins and turned his chariot to face the bull once more, urging his stallion into motion. His chariot's course took him parallel to the bull's course but in the opposite direction, and as they neared, the bull swung once more to face its tormentor.

Siptah's chariot raced by, no more than twenty paces from the bull, and as they passed, he leaned out and, with a muttered invocation to the gods, loosed an arrow at the turning bull. The arrow thumped into the chest of the bull, too far back to find the heart, but bringing it to a halt. It stood with feet splayed and looked at the receding chariot, uttering a bellow filled with pain and puzzlement.

Siptah turned his chariot once more and slowly approached the stricken beast. The bull turned to meet him, but slowly and painfully, allowing the king to loose another arrow into the beast's chest. It collapsed with a grunt, blood-flecked foam running from its mouth. The king yelled in triumph and leapt down from the chariot, clutching his bow and a single arrow. He limped toward the fallen bull, fitting his arrow to the string as he went. The bull groaned and rolled its eyes toward the approaching figure, but apart from its heaving flanks it was otherwise motionless.

The king limped around the bull and moved closer, lining up his arrow to finally dispatch the bull with an arrow to its heart. He drew back on the bowstring and leaned forward until the bronze tip was almost touching the bull's hide. A breath let out to steady himself, fingers starting to move, to relax...and the bull moved, lurching forward and to the side. The arrow grazed the beast's back, falling to the ground fifty paces away while the bull's shoulder sent Siptah flying backward. Lurching to its feet, the bull stood on unsteady legs and faced the fallen king. It coughed blood and started toward him as Siptah scrambled away.

Siptah saw his death approaching him and heard his heart hammering in his chest, the thunder of it seeming to shake the ground beneath him. He heard cries that he knew must be those of the watching hunters and felt shame that they should see him die lying on the ground. The king raised himself to a kneeling position and then awkwardly to his feet as the bull staggered closer, blood dripping from its mouth.

"I will not run from you, Great Bull of Kemet, for I am a king." Siptah reached out a hand and touched the bull on the head, between the out-spread horns, and a shadow passed near him, whispering in the hot, still air. "It is my death," he muttered.

Then the bull was falling, kneeling before him, its great head lowering to the dusty ground and Siptah saw a thin spear shaft sunk deep into the beast's side. He looked up and saw a chariot, and a man running toward him.

"Guard Captain Ahtep? You killed my bull?"

The Captain fell to his knees in the dusty ground. "No, Son of Re, for the bull was already dead on his feet. My spear merely knocked it over."

Senefer and the huntsmen crowded round, making sure the bull was dead and that the king was unhurt, offering him water and great praise.

"I have never seen its like, Son of Re," Senefer said. "You stood un-armed and faced down a deadly wounded bull, then reached out and touched it on the head...and it fell down dead at your feet."

"Ptah preserved me," Siptah said. "I will build him a temple."

They drove their chariots back to the waiting wagons, leaving a hand of huntsmen behind to dress the meat. Senefer sent one of the wagons back to the killing site to bring the spoils of the hunt, and the story of the young king's skill and bravery lost nothing in the telling. Bay greeted his nephew with pride in his eyes, for he had seen the drama unfolding from a distance, yet even he gasped when told the particulars of the king's deeds.

"Truly you are the chosen one of the gods."

Siptah grinned, his heart swelling with pride. "Find me a lion," he said. "I need to hunt something worthy of a king."

Chapter 13
Year 2 of Akhenre Siptah

While Siptah was away on his hunt, Queen Tausret put into motion her plans to identify more closely with the reigning king. As she told her now constant companion and adviser Ament, "I can no longer be seen as a remote and uncaring Regent, putting my grief and my son above the concerns of the Kingdoms. I must embrace the king as my son, and I can do this most effectively by putting myself on temple walls in association with the king."

"And what of Chancellor Bay?" Ament asked. "Will you seek to replace him in Siptah's affections?"

"I can scarcely do that...at least not yet, so I shall honour him by including him in the inscriptions of praise."

"The Amorite soars high," Ament remarked.

"He is accomplished," Tausret remarked, "and as long as he remembers his place, I will allow him a place in the king's light."

Tausret chose Per-Banebdjedet as the site of her first inscription, commissioning a stele in the Domain of the Ram Lord of Djedet. This Ram Lord was worshiped as the Ba or 'personality' of the god Asar, and as Per-Banebdjedet was the capital city of the Kha sepat, an inscription here would not only bring praise to the god, but also to the king and those associated with him. It would also serve to praise the Great One of the House of Ramesses, Usermaatre Ramesses in his form as the god Amun.

Ament looked up from the notes on the inscription that Tausret had been compiling. "Why the address to this man Pabes?"

Tausret looked around from her contemplation of the river through the window of the governor's palace. "He is the steward of the temple estates of Amun in Waset. The temple of Amun of Usermaatre-Setepenre Ramesses here in Per-Banebdjedet comes under his jurisdiction. By including him and enumerating his assets, I'm forcing him to act as guarantor for the new chapel I'm having built."

Ament smiled. "Cunning. And this Nedjem you mention? Why does he come in for criticism?"

"He's a priest in the Temple of Millions of Years of Baenre Merenptah. Competent but tight-fisted when it comes to spending temple gold. Pabes loathes him so I thought I'd deliver a reprimand."

"Why not just remove him from office?"

"As I said, he's competent enough."

Ament continued reading, putting down one sheet of papyrus and then another. "It's very...how should I put it...wordy...isn't it? I can't read half of these words...sort of don't need to as a soldier...but even so you're using ten words where I'd use two or three."

Tausret laughed. "This is just the common script. Wait until the scribes turn it into temple hieroglyphs. It'll be three times longer."

"All right, I can read half of what's here, but I understand only half of that. What's this? 'I was overseer of works for your eightfold adoring ba-boons which are in your forecourt.' What does that mean? Baboons? Did you mean to write something else?"

"Sometimes I forget you are just a soldier, Ament, and have had no in-struction in the ways of the gods."

Ament's lips twitched into a smile. "Not just a soldier, Great Wife. I'm a passable fisherman too."

"My apologies. Whatever else you are, you are not 'just' anything. Above all else you are a friend and a valued adviser in these straitened times."

"Thank you, Great Wife," Ament said with a grin. "So, the baboons?"

"The sun god Re is towed in a barque across the sky by four jackals and is adored in the court of the morning by four baboons. In the court of the evening is four more of each--so, eight baboons."

"Why baboons though?"

"Have you never watched them in the menagerie as the first rays of the morning sun strike their cage? They sit and face the rising sun and hold their arms out to worship the god."

"Really? I would never have thought it of an animal."

Tausret smiled. "It could just be that they welcome the heat of the sun after a chilly night, but it does look like they're offering up an act of wor-ship."

Ament nodded and kept reading. "I don't see anything about Bay. I thought you were going to include him in your inscriptions."

"In the right place. On this stele I'll put my own name as Daughter of Amun of Usermaatre-Setepenre and that of the king, but I'll leave Bay for another time."

"Good. It's more than he deserves."

Tausret made further notes and then had long discussions with scribes, priests and architects, debating the relative merits of erection chapels, pylons or steles, and the best way of displaying the inscription on them. It took several days, but by the time she and Ament left Per-Banebdjedet, stone was already being hauled in from stores scattered across Ta Mehu and masons had started work with their copper chisels.

The royal barge made many stops up and down the branches of the Great River, with Tausret visiting a score of temples in almost as many cities. In each one she discussed the importance of praising the god in the name of the king and his regent, and came to an agreement with each high priest. She would put her seal on a promissory note from the Treasury, enabling the priests to draw sufficient gold out to enable work to start. All of these inscriptions referred to Tausret as 'The Great Noblewoman of Every Land' as well as 'Daughter of Amun', 'King's Great Wife', and Regent, along with Akhenre Setepenre Merenptah-Siptah and all his titles. Somewhere amongst the wordy descriptions, she had Bay's name slipped in-- nothing particularly praiseworthy, just that he, as Chancellor, also supported the king.

In Iunu, Tausret spoke to the priests as usual, and then summoned a famous sculptor who had fashioned many images of kings. She outlined a special statue she wanted made that would highlight her status as regent and the dependence of the king upon her.

"It is unusual, Great Lady," sculptor Mutem said.

"But not unheard of," Tausret said. "Queen Ankhnesmeryre had herself carved with her child Pepy."

"Ah yes, Neferkare Pepy. I remember the statue in question. The boy-king was in full regalia seated upon the lap of his mother."

"That is what I want."

"But he was er, her natural son..." Mutem looked uncomfortable.

"That is immaterial," Tausret said. "She was there as regent to the young king and that is exactly why I will be there in this statue you will carve. You will depict me as ruling regent with Akhenre seated upon my lap."

"It shall be as you command, Great Lady."

Tausret had debated with herself whether to commission another statue with her son Seti-Merenptah seated upon her lap, but decided against it.

There would be time enough for that later, though perhaps he might feature in a description somewhere. It would not do for her young son to slip from the minds of the people during the years of Siptah's reign.

The Queen Regent returned to Men-nefer long enough to catch up on local government before setting out for the south, where she would be duplicating her efforts in the north and arranging for inscriptions and chapels to be constructed throughout Ta Shemau. Ament accompanied her again, willingly putting aside his duties as Overseer of Vineyards and Army Commander. The former duties he left in the hands of his foster-sons Ephrim and Jerem, while the latter could be adequately handled by junior officers.

They came again to the city of Waset, and both Tausret and Ament remembered happier former times there. The Hem-netjer of Amun greeted her on the quay and welcomed her into the house of the god, where they talked at length about affairs of state and the reasons for her visit.

"I should congratulate you, Hem-netjer Bakenkhons," Tausret said. "Former Hem-netjer Roma-Rui has adopted you into his house and made you his heir."

"Thank you, Majesty. I must admit I was surprised. Roma-Rui was never particularly loyal to Userkheperure, and I thought he resented my accession to the position."

"I think his action has something to do with Amenmesse's son being made king. That; and the fact that he is childless. Of what use is a hereditary title if you have no one to hand it on to? You have sons already and are Hem-netjer, so he manages to adopt you and become head of your house at the same time."

Bakenkhons smiled. "I will not let him influence my decisions," he said.

Tausret laughed. "I should hope not."

"How may Amun be of service to you, Majesty?"

"Rather, how may I be of service to Amun? I wish to display my piety and that of the king, but we must remember that the treasury coffers are not bottomless. Perhaps there are some repairs that can be made to existing structures instead of constructing whole new edifices?"

"Indeed, Majesty. The attention of the king...and of the regent...is most welcome.

"I can think of a few minor repairs within the Great Temple--a leaking roof, a bit of subsidence in one corner of the forecourt, refurbishing of some painted surfaces--nothing too expensive. Then there are a host of repairs to temples throughout Ta Shemau, some great, others small. I can have a list drawn up for your consideration, with an estimate of the cost of each."

"That would be useful," Tausret agreed. She paused to collect her thoughts. "I would like to refurbish the barque shrine of Userkheperure which lies inside the first pylon of the Great Temple also."

"A pious act, Majesty, though the barque shrine is in good repair."

"Perhaps the holy implements can be upgraded? Or the walls replastered and decorated? Either way, I wish our son Seti-Merenptah to be represented. He is no longer an infant and must soon take his place as his father's son."

"I shall give it my personal attention, Majesty."

"Thank you, Bakenkhons. Now, there are two other reasons for my visit to Waset. I must make sure work has started again on my tomb and that of the king, and I am of a mind to start my Mansion of Millions of Years."

"One cannot neglect such important works," the Hem-netjer agreed. "I can instruct the temple architects to advise you on the Mansion, at least."

Tausret started to rise from her chair, and Bakenkhons leapt to his feet. He cleared his throat and looked expectantly at the Regent. When she raised an eyebrow interrogatively, he spoke.

"There is one other act you might like to consider, Majesty, though again it is only repair work."

"Go on."

"You will no doubt be aware of the temple dedicated to Amun and Re-Horakhty at Amada in Kush that was originally built by Menkheperre. It was desecrated by the Heretic, but Menmaatre, Usermaatre and Baenre all made some restorations and of course added their own texts reminding the god of their service. Well, there is still work that needs to be done--in particular, the door jambs leading into the temple are damaged and need replacing.

"If I may be so bold, Majesty, replacing them with pristine new stone would leave some beautiful fresh surfaces on which to inscribe praiseworthy texts."

"How much would this cost?" Tausret asked, mentally calculating the reserves of gold still in the treasury. Bakenkhons named a sum and Tausret nodded. "That would be satisfactory."

"Excellent." Bakenkhons could not help rubbing his hands together and called in a temple scribe to take down some details of the required repair and construction. "Now I assume you will want the king carved on one jamb, and perhaps you on the other, Majesty?"

Tausret thought for several moments. She had committed to memory key phrases to be used in several inscriptions and these now needed modifying to suit the circumstances.

"No, the king is still in his minority. Naturally, I will feature on the right door jamb, standing and dressed as a queen, with the words 'God's Wife of Amun, the King's Great Wife, Lady of the Two Lands, Tausret Setepenmut, justified'. On the other you will have Chancellor Bay, kneeling and adoring the king, with the words 'Ramesse Kha'amen-teru Bay, friend of the king, Chancellor of the Entire Land'. The figure of Bay is to be facing columns of text reading 'Lord of the Two Lands, Akhenre Setepenre, and Lord of Appearances, Merenptah Siptah'."

Bakenkhons licked his lips and looked slightly agitated as the scribe took down the regent's words. "The...er, figures will look unbalanced, Majesty. I mean, one standing and one kneeling. Perhaps both figures could be represented standing?"

"That would give Chancellor Bay equal status to myself," Tausret replied sharply. "I, as God's Wife of Amun, stand as I enter the presence of the god, whereas Bay is simply an official who serves the king and therefore kneels in submission."

"Very good, Majesty. It shall be accomplished."

Tausret collected Ament on the way out of the temple and made her way across the river to the western shore. For a moment, she hesitated as she went to mount the chariot waiting for her, and then directed the driver to take her to the western palace.

"I am tired, Ament. I had thought to drive out to the Great Field today, but it is too hot. Tomorrow will be soon enough."

The servants of the western palace had been warned of the Queen Regent's arrival in Waset and had rooms prepared for her and her small retinue. Ament, ever mindful of Tausret's safety, immediately inspected the palace guards and made a few changes, instituting new passwords and procedures. A meal was prepared and tasted, and a cool scented bath prepared, after which Tausret relaxed in the palace gardens until nightfall.

The next morning, Tausret and Ament were driven out to the raised plain across from the city, and inspected the site for its suitability to house her Mansion. The Amun temple's architect, Senmut, was waiting for them.

"Mighty Lady, may you live forever," Senmut said, bowing deeply. "I am Senmut. Hem-netjer Bakenkhons has instructed me as to your requirements. Have you fixed upon a suitable site?"

"I hoped you could you advise me, Senmut."

"I would be honoured, Mighty Lady." The architect looked around and then strode off across the raised plain, skirting piles of rubble and the sharp drop-off of the escarpment. He stood and stared at the Mansion dedicated to Baenre for a few minutes, turned to look at Usermaatre's Mansion, and then returned to where Tausret and Ament were waiting.

"North of Baenre's Mansion, Mighty Lady, and south of Usermaatre's. It is the only logical place." Senmut proceeded to outline the main axis of the building.

"I don't suppose I can afford one the size of Usermaatre's, but I want it to be as large as Baenre's," Tausret said.

Senmut nodded and made a few notations on a clay tablet he carried. "There is a lot of rubble to be cleared away, and some rock to be cut through to create a level surface, even before we think about digging out the trenches or laying the foundation stones."

"How long will it take?"

Senmut started to shrug and then thought better of it. "That depends on how much gold you want to pour into it, Mighty Lady. A year to get the site prepared and another two to get the main structure up, perhaps. Five years in all?"

"Too long. Shorten the time."

"A smaller mansion, perhaps?"

"No. Find other ways."

Senmut bowed again, not wanting to argue with such an exalted person. "I shall draw up some detailed plans, Mighty Lady, together with some estimates of costs and times, and submit them for your approval."

"Very good, and while you are planning my Mansion, please allow for a small Mansion dedicated to Akhenre Siptah. Nothing elaborate or eye-catching--small and functional."

"As you command, Mighty Lady. An adjunct to your own mansion perhaps?"

"No." Tausret looked at the spaces between the existing mansions. "Over there somewhere," she said, pointing. "Between Menkheperre and Usermaatre."

"Yes, Mighty Lady. Hem-netjer Bakenkhons mentioned that you wished to have work on your tomb started again. Will you require my architectural services?"

"No, my tomb has already been partly constructed. I will see the scribe in the Place of Truth and arrange matters. You may leave me now, Senmut. Bring your plans to me as soon as they are ready, and we will discuss costs."

Senmut bowed again and departed, leaving Tausret and Ament on the raised plain near the Mansions of Millions of Years of her adopted father Baenre.

Chapter 14
Chancellor Ramesse Kha'amen-teru Bay speaks:

Truly, I am risen in the world and anything is within my grasp. Less than two years since my nephew Siptah became king and already I have become the power behind the throne of Kemet. Oh, I know that the Queen is officially Regent and thus rules the Kingdoms in all but name, but day by day my power grows and soon, I can see, I will rule in her stead. The greatest mistake she ever made was to confirm me in my position as Chancellor and Treasurer, for all the wealth of Kemet flows through my fingers and, as long as I am discreet, I can achieve much with the king's gold.

The priests have told Queen Tausret that it is the will of the gods that she accept and nurture the king during his minority, and that is what she is doing. For months now she has travelled up and down the Great River with her little dog Ament, spending the king's gold and having her name inscribed on temple walls and steles everywhere. I know, because the bills from the priests and governors cross my desk. She does everything in the king's name, so he gets the credit for all her actions, but she appends her own name to each inscription. Strange to say, she even adds my name to some of them. I think it is because she knows she cannot get rid of me just yet and still hold onto the love of young Siptah.

That boy is the means by which I will attain power. He is desperate to be loved and you can be sure that I have fostered his insecurities, telling him that the Queen is determined to control him and will find a way to prevent him ever becoming sole ruler unless I can act for him. That is not far off the truth, as I show him love and always support his efforts to become independent of the Regent. That is why I encourage him to hunt and pursue other manly pastimes, though without ever exposing him to real danger. I nearly lost the boy to a wild bull recently and that gave me a great scare. As the boy's loving uncle I can attain any height, but if he dies, I am nothing. Tausret would not let me live beyond his lifetime.

To secure myself against this, I am using the king's gold to buy myself favours from powerful people throughout the Kingdoms. The judicious outlay of gold and the promise of future favours gains me many friends, and if those men befriend me solely for what they can gain, what is wrong with that? When I am regent it will matter little, and when I am king it will matter not at all. Power is everything.

The gold flows steadily to priests of every important god, to court officials, to governors, to overseers who control the lifeblood of Kemet. I have even caused my name to be added to certain inscriptions saying things like 'He who establishes the king on the throne of his father', something that has only ever been said by gods or kings. Well, that too is no more than the truth, however unpalatable to the Queen and her supporters. Who was it who put forward Siptah's name in the face of those who hated his father? Who was it who bribed the priests to persuade Tausret the gods wanted him on the throne? Who is it who spends every waking moment gathering supporters to his cause? And who is it who dins the ears of the gods continually to protect Akhenre Siptah and to raise Ramesse Kha'amen-teru Bay to the throne after him?

Soon, I will be able to make my move. My nephew grows apace and though he will always be a cripple and scarcely half a king, yet must I raise him to that status in the eyes of all men. I shall send him off to war--oh, no, he will be in no danger, for I shall hedge him about with armed men and the enemy will be the weakest one I can find. Then, in a year or two, when all men can point to Akhenre Siptah as a true king of Kemet, I will succeed in throwing off the yoke of the Regent and allowing my boy to rule alone. Alone, that is, but for the real power behind the throne--me. I shall have myself crowned as co-ruler, the better to help and advise my nephew, and then, when the young king tragically dies, I shall take my place on the Double Throne.

I have in my possession two lists--one that details every priest, official, or army commander that I have ever bribed, and one that lists my enemies and those that refuse to be bribed. Tausret heads the latter list, of course, and it includes such men as her dog Ament, General of the South Setnakhte who has always hated the House of Amenmesse, and Ramesses, son of Setnakhte. Perhaps surprisingly, for he supported my initial efforts to get Siptah accepted, Tjaty Hori has become my enemy. When I tried to involve him in my schemes, he rejected me most insultingly. Luckily, I had revealed little of my plans, so he is unable to hurt me, but soon I will be in a position to hurt him, should it please me to do so. I will not forget those who reject me, and one day they will regret their decisions most bitterly.

Chapter 15
Year 2 of Akhenre Siptah

Akhenre Siptah was Lord of the Two Lands, undoubted king of Kemet, and as such had many duties despite his young age. He took his place in the law courts, and presided over any disputes that Tjaty Hori felt could be left to his inexperience. Hori guided the king in all legal matters, offered instruction and showed the boy how justice should be dispensed, stepping in whenever the boy-king made a mistake. Inevitably, Siptah hated being made to feel inadequate and longed for the day when his word became the law of the land.

The king was also High Priest of all the gods and while most services could be left to the ordinary priests to perform, he was expected to approach the gods on behalf of the people. He was god-on-earth and the gods would listen to him as they would to no one else. The problem was, the prayers to the gods were complex and long, and Siptah often found his attention wandering, especially in the daily dawn greetings to Re in the form of Khepri of the rising sun. He had received many scandalised looks from the priests when he yawned in the middle of a service.

His daily duties would have been intolerable if the grind of essential services had not been leavened by pleasure. Hunting was a staple, whether merely wildfowl in the reed beds or crocodiles on the river, or brief forays into the scrubland after gazelles. He still sought a lion, but those beasts had so far eluded his huntsmen--or so Bay informed him. However, there were other pleasures available within the palace.

The sons of court officials were encouraged by their fathers to strike up friendships with the young king in the hopes of preferment. After an initial flurry of interest, when boy after boy was introduced to the young monarch, his erstwhile companions had been winnowed away to a few whose interests matched those of Siptah, though they were a few years older than the king. They were Huni, the son of Henenu, the Overseer of Palace Wines; Sepi, the son of Meketre, Royal Butler; and Hay, the son of Maya, Deputy Treasurer of Ta Mehu. These three boys became the king's almost

92

constant companions during his leisure time, and they could often be found improving their skills with bow and arrow, playing games of Senet or throwing stones, or teasing the monkeys in the palace menagerie.

On a day a few months after he killed the wild bull, Siptah heard a rumour that a lion had been killing livestock on the edge of the desert near Per-Ramesses in the north. He became excited and immediately broke of the game of Senet he had been losing to Hay.

"At last, the lion I have been waiting for."

"You won't be allowed to," Sepi said.

"Of course he will," Huni said. "He's the king. He can do whatever he wants."

"Whatever the Regent allows him to do, you mean," Sepi corrected.

"Tausret need not know," Siptah said. "My uncle Bay will let me do it. He has already allowed me on hunts. This will be no different."

Siptah sent a servant to summon Bay and after a while he turned up on the balcony where the boys had been playing. As he was in the presence of the sons of court officials, Bay displayed none of the annoyance he was feeling at being dragged away from his work and merely sketched a bow toward his nephew.

"Ah, Uncle," Siptah said. "I did not need your huntsmen after all. There is a lion killing cattle near Per-Ramesses and I have decided to hunt it. Organise whatever is necessary and we shall leave tomorrow."

"I will see what can be done," Bay said. He left the boys excitedly making plans for the coming hunt and returned before the sun had advanced the shadows on the wall more than a hand span. "Alas, my lord, the Regent has forbidden the hunt as being too dangerous."

"She can't do that," Siptah exclaimed. "I want to do it. Tell her, Uncle."

"Regrettably, she can forbid you. She is the sole Regent. I am sorry, nephew. I know you had your heart set on a lion, but there will be others when the Regent has no power over you." Bay bowed again, and left the boys once more.

Siptah scowled and would have stamped his foot in anger had he not learned from bitter experience that the act made him stumble and look ridiculous. "She has no right to forbid me. I am the king, crowned and anointed, not some boy still with his sidelock."

"So tell her," Hay said.

"Hay's right," Huni added. "She may be Regent, but you are the anointed king."

"That's the whole point of being Regent though," Sepi said. "She has the power. It's just a pity your Uncle Bay isn't Regent."

"Perhaps he could be," Hay suggested. "Would that be possible?"

"What? You think Queen Tausret will just stand aside?"

"I just meant that maybe Bay could be regent as well as Queen Tausret," Hay replied. "That way, you could ask Bay for permission and he could officially grant it."

"The Queen would never agree."

"How do you know? Ask her, Akhenre."

"Or tell her. You are the king."

Siptah called a servant to him once more and ordered him to tell the Regent to attend upon him at once. The servant quailed visibly, but bowed and went off. Time passed and an overseer appeared. He bowed to the young king and cleared his throat nervously before speaking.

"My lord king, your summons was conveyed to the Queen Regent but she declines to appear before you. I am charged with giving you her exact words. Er, do you wish to hear them in private, my lord king?"

"Say what you will, Overseer. These are the king's friends and are in his confidence."

"As you will, my lord king. The Queen Regent's words are, 'if the boy who plays at being king wishes to see me, then he must come in person and petition me. Queen Tausret attends on no man or boy.'"

Sepi and Huni gasped aloud at the overseer's words, while Hay sucked his front teeth and shook his head. Siptah paled at the insult, but bit off the retort that sprang to his lips.

"You may leave us," he muttered to the overseer. Siptah turned away and put his hands on the balustrade of the balcony and gazed out at the gardens. Tears of chagrin threatened to flood his eyes and he angrily brushed them away.

"What will you do?" Hay asked.

"What can he do?" Huni asked. "He has been put in his place," he added in a whisper to Sepi.

"This challenge to your authority cannot go unanswered," Sepi said. "Shall I send for Chancellor Bay so that he might advise you?"

Siptah turned and glared at his friends. His eyes glittered with unshed tears but his voice was steady. "Leave me." He waited until the three youths had left his presence before taking a deep breath and letting it out shakily. "So," he muttered. "If I must come to you, I shall, but I am now determined that my uncle shall be regent."

Siptah went to his private suite and called his body servants. He bathed, selected perfumes and cosmetics to age his youthful face and dressed in royal clothing, donning ornaments and regalia befitting a king. Then he made his way to the Queen's quarters where she sat examining a selection of jewellery and had himself announced, limping into the room before the herald had finished his address.

"Send your servants out, Queen Tausret. What I have to say is not for their ears."

Tausret stared, her eyebrows lifting in surprise at the king's tone. She nodded to the Overseer of the Jewel Box, who gathered the servants together and ushered them from the room. When the door closed behind the last of them, the Queen beckoned Siptah forward.

"What game is this you play, Siptah? Can you not see I am busy?"

"No game, Lady, and I am properly addressed as King Akhenre."

Tausret smiled. "You will always be Siptah to me. You are scarcely older than my own son, and he still toddles around playing with his toys."

Siptah trembled with anger. "I am not a little boy any longer," he shouted. "I am a king."

"A true king would not need to proclaim it, Siptah. The evidence of it would be plain to see." She yawned ostentatiously. "What is it you came to say?"

"I am old enough to rule as king by myself. I don't need you as Regent any longer."

Tausret looked at the boy-king with a faint smile on her face. "Does this have something to do with my refusal to let you go on a lion hunt?"

"Yes...no...not just that. I am quite capable of making decisions on my own."

"That is not what Tjaty Hori says. He tells me you are making progress in the law courts, but you can still only handle the simpler cases. And as for your priestly duties...I have had three Hem-netjers complaining that you yawn and scratch yourself during the ceremonies." Tausret shook her head. "What must the gods think of your behaviour?"

Siptah scowled and looked down at the floor. "I am learning...and getting better all the time. Besides, as king I have a Tjaty and priests to do my bidding. I don't need to do everything myself."

"A king is the head priest of every temple in the land, Siptah, and represents the gods. Do you imagine the gods will look favourably on the Two Lands if you can't be bothered to pay attention during the rituals? And how can the people and nobles look up to a king who doesn't know the laws sufficiently well to adjudicate in even the hardest decisions?" Tausret regarded the boy with a softer expression on her face. "Must I explain your position to you again? You came to the throne for one reason only--Kemet needs a king and the son of Userkheperure Seti was too young. I might point out that your father killed my husband..."

"And you killed my father," Siptah blurted out.

"Is that what you believe? Well, I will not deny his death made my job simpler, but I did not give the order. In fact, my husband Userkheperure gave specific instructions that he not be harmed. I would have gone along with that."

"So who did kill him then?"

"I don't know. It would seem a man broke into the palace and stabbed him to death. When I heard, I told Tjaty Paraemheb to order a full investigation, but the murderer has not been found. Your father had many enemies after his general Sethi tore Ta Shemau apart."

"Why then did you make me king if my father was so bad?"

"Kemet needed a king and Seti-Merenptah was too young. I have told you this already."

"Why did you not just rule as regent with your son on the throne? Why does it matter if the king is two years or ten years?"

Tausret regarded the young king for another long moment. "If I am being honest, I would have preferred that, but my advisers convinced me you would make a good interim king."

"Interim?"

"Temporary. You are king until Seti-Merenptah is old enough, and then he will become co-ruler and eventually succeed you on the throne."

"I cannot pass the throne on to my son, should I have one?"

"No. That was the proviso for letting you become king. All this was explained to you before you were crowned."

Siptah shook his head. "I didn't know...or it wasn't explained to me. Did my Uncle Bay agree?"

"Yes. You can ask him if you like."

The young king was silent for a long time. He walked to a chair and sat down, his shoulders hunched, as he digested the unwelcome information. At length, he looked across at Tausret.

"I came to ask you to let my Uncle Bay become Regent instead of you."

Tausret shook her head. "He can't be Regent; he's a commoner. How could he possibly stand for the king when he is not royal?"

"But he is my family--my only family. I want him to play a part in my life."

"He already does that, Siptah. You spend far more time with him than you do with me."

"But he has no authority. Anything I want I must ask you for, and it would be much easier if I could just ask Uncle Bay. Please, Queen Tausret, can't you make my uncle the Regent?"

"No, Siptah; that is never going to happen. As I explained, he may be related to you but only because he was your mother's brother. He is an Amorite, a servant and a commoner. I am not going to let him rule Kemet through you."

"He is the king's uncle. Doesn't that count for something?"

"And he has a tomb in the Great Field among the kings. Is that not honour enough? Some would say it is too great an honour for a common man."

Siptah's shoulders slumped further and he swung his withered foot so his toes brushed the stone floor. He did not look up at the queen as he spoke.

"Why do you hate me so much?" he asked.

Tausret stared at the king who now looked like nothing more than a miserable child. "I don't hate you, Siptah."

"It feels like it. Bay is the only one who loves me."

"I'm sorry if it seems that way, but I only have the good of Kemet in my heart. You have a difficult path to tread, child, because of your father. He ripped the kingdoms apart and killed my husband who was the rightful king. The easiest thing would have been to wipe all memory of him from men's minds--but you exist. None of this is your fault, but you bear the burden. You are king of Kemet, for better or worse, to hold the kingdoms together until the wounds of civil war can heal. Then Seti-Merenptah will take his place on the throne alongside you and you will rule together."

Siptah considered his future, his swinging toes continuing to brush the floor. "Although I am king, I am treated as a child, and when I am no longer a child I must have a child beside me on the throne, knowing I can never truly be king in my own right. Is this fair, Queen Tausret? Am I always to be treated thus?"

"Such are the circumstances that led you to the throne, Siptah. The future is in the hands of the gods but..." Tausret hesitated, pity strong on her face. "Perhaps I can alleviate some of your sorrow. I cannot make your uncle Bay the Regent, but I can involve him more in the running of your affairs. Already I have included him in inscriptions and caused his image to be carved in monuments for your sake, but I will do more. I will create a title for him that allows him to be honoured on inscriptions in your name. Would that please you?"

"What title?"

"How about 'fan-bearer on the right of the king'? That is a prestigious title for a commoner."

"There are other fan-bearers."

"You want more?" Tausret thought for a few moments. "All right, here is a title that raises him higher than any other in the land of Kemet. In addition to 'fan-bearer on the right of the king', I will add 'king's messenger to Khor and Kush'. That gives him status above any other king's messenger and allows him to act throughout the lands of Kemet from the land of Khor in the north to the land of Kush in the south. Will that satisfy you, Siptah? It is unheard of for a commoner to bear those titles together, but such is my love for you, I will do it."

Siptah rose and limped across to where Tausret sat. He took her hands in his and bowed his head. "Thank you, Queen Tausret. I am pleased that you offer my uncle such honours. Will you also grant me leave to hunt my lion?"

Tausret smiled but shook her head. "One thing at a time, Akhenre Siptah. There will be other lions."

The young king left the presence of the Queen and made his way slowly through the palace to the chamber where Chancellor Bay sat alone, conducting the business of the Kingdoms.

"I hear you have been to see the Queen. Did you persuade her to let you hunt a lion where I failed?"

"No, Uncle, but that was not the only reason I went to see her."

Bay lowered the scroll he had been reading and looked at his young nephew. "What else did you discuss?"

"I asked her to make you Regent."

"Did you, by the gods? What did she say?"

"She said no, but rather insultingly, saying you were a commoner and an Amorite--as if that matters."

"It does to some people." Bay shrugged. "She was never going to agree, so you must not be too downhearted. There are other ways to achieve power..." Bay's voice trailed away as he saw the grin on the young king's face. "What?"

"She has agreed to give you what she says are some great honours. You are to be fan-bearer on the right of the king, and king's messenger to Khor and Kush."

"Khor *and* Kush? Are you sure?"

"That's what she said. I know about the fan-bearer but not about the messenger bit. She explained it but I didn't really understand. Is it really a great honour?"

"Oh yes. A messenger carries the king's words to a nation of the Nine Bows and can negotiate terms and truces on behalf of the king. Normally, a man is a messenger to a single nation, but Khor is the northernmost nation and Kush the southernmost, so what that title gives me is the right to talk to any nation on the king's behalf. I've never heard of anyone being given that title before."

"So although you are not Regent, you are more powerful than before?"

"Oh yes indeed. And let me assure you, it is but the first step. Together, you and I will overcome any opposition Queen Tausret puts in our way. You will become sole king, young Akhenre Siptah. Mark my words."

Chapter 16
Year 2 of Akhenre Siptah

Tjaty Hori and the king were in the law courts dispensing justice when there was a disturbance in the forecourt. Hori stopped the proceedings and sent a scribe to find out the cause, and the scribe returned a few moments later with a messenger in tow. Both men bowed before the Tjaty, and the messenger made a deeper bow toward the king.

"My lord Tjaty, Son of Re," said the messenger. "I come bearing serious news from the governor of the city of Perire."

"Wait." Hori dismissed the remaining petitioners and then bade the messenger speak.

"The Ribu have rebelled er, my lord...Son of Re." The messenger looked a little confused as to who he should be addressing.

"Report to me," Hori said. "Disregard the king's presence."

"Yes, my lord. Governor Nebmaktef of Perire bids me tell you that a small force of Ribu have crossed into Ta Mehu and have plundered several villages and driven off livestock. He sent the City Troop out to meet them, but they avoided battle, melting away as they approached and returning after the soldiers had left."

"How many Ribu?"

"Five hundred, my lord, maybe a thousand. They are only lightly armed and have no chariots."

"Why has Governor Nebmaktef sent me this message, rather than one that reports the Ribu has been destroyed?"

The messenger shuffled his feet. "Governor Nebmaktef says he has insufficient men to guard the city, the farms and neighbouring villages as well as march out to meet the Ribu. He asks that the king--Life! Health! Prosperity!--send a legion to destroy his enemies."

"And I will do it," Siptah exclaimed. "This is my chance to go to war, Hori." The king grabbed his walking stick and lurched to his feet. "I must get ready."

Hori hurriedly dismissed the messenger and called Siptah back. "Son of Re, even the king must consult his advisers, and in your case, the Regent will make the decision whether to send an army to Perire."

Siptah scowled. "What does a woman know of war? I will drive a chariot squadron at the enemy and destroy them utterly."

"Of course you will, Son of Re, but have you forgotten that Queen Tausret has fought the Ribu before, at the famous Battle of Perire in King Baenre's day? It may be that she will lead the army."

"She would not so insult me...would she? What will people think if a woman goes to war and the king stays at home? No..." Siptah shook his head and thumped his walking stick on the floor. "I must go."

"Nothing should be done precipitately, Son of Re," Hori said. "Let me call a War Council so these matters may be discussed and a decision made."

Siptah grumbled but agreed. He limped off to find Chancellor Bay, eager to discuss his exciting news. Somehow, Bay seemed to know all about it by the time he reached the Chancellor's chambers.

"You know already? Oh...well...it's exciting, isn't it? It means I can go to war. I can go, can't I? It would be just too unfair if I couldn't and the king should lead his army..."

"Calm yourself, Siptah. The news has only just come to Men-nefer. There will be a Council and the Regent will decide whether there is to be a war or not."

"But you'll argue for me, won't you? They'll listen to you."

Bay smiled. "I will make every effort on your behalf," he assured the boy.

A War Council was called for later that day, but Bay decided to call on Queen Tausret beforehand, wanting to argue Siptah's case in relative privacy. If the queen was vehemently opposed to the king's presence on the battlefield, it was better to know beforehand. It would be regarded as a sign of weakness if he was overruled in front of the whole Council. This way, he could openly support the Queen's decision and gain standing in front of the army officers. He found Tausret in the company of her frequent companion Ament.

"Regent," Bay said, offering up a slight bow of courtesy to Tausret but ignoring Ament. "You will have heard the serious news of the Ribu incursion?"

"Naturally, but I am unconvinced this is serious. Only five hundred men? All that's needed is a Troop of soldiers to run them out of Ta Mehu. I don't know what's wrong with Nebmaktef that he hasn't done that already."

"It does provide an opportunity though," Bay said.

Ament frowned. "What opportunity?"

Bay deigned to notice the erstwhile legion commander. "Ah, Ament. You are in good health, I trust?"

Ament dipped his head in reluctant courtesy. "Chancellor. What opportunity?"

"You must appreciate what this disturbance means for the palace and the king's education. Regent, it is the perfect opportunity to introduce the king to warfare. An enemy with few teeth, and we have the Ptah legion on hand. Ten days from now and Akhenre Siptah will be acclaimed as a king at the head of a victorious army."

"He is only a boy. Imagine the harm it would do if he cried at the sight of the enemy, or showed fear in front of his army officers. No, I shall send the Ptah legion under Besenmut and the king can wait a few more years before he faces danger."

"He has already faced danger, Regent. I know you will not let him hunt a lion, but he displayed great bravery with the bull recently."

"It's one thing to face an insensate animal from the safety of a chariot," Ament said. "Quite another to face an enemy capable of inflicting death from a distance."

"You did not see him against the bull," Bay objected. "On foot, and unarmed after his last arrow pierced its side, he stood there and faced its advance. He reached out and touched it on the head and it fell down dead."

"Well, he couldn't exactly run, could he?" Ament said.

"That comment is beneath you, Commander. A lesser man would not even have dismounted but faced the bull from the safety of the chariot. That boy may be crippled, but he is brave."

"Yet a bull is not the same as a human enemy," Tausret said. "I do not want to put the king in danger."

"How much danger would he be in?" Bay asked. "These are only tribesmen looking for a bit of plunder, a few cattle. Show them a few soldiers and they'll flee back to the wilderness they crawled out of."

"Scarcely any point in sending the king, then," Ament said. "Besenmut can handle it."

"But what an opportunity to let the king experience warfare."

"He doesn't need to," Tausret replied. "He will only be king a few more years."

"Of course, Regent, but the Ma'at of Kemet must surely be served by the Kingdoms having confidence in their king. What better way than to show him victorious at the head of his army? Never mind that the enemy is scarcely worthy of the name--the people will see only a victory and rejoice."

"And what do you get out of it, Bay?" Ament asked. "I've never known you put something forward without getting some benefit."

"I have only the good of Kemet at heart. It will be good for Siptah too. The semblance of war may take his mind off more dangerous activities, like hunting a lion."

"I've already told him he can't do that," Tausret said.

"But it won't stop him asking. Give him this and he'll put hunting aside--at least for the time being."

"You can guarantee his safety?"

"I shall make sure he is hedged about by competent men and sensible officers."

"Who will be in charge?" Ament asked. "Besenmut will be busy looking after his legion. Who will mind the king?"

"Perhaps you would care to do that, Ament?" Bay said with a small smile. "I can think of no one I would trust more."

Tausret stifled a laugh as she caught sight of Ament's expression. "Yes, I think that would be a good idea. You are to be Captain of the King's Bodyguard, Ament. Look after him at all times and make sure no hurt comes to him."

Ament scowled at Bay. "And if the king orders me to do something that might result in harm?"

"Use your judgment," Tausret said. "If it comes down to it, you obey your Regent rather than your king. Just make sure he experiences enough of war to satisfy him."

The king and his army set out two days later after dawn services to Re, with a somewhat under-strength Ptah legion. They marched north along the course of the westernmost branch of the Great River, Besenmut marching his men in a long column along dirt roads and cutting across fields and drainage ditches, while the chariot squadron raced ahead. Siptah revelled in the freedom of driving his own chariot, though Ament had detailed a strong bodyguard to match him in accompanying chariots. Time and again, when Ament judged the king was drawing too far ahead of the legion, he had to chase him down and encourage him to turn back.

"A good commander stays close to the source of his strength, Son of Re. You should keep in touch with the legion."

"Besenmut can manage, Ament. I want to forge ahead and meet the enemy."

Siptah shook the reins and urged his chariot forward once more. Ament cursed and followed, knowing the moment was drawing closer when he would have to order his men to escort the king back to the legion.

"Son of Re, you must think of your people. It would be a disaster if anything should happen to you."

"We know the enemy has no chariots, Ament. What can they do?"

Siptah drove off again before Ament could remind him that a single arrow could achieve what a squadron of chariots might not. This time when he caught up with the king, he ordered his men to block the king's way forward.

"This is as far as you go, Son of Re. We must turn back to the legion."

"You forget yourself, Ament. I am the king and I do not take orders from a mere Commander."

"I speak with the authority of the Regent, and it was at your Uncle's suggestion that I was appointed. I must insist, Son of Re."

Siptah grumbled, but allowed himself to be diverted from his course. He ordered Ament to ride back in his chariot and even relinquished the reins to his bodyguard so that he could talk unhindered.

"Why did my Uncle Bay have you appointed as my minder?"

Ament negotiated a rough patch of ground before he answered. "I don't think he had in mind that it was an honour for me."

"You don't like me, do you?" When Ament did not answer, Siptah pushed further. "Why are you my enemy, Commander Ament?"

"I am not your enemy, Akhenre Siptah, but I was your father's enemy."

Siptah frowned. "Of course, you were a commander in Userkheperure's army, weren't you? Did you ever see my father Menmire? Talk to him?"

"Yes, on both counts."

"What was he like? I was only a small child when I saw him last--not long after my mother died and before he became king."

"He should never have become king. He was never the heir to Baenre's throne, but usurped it and led Kemet into civil war. I cannot forgive him for that."

"But what was he like? Really like?"

Ament shrugged. "I'm probably not the person to ask. I only saw him in Waset when I went there to kill him."

Siptah's eyes opened wide. "You tried to kill him? During the war? But you didn't, of course. Why not? What happened?"

Ament shook his head. "Suffice it to say I did not have the opportunity when he was surrounded by his guards, his Tjaty, and his General."

"His men loved him. Bay said so."

"I don't doubt it, as we all loved Userkheperure. When it comes to it, it is not love that makes a man win, nor even strength of arms, but rather the will of the gods. We are all subject to that. Honour the gods and they will not forsake you."

"My father honoured the gods and they chose him to reign, anointing him in the coronation ceremony. That means he must have been the true king."

"How could he be when Userkheperure had been accepted and crowned before him?"

"Perhaps the gods had rejected him and chosen again."

Ament shrugged again. "Yet in the end, the gods forsook your father."

"And they have chosen me to succeed," Siptah said.

Ament opened his mouth to reply, but shouts from behind them interrupted their conversation. He looked round and saw a scouting chariot hurtling down the road toward them. The scout quickly overhauled them and as soon as they were within earshot, the driver was calling across his news.

"...found the enemy...Ribu...up ahead..."

Ament brought the squadron to a halt and beckoned the scout closer. "Tell us the news. Quickly, man."

The scout saluted. "Son of Re...Commander...the enemy has been found. They are a little south of the city of Perire, some hundred strong and..."

"Only a hundred?"

"Yes, Commander, though we saw dust to the north and east which might indicate other enemy forces."

"You did not think to investigate?"

"No sir...yes sir...that is, other scouts did so. I returned bearing the news."

"Very well, carry on and report to Commander Besenmut."

Siptah wriggled with excitement, and as soon as the scout had left, told Ament to return to his own chariot. "We must turn immediately and engage the enemy. We can be up to them in less than half a day."

Ament shook his head and started the horses moving south again. "We will wait for a full reconnaissance, Son of Re." He saw the anger and disappointment on the king's face. "Believe me in this, Akhenre, for I have had experience of war. Nothing is lost by learning of the enemy dispositions. Don't worry; you'll get your taste of war."

Chapter 17

A khenre Siptah speaks:

I am going to war!

The enemy has invaded Kemet and I have leapt to the defence of the kingdoms, leading a legion out of Men-nefer toward Perire where the vile Ribu are killing my people. I shall crush them completely, kill their leaders in single combat, cut off the hands of the fallen and lead their women and children captive into Men-nefer. My exploits will resound down the ages like those of Baenre and Usermaatre, and every temple shall bear the accounts of my great victory. In fact, I shall erect a great victory stele at Perire so that all men shall know of my victory down the long ages.

When the news of the foreign invasion came to Men-nefer, I ordered Chancellor Bay to arrange for my presence on campaign. I felt sure that the Regent would deny me my rights, but Bay must have argued brilliantly, for when the Council of War was called I was asked to attend and then, without having to demand my rights, Queen Tausret suggested I lead the Ptah legion into battle.

It was all I could do not to shout aloud my joy and leap to my feet with excitement. I blushed when I remembered it for my weak leg would certainly have caused me to fall over and shame myself before the assembled officers and officials. Instead, I maintained a solemn face and nodded my acceptance of the charge laid upon me. I am the king after all, and for the first time the Regent had allowed me a kingly dignity. Now was my opportunity to show I was a great War Leader and father to my people.

Uncle Bay came and talked to me for a long time the night before we set out. He told me of the Ribu and the terrible things they do to the innocent peasants of Ta Mehu. It sickened me and made me angry, so that I wanted to destroy the Ribu utterly. Perhaps that is what he wanted, for he smiled a lot when I voiced my indignation. He said, too, that I must not be concerned with my safety for the gods would look after me--and strong men had been charged with my protection as well.

I did not then know that Ament was to be my main protector. If I had, I might have objected and sought another Captain of the King's Bodyguard, for I feel uncomfortable in his presence. My uncle calls him the Regent's dog, and that is a good name for him. He follows her around, ready to do her bidding at all times, and Bay hints that he performs subtle and shameful acts for her. Well, he may be Captain of the Guard, but I am king, so he cannot do just as he wants. I tried to persuade Uncle Bay to come with me, but he says that war is no place for an administrator. He is probably right as all my men will need strength and skill to fight the Ribu.

We set out early, after morning services to the rising sun, and having offered brief libations to the other gods. I drove out of the northern gate of Men-nefer in my war chariot and the populace lined the road, cheering their king. At first I waved and grinned but then it occurred to me that a king should be more serious, so I turned my face from the adoring crowd and held myself in what I hoped was a regal bearing. I joined the Ptah legion just outside the city, and as I drove up, the other chariots in the squadron tore out from the ranks and surrounded me in an honour guard. I could not help laughing out loud at the sheer joy of it all. I was going to war and all these men were at my command.

Drums boomed out and rams' horns blew, and above the roar of chariot wheels I could feel more than hear the steady tramp of thousands of feet as the legion marched. Dust rose in a choking cloud, but that did not bother me as I was out the front in my chariot, leading the way into battle. All right, so there were other chariots with me, especially Ament and the men he had chosen as my bodyguard, but they could not lessen my swelling pride. The sun beat down on me and the cool north wind blew in my face. My blue leather war crown pressed down on my head, but I would not have put it aside for an instant. For this I was born--to reign over Kemet and to war against my enemies.

And so we came close to Perire after three days. Scouts returned saying they had found the enemy, and I desired more than anything to gather my chariots about me and hurl ourselves at the Ribu. Ament prevented me, forcing me to retreat to the safety of the legion. I was angry at his impertinence but I managed to hide it, for as my uncle says, he is merely the Regent's dog. There is little point in getting angry at the pi-dog that runs snapping at the chariot wheels, when it is the dog's owner who should be upbraided.

Besenmut ordered his men to march faster when the news of the enemy's proximity was reported, and it was mid-morning of the next day when we came in sight of the walls of Perire. Most men know of the battle fought here in Baenre's day, but fewer know that the Regent, Queen Tausret, also fought here. Whatever else I think of her, I allow that she displayed bravery that day, facing down the Ribu and holding them until Baenre could move his army up and crush them.

I met with Besenmut and his senior officers, and listened to the scouts' reports. It seems the enemy was not a regular army, but rather a mass of peasants and bandits. They had no regular military objectives but instead drifted from village to village, killing and plundering as they went. Where they could not carry away the spoils, they set fire to them and indeed, several plumes of smoke could be seen rising over the farmland near the river.

Besenmut laid out the battle plan and asked me for my approval. I freely admit (in private) that lacking experience I could not say if the plan was a good one, but I gave it what looked like consideration and offered my approval. Lest I be thought a complete beginner, I made a few minor changes and Besenmut willingly accepted them.

The horns are sounding again and I am strapped into my chariot, blue war crown on my head, gold gleaming at throat and chest, my bow in one hand and my arrows in front of me. I have a charioteer today, so that I might wage war without having to worry about controlling my horses. Ament and the Bodyguard are arrayed beside me and so hungrily do they stare at the enemy that I might forget they are not my friends either.

The Commander signals the army is ready and looks at me. I raise my hand with bow clutched in it and shout a challenge. My words crash back over me as nearly fifteen hundred throats cheer their king.

"Life! Health! Prosperity! For Akhenre, Kemet and the gods! Death to the Ribu!"

The men surge forward and I grip the rail of my chariot tightly as we start forward, picking up speed. At last, the hour is come when I will be measured against the deeds of past kings. I am determined that I will not be found wanting.

Chapter 18
Year 2 of Akhenre Siptah

The charge of the Ptah legion expended a lot of effort for very little result. Twelve hundred men on foot and thirty chariots smashed into the tiny enemy force and annihilated it almost before the king could loose his third arrow. Besenmut pulled his men into a semblance of order after the wild charge and set about collecting the spoils of war.

It amounted to very little. Eighty-seven right hands were harvested and piled before the king, along with a handful of spears, some crude bows, and a larger number of simple staves and assorted farming equipment. Siptah appeared not to notice the strange equipment of this invading army and only lamented that so few of the enemy had been killed.

"Three arrows I shot, Ament, and three men died," he exulted.

"Very good, Son of Re, but these were hardly enemy warriors. I mean, look at their arms--pitchforks and mattocks mostly. These are farmers, not fighters."

Siptah frowned and nudged a pile of implements with his walking stick. "These are probably spoils the Ribu were carrying off when we surprised them. Farmers wouldn't be carrying spears or bows."

Ament shrugged, and the king called for the army scribe.

"Take down the number of enemy killed and the spoils, scribe. Then write an account of my glorious victory, and don't forget that I led the charge and that with my bow I slew lots of the enemy."

"Three," Ament muttered. "Maybe."

The army resumed its march, bypassing the city of Perire. Scouts were sent out to find the enemy and they soon returned with the news of another small group of men to the northeast. Siptah ordered the chariots onward, and told Besenmut to follow with the soldiers. Ament remonstrated, despite the low quality of the previous group of enemy.

"You should not split your forces," he said. "Allow the men on foot time to come up in support."

"You are too timid," Siptah declared. "You saw how I crushed the last lot. I shall do so again, just with my chariots."

Ament signalled to his own chariots to follow the king and spent the short journey cursing under his breath. The charioteer was one of Ament's own men, but was shocked by the imprecations against the king. Wisely, he pretended not to hear.

Smoke rose ahead of the column of chariots as the road led them into lush fields bordering on the river. They found a smouldering village, and scattered corpses of women, children and livestock. Siptah drove past, following a thin dust cloud that hung in the still air. He pointed and cried out in excitement, urging his own horses onward.

Ahead of them, hurrying along the road, was a rabble of men driving beasts before them and laden with spoils. When they saw the chariots behind them, they scattered, some keeping to the road but others cutting across the fields. Siptah hesitated only for a moment before signalling to his chariots to fan out while he continued on down the packed earth road. At once, the narrow wheels of the chariots to either side of him cut through the turf and sank into the soft soil beneath, slowing their progress and disrupting the charging line of chariots. The pace of the king's own chariot continued unabated and soon he was alone, racing up the road toward the fleeing enemy.

Ament and his men, at the rear of the squadron, swore loudly and whipped their horses into a gallop, jostling and cursing as they pursued the king in single file down the narrow road. Ahead, Ament could see the king's chariot run down the hindmost fleeing men, Siptah himself leaning out and loosing arrows as fast as he could draw his bow. The other running men suddenly became aware that only a single chariot faced them and turned with weapons in hand. Copper blades caught the sunlight as spears stabbed, and all of a sudden a horse was down and the charioteer was falling, bright blood staining his tunic.

Ament raised a hoarse cry of horror and urged his own chariot on; now close enough to attract the attention of the enemy warriors surrounding the king's chariot. Moments later he charged into them, crushing men beneath hooves and wheels, his own spear stabbing and thrusting. Men threw themselves aside, and then turned to run as the rest of Ament's chariots arrived and, a little behind them, the rest of the squadron. The enemy was cut down, and several chariots headed off to chase down the rest of the enemy that had fled earlier.

Siptah stood in the body of his chariot, holding on as the living horse bucked and shied away from its dead companion. A man ran to cut the dead horse away and the king grinned as Ament turned and drove back.

"You are unhurt, Son of Re?"

Siptah lifted a hand to the blue leather of his war crown and fingered the rough streak of unstained leather where a blade had ripped its way past him.

"Untouched, Ament. You saw? How I fought against great odds, slaying my enemy so they fell like wheat before the reaper? It was magnificent."

"Tell that to your dead charioteer."

Siptah's smile slipped, and he turned to look at the man crumpled on the road. His lip trembled. "Poor Apet." He shook his head and looked away. "How many enemy died? I killed most of them."

Ament looked around at a dozen corpses, a few more scattered over the fields. He stepped down from his chariot and squatted beside one of the bodies, that of a grey-bearded man with a bloody wound in his chest.

"There's something odd here," Ament said, pointing at an ornament around the man's neck. He pulled at it, snapping the cord and examined it. "It's an amulet--a scarab. What is a Ribu doing wearing a scarab? They don't believe in our gods."

"So he robbed it off a Kemetu," Siptah said. "Is that an arrow wound in his chest? Is it from one of mine?"

"I think it's from a spear, Son of Re." Ament walked over to other bodies and gave them a cursory examination, lifting a few tunics and moving aside a few arms. Then he walked back to where the king was standing, drinking from a flask of water handed him by one of Ament's men.

"These men are cut," Ament said. "Circumcised."

"So?"

"The Ribu don't do that."

Siptah shrugged. "They're hardly more than beasts. Who can say what they get up to in their own lands?"

Ament frowned and opened his mouth to say something more but then thought better of it. He had his men clear the corpses from the road and harvested the right hands of each of them. He was finishing up as the rest of the chariot squadron returned and the first Troop of the Ptah legion came into view. The king ordered camp to be set up, though it was scarcely past noon, and retired to his tent.

Ament sought out Besenmut and showed him the fired clay scarab he had taken off the dead man.

"They're circumcised too. I don't think they're Ribu."

Besenmut fingered the scarab and drank from a cup of wine before answering. "Who is to say they are not Ribu who have taken up Kemetu ways?"

"There is one other thing I have not mentioned," Ament continued. "Two of the men were branded under the left arm. They're criminals, not foreigners."

"Can't they be both?"

"Of course, but take into account how badly armed they are, the lack of purpose in their movements, the circumcisions, and now the branding. Are these really Ribu we're facing?"

Besenmut looked at Ament. "What else could they be? The reports that came in from the Governor at Perire were of a Ribu incursion. Why would he lie?"

Ament shook his head. "I don't know. I could be wrong, but I think it's suspicious."

"Implying what though? These are still men taking up arms against the king. Are you saying we should ignore it just because they're not who they're supposed to be?"

"Of course not." Ament glowered and paced in Besenmut's tent. "Oh, forget I said anything. It doesn't matter whether they're Ribu or not. They must still be eradicated."

"Have you said anything to the king about this?"

"I told him they were circumcised but he shrugged it off."

"Then don't say anything more," Besenmut said. "This is his big chance to prove he's a warrior king. Don't spoil it for him."

Ament stared at the legion commander. "You knew." When Besenmut remained silent, he went on. "Who are these men? Really?"

"Criminals, bandits, a few disaffected peasants. Possibly even a few real Ribu. They've been promised gold if they put up a good show."

"But why?"

"I told you--to make the king look like a real king. An enemy invades Ta Mehu, he leads a legion out and crushes the enemy. Can you think of something else that would raise his self-esteem more?"

"Kemet lacks real enemies?"

Besenmut laughed. "Would you risk that headstrong boy by letting him battle the Sea Peoples or the Amurri? You've seen him in action, Ament.

Brave but reckless. We don't need a king of Kemet dying in battle and throwing the Two Lands into turmoil again. Far better to let him play at war without risk."

"Except for the soldiers who die while he plays his games. His charioteer was killed alongside him today."

"You can't make bread without grinding the barley. Soldiers know the risks."

Ament shook his head. "All so the king can feel like a man. Whose idea was this? Bay?"

"It was his suggestion, yes. I was happy to oblige."

"I thought you loathed the man. You were strongly in support of Seti-Merenptah at the succession council."

Besenmut inclined his head. "He's shown himself a capable minister since then and Akhenre is a decent enough king as long as he's guided."

"By Bay, I suppose you mean?"

"He is the boy's uncle."

"And what of Queen Tausret? The Regent? Shouldn't she be the one guiding him?"

"She has a lot to do, ruling in Akhenre's name. Why not let Bay help her? He's competent enough to be a regent alongside her." Besenmut stepped across and put his arm around Ament's shoulders. "Come, Ament, as fellow commanders, shouldn't we be thinking of the good of all Kemet? And what better way than by strengthening the king's status? Who loses by letting Akhenre become a strong king?"

"Even if it's a sham?"

"A sham now, perhaps, but the boy is cutting his teeth on something harmless. Let him learn the art of war today, and then tomorrow when one of the Nine Bows invades, we'll have a strong king to lead the army."

"What of Seti-Merenptah then?"

"What of him? Nothing has changed; he is still the heir. Look Ament, it could be ten years before the babe's old enough to sit on the throne and we need a proper king in the meantime. Better a strong king than a weakling who is king in name only."

"And the gold comes in handy too, I suppose?"

Besenmut's arm dropped from Ament's shoulders. "What are you implying?"

"Bay controls the treasury and you change your allegiance. How much gold did it take?"

"I don't know what you're talking about," Besenmut said stiffly. "If you're accusing me of taking a bribe, I resent it. I support the king, that's all."

Ament stared at the other legion commander. "We all support the king, Besenmut, but some of us have not forgotten our oaths."

"I think you had better leave, Ament, before I have you arrested."

"You don't have the power. My authority comes directly from the Regent."

"Then get back to Men-nefer and look after the Queen's interests, while I look after the king's."

"I have a job to do here, so I'm staying, but you'll regret the day you forsook Queen Tausret for Chancellor Bay."

The enemy, whether Ribu or something else, dispersed ahead of the advancing Ptah legion and the squadron of chariots led by the young king. He swept north and west around Perire, killing any stray person he found under arms, and then circled back around the city and made for the river again. The pile of hands obtained from the first two battles grew slowly and rotted faster in the heat, and carrying the sacks of hands became a duty Besenmut gave to defaulters.

Ament and his men remained close to the king, but he was no longer in any danger as the opposition to him had almost evaporated. So little resistance was put up that Siptah ordered villages burnt and fields trampled if he could find no Ribu to fight. Ament had been determined not to remonstrate with Siptah again, but he could not ignore these latest acts.

"Son of Re, is this wise?" Ament asked. "These are just the villages of poor peasant farmers. They are Kemetu, and the people you should be protecting, yet you wage war against them."

"Not against innocent Kemetu, Commander Ament, but against traitors. These villages have been sheltering the Ribu invaders. How else could the enemy just disappear so quickly? They must learn that their king will not countenance such treason."

"You are wrong, Son of Re. The Ribu--if they were ever here at all-- have gone back to their own lands. These people here are Kemetu men, women and children suffering under your hand."

"How dare you speak to me like that, Commander? I am the king and my word is law. I cannot be wrong."

"Then you have been led astray by false counsel and inaccurate reports," Ament said. "Give up this campaign and return to Men-nefer before you lose the goodwill of the people of Ta Mehu."

Siptah glared at Ament and turned his face from him. "If you were not the Regent's man I would have you executed. Now leave my presence and don't return. I don't want you near me."

Ament had no choice but to retire, though he wondered how he was going to protect the king if he was no longer allowed near him. Luckily, that was not a problem as the king decided he had had enough of warfare against a foe that would not face him and ordered the legion back to Men-nefer.

Siptah, with Besenmut's encouragement, decided to make a show of his victory over Kemet's enemies. He commandeered wagons from towns closest to the capital and loaded them with the weapons and farm implements he had captured, together with the severed hands of the fallen, and a number of so-called prisoners. None of the Ribu had actually been captured, so Besenmut rounded up a hundred or so peasants, bound them with copper chains and had them led behind the wagons. They were told to keep their mouths shut if they wanted to return to their villages afterward.

The king also declared that every soldier of the Ptah legion would receive a deben of silver, and every officer above Hundred rank a deben of gold for their part in the campaign. The Kemetu dead, numbering only five, including the king's charioteer and a man who died of snakebite, were brought home in honour and Siptah declared he would see them all buried at his expense. Neither the Regent, nor Bay was happy with this profligate expenditure, but as the king had announced it all publicly, there was nothing they could do.

The Ptah legion entered Men-nefer in triumph, the young king riding in his chariot at the front, resplendent in gold and wearing his blue war crown. The soldiers, looking forward to spending their wealth, cheered him until they were hoarse, and the populace joined in, rejoicing that they had a valiant young king to protect them. Siptah ordered cattle to be killed and the meat distributed, together with bread and beer, for everyone to celebrate his victory. Scribes were sent for, and the account of the campaign, outrageously embellished, was dictated for inclusion on victory steles to be set up near the north gate and at the site of the main victory near Perire.

Bay heard the report of Besenmut that night and was pleased with the outcome of the punitive expedition, while Tausret listened to Ament's report and was less pleased. Both rulers, however, recognised that Akhenre Siptah had grown in stature and would now be more difficult to control.

Chapter 19
Year 3 of Akhenre Siptah

The ben-ben or primordial mound, the preeminent land that rose from the original waters in the first act of creation, was honoured in the great pyramids of stone that housed the remains of the ancient kings of Kemet and in the capstones of steles that were erected to honour later kings. So too, the power within Kemet was also in the shape of a ben-ben, with the king at the apex, his Tjaties below him, through successive layers of officials, overseers and army commanders, down to the common people who formed the broad base of society.

In the days of Akhenre Siptah, however, the integrity of the capstone of power was shattered by the presence of a regent who was both above and below the king, and by powerful men moving up through the layers of society to grasp power for themselves. Ramesse Kha'amen-teru Bay was foremost of these, having seized control through the inexperience of his nephew the king and now vied with the official regent as the power behind the throne. He had brought men with him--men eager to exchange loyalty for gold and land, for honours and favour.

Bay had, through his offices of the Chancellor and Treasurer, redistributed the wealth of Kemet, buying men through the guise of loyalty to the king. Men had changed sides--not openly, as that would invite retribution by the still powerful Regent, but subtly, agreeing more often with Bay's ideas than with the Queen's. If the Queen Regent or her followers disagreed with Bay's pronouncements, then all he had to do was appeal to the king. Ultimate power still resided in the Regent, but the days of the king's minority were passing, and one day soon, men whispered, the king would claim full power and his word--and Bay's--would become Law. Better to be seen more loyal to the coming power than to the failing one.

Ament too, had risen in the Land. Though technically still just Commander of the Set legion, his army duties devolved more and more to his officers, while he performed other functions closer to the Queen Regent. He was often to be found hurrying from one part of Kemet to another, carrying out discreet orders from Tausret, or if within the palace at Mennefer, spending many hours in her company.

"Bay grows too powerful, my lady," Ament said one day, some months after the king's triumphant return from conquering the 'Ribu'. "On my way back from Waset, I saw inscriptions where his image appears with yours and the king's--and the same size. He elevates himself to the rank of Regent alongside you."

"Effectively, that is what he is," Tausret murmured. "There is little I can do about it."

Ament hid his feelings, but the apathy in the Queen's voice shocked him. It was indicative of her lack of interest that they now so often met in the palace gardens or the nearby menagerie rather than in one of the palace chambers or her suite.

"You are Regent and Great Wife, my lady. Of course you can do something about it. Say the word and I will do it for you."

Tausret sighed and looked across to where several small monkeys screeched and hooted in a large cage. "Do what exactly, Ament?"

"Whatever you want, my lady. Have Bay arrested or executed."

"That would risk tipping Kemet into civil war again. You must be aware of how powerful he has grown."

"Yes, but he is still a commoner. He may be Chancellor, but no noble would support him."

"He doesn't need nobles when he has the army behind him. By my count he has four legion commanders in his pay, maybe more. There is even talk that General of the North Iurudef has turned."

"Commanders and Generals can be replaced, my lady."

"Once they might have been," Tausret agreed. "If I tried to do it now, I might precipitate the civil war I'm trying to avoid."

Several small boys, sons of palace officials, were poking sticks at the monkeys who responded by screaming and hurling faeces at their tormentors. The boys laughed and dodged, and some of them threw stones back. The noise attracted a gardener, who ran off to find an overseer.

"So what do we do?" Ament demanded. "Give up, and hand Kemet to Bay on a platter?"

"What can I do?" Tausret asked. "When my husband died, I thought it would be a simple matter to rule as Regent until our son Seti-Merenptah came of age and then retire while he led Kemet to new heights of power and glory." She uttered a short, bitter laugh. "Siptah was forced upon me and with him came his uncle Bay and everything has been falling to pieces since then. Seti-Merenptah is still officially heir, but the chances of him actually ascending the throne are diminishing daily. I've tried to love Siptah, Ament, but it's hard--and I loathe Bay. Now I am in a cleft stick. I either continue as I am, letting Bay's power and influence grow slowly, or I strike out at him and risk a war I cannot be sure of winning."

"I can't believe the army would so forget itself as to rebel against you, my lady. The people love you and you have amply shown you care for Kemet."

"People's memories are short, and Bay has bought forgetfulness with gold."

"Kemet's gold, not his," Ament growled. "He uses his position as Treasurer to rob the Kingdoms."

An overseer appeared and remonstrated with the boys around the monkey cage. They laughed at the man and poked their tongues out at him.

"It is the king's gold," Tausret pointed out, "and the king has made it abundantly clear that he is happy for his gold to be spent where Bay sees fit."

"It is the king's gold--no matter who the king is. You have not given up on seeing Seti-Merenptah on the throne?"

"Userkheperure's son should succeed him," Tausret said. "I have not given up on him, but I cannot see how to implement it just yet."

Ament looked around carefully to make sure they were not overheard. The cacophony by the monkey cage died away as the boys ran off laughing, while the overseer followed, threatening to tell their fathers.

"Siptah's rule was only ever meant to be temporary," he said. "Elevate him now."

"He is too young."

"Too young to rule by himself, of course, but not too young to rule with you as regent. Siptah is also too young, so what is the difference?"

"The difference is that Siptah is now seen as an able king. Since the war with the Ribu..."

"The war with bandits and criminals in the pay of Bay, you mean," interrupted Ament.

Tausret glared at Ament for a few moments. "Maybe it is as you say, but Kemet sees him as a warrior king. There are even inscriptions to that effect, so it must be right."

Ament's hope of igniting emotion in his Queen's heart by interrupting her, faded. "Seti-Merenptah..."

120

"...is only four years old," Tausret snapped. "I know what you are doing, Ament, but my choices are limited. If I am to raise my son to the throne early, I must show that act as preferable to the alternative. At the moment, it is a choice between a child governed by his mother and a boy on the brink of adulthood who has substantial backing by officials and the army."

"Then remove that choice." Ament moved closer to Tausret and leaned over, murmuring into her ear. "Have Siptah killed. Or Bay...or both. No one will support a dead boy."

"I will not kill Siptah...or have him killed," Tausret said flatly. "Whoever his father was and whatever he did, the boy is innocent of wrongdoing."

"Then have Bay removed. Without his poisonous whisperings and treasonous acts, Siptah comes under your control again."

"Removing Bay would destroy the last vestige of regard that Siptah holds for me. Besides, Bay is doing no more for Siptah than I try to do for Seti-Merenptah--look after our families."

"Bay has no love for his nephew," Ament scoffed. "He sees him merely as a step to power."

"Perhaps, but Siptah loves him and I won't act against Bay unless there is no other way."

"There is no other way, my lady."

"I cannot believe that. Find a way, Ament. For me."

"An accident, then? I'll remove Bay in such a way that no blame rests at your door."

"No," Tausret said. "I forbid it. I will not have my son gain the throne by wading through blood. Find another way, Ament. That's an order."

Chapter 20
Year 3 of Akhenre Siptah

The northern border erupted into warfare as the Retenu rebelled against the harsh dictates of local Kemetu governors. General of the North Iurudef mobilised the legions and struck back in force, but the rebels melted away in the face of his aggression and when he withdrew, struck again. Iurudef sent messengers speeding south to Men-nefer, carrying reports which bypassed the Queen Regent and were delivered straight to Bay and the king. Bay immediately sent for Commander Besenmut in case there were military terms that needed explanation.

"I welcome the rebellion," Siptah declared. "It is a further opportunity to display my warrior skills."

"No one doubts them, Son of Re," Bay said. "However, we must consider this news carefully before acting."

"What's to consider? They have rebelled, I will crush them utterly and sell their women into slavery."

Bay turned to the army officer. "Commander Besenmut, what do you make of Iurudef's reports?"

Besenmut read through the scrolls again, his lips moving as he struggled with the phrases. "He hasn't had much success, has he? The Retenu are undisciplined but much more mobile than his legions."

"Yes, we know that," Bay said impatiently. "What are we going to do about it?"

"Reinforcements?" Besenmut hazarded.

"I will go up and lead them," Siptah said. "They just need to know their king leads them."

"I have no doubt that would hearten them," Bay replied, "but let us try to see the whole picture before we act."

"What whole picture? They are rebels and deserving of death."

"Indeed, Majesty, but we must decide whether the Kingdoms are best served by your presence on the border, or whether you should merely send more troops."

"I am the victor of Perire. What could be better for the Kingdoms than to see their victorious king once more on the march to the defence of Kemet?"

"You do not need to prove yourself on the field of battle, Majesty," Bay said. "You have amply demonstrated that already. Perhaps you will allow me to point out other considerations?" Siptah nodded, and Bay continued.

"First, Majesty, we are coming up to the hot part of the year, and it will be most uncomfortable on campaign. Flies, dust, heat, inconvenience and discomfort. Why subject yourself to these things when you don't have to? You have already proved yourself a great warrior king. Second, we already have the report of Iurudef that these Retenu rebels are proving hard to destroy. If you go against them, Majesty, and are unable to bring them to battle, you might cause men to lose confidence in their king."

Siptah scowled. "But I cannot just leave them alone, Bay. Then I'd look weak."

"Very true, Majesty. That is why you must send someone in your place to face the Retenu and bring them to heel. If they succeed, it redounds to your glory; if they don't, then you can punish them for failing their duty."

"Who should I send? Besenmut?"

Besenmut looked horrified and appealed silently to Bay, who smiled.

"Besenmut is loyal and it would be unfortunate if he was punished for failure. After all, if Iurudef has already failed, can a single Commander succeed? No, you must send someone whose failure would benefit you."

"Such as?"

"A supporter of the Queen Regent. Any failure on her part weakens her position and strengthens yours."

"Who would you suggest, Uncle?"

"Commander Ament of the Set legion."

"Oh, delightful." Besenmut clapped his hands and uttered a short laugh. "That busybody needs his legs cut out from under him."

"I take it you would not object to Ament failing this assignment, Majesty?" Bay asked.

"I suppose not, though I enjoyed talking to him on campaign...and he did look after me."

"Have no doubt that he is your enemy, Majesty. Whatever he does, he does to further Tausret's ambitions. This campaign is a perfect opportunity to weaken her position."

A palace servant brought the message to Commander Ament, pressed it into his hand, bowed and left him to read it. The message was from the king, written by one of the royal scribes, and was to the point, rather than bursting with the usual verbose phrases. Ament read it slowly, forming the words with his lips, and his brow darkened as he read. When he had finished, he swore under his breath, crumpled the message and strode off to find the Queen. He found her in a small chamber off an audience hall, looking over reports from the governors of the southern sepats.

"That son of a whore is getting rid of me," Ament declared, thrusting the crumpled note at Tausret.

The Queen took the note and smoothed it out. "What son of a whore is that?" she asked, a slight smile tugging at her lips.

"Bay, who else? It comes from the king, of course, but I can see his hand in it."

Tausret read the message. "A measure of honour is being offered you, Ament--providing you succeed."

"And if I don't, I'll find myself broken to the ranks. How can I possibly succeed? One legion where three have already failed? It's unrealistic."

"Clever, though," Tausret commented. "The only way Bay can get at me is through my friends and supporters, so he targets you for a difficult assignment, knowing that both of us will be damaged by your inevitable failure."

Ament bowed. "Thank you for believing in me," he said dryly.

"Well, do you honestly think you can do what Iurudef has failed to do? Three legions--Re, Heru, and Shu--failed to bring the Retenu to battle; do you think you can do better with just your Set legion?"

"Why does he limit me to just one legion? I could understand the Set legion being sent up to reinforce the northern legions, but being ordered to do it alone is ridiculous. I'm going to have to appeal the decision. Persuade the king to change his mind."

"I can't see it happening. Bay will control what Siptah says."

"Can't you do anything? You're the Regent."

"I can't overrule the king if Bay supports him," Tausret said. "I might be able to ease your burden a bit though. I could argue for Ptah legion to accompany you."

"No thank you. Besenmut would just be a liability." Ament scuffed at the stone floor with his sandalled feet. "I'll go, and do my best, but the gods are going to have to smile upon my efforts if I hope to live through this."

"How are those boys of yours?"

"Eh? Oh, they're well, thank you. Growing up."

"Take them with you, Ament."

"North?" Ament shook his head. "The army's no place for them. I'm happier for them to learn the management of a vineyard."

"They're Retenu," Tausret observed. "They might be able to offer some insights into the thinking of the rebels."

"All the more reason to leave them behind, my lady. I would not want them to feel they were expected to betray their people."

"Kemetu are their people now. Give them the choice, Ament. They might surprise you."

The Set legion was based near Iunu, and Ament sent word that they were to get ready and make their way northeast to Per-Ramesses and wait for him there. He took leave of Tausret and made his way to his estate at Per-Bast, spending a day or two with his sister Ti-ament and her family, and going through the accounts of his vineyard with his adopted sons Jerem and Ephrim.

"I am going to rejoin my legion at Per-Ramesses," Ament told them. "I have been ordered to put down the Retenu rebellion."

The two boys looked at each other. Jerem lifted his eyebrows questioningly and his elder brother Ephrim nodded. "We would accompany you, sir."

"Why? I will be killing members of your tribe. You would be better off out of that."

"Not our tribe, sir," Ephrim protested. "We are Kemetu now."

"And your sons, father," Jerem added. "It is the duty of sons to help their father."

"And their duty to obey their father," Ament said. "If I say you stay behind, you do."

"Please do not order us to do that, sir," Ephrim said. "We desire only to be of service to you. A legion commander must have servants to look after his needs--why not employ us for those duties?"

"Please, father," Jerem begged.

Ament gave in, and two days later they caught a boat for the trip to Per-Ramesses. Once there in the old capital city, Ament spent some time inspecting his legion, soundly castigating his junior officers for real and imagined faults, and putting the men through some rigorous exercises, shaking loose the dust of their recent inactivity. Then, with a baggage train trailing behind them, the Set legion marched north to the border.

General Iurudef read over the orders he had received. "You are to bring the Retenu to battle and destroy them or you are to negotiate with their leaders, but either way you must bring peace to the border." He shook his head. "It doesn't make sense, Commander Ament, but I am expressly forbidden to offer you any help in your mission against the Retenu."

"That was my understanding," Ament replied gloomily.

"I don't know what the king's thinking of," Iurudef went on. "His councillors can't have told him the true situation."

"I think that is the reason. Bay is behind this."

Iurudef looked searchingly at the other man. "This is deliberate? You are being set up to fail? Why? How have you offended him?"

"My only offence is my support of the Queen Regent."

Iurudef grunted. "What will you do?"

"Obey my orders to the best of my ability." Ament shrugged. "After that, it is with the gods."

Ament sent out scouting chariots to scour the land near the border and soon received word of the presence of armed men. He mobilised the Set legion and set off to find them, but as General Iurudef had found, the Retenu did not seem keen on meeting the might of the Kemetu legions on the battlefield. The enemy melted away in front of them, disappearing into the hills and scrubland, only to emerge on the legion's flanks under cover of darkness and inflict casualties.

The tactics of the Retenu drew the Set legion deeper into enemy territory until they lost touch with the passive northern legions within their camps. Then the Retenu became more adventurous, even attacking in the daytime. Small groups of men would hide in the gullies and ravines, swarming out to harass the marching soldiers, and vanishing again as the legion flexed itself to retaliate. The country was too broken and stony to allow scouting by chariots, so foot patrols were Ament's only option. These of necessity were small, and vulnerable to surprise attack, so after half a month, Ament was forced to withdraw his legion to the coastal plains. There he set up camp and licked his wounds while he considered the options open to him.

Chapter 21

Commander Ament speaks:

My expedition against the Retenu was every bit as hopeless as I had feared. General Iurudef had striven to put down the rebellion with three legions at his disposal but had not succeeded in even bringing them to battle. How could I hope to do so with only my loyal Set legion? Half a month in the rugged territory north of the border showed up the hopelessness of my position, and I camped to think things through. Bay's plan had worked, and any respect I had garnered through years of loyal service would rapidly disintegrate if I failed in the task I had been set.

And then, as I sat depressed in my tent, I received news that shattered me like a bronze-tipped spear in the heart--my adopted sons Ephrim and Jerem had run off in the night.

I know they are Retenu by birth. They were captured during Baenre's campaigns and sent to the mines in the Timna Valley, from where I rescued them and brought them back with me to Kemet. Queen Tausret made them my servants and I have always treated them well. Indeed, I came to think of them as sons and I thought they regarded me in the same light--but it appears not. When faced with a military excursion against their people, they threw off the outward appearance of being Kemetu and have fled back to their tribe.

I was heartbroken at first, and then angry that they had taken me for a fool. I ranted and swore to track them down and recapture them, returning them to their servitude at Timna, but gradually I calmed down and resigned myself to the fact that they had never really become Kemetu. They could carry very little information to the enemy that their scouts did not already know. They were peasant boys plucked violently from their tribe, and once a Retenu, always a Retenu, it seemed. Well, no matter, I had more important things to worry about.

I called my Troop Leaders into council and discussed the choices before us. They knew as well as I that this expedition was designed to discredit me, but their own reputations would be brought into question if we failed in our duty, so they were eager to find a solution.

"We must lay a trap for them," Leader Khetef said. "Offer an opportunity to do us some real damage and draw them out into the open where we can crush them."

"They are reluctant to face us," Leader Bakaa replied. "They do enough damage with their night-time raids. Why would they risk all by confronting us?"

"Perhaps if there was a sufficient inducement," I said. "Khetef and Bakaa, work together on this and come up with a workable plan."

"Raid their villages," Leader Penre opined. "Make them angry enough to face us."

"They're angry now with their supposed list of grievances against their governors," I said. "Can a few raids tip them over into carelessness?"

"Take hostages," Leader Djetmen said. "Threaten to kill them unless the leaders come and talk. Then when they do, slaughter them."

"Why would they believe we wanted to talk anyway?" Leader Hor'heb asked. "I doubt they trust any Kemetu."

"Besides," Bakaa added, "the Retenu throw up leaders as fast as you cut them down. Rid ourselves of this crop and more will spring up--and they certainly won't trust us again."

I considered the opinions of my Troop Leaders for a time. "I'm inclined to try talking," I said. "Really talking. By all means let's take some prisoners, but we treat them well and let it be known we will give safe passage to any leader who will bargain for the lives of the prisoners."

"Would they believe us though, sir?" Hor'heb asked.

"If they don't, we're in no worse a situation than we are now," Khetef said.

"Except we'll then have to kill the hostages," Penre said. "If we released them, we'd look weak."

I dismissed my Troop Leaders and thought about the possibilities they had raised. Direct confrontation had proved fruitless, and unless Khetef and Bakaa came up with a decent plan, I decided I would have to try talking to the leaders of the rebellion and seeing whether we could sort out matters with words instead of swords. If I could get a message to them, of course.

I sent out scouting parties and they found small villages close by. The legion surrounded one at dawn and descended on it, the men armed with staves instead of weapons. Thus we managed to capture nearly fifty men, women and children alive and with no more hurt than a few broken bones and bruises.

I had two uninjured young men brought before me and told them I wanted to talk to the leaders of the rebellion. I offered safe passage for any who came to talk to me and promised to release all the prisoners unharmed after I had spoken to them. I don't think they believed me, but they said they would carry my words to the rebels--"if we can find them, for we are not rebels ourselves"--and bring an answer back.

I had the legion set up camp near the village and erect a secure pen for the prisoners. Then I sat down to wait. It was quite possible that the young men would never return, taking the opportunity to escape, but I had to try. If they had not returned after three days, I would select another two and send them forth.

On the evening of the second day, the perimeter guards reported the approach of two men, and I prepared to receive the messengers I had sent forth. Instead, Ephrim and Jerem entered my tent under guard and fell to their knees before me.

"Why have you come here?" I asked. My voice threatened to break with emotion and I took a deep breath before I continued. "You betrayed the faith I had in you by deserting your posts."

Ephrim stretched out his arms in Kemetu fashion and entreated me. "Harden not your heart toward us father, for we have not betrayed you or Kemet. Hear instead what we have to say and then judge us."

I nodded, not trusting my voice, and signed for them to continue.

"Father, you know that we were born to the Hashimite tribe of the Retenu, before we passed into captivity and thence into your service where you did us the honour of raising us as your sons. We regard you as our father, and should you cease to regard us as your sons we would wish to die."

Jerem echoed the sentiments of his brother.

"Go on," I said.

"We recognised one of the fallen Retenu as being a distant relative, and thus knew that we faced remnants of the Hashimite tribe."

"Why did you not tell me this?" I asked. "It might have affected how I fought the rebels."

"Forgive us, father," Jerem said. "I reasoned that we could achieve more by contacting our family, and I convinced Ephrim that we should try."

"It is as my brother says," Ephrim said. "We left in secret, knowing that you would prevent us going..."

"Yes, I would have. It was a foolish risk to take."

"But we made contact with Jethanah, a cousin and leader of the Hashimites, who is one who rebelled against the hard-hearted Kemetu governors. Father, we have persuaded him that talking to you may achieve more than force of arms. Were we wrong?"

I stood and looked at my sons, for they were indeed as sons to me, no matter what their origins. "You were not wrong," I said, "for I have this day sent out messengers to the rebels to bring them to the bargaining table."

"Come with us, father," Ephrim said. "We will take you straight to Jethanah that you might resolve this rebellion without further ado."

I nodded. "I will talk to him. Bid him come here without fear and..."

"Father," Jerem interrupted, "he will not come here for he mistrusts the Kemetu."

"He knows I am an army commander and envoy of the king? Does he doubt my honour?"

"He knows only the false tongues of the Kemetu governor of this region. In his eyes, all Kemetu are the same. He bids you come to him if you have truth in your heart and seek justice for all."

"Where then would you have us meet?"

"At the rock that looks like a lion, half a day east of here, at noon tomorrow."

"I know it," Troop Commander Penre said. "We can throw a cordon around the area if we move tonight. By noon we will have him in chains."

"No," I said. "I will meet him with only my sons for company...and perhaps a scribe to take down our words if we should reach agreement."

"Sir, you cannot trust this Hashimite dog..."

"You forget my sons are Hashimite. I trust them and I trust the word of their tribal chieftain if they will vouch for him."

"We do, Father," Ephrim said. "Jethanah has given his word that you shall come to no harm if you come in peace."

And so I did. You may suppose I had taken leave of my senses to trust my safety to two boys who had suddenly remembered their tribe, and to their chief who had already displayed his lack of loyalty by rising in rebellion against us. Well, maybe I had, but maybe I had little to lose. I could continue trying to bring the Retenu to battle, or I could seek another path to my destination. Siptah and Bay had made it plain that disgrace awaited me in Men-nefer if I failed in my mission, so if death awaited me at the hands of Jethanah, then death was preferable.

We left the camp the next morning before daybreak in four chariots, one each for me, my sons and an army scribe. As the sun approached its zenith we reached the vicinity of Lion Rock, dismounted, and approached the landmark on foot. Jethanah and a handful of his men were already there, nervously awaiting our arrival. My sons effected an introduction and lessened the tension somewhat, reassuring the rebel leader sufficiently so he felt safe enough to dismiss his tribesmen. We talked, and I found Jethanah a reasonable man driven to an act of rebellion by, if his accusations were correct, the crimes of the Kemetu officials set over him. I had been given power to negotiate terms, so I did so, and by sunset the rebellion was essentially over.

Chapter 22
Year 3 of Akhenre Siptah

Commander Ament returned the Set legion to their station at Iunu and made his way swiftly down to Men-nefer where he reported to the king and assembled court officials in the main audience chamber. He entered when called, quailed momentarily when he saw the crowded chamber, and advanced down the centre of the room toward the raised dais and ornate thrones. Several people were on the dais, but Ament's gaze rested solely upon the king and Chancellor Bay standing by him.

The crowd of nobles and officials fell silent as Ament moved with measured step to the edge of the dais, where he fell to his knees and stretched out his arms toward the slight figure of the king.

"Son of Re, Lord of the Two Lands, Great One of Kemet, Lord of Appearances, Akhenre Setepenre Siptah--Life! Health! Prosperity! I have returned to bear witness that I have obeyed your orders and fulfilled the mission entrusted to me--namely, that I should end the rebellion of the Retenu."

The king stared at the kneeling figure in silence, and the watching officials and nobles caught in his silence a hint of disapproval and watched to see if this favourite of the regent would suffer some penalty. Tjaty Hori stirred and whispered something in the king's ear, but it was another voice that broke the silence.

"Arise, Commander Ament. You may stand to deliver your report."

Ament saw for the first time that Tausret sat on the other throne and a smile flickered across his face as he got to his feet. He bowed toward her and then faced the king again.

"I have not given permission for this man to stand, Lady Tausret," Siptah complained.

"Indeed not, my lord," Tausret said in a pleasant tone. "I assumed it was the excitement of the moment that made you omit a common courtesy, so I took it upon myself to greet the man who has ended the rebellion in your name."

Siptah scowled and once more managed to look like a small boy playing at being a king. "Oh, very well, get on with it then, Ament."

"Son of Re," Bay said quietly. "I have seen part of the written report submitted by Commander Ament already, and it might be better to hear his words in private."

Siptah cleared his throat and wiped his nose on his sleeve. "It has been a long and boring morning," he said. "I could do with a cup of wine." He waved a hand dismissively at the officials and nobles. "Go on, get out. This audience is at an end."

Bay led the way into a smaller chamber, followed by the king, Hori, Tausret and Ament. Commander Besenmut was sent for and quickly arrived. A servant was dispatched for wine and some simple fare, and other servants distributed wine and dates. Siptah took a cup and seated himself, looking toward his uncle impatiently.

"Well? Can I hear this report now or do you have some other objection?"

"None at all, Son of Re. Commander Ament, you may present your report."

Ament bowed to the other people in the room, and then again to the king. "Son of Re, I have tendered my full written report to the royal scribes for inclusion in the records of the Two Kingdoms, but it is my honour to speak of my actions with my own lips.

"Son of Re, upon receiving your command to put an end to the rebellion of the Retenu by any means possible, I made my way to the northern borders with the Set legion, and there sought out the enemy. They proved difficult to find and impossible to bring to battle, so after a month, I resolved to seek another way to end the conflict, namely, by negotiation rather than by force of arms."

Siptah yawned and coughed. "Why would I send a legion if I wanted a peace treaty?" he asked. "Are all my commanders lacking in courage? Must I conquer all Kemet's enemies personally?"

"Son of Re, my orders allowed that I could use any means necessary to end the rebellion, and I have done so. Will you hear my report, Great One?"

"Go on."

"I found out that the main rebel leader was one Jethanah of the Hashimite tribe, and I arranged a meeting to discuss the reasons for the rebellion and..."

"I'd have surrounded the meeting place with my legion and captured the rebel leader," Besenmut interrupted.

"I had given my word that he would have safe conduct," Ament said.

Tjaty Hori clapped his hands together softly. "A man of honour," he murmured, and Tausret smiled at both him and Ament.

"Continue," Bay said.

"I met with Jethanah the Hashimite and listened to what he had to say. He told me of the abuses of the Kemetu governor Ahmose, and instanced eight specific cases of abuse..."

"Naturally he told lies," Besenmut said.

"...and though he did not have specific charges he could bring against Governor Mentuneb as the Hashimite tribe was not under his jurisdiction, he provided me with two instances of abuse passed on to him by Nathael, another tribal chieftain."

"And of course we have heard charges brought against governors before," Bay said. "They are always unfounded, so naturally the bringers of such charges are rightly punished."

"I fear he is right, Commander Ament," Tjaty Hori said. "Whenever the tribes have a bad harvest or suffer from some unexpected disease, they find they cannot pay their taxes and seek to avoid payment by complaining about those officials set over them. You cannot put any reliance on the word of a savage tribesman."

"Nor did I," Ament said. "I investigated, using the powers given to me by royal command, and I found that two of the charges laid at the feet of Governor Ahmose were true."

"Only two?" Bay asked. "Out of eight? It sounds like Ahmose was guilty of little more than overzealousness."

"There was evidence for the other charges, but not incontrovertible. For the two I could prove, the charges were murder and rape."

"Serious charges," Hori said. "You had proof, you said?"

"Yes, Tjaty. I interviewed many men and even put some servants to the question..."

"I think you might have overstepped your authority there," Bay murmured.

"Not so, Chancellor," Ament retorted, "for my orders clearly said 'by whatever means necessary'. In the event, the confessions of the servants under torture revealed the guilt of Governor Ahmose."

"A man will say anything under torture," Bay said.

"Of course, and an accusation made under such circumstances cannot be acted upon in the absence of other proof."

"And there was other proof?" Hori asked.

"Yes, Tjaty. There were three other witnesses to the murder and two to the rape."

"The governor actually committed these crimes?"

"Not in person, but he ordered them. That is why I simply put him in chains and ordered him to be held at Per-Ramesses awaiting your majesty's pleasure."

"And the guilty men? The ones who actually killed and raped on the orders of the governor?"

"I had them executed."

"You should have had them set down to us so that we might rule on their guilt," Bay said.

"I could not risk that, Chancellor."

"What do you mean? Are you implying I would be less than just?"

Ament bowed, a sardonic expression on his face. "Of course not, Chancellor, but I needed to show Jethanah that Kemetu justice was swift and sure. The leaders of the rebellion are now satisfied that their wrongs have been righted and have returned to their farms and villages. The Retenu are once more at peace."

"That wasn't all you did though, was it?" Bay asked. "I read that part of your report when a scribe drew my attention to it."

"The Hashimites--and other tribes--have suffered greatly at the hands of the governors and, to a lesser extent, from our military incursions. I took it upon myself to remit their taxes for next year..."

"But those are my taxes," Siptah protested. "You must make up my loss personally."

"Don't be ridiculous," Tausret snapped. "Ament's actions have saved the Treasury a huge amount of gold by cutting short a potentially costly and protracted war. The taxes from a few poor tribes are nothing compared to that. Tell him, Bay. Tell the king just how beneficial Ament's actions are."

Bay scowled but nodded. "It is true, Son of Re. The taxes are as nothing."

"Well, he shouldn't have done it without asking me first," Siptah complained. He lifted the wine cup to his lips and drank, swallowing with an obvious effort. "My throat feels sore," he muttered.

"Son of Re," Hori interjected softly. "You had, in effect, already done so by making Commander Ament your envoy."

"I don't like it," Siptah grumbled. "This whole exercise stinks. The rebels should have been crushed instead of pardoned. What will the other nations think when they hear that the king of Kemet is so weak he cannot put down a simple rebellion but must buy them off instead?"

"I would imagine they will praise your justice and mercy," Tausret observed. "The Nations know that Kemet has a strong army, which is why they leave us in peace. Through Commander Ament, you have shown them we have wisdom as well."

"Oh, very well. I don't suppose there's much I can do about it now," Siptah said. He wiped at his eyes and then his nose.

"Are you feeling well, Majesty?" Bay asked. "Shall I send for a physician?"

Siptah shook his head. "I'm tired. I just want to lie down for a bit." He got up and limped toward the door. "Perhaps some honeyed milk, Bay. My throat feels sore."

The king got his milk and honey but he did not have long to enjoy it, because Bay sent for the court physician who, backed up by the Chancellor, threw away the sweet and rather soothing drink and replaced it with something rather less palatable. First, he sent for a lactating mother and had her express milk into a cup. He then mixed in a little ibis dung, wrote out a prayer on a scrap of papyrus which he then burnt and stirred the ashes into the milk.

"Here, Son of Re. Drink this."

Siptah looked to his uncle for support but found none, so he shrugged and drained the cup, grimacing at the taste.

The physician then added ground garlic to fresh river water and vinegar, and placed the jar within easy reach of the king's bed. "A cupful twelve times a day."

"Is that all?" Siptah grumbled.

"Of course not, Son of Re," the physician replied. "I will notify the priests and they will come to your bedside and say prayers over you."

The physician left to find the priests and Bay stirred the contents of the jar with a forefinger. "Can I trust you to drink a cup every hour or must I send a servant to see you do it?"

"I'll do it. Now go away; I'm tired and I don't feel well."

Bay bowed and left the king in his darkened room. He went about his duties, but had one of the king's servants report to him on the king's condition three times a day.

"The king is restless, my lord, and coughs a lot," the servant said at dusk.

"He did not sleep well, my lord, and lay in a sweat," said the servant at dawn.

"He complains of the cold, my lord, but throws off the covers," the servant said at noon.

"The king's breath is laboured, my lord. He sweats profusely," said the servant at dusk on the second day.

The court physician was sent for again, and he arrived laden with herbs and medicines. Mallow leaves were added to boiling water and the vapour wafted over the king's face. Onions and garlic were crushed and mixed with honey and the sticky mess applied to the royal throat. More mother's milk was gathered and servants scoured the palace grounds for fresh ibis dung, and a phalanx of priests recited prayers for the king's recovery.

Bay left the professionals to their work and went in search of the only man he even half-trusted--Commander Besenmut of the Ptah legion. He found him taking his ease on a broad veranda lit by a single torch.

"How is the king?" Besenmut asked.

"That is with the gods, but the priests are dinning their ears as we speak. The physician says it is nothing more than a common fever and will succumb to his treatment."

"Thank the gods for that."

Bay looked around and then took Besenmut by the elbow, leading him out of the palace and into the gardens near the menagerie. There in the darkness they could talk unseen, though there was always the danger of someone listening in the shadows.

"The king's health concerns me," Bay said.

"But you just said the physician was not concerned."

"Not this time, but what about the next illness?"

"What do you mean?"

"The king is physically weak and any serious illness could kill him. If he died..."

Besenmut peered at the shadowed face of the Chancellor. "That could happen to any man...any king."

"And what do you think would happen to us?" Bay made an angry gesture. "I'll tell you. We would follow him into death within a day. Do you think Queen Tausret would let us live?"

"We have done nothing worthy of death," Besenmut said uneasily.

"Have we not? I have been gathering power to myself at the expense of the Queen and you have openly thrown in your lot with me. Will you scurry back to Tausret's skirts and beg forgiveness? Will you turn on me and deliver me to her dog Ament?"

"Never, my lord...but...what are we to do then? Do you really think the king will die?"

"Not this time, gods willing, but we need to strengthen our position."

"Agreed," Besenmut said. "But how?"

"Who stands in our way?" Bay asked in a low voice. "The Queen, her son, and her dog. Remove them and no man can touch us."

"Ament is easy enough, but for the others...that is treason, my lord."

"Nobody would charge us with treason is we succeeded. The king would protect us anyway."

"You are certain of that?"

"It is in his interest to be rid of her and her son."

"How? How would you..."

Bay could smell the fear sweat on the other man and smiled in the dark. "Let me worry about that, Commander. You just need to gather the army behind us. How are you doing with that?"

"Emsaf of Heru is with us, as are Samut and Panhesy. Iurudef possibly. The rest of the northern legions...with the exception of Set...will follow him. The south is in Setnakhte's purse. He bitterly opposes the king because of who he is and you by extension, my lord."

"That's not enough."

"There's Tjaty Hori too..."

"Hori has taken against us."

"Why?"

"I don't know. Perhaps he just lacks the courage to offer full support to the king, or perhaps he believes he should be loyal to Userkheperure's son rather than Amenmesse's."

"We cannot succeed with half an army and the civil administration against us," Besenmut said. "Queen Tausret has only to give the order and our heads will leap from our shoulders."

"Not for much longer," Bay said. "I am within a breath of becoming a regent alongside her, and the king is on my side. Together we can defeat her no matter how large her army."

"Providing the king lives. Faced with a choice between the son of a queen and an Amorite servant, no guessing which way the army will jump."

"All right, all right, I know. Everything depends on the king being alive when we make our move. We'll just have to make sure the queen and her boy are no longer there to contend for the throne."

Besenmut was silent for a time. "How?" he asked at length.

Chapter 23
Year 3 of Akhenre Siptah

Siptah recovered from his illness and, encouraged by his uncle Bay, set about taking more responsibility for the governing of the Kingdoms upon himself. He called Tjaty Hori to him and ordered him to start compiling lists of the scribes, priests and officials throughout the northern kingdom. When Hori asked the reason, the king replied that it was time to make some changes. Hori excused himself and went to see the Queen Regent.

"It is too much, Majesty," Hori said. "Ta Mehu is running efficiently, yet the king wants to start making changes."

Tausret smiled and shook her head when she heard Hori's complaint. "The boy is growing up, it seems. Do you want me to have a word with him?"

"Please, Majesty."

Tausret did not hurry to see the young king, but called in to see him as he partook of the noon meal two days later as if casually passing.

"Greetings, Son of Re," she said, accepting a cup of wine from an attentive servant. "I trust you are fully recovered from your illness?"

Siptah half rose from his chair before remembering he was king and was expected to remain seated. He hesitated and gestured, sending another servant scurrying for a chair for the Regent.

"May I offer you food?" Siptah asked. "The roast goose is particularly fine today, and the honey cakes are delicious, though they hurt my teeth."

"Thank you. Just a small piece of goose." She waited until she had been served and had tasted the slice of meat before continuing.

"How are your studies going, Son of Re? I hope Tjaty Hori is instructing you properly in legal matters."

"I look forward to him allowing me to judge a proper case in the law courts. All he allows me is to listen in and sometimes give my opinion. It's not fair. I'm the king and the people look to me for judgment."

"That is true." Tausret sipped her wine. "This is a good pressing, Son of Re. I think the grapes come from Commander Ament's vineyards in Per-Bast." She smiled inwardly at Siptah's sudden grimace. "Would you like me to talk to Tjaty Hori about letting you play a greater role in the law courts?"

"He should give me no more than my due."

"And what of your priestly duties? You are managing those?"

"I don't like having to get up while it is still dark."

"The king, as High Priest of every god, is essential for the proper worship of the gods, as I'm sure has been explained to you. Your daily intercession establishes Ma'at, keeps the sun shining and the crops growing. It is a great responsibility."

"It makes me very tired."

"Indeed, Son of Re." Tausret sipped again. "But that is why we have thousands of lesser priests to lift some of the burden from your young shoulders." She paused and then said, "Hori tells me you want a list of every scribe, priest and official in Ta Mehu. May I ask why?"

"It's not a secret, is it? Even if it was, a king should be allowed to see it. I asked Hori for them two days ago but I think he's ignoring my order. He should be punished."

"It's not a secret," Tausret said with a smile. "You will understand that a great many people are on those lists and it takes time for them to be prepared. Longer than two days. Hori will produce them. He is loyal and efficient, and I value him highly."

Siptah grunted and applied himself to another honey cake, wincing as the sweetness found a rotting tooth.

"You didn't tell me why you wanted the list," Tausret said after a few moments.

"I just wanted to know who did what in the north."

"Many of those men have served since the days of your grandfather Baenre, you know. They were carefully selected and any that did not measure up to the tasks asked of them were replaced. Hori tells me they run the Kingdom very efficiently."

"That is good to know."

"It would be a mistake to replace them."

"Bay said..." Siptah bit his lip and flushed.

"What did your uncle Bay say?"

"He said I should know every man who served me, so that no man could cheat me."

"A commendable notion," Tausret said. "But it would still be a mistake to replace them."

Siptah scowled. "Am I powerless, then, though I am king? Will you block me in everything?"

"By no means, Son of Re. It is my function as Regent to rule for you until you are old enough and experienced enough to rule by yourself. Examine the lists by all means, ask questions of every man, increase in knowledge. One day you will be called upon to make decisions on your own, but until then you should heed the word of all your advisers, not just your uncle Bay."

Siptah finished his meal after Tausret left, and then hurried off to find his uncle Bay. He burst in upon the older man in his private suite where he was enjoying the company of a young palace servant. The girl looked horrified by the sudden appearance of the king, scrambled off the bed and fell to the floor, abasing herself.

The king stared interestedly at the naked girl for a few moments and then dismissed her. He waited while she grabbed her dress and fled the room, and then addressed Bay, who was adjusting his clothing.

"She told me I couldn't make any changes."

"Who told you what?" Bay asked. "Anyway, my lord, it is bad manners to just burst in on people...even if you are the king."

"Sorry, uncle, but Tausret said I mustn't make any changes to the roll of priests and officials. That's not right, is it? I can make changes."

"Tell me exactly what she said."

Siptah told him, and Bay thought for a while. "Her attention is fixed on Ta Mehu now, so perhaps we can look elsewhere. I'm sure Ta Shemau has people who should be replaced. Let me think on it."

Bay sat down with Siptah a few days later and produced a long list of names and positions from the temples of Ta Shemau and the court at Waset. Siptah stared at it and then frowned.

"How did you get it so quickly, uncle? Hori hasn't even produced the northern rolls yet. You wouldn't have had time to send to Waset for them...unless you sent for them ages ago."

"I have been considering who our friends are in the south for some time, my lord. This might be an opportune time to make some changes. Men loyal to us should be rewarded."

"But I don't know any of these men," Siptah said, tapping a finger on the long scroll.

"That is why you have me, my lord. I can tell you exactly who must be replaced and who to put in their place. I only need your authority to see it done."

"Won't I need Tausret's permission?"

"Not if we act decisively. By the time she finds out it will be too late. She won't dare countermand you for fear of weakening the throne."

"So I can do what I like? Why didn't you tell me this before, Uncle? I don't have to obey her and I..."

"Don't be foolish, boy," Bay snapped. "That is not at all what I said. Tausret is still your regent but if you act swiftly and decisively behind her back in certain ways, it is not in her interests to change things back."

"You shouldn't speak to me like that," Siptah said. "Even if you are my uncle."

"You are right, Majesty. I apologise. Now, may we proceed with our selections? We should have our men in place before she hears what we are doing."

"I wish you were the regent."

"We've been through this before, Majesty, though for all practical purposes I am a regent as long as you back me. Working together we can counter Tausret."

"I'm going to issue orders that henceforth your image must be of equal size to Tausret's, and the inscriptions must stress your importance."

"I am honoured, Majesty, but all I seek is a stable Kemet ruled by its rightful king in peace."

"Very soon now, Uncle. With you as my trusted adviser I don't need another regent. Besides, I'm almost old enough to rule by myself. King Nebkheperure was even younger when he ruled alone, though he had his uncle to help him...just like me."

"And you will make a wonderful king, Majesty, but if this great day is to dawn we must put you in an unassailable position by making judicious appointments to select positions throughout Kemet."

Siptah nodded and picked up the long scroll. "Where first, Uncle?"

"King's Son of Kush. The most powerful position outside of the Two Kingdoms."

"That's held by Setuy, isn't it? I thought he was loyal."

"Perhaps, but my spies tell me he is on friendly terms with Tjaty Paraemheb and has received General Setnakhte."

"That's not good?"

"Indeed not, Majesty. That is why we must replace Setuy."

"Wouldn't it be better to replace Setnakhte and Paraemheb?"

"Not entirely possible, Majesty. At least, not Setnakhte. Paraemheb was implicated in the death of your father, or so my spies tell me."

"Then I want him gone."

"I'll see what I can arrange..." Bay's voice trailed off and he frowned.

"What?"

"If Paraemheb goes, there will have to be a new Tjaty, and I think Hori would be perfect for the job. Useful to get him out from Men-nefer too."

"Hori the Tjaty?"

"Yes."

Siptah shrugged. "So who replaces Setuy as King's Son?"

"Hori, son of Kama. He is already First Charioteer of His Majesty, and King's Messenger to Every Land. Experienced and loyal."

"Good. Er, how do I appoint him?"

"I will have the necessary documents drawn up and attach your seal to them. Your approval is all I need."

"Who else?"

"Army officers."

"I can do that? I thought Setnakhte controlled the southern army."

"He does...but there are ways. For instance, the garrison at Khenu..."

"Where?"

"Khenu, Majesty. It is a quarry near the Kushite border. The garrison there lost a senior officer from an accident, and another to fever. I have it in mind to replace them with two men loyal to me...to you...by the name of Yuy and Anhurnakhte."

"Do so if you see fit. What else?"

"There are numerous priests..."

"Priests? Why would I want to replace priests?"

"You remember Roma-Rui who was Hem-netjer of Amun in Waset? He was firmly on your father's side until the last king replaced him with someone more politically expedient. I think it is time to replace the present incumbent."

"With Roma-Rui again?"

Bay shook his head. "His usefulness is long past. No, there is another Hori who is presently High Priest in Khent-Min. You should move him to Waset to replace Mahuhy."

"Whatever you think is best, Uncle."

"The High Priest of Ptah of the Mansions of Millions of Years on the West Bank has recently died. He has two sons, Minmose and Rahotep, who deserve high positions. I propose you make Rahotep High Priest of Ptah in his father's place and Minmose High Priest of Amun alongside him."

"I thought you wanted Hori as High Priest of Amun?"

Bay sighed, and tapped the list. "Hori for Waset, Minmose for the Mansions."

"Oh."

"There are other replacements you should make to key positions in the south, Majesty. The priests of Amun remember your father's support and I have been at great pains to portray you as your father's son, rather than as merely the successor to Userkheperure. You need to channel more gold to the temples there, and luckily I am Treasurer, so that should not be a problem."

Siptah yawned and stretched. "Do whatever you deem necessary, Uncle. I have full trust in you."

"Your trust gladdens my heart, Majesty."

"It is a hot afternoon, and I am tired after my meal. I think I will lie down."

"And the replacements?"

"I'm sure you don't need me for that. Replace whom you will, Uncle. I know I can entrust Kemet to your capable hands."

Chapter 24

Regent Tausret speaks:

I laughed when I heard the latest ploy of Chancellor Bay. Tjaty Hori carried the tale to me of the lists from Ta Mehu, wanting me to forbid it for fear that Bay would strip away all support for me and for my young son. Then when he heard that lists from the southern Kingdom had been sent north, he became almost apoplectic, sputtering his indignation and so forgetting himself as to shout in my presence. I forgave his indiscretion, of course, but also forbade him to hinder Bay's attempts. He stamped off feeling very ill-used.

Poor Hori. If he would stop to think about it, he would realise I must know more than I am revealing. I have my own spies within the king's circle and Bay's entourage, and I hear what has transpired within half a day. Forgive me if I do not reveal exactly who my sources are, but while Hori knows of the existence of the southern lists I know what changes have been made. I agree with most of them.

That surprises you, I'll warrant. Well, governing Kemet is a balancing act at the moment. I have to, like a tumbler or common entertainer does with coloured balls, juggle the powers within society. If I clamp down on Bay's ambition, limiting his power, maybe even stripping him of honours and position--as I am quite capable of doing--what do you think would be the result? Seeing power slipping away, he might act precipitately, plunging our Kingdoms back into civil war. That I cannot allow, yet I cannot go too far in the other direction. If I give Bay too much power, he will seize the rest and both I and my son will be immured in our tombs before our times. Too much or too little are equally injurious.

No, it is a delicate balancing act, allowing him some power but not too much, keeping him happy but denying him the ultimate prize of the throne. I am sure that is his aim, for if he managed to do away with me and set up young Siptah of the withered leg as full king--how long would a crippled boy last on the throne without my protection? Not long is my guess. Something would happen to Siptah and the only person capable of mounting the throne would be the man who holds army commanders in his fists, who funnels Treasury gold into the coffers of priests, who bribes officials and servants throughout Kemet--the man who styles himself Ramesse Kha'amen-teru Bay.

Now, I may agree with some of Bay's replacements, such as Hori son of Kama, and be prepared to allow others, such as Tjaty Hori, but I must protect myself at the same time. Someone needs to whisper in their ears, reminding them of the reality of the situation. I cannot summon them without making my concerns public, and I cannot spare the time to journey all over the Kingdoms and Kush, so I must send a trusted deputy. I have officials by the hundred, but so many of them belong to little groups who think of their own advancement or connive with powerful men, rather than owing the proper allegiance to their Queen Regent and the legitimate son of Userkheperure Seti. So I suppose that there are not so many I can call on--really just one. Who else but Ament?

I sent for him and saw him in private, or at least as private as a man and woman can be in a royal palace. I am surrounded by servants at all times, even when I sleep or attend to the baser functions of my body, so much so that I block them from my conscious mind and tell myself I am alone. On this occasion, when Ament came to me, I had no more than three servants in attendance, all employed in cleaning the corners of my room. I paid them no attention, as was proper, but spoke in low tones to Ament, to achieve some degree of privacy. I could have just dismissed the servants, but this would only have served to draw attention to Ament's presence.

Ament knelt in my presence, and when I stepped forward to raise him up, he grasped my hands and kissed them. This was a shocking breach of protocol and I could almost hear the gasps of the servants, though they all managed to avert their eyes and look busy. I knew they would carry word to the rest of the palace, so I bade Ament rise, addressing him as 'loyal and favoured friend', and then offered him wine and a chair next to mine.

Ament sipped his wine. "How may I serve you, my lady?"

"Bay has made many alterations to the lists of priests, scribes and officials in Ta Shemau and Kush, convincing the king that they are necessary. In reality, they are useful only to Bay, inasmuch as he believes they will be grateful to him for their elevation and thus loyal."

"You should have him removed, Lady. I'll do it; just give the command."

"That is not my will, Ament, as I have made plain before. As long as my own son is too young for the throne, I need Siptah, and to keep him pliable I need his uncle Bay. When my Seti-Merenptah is old enough I will loose the leash and you may strike Bay down."

"Like the hunting dog I am, eh?" Ament smiled. "Yes, I know what they call me and I consider it an honour to be called your dog, for a dog is loyal unto death."

"For now, dear friend, I have another task for you. As I said, Bay seeks to alter the balance of power in the south by appointing men he thinks will favour him should it become a contest between us. I would have you go to each one and quietly remind them of the realities of power within Kemet. I am Regent, a position Bay can never hold, for he cannot be priest and represent the people in front of the gods."

"Only quietly? What if they will not listen to reason?"

"No more than that, Ament. I would know what each man thinks, whether he will remain loyal to me or cast his lot with Bay. When you know, carry word to General Setnakhte, so that he knows the loyalty of men in the south, then come back and tell me."

"If that is what you want, my lady. Who are these men that Bay chooses?"

"Hori, son of Kama is chief amongst them. He replaces Setuy as King's Son of Kush. Our own Tjaty Hori of the North is to replace Paraemheb who will retire. Another Hori as Hem-netjer of Amun in Waset, and Minmose as High Priest of Amun on the Western Bank. There are other names on the list I will give you. You can study them at your leisure. As for the army officers, Bay has no real jurisdiction over them, though the king, of course, can make such changes as he will. Do not approach them yourself, but tell Setnakhte. If he wants them removed, he will find the means."

"You trust Setnakhte that much?" Ament asked.

"He hates the memory of Menmire Amenmesse and through him, his son Akhenre Siptah," I said simply. "He was utterly loyal to Userkheperure Seti, and now to Seti-Merenptah. I trust him almost as much as I trust you, old friend."

Chapter 25
Year 4 of Akhenre Siptah

Night still held the palace of Men-nefer firmly in its dark grip as the servants stirred from their slumbers, yawned, stretched and scratched, stumbling off to the middens to relieve the pressure on bladders and bowels and then to the kitchens for a bite of day-old bread before they started their duties. They shivered in the chill morning air and looked to the east where the more hopeful ones among them declared they could see the first paling of the stars.

It was not just the servants who awoke long before dawn. The rising of the sun god was not something that could be left to chance. Unless suitably propitiated and cajoled, the god might choose to remain below the horizon and deprive Kemet of light and heat. The king, as High Priest of every god, shouldered the responsibility for this monumental daily task. Of course, Kemet had thousands of priests and the priests of Re could perform the ceremonies in the hundreds of temples scattered through the Two Lands, but it was accepted that the king would conduct the rites where possible.

On a typical morning, the king went through a long and thorough cleansing upon awakening. His body was purged of unwholesome substances and washed with clean river water. Perfumes and makeup followed, and pristine linens draped his young body before he was led out to an open place with an uninterrupted view of the eastern horizon. He poured a lustration of pure water, lifting up his high-pitched voice in praise of Re, stumbling over the phrases and being corrected by the local High Priest. With help, he worked his way through the rites, and waited with arms uplifted for the first rays of the sun to stab over the low hills to the east. So far, despite many faults in the performance, the sun god had seen fit to hearken to his son-on-earth and bless Kemet with his life-giving rays. It remained to be seen whether this would always be the case.

Akhenre Siptah was, however, not up to the task at present. He was still only a child and struggled to remember the correct phrases and the actions needed at each phase of the ceremony. The priests of Re, experienced in the ways of the god, interceded when necessary, their selfless actions ensuring the blessings of the god. And so it went with the other gods of the Kemetu pantheon. Other ceremonies may not have been quite so necessary, but the Ma'at of Kemet depended on the daily recitation of the rites of every god, and the offering up of the appropriate sacrifices.

Tausret helped where she could, but she had her own duties as God's Wife of Amun each day. She had been consecrated in this holy office as a young girl, and it was her duty to serve the god on a daily basis. The rites could be observed at any of Amun's temples, though the Great Temple in Waset was the one where she could most feel the physical presence of the god. Amun's temples were dark, even in the daytime, and the inner sanctuary where the god resided was windowless. Lit only by flickering oil lamps, the shadows moved in the sanctuary and the great golden statue of the god appeared to nod and follow her movements with sightless eyes.

Dressed in sheer linen that clung to her body, Tausret moved with the priests of Amun through the temple each morning. Acolytes bore the burdens of the god's needs--food, drink and clothing. In the outer sanctuary, the priests called out to awaken the god, and Tausret sang a song of welcome to her divine husband. The acolytes spread pristine linen on the floor and set out dishes of every food that might entice a god's appetite--beef, lamb, duck and goose, roasted and braised with herbs, vegetables in profusion, fresh baked fragrant bread, sweet tarts and cakes flavoured with herbs and honey, ripe dates and figs, and pots of freshly brewed beer and the richest wines.

Nobody but the God's Wife and the highest priests could view the body of the god when first he awakened, so the acolytes and junior priests withdrew now, chanting praises as they went. When they had departed, the priests opened the wooden doors that led to the inner sanctuary and lifted their oil lamps high, shedding a buttery glow over the linen-clad golden statue of the god. Poles were inserted into the base of the statue and the priests heaved on these, lifting the god aloft and staggering with it into the outer sanctuary. Here they reverently stripped the linens from the body of the god and washed it down with pure blessed river water before drying it with linen cloths.

Tausret moved close to the statue of her divine husband and took hold of the giant extended phallus, stroking it and guiding the god toward a metaphysical ejaculation. The seed of the god created the world anew each day, and without this symbolic act, the life force within Kemet would wither and die. When the sexual act was over, Tausret herself washed and dried the god's member, and then the priests dressed the statue in fresh linen clothes that had never been worn. The old clothes were collected together and taken out to be burnt lest they be used for any lesser purpose.

Then the god broke his fast. One by one, the priests lifted plates of food or pots of drink, wafting the aromas beneath the golden nose of Amun. The god did not move or visibly partake of the offering, but the priests understood that just as the vital seed of Amun had been spread through the land by the symbolic sex act of the God's Wife, so too was the vital essence of the food and drink taken up and used by his golden body. When every dish had been presented, they were gathered together and taken back to the priests' quarters where they would later partake of the god's leavings. The god himself was returned to the inner sanctuary to dream away the day and night before being aroused again in the eternal cycle of life.

Tausret broke her fast upon her return to the palace each morning. She stripped off her special dress and wig and washed herself thoroughly as if she had once more committed a sexual act, and then once dressed in fresh linens, ate a simple meal before taking up her duties as Regent. In the absence of Ament, who had recently departed for the south on a delicate mission, she had few people she felt she could confide in. Tjaty Montu, newly raised to the office after Hori's departure for the south, was one of these. Montu was a friend of Hori, and had been well schooled in the intricacies of Ta Mehu politics.

"Chancellor Bay is making sweeping changes to the priest and scribe lists of Ta Mehu, Great Lady."

Tausret nodded. "I have seen them."

"You are not concerned?"

"Should I be?"

"Great Lady, the man is gathering power to himself with both hands. He is uncle to the king, Chancellor and Treasurer, and has taken upon himself such titles as 'head of the bodyguard of the Great King' and 'he who establishes the king upon the throne of his father'. It is too much, Majesty."

"Truly he is an Irsu, a self-made man," Tausret said with a half-smile.

"You must act to curtail him, Majesty, before he grasps the title of Regent and...and more."

"He cannot be regent, Montu. You know that. Nor can he strive for greater powers. He has reached his limit."

"The king could grant him more."

"Not while I am regent."

"In another three years...maybe even two...he will be old enough to rule as king without a regent. What will happen then?"

"He will never be sole ruler. The agreement was that he would be king only until Seti-Merenptah was able to ascend the throne."

"And if he begets an heir? A son of his loins? What then?"

Tausret smiled. "Is that likely? He starts to show an interest in the palace girls, I know, but none of them are of sufficient status to be mother of a future king. Let him seek pleasure where he will, and if a child occurs...well, even a temporary king should have children. It changes nothing."

"If Siptah begets an heir, Bay will not be content to let him be put aside in a few years' time. If nothing else, he would lose all his own status and wealth."

"He cannot rise further, for he is a commoner and a son of servants. Already he is higher than he should be."

"But he fixes his gaze on the highest position, Great Lady."

"King? He cannot be king, for a king is trained to that position from childhood. A king must be a son of a king, an intermediate between the gods and men, High Priest of Every God. Bay is not a priest--he cannot be a priest--and thus he cannot be a king. Even he knows this."

"He talks to his supporters of Kheperkheperure-Irimaat Ay, the commoner uncle of Nebkheperure Tutankhamen, who became king after him."

"Ay was a commoner, but he was also a priest of Amun, and later of the Aten," Tausret said. "Bay is a fool if he reads any more into that relationship."

"Whether or not he makes the connection is unimportant, Great Lady. It is his supporters that will raise him up if the opportunity arises. He is dangerous, Majesty, and you should curb him now, before it is too late."

"Your concern is noted, Tjaty Montu, but I will not act while Siptah needs his uncle. The boy is more controllable if he believes himself to be in a strong position. I am aware of the threat Bay poses and I have hedged him about with loyal men. I do not believe he is capable of real harm."

"May that be the will of the gods," Montu said fervently. "But what about my position? Some men say that Bay could become Tjaty in my place...or even Tjaty of the combined kingdoms."

"That will never happen. A Tjaty is more than just a mere palace official and overseer of the wealth of the kingdoms. He must stand in for the king and conduct affairs of state as well as sitting in judgment. Bay does not have that training."

"The king himself has voiced the thought that Bay should be Tjaty, Majesty."

"Then that is a sign--if one was needed--that he is unready for true rulership. He still needs a regent to rule for him and make the important decisions." Tausret smiled. "It is fortunate that I am willing to continue that onerous task."

Not everything in the life of Tausret was an onerous task, of course, as she had the leisure to spend time on pleasurable pursuits. Although some thirty-seven years of age, a time of life when most women in Kemet were already stooped and experiencing joint pain, hair greying and lines steadily conquering the face, teeth rotting in the mouth, and looking with some longing at the peace of the tomb, Tausret still thought of herself as young. A good diet and active life, coupled with a natural vitality that had enabled members of her family to reach a ripe old age, had conspired to keep her bright-eyed and energetic. She still had her monthly courses and had not ruled out the possibility of a future marriage or at least an entertaining liaison with a suitable partner, so she took care of her appearance.

Tausret had her ladies prepare fresh unguents and creams daily, and cosmetics were ground and mixed regularly. Every morning, after returning from her duties as God's Wife of Amun, she bathed and donned clean clothing, and then sat for over an hour as her ladies applied astringent creams to tighten the skin, kohl around the eyes to increase her beauty and offer her magical protection. She knew that the almond-shaped eye resembled the hawk's eye of Heru miraculously restored after his battle with the god Set. Merely reproducing the shape of the god's restored eye offered its wearer the same protection. It was a matter of record that people wearing kohl around their eyes were protected from the glare of the noonday sun and, when eye diseases struck the commoners during the months of the inundation, the ladies of the court were much less likely to suffer from these afflictions. What else could it be but the protection of Heru?

Tausret had inherited the red hair that was a feature of the House of Ramesses, and though she kept it trimmed short and wore black wigs on every formal occasion, the rays of the sun had a much greater effect on her skin than on most Kemetu. Consequently, she spent as much time as possible indoors, frequenting the cool shadows of palace and temple, and when she had to travel on official business, made much use of awnings and sun-shades. Her skin remained lighter in colour than most other palace women, and her beauty remained when others were losing theirs.

Her great love was jewellery, and she often entertained skilled craftsmen who would display their latest offerings. Tausret eschewed the use of the plated gold so loved by men, who wore thick and heavy rings, armbands and pectorals of the precious metal, but she loved precious and semi-precious stones set in delicate frameworks of gold or silver wire, both in the form of necklaces or as small pieces pinned to clothing or braided into a wig. Some jewellery was just ornamentation, but certain pieces served another function--a magical one--by calling down the protection of the gods or warding off demons. Scarabs carved from turquoise or malachite were her favourites, and they were always inscribed with a protective prayer or ward.

Hundreds of people lived within the palace and Tausret rarely had the luxury of being alone. Whether in her bedchamber at night, attending to the needs of nature, at mealtimes, or just strolling within the palace gardens, there were always people on hand from a myriad court officials of one sort or another, to servants, to other members of the royal family. There were fewer of these family members in recent times. Usermaatre Ramesses had wives and concubines at every turn, and there were always royal children underfoot. Baenre Merenptah had fewer, and Userkheperure Seti had only two wives and now only one surviving child, so the rooms of the palace were much more sparsely populated.

Because Tausret had grown up in palaces, she hardly noticed the swarms of people, and it was accepted behaviour that servants were ignored. So it was that there were very few secrets within the palace and though, if she had been asked, Tausret would have said that she was unattended when talking to Tjaty Montu, her words had been carried to both the king and his Chancellor before the day was out.

Chapter 26
Year 4 of Akhenre Siptah

I t was this same ubiquitous presence of servants that plagued Chancellor Bay. The words of Queen Tausret angered him. He was careful not to express his thoughts but instead considered the implications carefully. Then he went in search of the young king, and found him enjoying a game of Senet with the son of one of the palace Chamberlains. As usual, servants hovered around the periphery of the room, busying themselves with sundry duties or awaiting instructions.

"Son of Re," Bay said. "I would have words with you."

"As you wish," Siptah replied offhandedly. "Would you believe I am winning again?"

"Given your skill in the game, Majesty, nothing would surprise me." Bay looked at the son of the Chamberlain and winked. The boy blushed and looked away.

"What did you want to say, Uncle?"

Bay hesitated, wondering how to prise the king away from his playmate. "I thought you might like to go hunting. I can arrange it."

Siptah looked up from the game, one of the pegs in his hand. "Hunting what?"

"Gazelles...or ostrich. There are some wild asses east of here, I hear."

The king scowled. "I was hoping you were going to say lion. I've hunted gazelle and ostrich before and they're boring." He made his move on the Senet board, but was obviously distracted as the move weakened his position considerably.

His opponent frowned, perhaps wondering how he could lose the game without making it too obvious. He reached out to a peg, hesitated, and then drew back.

Bay lowered his voice and squatted beside Siptah. "Majesty, it is important that you give no sign that may attract the attention of your servants, but I have other news for you."

Siptah stared at the Senet board, visibly angry at the move he had just made. "What news?" he muttered.

"Majesty," Bay whispered. "They are not wild asses east of here but a lion."

"Lion!" Siptah exclaimed. "You have found me a lion? Then of course let us go hunting. Immediately."

Bay put a finger to his lips and then said loudly, for the benefit of the listening servants, "Of course not a lion, Majesty. You know the Regent would not allow that. Perhaps I expressed myself clumsily when I said the other word. I meant to say only that there are wild asses to be hunted and that this might make up in some small way for the animal you are not allowed to hunt." He winked at the king, hoping that he would understand what he was saying.

"There isn't a lion?" Siptah frowned and suddenly his face cleared. "Oh, yes, I see. Well..." he continued loudly, "let us go and hunt these wild asses immediately." He scrambled to his feet, knocking over the Senet board and his playmate bowed and backed away from the royal presence, his relief at not having to try to lose the game apparent on his face.

"When do we leave?" Siptah demanded.

"I will have to inform the Regent and put together an expedition, but as it will be a quick trip into the wilderness, we could probably depart the day after tomorrow."

"I will go and start practicing with my bow at once then."

Tausret knew all about the conversation before Bay informed her that the king would go hunting, but she kept silent, knowing from her own hunters that lions had not been seen east of the city. She presumed that Siptah had just got carried away by thought of hunting the large carnivore and that Bay was, for once, truthful in his utterances. The Regent gave her permission and Bay thanked her. It was all very civil.

The expedition set out, the hunting chariots being loaded onto a ferry to cross the Great River, and headed eastward across the river plain and into the dry scrubland on the borders of the red desert. Bay rode with the king in a heavy three-man chariot, while two smaller ones followed. Further back, three ox-drawn wagons contained the minimum comforts a king had a right to expect, even in the wilderness. Siptah chattered, hardly able to contain his excitement, though he first expressed some doubt at the preparations his uncle had made.

"I don't know why you chose a heavy chariot, Uncle. We won't be able to go over rough ground at any speed. I suppose the other chariots will do, but three wagons only? We might be gone some days."

"I wanted the three-man chariot so I could ride with you, Son of Re," Bay said. "There are things we must discuss."

"You're not going to spoil this hunt with serious talk are you? I want to enjoy myself."

"Not at all, Majesty, but enjoy yourself for now. Take pleasure in the freedom of the road, the heat of the sun and the cries of the circling hawk, and be not concerned. I will talk to you later."

The opportunity came the next day. Bay had sent the hunters out at dawn to check for spoor, and later in the morning suggested that they drive out alone. Siptah looked at his uncle as if trying to discern the reason behind his suggestion and then shrugged.

"Why not?"

A mere half hour brought them to a gully with scattered thorn trees along its edges and here Bay ordered the charioteer to wait while he and the king proceeded on foot.

"Why can't Ahmose wait here and we take the chariot?" Siptah demanded. "It's too hot to be walking around in this wilderness. And besides, my leg hurts."

"You will see the reason for my request soon enough, Majesty."

Siptah grumbled in a most unkingly manner but dismounted and, with the aid of his cane, lurched along behind his uncle.

"How far are we going?"

"Not far, Majesty. Just up that hill."

"I can't climb up there."

"With my help you can."

Bay soon had to drop back and support Siptah as they hauled themselves upward over small boulders and through loose rock. They slipped and almost fell several times, but after less than an hour they sat, panting and sweating, on a rock at the top. The hill was, in reality, not even as high as the pylons of the Temple of Ptah in Men-nefer, but it felt like they had conquered a mountain.

"I'm thirsty," Siptah said.

"I regret to say I did not bring any water with me, Majesty."

"Then we must go back down to the chariot at once. That was a silly mistake, Uncle."

"In a little while. There are some things we must discuss while we are alone."

"Couldn't you have said them back at the palace? Or even at the camp? It's hot and I'm thirsty, so..."

"Tausret means to kill you, Son of Re."

"What?"

"My spies have brought me word that she discussed how to get rid of you...and me, of course...with Tjaty Montu."

"That's...that's...she can't do that. I mean, people wouldn't let her. Would they? I'm the king. You can't just kill the king." Tears formed in Siptah's eyes.

"At the moment she is only discussing the possibility, Majesty. That gives us some time, so we must discuss how we can turn this to our advantage. Now do you see why I insisted we come all the way out here, where no man can possibly overhear us?"

Siptah nodded and wiped away his tears. "You have a plan, don't you, Uncle?"

"Indeed I do, Majesty, but it is a risky one and we will have to stake everything on it."

"Tell me."

"We kill her instead."

Siptah stared and licked his lips. "Is...is it possible?"

"Anything is possible if one is forthright and brave."

"But to kill a woman..."

"Not just a woman, but a powerful regent. That is why she must go. She has tasted the power of rulership and will not give it up. The only obstacle between her and the throne is you, Majesty. Kill you and she can reign as King of Kemet."

"She's a woman," Siptah scoffed. "She can't be king."

"It has happened before, Majesty. Were you taught nothing of the history of the kings of Kemet? Maatkare Hatshepsut was her name. She desired the throne and grasped it, defying custom and the gods to rule as king over all Kemet."

"The gods put me on the throne," Siptah declared. "They would not let a usurper take my place."

"The gods might have little to say about a dagger in the night or a poisoned cup," Bay said dryly. "They make their will known by signs and portents, but rarely step down onto the earth and interfere in the affairs of man."

"Then I'll have to kill Tausret first. How should I do it? Have her arrested and executed? But on what charge?"

"Unfortunately, she is too powerful for that to succeed. An attempt to arrest her would doubtless precipitate your overthrow as she has powerful friends."

"Ament, you mean? I suppose we will have to have him killed too."

"Yes, Majesty, and to be complete we must remove Seti-Merenptah as well."

"But he's only a baby."

"And the son of the previous king's loins. Even if we removed Tausret, he would remain as a rallying point for traitors. He must go too."

Siptah looked unhappy. "I don't like the idea of killing a child. I'm not sure I could do it."

"You won't have to. I will arrange for the deaths myself. All you are required to do is look suitably surprised and dismayed."

"Then you should not have told me, Uncle. I can't keep a secret like that and not look guilty when I'm found out."

"You will have to, Majesty. The reason I'm telling you beforehand is in case something goes wrong. Then you can act to preserve my life."

"What do you mean by 'something goes wrong'? If you try and kill Tausret and fail, you won't get a second chance. In fact," Siptah added morosely, "we'll probably both die very quickly."

"I won't fail, Majesty. First I remove the Queen's dog Ament--by an accident. Then I remove the boy, either by accident or poison. Lastly, when Tausret is prostrate with grief I will have her killed. Nothing can go wrong if it is properly planned."

The king sat and looked out over the desert landscape, the heated air rippling and making the rocks and gullies waver as if seen through water. "When?" he asked.

"Soon. We know that she is thinking of our deaths, so we must move before she does. Leave it with me, Majesty. I will find the correct time and method, and the first you will know of it is when they bring you the news."

Siptah sat a while longer and then sighed. "I suppose we'd better go hunt that lion then."

"There is no lion. I lied to get you out of the palace."

"You could have told me the truth, Uncle. I don't like being lied to."

"You would not have come out for any lesser beast and it was imperative that you learn of my plan where no one can overhear us."

"Well, I've learned of it now. Can we go and do some hunting? I feel like I want to kill something."

Bay and Siptah returned to the chariot and the waiting charioteer, who looked relieved that they had come to no harm. They returned to the camp and from there followed the hunters out as they searched the surrounding countryside for game. Not only were there no lions, but the wild asses had fled too, and all Siptah had to show for his hunting expedition was a pair of gazelles, dispatched by the king's bow as they stood grazing.

The return to Men-nefer went almost unannounced, but the Queen Regent was on hand to welcome them back. Tausret stared at Bay for a few moments before turning her attention to the king.

"You are well?" she asked. "I heard a rumour that you had gone out after a lion, though Bay informed me beforehand it was just to hunt for wild asses."

"As you can see, Lady Tausret, we found neither," Siptah replied.

"That is good, for I would not like to see you endangered. Kemet needs its king."

"I have the right to do as I see fit, and if I want to hunt, I shall. Even lions," he added boldly.

Tausret smiled but her eyes glittered as she stared into the youth's eyes. "When you are full king, you may do as you please, Son of Re, but until that day dawns you will do as I say."

Siptah drew himself up, though he had to lean heavily on his cane. He met Tausret's gaze but his lip trembled as he spoke. "I am still the king, crowned and anointed by Amun and all the gods, and I will not be spoken to in that way."

"Will you not?" Tausret asked with a smile. "I must remember that." She turned and strode from the room, leaving Siptah to glower after her.

"I know what you mean to do," he whispered, "but I shall strike first. Then you will see I am truly king."

Chapter 27

R amesse Kha'amen-teru Bay speaks:

I am gripped by excitement, for at last my plans are in motion. Soon, I will rid myself of my enemies and rise to the position ordained by the gods of Kemet and my native Amurri. My parents came to this land under bondage, but I worked hard and rose through the ranks of servant to official and from thence to Chancellor and Treasurer of all Kemet. I put my sister Suterere into the bed of Messuwy, son of King Baenre and their only son was Akhenre Siptah who is now king over all of Kemet. Thus I am uncle to the king, trusted adviser and he who established him upon the throne of his father in the face of opposition from Queen Tausret, widow of King Userkheperure Seti.

But I would be so much more--and now the opportunity arises. Tausret accepted Siptah as king and placed herself in authority over him as Regent until such time as her infant son Seti-Merenptah came of age. Siptah was only ever going to be an interim king if she had her way, but I would make him true king. I have striven to make myself more important in the king's life, but she blocks me at every turn. Siptah petitioned that I be made Regent alongside her, but she refused. He asked that I be made Tjaty, but she laughed. It is plain that she denies me so that her unnatural control over the king will remain total. Then, when her son is old enough, she will murder poor Siptah and probably me too, continuing to rule as Regent over her son. Perhaps she even means to rule as King herself.

It has happened before, if the scrolls of Kemetu history are true. Maatkare Hatshepsut ruled as regent, thrusting aside the legitimate claims of Menkheperre Djetmose, and later elevated herself to the status of King, even showing herself in men's clothing. Such an unnatural thing could happen again unless I am vigilant, but I am resolved that her overweening ambitions shall come to naught. She shall fall into death and her son with her, leaving no one to challenge the rule of my nephew Akhenre Siptah.

The problem is how to bring it about. Obviously, I cannot just walk up to her and plunge a dagger into her breast. It would achieve the desired result but at the cost of my own death, and that is too high a cost. Therefore I must find someone else to do the deed, with all the risks that entails. Well, I have men willing to do my bidding as long as there is reward in it for them, so the problem is not an insuperable one. I just wish I had someone I can confide in, to discuss the problem and its solution, but there is no one for I can trust no one. You may wonder why I told the king of my designs as he is a boy and has not yet learned to keep his counsel. It is not that I trust him to keep quiet, but rather to provide me with an escape if things go wrong. If I am accused to his face, I do not want a look of shock and distaste to overwhelm him. I want him to at least order a proper investigation as I know I can survive that. What I cannot survive is a quick and unthinking denouncement by the king. Thus I have ensnared the king in my plotting.

I have three deaths to encompass--the Regent, her son, and her dog--and in that order of importance. If Ament is the only one left alive, he is impotent, a mere soldier. If only the child lives, others may rally around him but he will be easier to kill if his mother does not live. But leave Tausret alive with the others dead and she will surely wreak vengeance.

Ament is perhaps the easiest of these to kill, for he is a man secure in his own abilities and who moves freely and without any other guard but his own right arm. He could be set upon in the streets by a band of thugs, making it look like a simple robbery, or a dagger could be slipped between his ribs on a dark night. Less confrontationally, poison might work, for while the royal meals are carefully prepared, watched and tasted, no one is overly concerned with a dish served to a soldier.

The child's death is probably easy to bring about too. So many children die each year that it is a miracle anyone survives to adulthood. Disease kills most, followed by simple accidents. The problem is that disease is sent by the gods and I can think of no good way to make it happen. That leaves an accident, but first there are the child's guardians to be got rid of. There are few royal children in the palace these days--a handful of sons and daughters of distant scions of the ruling family--and those that have survived are watched carefully. However, it only takes a moment's inattention.

Tausret's death may be difficult though. She is guarded by Ament her dog and rarely visits places where a murder attempt might be made, so direct violence is unlikely to succeed. Her food and drink is prepared carefully and tasted, so poison will not work. An accident? Well, accidents happen but I cannot wait for something that may never occur--so what do I do? It seems to me that timing is everything. Kill Ament first and her dog can no longer protect her. Kill the child and she may be so overcome with grief she becomes careless.

Yes, the more I think on it, the more likely my plan will succeed, but I must take the risk of leaving Tausret to the last. Ament's death will seemingly be by chance, and the child's by a boyhood accident. Then in the throes a grief, she is careless and an opportunity presents itself...yes, I think it will work.

There is much to do. I must investigate the daily lives of my trio of targets and look for weaknesses in their shells of protection. Measure carefully and then strike.

Chapter 28
Year 4 of Akhenre Siptah

S eti-Merenptah had grown into a strong and healthy young boy and now, at the age of five, he had discovered the joy of being able to go almost anywhere within the palace and do anything without being told off. He rarely wore clothing as he ran through the corridors and rooms; his side lock bobbing on his otherwise shaved head. Other children, mostly the sons (and a few daughters) of high palace officials played with him, and a handful of palace nurses and servants followed, ready to soothe away a hurt, clean up a mess, or administer a sharp reprimand to any child save the royal heir.

One of the favourite places to play was the warren of storerooms near the servants' quarters at the rear of the palace. Here were rooms filled with jars, with furniture, with bedding, and with the myriad of other accoutrements without which a well-ordered household would founder. Hours could be spent fossicking through the contents of the dimly lit rooms, or climbing piles of linen, striving to climb higher than anyone else and shrieking with delight as the piles collapsed, spilling them to the floor.

The Chancellor happened upon the little knot of children one day as they played among the linen piles, and stood near two nurses as they kept watchful eyes on their charges. The nurses looked at Bay out of the corners of their eyes, but were afraid to speak to such an exalted personage. Bay, in turn, ignored the nurses but watched the children at play. He saw the other children deferring to Seti-Merenptah, allowing him to climb higher, and when he slipped and fell, waited for a heartbeat to see if the royal son would laugh or cry before joining in.

Bay thought to himself how easy it would be to press the boy's face into the pile of linen until he stopped breathing.

Another favourite place was the kitchen. The ovens were housed in a large lean-to arrangement at the rear of the palace where large fires were stoked beneath mud-brick edifices in which breads were baked. Other fires blazed in pits above which hung whole beasts--sheep, goats, cattle and pigs, as well as geese and ducks--slowly being turned while the fat dripped off sizzling into the fires or was collected into flat earthenware pans. To one side of the lean-to was a large storage shed housing huge wide-necked jars. Baked barley bread was crumbled into these jars along with honey and a variety of spices and herbs before being topped up with water and a handful of dried grape skins. The skins provided natural yeast and soon the vats were bubbling away as the brew turned into barley beer.

The aromas of beer, bread, and roasting meats drew the children like flies to dung, and there was always keen competition to see who could filch some ripe fruit, or a piece of oven-hot bread, dip a finger into a honey pot, or hoist themselves up to lick the pungent foam from the necks of the beer jars. Bay would follow the children here too, and watch as they scurried and ran around the legs of the many cooks and servants preparing food, twisting away from the heat of the ovens, and laughing with delight as they stole a scrap of food.

Bay thought to himself how easy it would be to nudge a running boy so he fell into an open fire, or to swiftly upend him into a beer jar, leaving him to thrash and drown.

If there was any place within the palace complex that was sure to attract small children, it was the expanse of gardens with gravel paths, shady trees, rush-bordered pools, flowerbeds, and menagerie. It was this latter attraction that always drew them outside, with its strange smells and sights. They loved standing outside the monkey cage screaming with laughter and throwing stones at the agile beasts, or looking down into pits where lions, panthers or bears prowled. Other enclosures housed exotic animals from Kush and beyond--dog-headed apes, black-and-white painted horses, creatures with impossibly long necks, or heavy bull-like creatures with a huge head and long horns on their noses. Here the children would be struck dumb as they stared wide-eyed at the wonders from foreign lands.

Bay thought to himself how easy it would be to push a boy into a lion or a leopard pit and slip away quietly as men cried aloud and women tore their hair and garments in horror, while sending for the keepers of the menagerie.

The heat of the day would often drive the children indoors again, but sometimes they would play under the wide-spreading shade trees and seek amusement there. Scarab beetles could be found rolling little balls of dung purloined from the menagerie enclosures, or columns of ants marching like soldiers coming back from war, each carrying a piece of the spoils--a seed, a scrap of leaf, a limb from a dead spider. Butterflies fluttered around the flowering shrubs, brown and orange and yellow and blue, while bees foraged in the blossoms, eager to work while the butterflies played. Flies swarmed, attracted by the animal dung, and as the children played or watched the little animals of the gardens; their hands would flick constantly, waving away the insistent flies.

Pools of clear water, set about with rushes and papyrus, dotted the garden, and these cool places drew the children. They searched the edges of the pools for frogs and dipped little nets into the clear water in pursuit of tiny silver fish, laughing with delight and splashing each other with abandon. For those children less adventurous, they could sit and watch the dragonflies flitting above the pools, tiny red and blue jewels that hunted and ate flies on the wing. The nurses stayed close when the children were near the ponds, vigilant in case one of their charges should fall in, or in case they would disturb a cobra amongst the plants growing luxuriantly by the water's edge.

Bay thought to himself how easy it might be, if the nurses could be distracted, to push a boy into a pond and hold his head under until he drowned. Accidents happened.

Days passed, and Bay kept watch on the palace children as unobtrusively as he could, looking for when an opportunity might present itself, but knowing that the time was not yet ripe for action. He took his findings to the only other person who knew his mind and with whom he could share his thoughts.

"I could do it myself. As long as nobody actually saw me push him, none would dare accuse me--even her."

"Majesty, no. You must appear to be entirely blameless in this affair. Even a hint that you were involved could bring her wrath down on you. In the first wild moments of grief she may lash out at any she thinks have harmed her, and even your exalted status may not protect you. Leave the act to me, Majesty. I will either do it myself or employ a trusted man."

"Which method do you favour, Uncle?" Siptah asked curiously. "I think the fire pit as I hate him and that would hurt the most."

"That is an unworthy thought, Majesty. The child's only fault is who he is, and the gods made him that."

Siptah grimaced. "He stands in the way though."

"Yes he does, but unless I have no alternative I shall wish no such cruel death on him. I shall try to find a method that is quick and painless."

"Poison? I've heard that some poisons are very fast."

"Perhaps." Bay sat for a few minutes in thought. "I have not made my mind up yet. I only wanted to tell you of my findings so far, so that you would not worry that nothing was being done to safeguard your life."

"Don't delay too long, Uncle. You told me yourself that the Regent desires my death...our deaths...and if you wait too long it may be too late."

"I must have everything planned before I strike, so there is no possibility of failure. Have patience, Majesty, and all will be well."

Bay knew he could not follow Ament around in the same way, as the Commander would soon notice him and wonder what he was doing, so he detailed a pair of his close servants to do so.

When Ament was not with the Regent, he was most likely to be found in the Men-nefer legion barracks, where although he detested Commander Besenmut, was on friendly terms with some of the senior officers and often whiled away the hours over a pot of beer. They discussed battles, training methods and weapons, arguing fiercely and thumping the table with fists to emphasise points. Bay's men brought back their ideas.

"They become quite heated in their arguments sometimes, Master. It might be possible to escalate an argument to the point of blows. A man with a dagger..."

"Which man?" Bay asked. "You have someone in mind? One of the officers he has perhaps slighted or who holds a grudge."

"No, Master. We just thought that if we could get a man there, he could..."

"Any man I tried to introduce would be viewed with suspicion. Besides, they would surely kill him."

"Perhaps we could poison the officer's food?"

"Could you be certain that Ament alone would eat it? No, it is too risky. Find me something else."

Bay's men followed Ament to Iunu when he went to resume command of the Set legion, but the situation there was even worse than in Men-nefer.

The Set legion was fiercely loyal to Ament and Bay's men could tell at once that they had no chance of subverting any officer, or of introducing an assassin into their ranks.

"Find me something I can use or find other employment," Bay ordered.

They followed him to Per-Bast, for Ament was still Overseer of Vineyards there, and owned a vineyard adjacent to the one gifted to his sister and her foreign husband by Baenre Merenptah. His sister now had many children and Ament enjoyed the company of his nephews and nieces, as well as the attentions of his adopted sons Jerem and Ephrim. Bay's men spent many days in the city of Per-Bast and took many opportunities to observe the Overseer as he did his rounds of the vineyards and inspected their produce.

"You have something for me?" Bay asked when his spies reported back to him.

"Yes, Master, I think we have." They went on to tell Bay of Ament's duties as Overseer and the jars of wine that were sent to the palace from his estates. "Furthermore," they said, "he is very fond of particular foreign dishes his sister prepares."

"And why should that be of interest to me?"

The spies smiled. "If such food arrived at the palace addressed to Commander Ament, purporting to come from his sister, he would accept it without question, and greedily consume it."

"Ah, I see," Bay said. "You have done well and shall be rewarded."

Bay's plans were starting to come together. He now had some ideas about how he could kill Ament and Seti-Merenptah, but there was still the problem of Queen Tausret. Next to the king, she was the most exalted personage in all of Kemet and was at all times all but surrounded by officials and courtiers. Even when alone, she was not, as the ubiquitous servants formed an unofficial presence that served to guard her. It would take exceptional circumstances for that cordon of people to be penetrated and breached. Any man who sought the life of the Regent would be almost certain to be apprehended, after the deed if not before, and must be prepared to die. Bay would have to offer a considerable incentive to get a willing assassin.

Bay gave the problem much thought, but could come to no conclusion regarding Tausret's death, so he decided he would try for Ament and the child, perhaps by the same method. He was aware of the poison that had been used to kill Baenre Merenptah and knew where to find a small amount of it, though it would have to be administered in a different way.

The poison, when it arrived, was a tiny amount of powder sealed in the tip of a cow's horn. Bay weighed it carefully in his hand, his heart beating fast as he contemplated the death he held. He called a trusted servant, a fellow Amorite by the name of Sensek, and bade him hide the horn where it could be quickly accessed but not easily found.

"You do not want me to administer it, Master?" Sensek asked.

"The opportunity is scarcely likely to arise," Bay replied. "If it does, tell me of it."

Sensek went off with the poison, while Bay, who realised the amount of poison in the horn was enough to kill a child but not a child and an adult, considered where he could lay hands on more. He thought he might have to send to the city of Khent-Min for more as that had been where Messuwy's man had obtained the unguent that had killed Baenre.

Sensek, in the meantime, hid the horn carefully on his person and, knowing the intended target, kept a close eye on Seti-Merenptah, looking for a chance to administer it. In his mind, he believed that the path to personal power lay in performing great deeds for his master. Poisoning the young prince would be such a great deed.

His opportunity came a few days later on a hot day when the young prince was at play near the menagerie with several other children. One of the nurses brought out honey cakes and milk and called to the children. Sensek saw his chance immediately but could not get close to the children's refreshments while the nurse remained close by. He stayed close, the horn unstoppered, watching as the nurse poured milk into a silver cup and several wooden ones. The Amorite smiled when he saw the royal cup being prepared and called out to the nurse, pointing at a nearby pond.

"I think I saw a child fall in the pond."

The nurse ran toward the pond and Sensek swiftly shook the powdered poison into the silver cup, stirring it in with his finger and then stepping away into the shadows of a tamarind tree, from whence he could observe the outcome. He absently wiped his finger on his kilt as he watched the nurse return to her place and the children come running. The prince was a few paces behind the other children, chattering away to another small boy, and one of the first boys to reach the refreshment grabbed the prince's silver cup and raised it to his lips.

"No, Hortep," the nurse cried. "That is Seti's cup. Drink from your own." She reached across and plucked the cup from the child's hand, leaving a smear of milk on Hortep's upper lip.

The boy licked it off and reached for a honey cake, taking a bite out of it before grimacing and spitting out his mouthful. He clutched his stomach and stared at the nurse.

"It hurts."

The other children, including Prince Seti, stood around and stared at little Hortep, who was now rolling on the ground, crying. Nobody had stopping eating their cakes and drinking their milk, except Seti, who chewed on a honey cake but had a hand out for the silver cup that the nurse still held. The nurse dropped to her knees beside the stricken boy, setting the cup down awkwardly on the grass, oblivious to it falling over and spilling the milk.

Under the tamarind tree, Sensek cursed when he saw the poisoned milk spill to the ground and slipped away, putting some distance between him and the children. Already the nurse's screams were attracting attention. He made his way back into the palace by way of the kitchens, and unobtrusively dropped the horn vial into one of the fire pits, before finding Bay and reporting.

"You fool," Bay said. "I asked you to tell me if an opportunity arose, not snatch at it and ruin whatever chance we had."

"It would have worked, Master, if that greedy child had not grabbed the Prince's cup."

"And now you have alerted them to the danger, making it even harder to get close. What have you done with the empty horn?"

"Destroyed it."

"Good, now get out of the palace, lie low in the city."

Bay watched his man leave and knew that he had another problem--one that needed his immediate attention. He sent a servant to find another of his men, and had him admitted as soon as he arrived.

"Get rid of Sensek, as soon as possible."

"Permanently?"

"Of course, permanently, but make it look like an accident. A tavern brawl or street robbery gone wrong."

"Yes, Master."

"They have tried to kill my son."

"Thank the gods they did not succeed, my lady, but...who are 'they'?"

"Bay of course. Do you doubt it?"

"Can you prove it?"

"No, but it reeks of him. Find out, Ament."

Ament reported back a day later.

"The nurse in charge says there was a man near the children. He called out to her, telling her a child had fallen into a pool. She went to look, leaving the cakes and milk unattended and, after finding no child in or near the pool, returned to find the man gone."

"Did she know the man?"

"No, my lady, but her description was of one Sensek, an Amorite servant."

"Amorite. Like Bay."

Ament nodded. "There was no obvious connection with Bay, save that of their race."

"Was?"

"He was found dead in the city this morning. It seems he was stabbed and robbed."

"Or got rid of."

"Very likely, my lady."

"Nothing to connect him to Bay?"

"Only him being an Amorite. But there are several Amorite servants in the palace, most of them with no connection to Bay."

"What of the boy that was poisoned?"

"He will live, my lady. The poison was in the milk, but introduced into the Prince's cup alone. The boy only sipped from it."

Tausret shuddered and wrapped her arms around her body. "So close, Ament. I should have known he would try something like this and guarded against it. Well, that changes today. No food or drink comes near Seti-Merenptah without being tasted, and I will have a squad of soldiers attendant upon him at all times. He will not leave the palace precincts unless accompanied by at least a squad."

"You would make him a prisoner despite being heir, my lady," Ament murmured.

"Better a prisoner than...than..." Tausret shuddered again.

"Reassign me, lady. Make me guard and tutor to the boy and I will stick with him at all times, never letting him out of my sight."

"You have duties of your own."

"Nothing that cannot be managed by others, my lady. My sons can handle my duties as Overseer of Vineyards, and I have capable officers in my Set legion." Ament looked at Tausret and saw that she was undecided. "My lady, I would count it a signal honour to guard your son who will be the next King of Kemet. I would willingly offer up my life to protect him."

"I know you would, dear Ament..." Tausret nodded. "Very well. A better friend and protector no man could have, but call on whatever help you need."

"With my life, my lady," Ament said solemnly. Then he grinned. "I'd better go and tell him the news."

Chapter 29
Year 5 of Akhenre Siptah

Ament now lived close to Seti-Merenptah's rooms in the palace with a hand-picked guard on the doors and outside the windows at night, but the guards were almost unnoticeable during the day, withdrawing to allow their charge the semblance of privacy. The little boy quickly grew accustomed to Ament's frequent presence and grew to love his stories, his attention and his company, complaining loudly on those rare occasions when Ament was called away to attend to some other duty. On those occasions the guards moved in closer and Seti-Merenptah was allowed less freedom of movement.

"I don't know why you allow Bay to live," Ament said boldly one day, several months after the attempt on Seti-Merenptah's life. "You are the Regent, after all."

"Believe me, there is nothing I would like more, but I cannot just act against the king's uncle without proof. Siptah is almost old enough to rule alone, and acting against Bay without proof may just precipitate a civil war. I cannot risk that until my son is ready to take his place on the throne. Another year or two, perhaps."

Seti-Merenptah knew exactly who he was, and what his future was likely to be as the son of Userkheperure Seti and God's Wife of Amun, Queen Tausret. This gave him a sense of self-importance and it had led to rebellion against his tutors on more than one occasion. They tried to drum into him the history of the kings of Kemet, technicalities of the law, priestly duties and incantations, or the subtleties of hieroglyphs and cursive writing, but it was always a struggle. The boy would much rather be at play, or wandering around the stables, or training with his toy bow and arrow.

Ament was a good influence on Seti-Merenptah when it came to learning. The boy so loved his constant companion that he would rather suffer a whole morning's instruction by his tutors than risk the old soldier's displeasure and perhaps even miss out on a story. So every morning, Ament would deliver him to his tutors and sit in the shade of the stone columns or by a sunlit window while Seti-Merenptah struggled with the intricacies of a royal education. At noon they took a meal together, with the heir not tasting a morsel that had not come from the common dish and been thoroughly tested by several people. Ament would eat too, again from the common dish, and then after a short respite in the heat of the day, he would lead the boy out to enjoy the afternoon.

It might have seemed like play to the boy, but Ament made sure that most things he did had some practical application. In the stables, Seti-Merenptah learned to care for horses; sitting on the palace walls, they would look down into the streets of the city, where Ament would point out what people were doing and why. In the palace gardens, they observed the animals in their cages and pits and Ament spun stories about the lands they came from and which king of Kemet it was that brought that land into subjugation. Other times, Ament would produce a straw and wicker gazelle and Seti-Merenptah would stand a few paces away with his little bow and a handful of arrows and try to hit it. Sometimes, servants or officials would stand around and watch the young prince's activities, applauding a fine effort or calling out encouragement.

But if there was one pastime the boy loved above all others, it was wading in the mud and reeds on the edges of the garden ponds hunting for frogs. If Ament or the nurse on duty did not call a halt to the activity, Seti-Merenptah would stay there till it grew too dark to see and he missed his supper. Ament, having been the son of a fisherman before he became a soldier, fashioned a little net for the boy and strung it between two thin sticks so he could scoop fish or frogs from the water with a lunge, or drop the net over them with a shout of glee. His catch would be transferred, with squeals of excitement, to a pot of water.

Even here, Ament tried to instil some educative advantage. He showed how the silvery scales of fish and their shape, made them very suited to life in water, and he explained how the frog exceeded all other animals in its fertility, flooding the ponds with tadpoles in the spring. This was why, he said, the goddess of fertility, Heqet, took the form of a frog or a woman with the head of a frog.

There was always a danger of snakes among the rushes and reeds, and on one occasion, Ament scooped the boy up out of harm's way and pointed out the black sinuous body of Iaret, the risen one of the goddess Wadjet, the royal cobra.

"Leave it alone and it will leave you alone--most times. Never provoke it, for its bite is death."

After the first time, Ament would scour the pond edges for the deadly snakes before the boy came anywhere near it, and if he found one would coax it into a wicker basket and have it taken outside the city boundaries to be released. He never considered killing one as they were the sacred protectors of the royal family and he respected them too much. After clearing the vegetation of its ophidian dangers, it might be several days before a new one took up residence, but Ament was ever vigilant.

Ament received packages of food from his sister from time to time, and a favourite dish was a thin pastry shell stuffed with almonds, honey and spices. It was a dish that stemmed from the northern regions of the Great Sea beyond the lands controlled by Kemet, and the recipe had come to her through her Kaftor husband. The packages, when they arrived, were often battered and oozing sweet stickiness, but Ament eagerly opened them and often shared them with Seti-Merenptah, who loved all things sweet.

On this occasion, the young prince had had a troubled night and had fallen asleep after the noon meal. The package was delivered to Ament, who took it around to the Prince's quarters to share it, but found him asleep. Instead, he opened it in the privacy of his own room. He noted that the seal on the jar had been broken and the chipped neck was sticky, but looked inside the shallow pot and smiled. It was filled with almond sweetmeats, and he dipped a finger into the sticky mess and sucked it, murmuring with delight.

"Little Seti would love this," he murmured to himself. "If he had not been asleep, we would have eaten it all by now. I must remember to take him some when he wakes." Ament lifted one of the cakes from the pot and took a small bite, savouring the flavours of almond, of honey, of cumin, "and something else...something almost bitter..." He put the cake down and licked his fingers again.

His lips tingled and he rubbed them absently as he put the jar containing the cakes to one side. He stepped outside his room, intending to make his way down to the barracks, but had not gone more than twenty paces before he broke out in a sweat and had to steady himself against a wall as his legs jerked. A servant hurried over when he beckoned.

"Commander Ament, you are not well?"

"I...I don't know..." His stomach clenched and he tasted again the almonds and honey and cumin. "Poison," he gasped, clutching at the servant. "Fetch a physician." As the servant ran off, Ament fell to his knees, feeling his heart start to race and his vision blur. He stuck a finger down his throat, gagged, and thrust it further down, collapsing onto hands and knees as his stomach heaved and a burning taste filled his mouth.

The physician arrived very soon after to find Ament curled up on the floor in a puddle of vomit, moaning weakly and shaking. While assistants carried Ament to a nearby room and laid him on a makeshift bed, the physician bent over and sniffed the vomit, and then dipped a fingertip into the mess and touched the tip of his tongue with it. He grimaced and spat it out before hurrying after his patient.

"Find me charred wood and scrape the black off it," he ordered one of his assistants. To another he said, "bring me an emetic," and to a third, "darken the room with curtains." A fourth was sent to take the news to the Regent.

Tausret arrived shortly after the emetic had done its work and the vomit was being cleaned from the bed and the convulsing man on it.

"What is the poison?" Tausret asked the physician.

"It is sometimes called 'the choker', Majesty. Uncommon and expensive, as the poison comes from far to the east."

"But you can cure it? He will live, won't he?"

"It is almost invariably fatal, Majesty, but it seems Commander Ament made himself vomit as soon as he realised the effects were upon him. I also administered an emetic and now..." The physician beckoned as his assistant entered the room with a small dish full of black lumps and powder. He instructed him to feed Ament as much of the charcoal as he could, telling him to massage his throat to make him swallow.

"Charcoal?" Tausret queried.

"It has been known to work, but no one knows how."

"So he'll live?"

"That is in the hands of the gods."

"I shall have a hundred prayers offered up for him."

"Thank you, Majesty."

"In what was the poison administered?" Tausret asked.

"From the contents of his stomach it was either something he ate at the noon meal..."

"He ate from the common dish and everything was tasted besides."

177

"Then it was the almond sweetmeat. He is fortunate he consumed no more than a bite."

"I will have his rooms searched for the remainder. Look after him, physician, for this man is important to me."

Tausret left the physician to his work and went to her son's room where he was awoken from his sleep to be told that Ament was indisposed and could not play with him that afternoon. "Play inside, this once, my beloved son," she said. She drew the nurse aside and whispered to her. "Be vigilant. My enemy has struck at me and I fear for the life of my child."

"No one will get past me, Majesty," the nurse assured her.

"I will put armed men outside the door. No one is to pass in or out without my permission."

Seti-Merenptah played happily enough within his room for a while, moving little clay and wood figurines around, pretending they were his armies, but then grew bored. He could hear the sounds of other children outside and pleaded with his nurse to be allowed out. She refused and suggested that he perhaps sit by the window and watch the other children instead.

"Your mother the Queen commands you stay in your room today."

"But I haven't done anything wrong. It's not fair."

Seti-Merenptah sat by the window, but with a scowl on his face. He could hear but not see the other children as they ran and called near the menagerie, but he could see his favourite pond. The sun sparkled on water ruffled by a cool breeze, and the reeds and rushes round the edge swayed back and forth. A feeling of longing came over him, and then he saw a man carrying a large wicker basket. The man approached the pond, looked around as if to see if anyone was watching, and then squatted down.

"Nurse Henet," Seti-Merenptah called. "What is that man doing?"

"What man is that, child?" came Henet's voice from the next room.

"The one by the pond. He's carrying a large wicker basket."

"How should I know? Now play quietly, child. I'm busy."

After a moment, the man took the cover off the basket, tipped it toward the water and sprang back a pace.

"Oh, do look, Henet. Something's happening."

Henet grumbled, but came into the room and looked out of the window. "It's just a man with a basket. Now, go and play, I'm busy." She turned and bustled off.

Moments later, the man by the pond reached for the now obviously empty basket, and hurried away with it, after giving the palace a searching look.

"What is he doing?" Seti-Merenptah asked himself. He thought of calling out to his nurse again but she had not seemed interested, so he remained silent, staring at the pond and the mystery in its reeds and rushes. At last he could stand it no longer, and after looking to see if he was observed (he wasn't) climbed over the window sill and dropped into low bushes. He waited a moment for his nurse's angry reprimand and when it did not come, ran across the gardens to the pond.

The breeze was cool on his skin, and the sun's rays warm, but he felt a tingle of excitement as he stared at the muddy ground and low but thick vegetation that bordered the pool. Seti-Merenptah stepped forward slowly, following the trail of crushed plants that the man had left. Mud squeezed between his toes and he looked around avidly for whatever it was the man had tipped out of the basket. The plants right at the water's edge seemed undisturbed and were thicker, taller, rising to his waist, so after a brief hesitation, Seti-Merenptah stepped through, pushing blindly into the reeds, his bare foot seeking purchase on the slippery ground.

Something moved beneath his foot as he put his weight on it and he felt a sudden blow to his calf, followed instantly by flooding pain. He screamed and stumbled back, his limbs already failing him as he fell onto the ground beside the pool. The pain enveloped him and he screamed again, dimly hearing answering shouts drawing nearer. His vision blurred and despite the horrible pain in his leg, he started to feel like he wanted to sleep. The first person reached him and called to his nurse who screamed and ran to him, cradling him in her arms. Seti-Merenptah lost consciousness as his nurse picked him up.

They carried him inside the palace and called the physician, recognising the puncture wounds on the boy's calf as having been made by a snake. Two men thrashed at the poolside vegetation with sticks but retreated when they heard an angry hiss and saw the spread hood of a cobra rise up out of the reeds.

"Iaret," they told the physician. "The risen one of Wadjet is responsible."

"Then there is no hope. Send for the Queen for her son is dying."

Tausret arrived, but Seti-Merenptah was already past all help and comfort, his little chest heaving as he struggled against the creeping paralysis of the cobra's venom. She wailed aloud, and sent runners to the priests of every god, but minutes later the little prince's body shuddered and he died in his mother's arms.

Chapter 30

Queen Tausret speaks:

Truly I am the most unfortunate of women. My darling boy has been snatched from me, leaving me alone. And the way in which he died...in pain and terror, looking to me for help and I could offer none. Ah, Seti-Merenptah, my beloved, the light and hope of Kemet, favoured one of the gods...what am I saying? If ever I needed proof that the gods have turned against the House of Ramesses it lies in the method they chose in my son's death. Wadjet, goddess protector of the Royal House has struck down the heir by her symbol of the risen one, leaving none to succeed his father Userkheperure Seti.

The line of Userkheperure Seti has come to an end, and now all rests on the scrawny shoulders of the present king Akhenre Siptah, son of the traitor Amenmesse. He is an unlikely king, but now he is the only one we have. Ah, Seti-Merenptah, my beloved...why have you been taken from me?

Days pass, and I grieve. I wail and throw dust upon my head, rending my clothes and scratching my face in my agony--and the palace grieves with me. The constant cries of women reverberate through the halls and rooms of the palace, and the sounds of the city of Men-nefer are muted. I am told that the whole country is stunned by the death of my little boy...it is too much. I cry again, deep, racking sobs that tear my heart from my chest...

What can I do? I do not know a single woman who has not lost children and there are many like me who have lost all their children--yet they have husbands to sow their fields once more, and I have none. Truly, I am alone in the world.

Every official has called upon me, offering up their condolences and public sorrow, chief among them the king and Chancellor Bay. When my grief was fresh upon my face and in my heart, I accepted their words without weighing them, but time has passed and I lie awake at night thinking of my little boy now lying in the Place of Beauty...

I consider Bay and think that his outward show of grief must be tempered by relief. The agreement we reached nearly five years ago was that I would rule as Regent and that Siptah would be king until Seti-Merenptah came of age. But now that the heir is dead, there is no one to replace the king on the throne. Siptah is secure, and Bay's position has been immeasurably strengthened. What will he do when the time of mourning has passed?

With an effort I have thrust my grief behind me. I am still the Regent and Kemet has need of me, though I think my usefulness has ended. The balance of power has changed and soon I will face a man and a boy determined to wrest the last vestige of power from me. I am tired, worn out, and lack the will to continue, so perhaps I should let Akhenre Siptah become king in fact as well as name, and allow Bay to seize the power for which he hungers. I can retire to estates in Per-Ramesses and let the last scion of the House of Ramesses do as he wills for good or ill. Why should I care any longer?

Ament came to see me, having risen shakily from his sickbed. He looked old and worn and the death of Seti-Merenptah obviously weighed heavily upon him, for his first words to me were not of support but of self-blame.

"Kill me, Lady Tausret, for I do not deserve to live. I have failed you and I have failed your son whom I regarded as if my own. I let my guard down and he died, so the blame is mine."

His words brought the tears fresh to my eyes, but I sought to ease his pain. "Do not blame yourself, dear Ament, for the gods themselves struck down my son. Wadjet herself sent the sacred cobra."

"And yet I scoured the edges of that pool for snakes just the day before, as I do constantly. There were none. Or none that I could find. Perhaps I did not look hard enough."

"Nobody blames you, Ament, least of all I. I know full well the love you bear for me and for my son, and if you had been with him that day, this would never have happened." I stretched out my hand and touched his arm gently. "What caused your sickness? Was it poisoning, as I have heard?"

Ament made an effort to thrust away his pain and answer me. "The physician told me it was a rare poison from the east, administered in a jar of almond and honey cakes sent by my sister. The seal was broken but I thought nothing of it. It was a virulent poison and if I had taken more than a bite of cake and licked the sweetness from my fingers more, I would now be dead."

"The man who broke the seal introduced the poison, no doubt. It was addressed to you. Who would wish you dead?"

Ament smiled wryly. "I can think of a few names, and you can be sure I will be making enquiries. I'm just thankful the physician was near at hand and recognised the poison."

"I will reward him with gold for saving your life...what is wrong?"

"I've just realised that if Seti-Merenptah had been awake, I would have shared the cakes with him and we would both be dead. I always shared the cakes my sister sent...people knew that. This may have been an attempt on his life, my Lady."

"Or just on yours, Ament," I said. "Chance prevented my son from eating the poisoned cakes, but the gods themselves led him down the path to his death by their holy instrument. You are not to blame, Ament."

"I found no snake there the day before. I looked, but not well enough."

"Do you not imagine the gods could place a snake there at any time? After you had searched? We cannot fight the gods, Ament, but must accept their will, no matter how hard it is to bear. And I have need of you, my friend. I am all alone in the world now--without a husband and without a son--and beset by men and women who seek only their own advantage. I need a friend, a true friend. I need you, Ament, as I have before."

Ament sighed and shook his head. "I am here for you as ever, my Lady. What would you have me do?"

183

"Advise me. While my son lived, I had a purpose in life, namely, making sure that he ascended the throne of his father. But now the last of Userkheperure's line is dead, so where lies my purpose? Siptah is my nephew and I would be content to let him rule alone were it not for the presence and influence of Bay. Should I just step aside, retire to my family estates and let Bay rule in my place, or should I do something else? But if something else, then what? The lamp that lit my path has gone out and I stand here in darkness."

Ament nodded and thought for a while before saying, "Do nothing precipitate, my Lady. An action once taken is harder to undo than one merely considered. You are still Regent, and were going to remain so for another year or two anyway, until Siptah came of age. Nothing has changed there.

"As for Bay, well, your presence deters him from actions that might harm the Ma'at of Kemet. He is an ambitious man and related to the king. That might be enough to lead him into wrongdoing, though I hesitate to blame him for trying to poison me or cause a snake to bit your son. I have not even looked to see if his hand is in this matter.

"So my advice for now, Lady, is be Regent, govern Kemet, encourage Siptah to be the best king he can be. After all, he is the grandson of Baenre Merenptah, if not the son of Userkheperure Seti."

"You have spoken wisely, dear Ament," I said. "I shall heed your advice and do nothing to change what is. You shall determine who sent you the poison and if it was meant for my son as well. If it was, then I shall visit my vengeance upon them, both for your sake and for that of my son."

Chapter 31
Year 5 of Akhenre Siptah

T he shock of the heir's death gripped the palace and its grip was slow to loosen. People fell silent as Tausret appeared, and business was conducted in hushed tones, even as they watched avidly for signs of what the future might hold. Seti-Merenptah had been well liked, but he had been an infant and a lot of the favour shown him had been because of who he was. It was open knowledge that he would ascend the throne when he came of age, but now that he had been removed, there was really only one person to back in the long term--King Akhenre Siptah. The only area of doubt remaining was whether Queen Tausret would now step down as Regent and hand over the support and care of the king to his uncle Ramesse Kha'amen-teru Bay.

Factions that had divided the palace became less pronounced for a time--after all, what was the point of supporting a dead child? Then those who had supported Seti-Merenptah and Queen Tausret saw that the other faction was gaining support and felt betrayed. They started to voice suspicions that the child's death had not been an accident and hinted at a conspiracy to grasp power. Supporters of Bay resented this interpretation and the palace people became polarised once more.

Besenmut, Commander of the Ptah legion was promoted to Fan Bearer on the King's Right Hand, and felt his position to be such that he should try and convert some of the Queen's supporters to his own side. On the suggestion of Bay, he took Tjaty Mentu aside and spoke to him.

"This sad news of the Prince's death grieves us all, Tjaty Mentu," Besenmut said. "But it does also simplify matters."

"Simplify? How?"

"There has been debate over the succession..."

"There has been no such debate," Mentu interrupted. "The agreement was plain--Akhenre Siptah ruled as king under the regency of Queen Tausret until Prince Seti-Merenptah came of age, at which point he would step aside for the son of Userkheperure."

"But now the son is dead and the agreement comes to nothing. Akhenre is king."

"There is still no debate," Mentu pointed out. "Of course Akhenre is king. Where lies the problem?"

"The problem lies in the regency," Besenmut declared. "Queen Tausret should step down immediately and hand over power to the king, now that her son is dead."

"As no doubt she will do at the proper time," Mentu countered. "But that time is not yet. What has changed in the last few days? The regency is proper while the king is young--has he magically matured in the last few days?"

"You should support Siptah."

"I do."

"Then why will you not support him in this?"

Mentu sighed. "If the Queen steps down, who will rule the king?"

"He will rule himself."

"He is not ready to do so."

"Then Bay will help him."

"If the king still needs help then why not let the Queen continue to exercise her powers as Regent?"

"I am only thinking of the Queen in this her time of grief. Why not lessen her load?"

"So this is a selfless act on your part, is it Besenmut? I thought this was all about who controls the king, but it seems I was mistaken." Mentu held up a hand as the legion commander opened his mouth. "I suggest we leave this to those most concerned. Queen Tausret knows what she is doing and if the load becomes too much to bear, I have no doubt she will make the appropriate decisions. And let me stress that it should be her decision, not one forced upon her. Is that what you want to do? To force a decision upon the Queen?"

"Of course not. I seek only what is best for the king and Kemet...and the Queen."

"Then let us speak no more of it." Mentu turned and strode off, leaving Besenmut staring after him.

Besenmut reported the conversation to Bay, who shrugged. "Tjaty Mentu is the Queen's dog, like her other one. It comes to naught in the end, anyway. Another year at the most and the king will be able to take up the reins of government for himself, and then those loyal to him--like yourself--will come into their reward."

"And the dogs?"

"They will yap and whine but achieve nothing."

Bay found he had also to reassure Siptah, who had become quite nervous after the death of Seti-Merenptah. The difficulty was to get him alone, where they could not be overheard, and the palace gardens proved to be the best place for this after the heat of the day had passed. He would have preferred to go out into the wilderness on a hunt as he had before, but he thought it might seem suspicious at this time. Instead, he used the death of the little prince as an excuse for thoroughly searching the garden for snakes and then clearing it of all people so that the king could relax in complete safety.

"Was this really necessary?" Siptah asked when he was seated comfortably under the shade of an awning, the breeze cool upon his body. "I don't mind other people in the garden as long as they don't talk to me."

"It is better not to run the risk of being overheard. We need to discuss the death."

"You didn't do very well then, did you? I thought you said you'd kill Ament first, then the boy and then his mother. Well, the boy's dead but by an accident, and Ament and the Queen still live."

"Some god smiled on Ament that day," Bay replied. "He was sent a poisoned dish of cakes which under normal circumstances he would have shared with the prince immediately. As we know, the prince was tired, so Ament tasted the poisoned cakes alone and almost died."

"Almost isn't good enough, Uncle."

Bay glared at his royal nephew. "I am aware of that, but the amount he ate should have been enough. It would have been if that physician had not recognised the poison and purged his body of it."

"So you failed. Thank the gods they saw fit to remove the boy themselves."

"Sometimes the gods need a little help."

"Meaning what?"

"Meaning that I knew by a little after midday when Ament succumbed that the poison wasn't going to kill, so I made other arrangements, and unbeknownst to him, Ament actually helped me. He had made a point these last months of clearing the pond edges of snakes, making the garden safe for the prince to play in. He transported the snakes he caught in wicker baskets and releasing them outside the city." Bay smiled. "I had a man reverse that work."

Siptah stared at his uncle. "You put the sacred cobra into the garden? Not the gods?"

"As I said, sometimes the gods need our help. Anyway, you could argue that the sacred cobra would not bite the child if it was not the will of the gods. It did, so you could say the gods themselves wanted him dead."

"And Tausret? You said you were going to kill her while she grieved."

"I considered it, but I don't think it's necessary. She is talking of stepping down."

"Good."

"If she comes to you and tells you she is doing so, you must not express joy at the thought, nor must you express any doubt that you will be able to fulfil all your duties as king. Rather, you should give thanks for the wonderful way in which she has raised you, and assure her that you will consult her regularly."

Siptah made a face. "I won't have to, will I?"

"Not unless you want to, but until she actually does step down you must give the outward appearance of being grateful for the help and instruction she has given you that now enables you to rule alone. You'll be able to do that?"

The king nodded, but his thoughts were elsewhere. "Ament knows he was poisoned. Won't he know you did it?"

"Very likely, but knowing and being able to prove it are two different things."

"The man who poisoned Ament's cakes? Will he talk?"

"He is no longer in Men-nefer."

"And the man who brought the snake in?"

"He won't talk and besides, no one saw him."

"You are certain of that?"

"Yes."

"So we are safe?"

"Define safe." Bay saw the worried expression on the king's face and re-lented. "You are in no danger, for you are the king and above the law. I am your humble servant and despite doing all things for you, I could be blamed for certain things and held accountable. In that event, I ask only the protection of your right hand and a suitable reward when the regency is ended."

"And you shall have it, Uncle. If it is within my power, you shall have whatever your heart desires."

Bay smiled. "You have been a good son of your father, Akhenre Siptah, and he would be proud of you. Never forget that Menmire Amenmesse was a true son of Baenre and rightful king of all Kemet. As your father's only son, you too will make an excellent king."

Chapter 32
Year 5 of Akhenre Siptah

Ament had tried to track down the person who had administered the poison to his sister's cakes, but had failed. He journeyed northeast to Per-Bast and talked to his sister, finding out from her who had been charged with the delivery of the sealed jar of sticky cakes. By stages, and by the judicious use of beer, wine and gold as means of loosening the tongues of witnesses, he had managed to trace the path by which the cakes reached him.

A porter by the name of Ked had taken the sealed jar to the docks of Per-Bast, and there found a fisherman called Bak willing to transport it to Men-nefer along with other produce he meant to take to market there. Upon his arrival in the capital city, Bak had passed the jar (still sealed), along with a small payment, to a palace servant by the name of Nehi, who swore he would take it to the Overseer of the King's Table, Djetmose.

Djetmose remembered the jar because at some stage in its journey it must have been overturned as the jar had leaked and was sticky. The overseer had licked his fingers and recalled the taste of honey and almonds. Evidently the jar had not yet been poisoned as Djetmose was in good health and had suffered no more than toothache between then and now. The jar had been handed on to a palace servant called Mose who, having other duties to perform, had set the jar aside for later delivery to Commander Ament's quarters.

"I returned to it no more than a few minutes later, Commander," Mose said. "Well, perhaps an hour or so," he amended. "I found the seal broken and thought to find the contents stolen but when I looked inside, the jar was full."

"You did not taste the contents?" Ament asked.

"No, Commander," Mose replied indignantly. "I delivered the jar to your rooms."

"And you have suffered no illness since then?"

"No, Commander."

Ament knew the poisoner had taken advantage of the unattended jar, but was disturbed by the effort that had gone into the attack. This was no random attempt but one that had been carefully planned. The man responsible had known that sweetmeats arrived from his sister and probably the route through the palace when it arrived. It was quite possible that he had known the jar would be unattended for some time too.

"Who would have had access to the jar in your absence?" he asked.

"No one, Commander...or rather, anyone. The room is not locked or normally attended, so anyone could have come in."

"You saw nobody acting suspiciously? Furtively?"

"No, Commander."

"And these duties that required you to set the jar aside for later delivery? What were they?"

"Just normal duties, Commander. Nothing out of the ordinary. Fetching and carrying mostly."

"Who gave you the orders?"

"I am answerable to Overseer Djetmose, Commander. If he tells me to do something, I do it. No questions asked."

Ament dismissed the servant, knowing he would get no more out of him. He knew when the poison had been added, but had no way of finding out the identity of the poisoner. No doubt someone among the swarming multitude of servants had seen him, but as servants were generally trained not to see what did not concern them, he doubted any useful information could be gained from countless interrogations. He would have to try something else.

He tried his system of spies and informants. Every person of note, and quite a few who merely wished to be, employed spies through a series of favours and gifts as a means of advancing themselves or gaining an advantage over their fellow servants. Because servants were everywhere within the palace, it was quite possible that someone knew something. It turned out they did, but not what Ament was expecting.

Among the many bits of gossip was, "Nurse Henet is wearing a new piece of jewellery."

"Why should that concern me?"

The man shrugged. "It's just what I heard."

"Who is Nurse Henet anyway?"

"She is...was nurse to the young prince what died."

"Ah, yes, of course. I'd forgotten her name but I remember her."

Ament dismissed the man and thought about the snippet of information. Was it in any way related to the poisoning of the cakes? Ament could not see a connection but that did not necessarily mean anything. The connection could be tenuous or indeed, nonexistent. He sighed and shook his head, feeling overwhelmed by the lack of useful information. The fact that the nurse was Seti-Merenptah's was probably no more than a coincidence, but the poisoned cakes had been meant for both him and the prince, and if he had taken them to the prince, the nurse would have had to allow him the sweetmeat. Ament supposed it could do no harm to talk to Henet, though he could not see any reasonable avenue for interrogation.

He found the nurse weeping in the rooms she had recently shared with the prince. She looked up, bleary-eyed, as he entered and fell to her knees when he identified himself.

"Oh, sir," Henet wailed, clasping Ament's feet in her hands. "I miss the little boy. I loved 'im, see, and would 'ave done anything to save 'im from 'urt."

Ament stooped and raised the nurse up, guiding her to a chair. "I'm sure you did, Henet. No one doubts you loved the little prince."

"'E was...'e was like me own boy. I suckled 'im when 'e was little, you know. Fed 'im from me own body. Can't get closer than that, less 'e was me own."

"I know. I saw you with him often enough to know you loved him. I loved him too."

"Oh, sir, everyone knows you did." Henet dabbed at her eyes with a cloth and ventured a weak smile. "You was like a father to 'im."

Ament could not think of any subtle way to broach the subject, so just plunged ahead. "I hear you have a new piece of jewellery, Henet. May I see it?"

The nurse hesitated and then got up and went to a small wooden chest in the corner of the room. She lifted some clothing and picked up a necklace, passing it to Ament.

"Very nice." Ament turned it over in his hands. It was made of faience; bright blue glazing set in copper, and was well made. He estimated its worth as considerably more than the nurse would earn in a month. "Where did you get it?"

"Oh, sir, I didn't steal it."

"I'm not saying you did, Henet, but were you given it?"

"Yes, sir."

"You have a wealthy admirer then. Anyone I might know?"

"It weren't a gift from a lover, like," Henet said, her lips twitching with faint mirth. "And I don't think you'd know 'im, sir."

"Try me."

Another hesitation. "Mensay, sir."

Ament frowned. "I don't know him. Why did he give it to you?"

Henet shrugged and looked away. "P'raps 'e just likes me."

"If a man gives a woman a gift this valuable it's because he wants something from her. You've told me he wasn't a lover, so come on, Henet. What did he want?"

To Ament's surprise, Henet burst into tears. "I...I didn't do nothing, sir. Honestly. 'E just...'e just wanted me to say nothing, but...but I don't know what 'e wanted me to say nothing about."

Ament soothed the upset woman and waited until she had cried herself into sobbing gulps before squatting beside her. "This man...this Mensay...what exactly did he say to you?"

"I can't remember, sir."

"When did he give you the necklace?"

Henet hiccupped. "The day after...after little Seti..." She blew her nose on the cloth.

"He came here? To your room?"

"Yes, sir. 'E said...I just remembered, sir. 'E said I was to forget what I seen and 'eard. Just that, sir. I didn't know what 'e meant, so I nods like, 'e gives me the necklace and says, 'Say nothing' and goes."

"What do you think he meant?"

"I don't know, sir."

"What do you think he might have meant, Henet?" when the nurse shook her head, Ament went on. "Anything at all. What did you see on the day the prince died? What did you hear? Think, Henet, it could be important."

"I didn't hear nothing, sir, I swear. Only what the little prince says."

Ament grunted in annoyance. "Nothing else? A man's voice...or a woman's?"

"No sir, just little Seti...but 'e spoke about a man only I didn't listen proper like. I was busy and..." Henet started crying again. "I told 'im to go and play. P'raps if I 'adn't, 'e might still be alive."

"Come on now, Henet, dry your eyes and think hard. You want to help little Seti's mother, the Queen, don't you? She would like to know anything Seti said that day."

Henet blew her nose again and sniffed. "Well, 'e's playing and I'm in the next room looking for my wool, an 'e says something about a man outside." She frowned, concentrating. "'E said 'e 'ad a basket."

"The prince had a basket?"

"No, sir, the man. The prince calls again and I go out and look but it's just a man standing near the pond with a large basket. I tells the prince to go and play and I go and look for my wool again. Never did find it, sir, because...because..." She burst into tears again.

Ament sat back on his heels and watched the nurse cry, thinking about a man near the pool with a basket, of the cobras he used to catch in baskets and take away, and of a man who had tried to poison the prince a few days before.

"The same man?" Ament muttered. "Can't be; they found Sensek dead. Another Amorite perhaps? Another tie to Bay?"

"Henet, did the man look like an Amorite?"

"I don't know, sir. I don't know any Amorites."

"Like Chancellor Bay."

"Oh, sir, it weren't 'im."

"Never mind, would you recognise the man with the basket if you saw him again?"

The nurse looked doubtful but nodded. "Maybe, sir."

"Good. Now, tidy yourself up and be prepared to enter the Queen's presence. I am going to see if I can find this man with the basket and have you identify him."

Ament went straight to see Tausret and was admitted to her presence at once. She immediately dismissed the servants and beckoned him closer.

"You have some news. I can see it in your face."

Ament nodded. "News, but not what I was expecting, my Lady. I was investigating the person who poisoned my cakes but a path led me to Henet, your son's nurse."

"I know her. She is a good woman and was devoted to Seti."

"That was my impression, my Lady. However, there is something else. It seems that she heard your son talking about a man with a basket near the pond, and she even caught a glimpse of this man."

"Who was this man?"

"I don't know, but whoever it was, someone felt it important enough to go to Henet the day after and attempt to buy her silence with a faience necklace."

Tausret considered this for a few moments. "What was important enough in what she saw or heard that warranted a bribe?"

"That is what I have been unable to find out. I questioned Henet, of course, and while she may be able to recognise the man if she saw him again, there is no evidence that the man is important to either your son's death or the attempted poisoning."

"Bring Henet to me, Ament. It may be that she will talk to another woman more than she will to a man. Besides, we have each of us lost our son, and that is a bond between us."

"I prepared her for that eventuality, my Lady. With your permission I shall go and fetch her myself."

Ament returned minutes later, looking grim. "She is dead, my Lady."

"How?"

"It would seem she was smothered, for I found her lying on her bed and a pillow on the floor beside her." Ament grimaced. "I should have brought her with me rather than coming to see you first. Now we shall never know the identity of the man with the basket."

"Is it really important, though? I mean, what is the significance of a man with a basket?"

"Ah, my Lady, I fear there is a very great significance. It is common knowledge within the palace that I have, of late, scoured the edges of the ponds where the prince played; removing any snake I found in the reeds and water plants. I would trap them in a basket and carry them outside the city walls. I had searched that very pond the day before."

"You are not to blame, Ament."

"I think you are right, my Lady, but someone saw me take cobras away and brought one back by the same method. If that is in fact what happened, then your son was murdered on the same day I was poisoned. That is not a coincidence, but the action of an enemy."

"The Great Enemy--Bay."

"I think so, my Lady, though how we prove it, I don't know."

"We do not have to prove it; though it is likely Bay planned it with or without the knowledge of Siptah. One thing is certain, we cannot bring the king to trial and it would be dangerous to arrest Bay."

"Then we are helpless in the face of their enmity?"

"Not helpless, but we must be on our guard."

Chapter 33

Setnakhte speaks:

The death of Prince Seti-Merenptah has altered everything. Kings of the House of Ramesses are ordained by the gods, descending from the great Usermaatre Ramesses to his son Baenre Merenptah, from Baenre to his son Userkheperure Seti, and from Userkheperure to the rightful heir of the throne of the Two Lands, Seti-Merenptah. The one they call Menmire Amenmesse, elder son of Baenre, was an anomaly, a pretender who tore the Kingdoms apart, and his son after him called Akhenre Siptah. Neither Menmire nor Akhenre are legitimate kings, but the issue of the loins of Userkheperure has passed from the earth, and Kemet is without a king.

I cannot accept Akhenre, and I have made my position clear. I have allowed this pretender to sit on the throne only because the true king was too young to take up the throne in his own right. His mother, Queen Tausret, Great Wife of Userkheperure, should have exercised what power she had to become regent in her son's name. It has been done before, most notably when Maatkare Hatshepsut ruled as regent for Menkheperre Djetmose--and I would have accepted that without question.

Instead, she gave in to traitors and allowed the pretender's son Siptah to be anointed king, although with her retaining some control as regent. But now, her son lies dead and the legitimate line of Ramesses has come to an end. What is to become of the Two Lands? I am not sure that I can continue to serve Akhenre Siptah now that all hope of the true succession has vanished. I think I must resign as General of the Southern Army and retire to my estates with my wife and son.

I called them to me that I might explain my position and do them the courtesy of making them a part of my deliberations.

"Beloved Tiy-Merenese, wife of my youth and keeper of my heart, sit beside me. Ramesses, strong issue of my loins, come stand where I can take strength from your countenance. I have news to impart that must affect our family greatly, and I wish you to hear it from my lips first."

"Then speak, husband, for I am a loving and dutiful wife and will follow where you lead."

"And I shall always be your strong right hand, father. Tell us your news."

I felt a flood of warmth in my chest at these words. Could any man hope for a more loving wife or dutiful son?

"Know then that Prince Seti-Merenptah, Heir to the throne of Kemet, and indeed the rightful heir of Userkheperure Seti, is dead. The usurper Siptah is now firmly in place with no legitimate issue to supplant him. You know I have always been loyal to the last legitimate king of the House of Ramesses, Userkheperure, and I have suffered the presence of the usurper solely because the rightful heir would one day take up the heka and nekhakha of kingly authority, but now he is dead and I can serve the usurper no more."

"What do you mean, husband?" Tiy-Merenese asked.

"I must resign my position and go into retirement. It will mean we will have less income and must dismiss many of our servants, but I am sure we will, in time, be able to live quite comfortably. Our estates are small but productive."

My wife sighed, but gave me a brave smile. "If that is what you have decided, husband, then we shall obey."

I looked at my son standing silently in front of me, and saw the frown on his brow. Rising thirty inundations now, he was a mature man with his own firm views on the world--views that I wanted to hear, yet he stood there saying nothing.

"Well, Ramesses, have you nothing to say?"

"Forgive me, father, but I thought you had not yet finished speaking. I felt certain that the words of despair and defeat that dripped from your lips were to be followed by a message of hope for the future."

I bristled at the disrespect in my son's voice. "I have told you of our future," I said. "It lies on our estates."

"That is a future for peasants and farmers," Ramesses said. "You are a son of the great Usermaatre and a soldier of note. I would not have believed you would run from your fate when the will of the gods is written plain before you."

"How dare you?" I asked, fury rising in me.

"My son, that is no way to speak to your father," Tiy-Merenese said. "Fall on your knees at once and beg his forgiveness."

Ramesses stared at me, determination written upon his face. "Well, father, what is it you desire? My apologies for my outspokenness or will you hear me out?"

I choked back my anger and said, "Speak then. I will hear you."

"Father, I have ever been a faithful and loyal son, willing to spend my days in your shadow as you rose to greatness under the kings of Kemet. I know you for the steadfast man of principle you are and I honour you for it. You have served the kings of Kemet as a soldier, as an officer, as legion commander, and as General of the Southern Army, swearing allegiance to every legitimate scion of the great Usermaatre.

"Therefore it grieves me to hear you say that now, as Kemet enters into its most grievous time, when the last legitimate king has died and that his infant son has died without issue, you will let a usurper and pretender sit upon the throne unchallenged. This is not the father I know and love.

"If I have offended you, father, then I will remove myself from your presence and go to fight the pretender with whatever loyal men I can find in the Kingdoms. But I cannot go to our estates and raise cattle, tend vineyards, and while away my days eating and drinking, leaving our beloved Kemet to fester under the heel of the pretender and his uncle."

I sat silent while I digested his words, and Ramesses stood proudly in front of me, challenging me. There was some truth in what he said, but he had not thought it through.

"You have given me a young man's response," I said mildly. "But I am old and look upon retirement with favourable eyes. What would you have me do, son of my loins?"

"You are a leader of men and control an army second to none. Rise up and overthrow this Siptah and his Amorite uncle, Bay. You will earn the thanks of all Kemet."

"For plunging the Kingdoms back into civil war, brother against brother? No one would thank me for that. Besides, to what end would I fight? Who would I replace on the throne once Siptah and Bay have gone?"

He hesitated. "Queen Tausret is regent and was Userkheperure's Great Wife and God's Wife of Amun..."

"But she is not king and can never be," I said. "Women may be many things, including regent during the minority of their royal sons, but they can never be king."

"Maatkare Hatshepsut was," Ramesses said, reminding me of my previous thoughts.

"Different times," I countered. "Besides, look what happened to her, overthrown and all but forgotten except as an object lesson not to let women grow too powerful."

"Then someone else."

"Who?" I asked. "You would cast down the present king without having anyone else to step up and take over?"

"There is somebody. Surely you can see that?"

"Userkheperure Seti was the last legitimate king of the House of Ramesses," I declared. "There is no other, so let that be an end of it."

"So you will just let Siptah become full king and let Kemet suffer under the ministrations of Bay when there is an obvious solution?"

"What obvious solution?" I asked.

"Seize the throne for yourself."

I stared at my son, my heart gripped with horror, but a feeling of ex-citement growing in me at the thought. I knew what it was like to go into battle at the head of an army--I had even worn the blue leather war crown as a ruse--but this was not some play-acting, some subterfuge, he was talk-ing about. This was real, and it was madness.

"Are you mad?"

"Why not, father? You are a son of Usermaatre Ramesses, just like Baenre Merenptah was. When the line of the legitimate heir dies out, the line of the next son takes his place. You are a younger brother of Baenre, and now that his legitimate son and grandson have died without issue, it is your duty to become king. Reach out your hand for the throne and thou-sands will flock to your banner. Even Queen Tausret will not oppose you once she sees the legitimacy of your claim."

"My mother was a mere concubine," I said.

"Forget her," Ramesses countered. "You spring from the loins of Us-ermaatre and his heart beats within you."

"There are other sons..."

"A hundred sons and grandsons and great-grandsons, for your father was prolific as befitted the Bull of Heru, but none of them are as capable as you. They are low-ranking government officials, or scribes or priests. Per-haps a few are even soldiers, but none command at legion level and none are General of the Armies--save you. Father, can you not see that you are best qualified to rule Kemet now that the line of Userkheperure is dead? Mother, speak to him."

"Our son is right, husband," Tiy-Merenese said. "The gods have handed you the throne. All you have to do is reach out and take it."

I shook my head, feeling overwhelmed at the thought. I had dedicated my life to the service of the kings of Kemet, knowing that my own position as one of the lesser sons of Usermaatre precluded me from the succession. It was never mine and it never entered my consideration, though I admit that once or twice I had felt that I could do as well as the king. Now the throne beckoned me, but could I take that final step and overthrow a lifetime of obedience?

"I never thought to be king," I said. "I don't know that I could be one."

"Baenre Merenptah was thirteenth son of Usermaatre. He would never have considered the possibility of becoming king--yet he did. You are...what? Twentieth son? Thirtieth?"

"Something like that," I muttered.

"And even less likely to become king--yet you could be. Father, no one can force you, but think upon it, I beg you. I can think of no one more capable of being Lord of the Two Lands."

I sighed, feeling my feet being set on another path. Anxiety gripped me, but also excitement. "I will think on it," I said. And with that, my son Ramesses had to be content.

Chapter 34
Year 5 of Akhenre Siptah

An invitation came to the palace from the priests at Iunu, requesting that the Queen, as Regent, preside over the inauguration of a new shrine. Tausret declined, but suggested to the king that Bay should attend as he was high in the king's estimation. Siptah was very pleased with this suggestion and put it forward as his own idea, with the result that Bay willingly accepted. He may not have been so pleased to attend if he had thought that it was a way to separate him from the king's presence. Ament offered to accompany Bay with an honour guard of palace soldiers, and Bay reluctantly acceded to this offer providing it was Besenmut and a squad of the Ptah legion that accompanied them.

"He doesn't trust me," Ament said to Tausret.

The Queen laughed, warming Ament's heart. "Even Bay can show wisdom sometimes. Just make sure you get him alone at some point and question him. I need to be sure if he acted alone or with the acquiescence of the king."

"What will you be doing, my Lady?"

"I'll be talking to Siptah. I think I'll be able to work on him without Bay there to put words in his mouth."

"There's still not much you can do, even if the king did agree to it. He's above the law."

"Well, we'll see, won't we?"

Bay travelled by barge to Iunu, with Ament and a contingent of the Ptah legion crowding aboard the craft with them. Ament tried to talk to Bay during the short voyage downriver, but Besenmut made sure they were never alone.

"Why do you need to see him alone?" Besenmut demanded.

"That is my own business. Now will you withdraw and let us talk?"

"Chancellor Bay?"

Bay looked at Ament and yawned. "I cannot think of anything I wish to discuss with you, Ament. Go away and let me enjoy the breezes."

So Ament had no option but to withdraw. He spent the two days and a night cloistered with soldiers of the Ptah legion who looked at him askance as they had been told he was a traitor to King Akhenre.

It was scarcely better once they landed at Iunu, though here he could escape from the barbed comments of the soldiers and officers. The Set legion was based near Iunu, so he took the opportunity to inspect his men and spend some convivial time in the presence of his officers. The next day, Ament went back into the city and watched from a distance as Bay went about his official duties, meeting with the priests and officiating with them as the god was called down into his newly constructed stone home.

Bay attended a feast at the Hem-netjer of Atum's house, but Ament was not invited. He waited outside, wrapped in a woollen military cloak against the chill of the night, hoping to approach Bay as he walked back to his lodgings. Besenmut and his soldiers quickly surrounded the Chancellor as he left, though, and Ament was not able to get near to Bay. As the men marched away, Ament called after them, "I know who brought the basket to the palace garden." It was as if he had not spoken, and Ament returned to his own lodgings with his Set officers feeling quite dejected. In the morning, though, he was surprised when two junior officers of the Ptah legion turned up and demanded he accompany them.

"Where to?"

"Chancellor Bay demands your presence at once."

Ament nodded, but first issued instructions to the officers of Set, before accompanying the Ptah officers into the city again. An honour guard followed him and waited outside the temple of Atum. The forecourt of the temple was deserted; with soldiers turning away people at all the entrances. Besenmut met Ament and his two summoners and brought him to Bay in a shaded part of the forecourt.

"What did you mean by that comment about a basket?" Bay demanded.

Ament looked at Besenmut. "Send your lapdog away first."

"Commander Besenmut is a trusted confidant. You may talk in front of him."

"You are certain of that?" When Bay did not react, Ament shrugged. "Very well. You tried to have me killed, Bay. What did you hope to gain?"

Bay yawned. "I deny that. Do you have proof?"

"Maybe not enough to convince a judge."

"I thought not."

"Then there is the basket with the snake," Ament went on. "Your man was seen and recognised. When we catch him he will talk."

Bay's expression did not change, and Ament knew his bluff had failed. The man was probably already dead.

"What snake?" Besenmut demanded. "Are you accusing Lord Bay of complicity in the death of the Prince? How dare you? My lord, let me call my men and have this dog killed and his body thrown into the street. It would be no more than he deserves."

"I might point out that the Set legion followed me into the city and they are more than a match for these Ptah soldiers."

"You would already be dead by the time they got here," Besenmut sneered.

"Then you would shortly follow me, as would Chancellor Bay and any other who opposed them. They have their orders."

"What is it you want?" Bay asked.

"A private talk, no more."

Bay thought for a few moments and then spoke to Besenmut. "Remain in sight but withdraw out of earshot, you and your men."

"My Lord, I must protest. He means you harm."

"Then search him first to make sure he has no weapon."

Ament allowed himself to be searched and straightened his clothing as he watched Besenmut and his soldiers march away. Then he turned back to Bay with a hostile stare.

"You may deny it, Chancellor, but we both know you tried to poison me and that you killed Prince Seti-Merenptah."

"Actually, I do deny it--that I did those things myself, by my own hand. I wish I had as you would certainly be dead by now, but in both cases I have to admit I only caused them to happen."

"You admit it?"

"Why not? We both know I stand to gain everything."

"But now that I know..."

"You will be able to do nothing. Bring charges against me and you will see. The king will dismiss them out of hand." Bay smiled and watched Ament. "By all rights you should be dead, Commander. That was a very virulent poison. Still, it will not matter soon. Another month or so and the king will demand of the Council that the regent is dismissed. They will grant it, I feel sure, and then the Queen will retire to her estates and you...well, there will be no one left to protect you."

"You are so certain of success?"

"Oh, yes. I know who is for me and who is against. I have the numbers in the King's Council and in the army. There is nothing you or the Queen can do."

"Then why wait a month or two? Why not act now?"

"The king turns fifteen in a month's time. There are some that might argue that a regent is needed until then, but none will argue that beyond then--especially when the king raises me to the status of God's Father and Tjaty of both kingdoms. He might even make me Heir until he produces a son of his own body."

"You mean to be king. How long will Akhenre survive your elevation?"

Bay just smiled.

"What if I tell people of your ambitions? Of what you have already done?"

"Who would believe you? Accuse me and I will deny it and counter charge you with spreading dissension and treason. The king will support me, I assure you of that."

"Queen Tausret..."

"Will shortly be powerless. She has already lost her reason for living and will soon find her regency stripped from her. After that, she is nothing without the king's permission, and the king will do as I say."

Bay beckoned to Besenmut. "Keep Commander Ament under guard until I have left the city, and then release him. The Queen's dog is now toothless."

"He does still command the Set legion."

"Hmm." Bay thought for a moment. "Who is your most trusted officer here in Iunu?"

"Leader of Fifty Wenemef, my Lord."

Bay barked a short laugh. "It is his lucky day. I will write out an order raising him to the rank of legion commander. He will assume command of the Set legion. Satisfied?"

"If you say so, my Lord, but may I have Ament killed?"

"No, I want him to witness my final victory, but if it pleases you, you may kill him after that."

"Thank you, my Lord. I shall look forward to it."

Queen Tausret called informally on Siptah while he ate on a wide shaded veranda overlooking the Great River. A pleasantly cool north wind blew, ruffling the water and swaying the tops of the palm trees. Servants stood around the king's table attentive to his needs and a small group of entertainers played music and danced for the king's pleasure. Three young women plucked on stringed instruments or shook a sistrum, while two girls, nubile and naked save for a thin girdle round their waists, swayed and stepped in time with the music.

Siptah scowled when Tausret appeared, and threw down the duck leg he had been gnawing on. He wiped his hands on a crumpled linen cloth and stared at the approaching regent.

"What do you want?"

"I think we need to talk. In private."

"So talk. There's nothing of interest you cannot say in front of the servants."

"It concerns your Uncle Bay and certain actions he has taken recently that threaten to destabilise the Kingdoms. If you want to talk about that openly, we can do so, but the gossip will be all over the city by sunset and I dare say Bay will not be pleased."

"Oh, very well. Get out, all of you."

The servants bowed and left quickly, while the musicians ceased in a discordant flurry and the naked girls fled. Siptah waved a hand toward a chair and selected a ripe fig, inspecting the skin for blemishes.

"What do you want to say? Know that anything you say will be reported to Bay."

"You rely on him for everything, do you? It makes me wonder who really rules Kemet."

"You are impertinent, Lady. I am the king, and I rule Kemet."

"Or at least as much as I let you."

Siptah glared at Tausret and bit into the fig. "Have you come here just to insult me then? You will not always be regent, you know."

"Is that what Bay tells you? He drips poisoned words in your ear."

Siptah shifted in his chair and looked away, chewing on the piece of fruit.

"Speaking of poison," Tausret went on, "you want to be careful what you lend your name to."

"I don't know what you mean."

"Don't you?" Tausret stared at the young king who refused to meet her gaze. "Your uncle and trusted adviser Bay had poison put into some honey cakes intended for Commander Ament and...and my son. It was only by great good fortune that the scheme did not succeed."

"I don't believe you."

"Shall I send for the physician who treated Ament? He tested the cakes on a dog. It quickly died in agony."

"Not that. I don't believe Bay had anything to do with it."

"Then there is the matter of the snake, the cobra in the basket that killed my only son." Tausret's voice quivered as she spoke but she forced down her emotions, determined to carry through her plans dispassionately.

"I...I don't know what you mean."

"No? I understood that Bay confided in you. Did he not discuss with you the need to remove me and my son before I could act to put my son on the throne?"

Siptah's lips quivered. "How...how dare you accuse me of that? I had nothing to do with it."

"My sources say differently." Tausret leaned forward and studied Siptah's face intently. "Not even a king can kill innocent children with impunity. When the army and nobles hear of this they will rise up and overthrow you. Even your supporters will disown you. You will go to prison at the very least and end your days in squalor and misery. Do you see now where Bay's advice has led you? You have become a child murderer and the gods will curse you."

"No. I had nothing to do with that, with the death of your son. Bay told me...but I didn't agree with it." Siptah shifted uncomfortably on his chair and averted his eyes from Tausret's face.

"Are you telling me that Bay acted alone in the killing of my son?"

"I didn't have anything to do with that, I swear."

"So Bay acted alone? Without your knowledge and permission?"

"Yes. Yes, he must have." Siptah's eyes glistened as he stared back at the Regent. "I didn't tell him to...to do that...to do anything. If he did anything it was without my knowledge."

"Do you regret the death of my son? Of my innocent child?"

"Yes, of course. It was Bay, I tell you, not me."

"Then Bay is guilty of murder. Do you accept that?"

"I...I suppose so."

"What is the penalty for murder?"

Siptah went pale. "No. He is my uncle and I love him. I won't allow it."

"If you do not, people will believe you had a hand in it. He must be punished."

"I will not execute him."

Tausret leaned back in her chair, her look now more one of curiosity than accusation. "What punishment then? He must be punished; you do realise that?"

"I suppose so, but I will not have him harmed. He is my mother's brother."

"It is your duty to uphold the law. I could have him arraigned before you and tried officially. You would have to exact some severe penalty then. Or there might be something else we could do."

Siptah looked up. "What?"

"Nothing will bring my son back from the dead, and such is my love for Kemet that I do not desire to see chaos descend on the land. Bay is the one responsible. He is the one offering malicious advice. Have him stripped of his offices and sent to one of his estates, never to take part in any aspect of government again. I would be satisfied with that."

"Never?" Siptah queried. "I could not ask him for advice?"

"Soon you will not need anyone's advice. In another month, I will step down as Regent and let you rule by yourself. You will need neither Bay nor me."

"Full king? Without you telling me what to do all the time?" Siptah's eyes gleamed with growing excitement.

"That's right. Exile Bay to one of his estates and strip him of any influence, and I will be content."

"I...I'll need to think on it."

"No. Bay will return from Iunu in a day or two, and once he hears of this, there is no telling what he might do. This happens now or not at all. In the event you do not agree to act immediately, I shall present Bay's guilt and your complicity to the full Council while I am still Regent and depose you. It is your choice...Son of Re."

Siptah struggled to control facial expressions of unease and fear. "I shall have a scribe draw up the document."

"No need. I have already had one drawn up. All it requires is your official seal. Send for the seal and Tjaty Mentu to witness it, and we can be done."

"What does your document say?"

"Just what we discussed." Tausret drew out a rolled up scroll from her robes and, pushing the dishes aside, unrolled it on the table. "You see?"

'Know this,' it read, 'that Ramesse Kha'amen-teru Bay, Chancellor and Treasurer of all Kemet, has forfeited the love and trust of his king, Akhenre Siptah, Son of Re, Lord of the Two Lands, Life! Prosperity! Health! He is forthwith to be stripped of his offices, titles, and chattels, and be confined under guard in the only estate left to him, namely that one in the city of Per-Bast, there to await such fate as the king shall decide upon.

'Dated in the royal palace of Men-nefer, on this twenty-second day of Shemu III, Year Five of the reign of Akhenre Siptah, Life! Prosperity! Health!'

Tjaty Mentu arrived, with the royal seal and, having been prepared by Tausret for this eventuality, affixed the seal to the document and had the king add the symbols for his throne name just above the seal.

"There, that's done," Tausret said, rolling up the scroll and handing it to Mentu. "I shall enact this ruling as soon as Bay returns from Iunu. May I suggest, Son of Re, that you spare yourself any unpleasantness that might arise from the arrest by absenting yourself from the palace for a few days?"

Siptah nodded. "Yes, I shall go upriver and hunt wildfowl in the reed beds. Send word to me when everything is complete."

Chapter 35
Year 5 of Akhenre Siptah

Bay arrived back in Men-nefer the next day and was a little chagrined that his nephew had not awaited his return. He shrugged his shoulders when told the king had gone hunting wildfowl and would be back in a few days. Ament arrived the day after and went straight in to see the queen.

"He admitted everything to me, but defied me to prove any of it. On top of that, he signed an order stripping me of my command and handing it to Wenemef, some creature of Besenmut."

"That is easily overturned," Tausret said. "I shall send an official document north immediately, ordering that Wenemef be arrested and that the legion come down to Men-nefer with all speed."

"Has something happened, my Lady?"

"Indeed it has. Siptah as good as admitted he knew of the killing, but blamed it all on Bay. I bullied him a bit, pretending that we had proof and he signed Bay's arrest warrant."

"Death?"

"No, he would not agree to death, but that little fact will not stop me. Bay ordered my son to be killed and I will have my revenge."

"Unless he is killed he will find a way back into the king's favour. Siptah is weak and malleable."

"That is taken care of. There was room on the arrest document to add the death penalty," Tausret said. She went to a chest by a wall and opened it, taking out a scroll. "See for yourself."

Ament unrolled the scroll and looked at the cursive writing by the Queen's scribe. He disregarded the usual honorifics and read the main text carefully. "It says he is stripped of his titles and property and is to be confined on his estate awaiting the king's pleasure...then you have added the death penalty. It doesn't read well. As it stands it is fairly obvious the death part has been added. I mean, why stipulate confinement on his estate if he's going to be killed?"

"It won't matter. The Council will accept his death after the event. They won't be shown it until he's dead."

Ament grunted and turned his attention back to the document. After a few moments he nodded. "There might be a way to make it appear more legitimate," he said. "All you need is a conditional phrase inserted here...I think there might be room if your scribe is careful."

"Saying what?"

"Something like, 'If the prisoner resists arrest, he is to be executed immediately.' Then you have Bay stripped of his titles and property, confined on his estate unless he resists arrest, at which point he is to be executed. And, of course, he will resist arrest. It should work, and will certainly look more legitimate, though the king will know the difference immediately."

"By the time he sees it, it will be too late."

"He could still cause trouble."

"Bay is his main support. With him gone there is little he can do. I will still be regent and I can overrule any of his commands."

"Unless he calls upon Besenmut and the Ptah legion," Ament said. "Besenmut is Bay's man, bought and paid for. A single legion could take the city and have you killed."

"All the more reason for the loyal Set legion to be here then. Commander Ament, you will wait until the Set legion is here, at which time you will arrest Bay and execute him, and at the same time, neutralise Besenmut. How you do that is up to you. Agreed?"

"Your word is my command, my Lady." Ament grinned. "My pleasure too."

Two days later, the scout chariots of the Set legion appeared on the east bank of the river, and Ament took a ferry over to meet with them. He, and the chariots, raced off into the northeast where the main body of the legion was marching steadily toward the capital.

"Wenemef is under arrest?" were his first words to his deputy commander Mose.

"Yes sir, along with a squad of his men. As soon as orders came from the Regent."

"Good. Kill them at once."

Mose snapped off the necessary instructions and soldiers raced to carry out the orders. "What's happening, Commander?" he asked. "Even on the march, we hear rumours."

"Chancellor Bay had the young Prince assassinated, and plans to topple the regent. We're going to make sure he fails in that at least."

Mose looked worried. "Bay has the Ptah legion in his fist. Besenmut has been his dog for some time now...Emsaf of Heru too."

"Heru is in the north, and only Ptah is in the city. I'm counting on you to be able to neutralise them."

A slow grin spread over the deputy's face. "We'll go through them like shit through a goose, sir. I take it we can use force?"

"If necessary, but try to avoid undue bloodshed."

"And Bay?"

"Arrested, then executed, but only on my command."

The Set legion resumed its march and later that day arrived on the plains across the river from Men-nefer. Mose immediately started ferrying the legion across in small boats, while Ament took a squad across immediately and went in search of Bay. He found him in the Treasury offices, going through accounts with officials and scribes.

Bay looked up at Ament and then past him as the soldiers entered the room. "Couldn't stay away eh, Ament? What do you think you're doing now, with these soldiers?"

"Huni," Ament said to the squad leader, and pointing at the officials and scribes. "Clear these men from the room." To Bay he said, "You're under arrest."

Bay stared, and then laughed. "You're a fool. You have no power over me. When the king hears, he'll have your head."

"By the time the king hears, you'll have lost yours."

Bay went pale, but held out his hand. "No arrest warrant is legal without the king's seal. I demand to see it."

Ament took the scroll out and opened it so Bay could read the warrant. Bay peered at the script, relief flowing over his face as he read.

"This says you are to take me into custody. It says nothing about having my head unless I resist arrest." He bared his teeth in a humourless smile. "I have no intention of resisting arrest. I don't need to. The king will restore me when he returns from his hunting trip."

"Whatever you say, Chancellor...ah no, that's right, you are stripped of your titles, so you may no longer be addressed as Chancellor. So, Bay, please accompany Huni here, while I prepare your accommodations."

The squad marched Bay out into the hallways of the palace and set off in the direction of the main entrance. Servants stared and drew back as the soldiers tramped by and several ducked aside and ran. They were approaching the entrance when they heard the sounds of running feet, shouted commands and the clatter of arms. Fifty Ptah legion soldiers poured out in front of Ament's squad and blocked their way with spears levelled.

Commander Besenmut pushed to the front. "Surrender, Commander Ament. You have failed in your attempt to rebel against the legal authority of Kemet."

"Stand back, Besenmut," Ament replied. "I have here a warrant for the arrest of Bay. You would do well not to interfere. Now stand aside."

"Or what? You have a mere squad of men and we outnumber you."

"Huni," Ament said in a clear, calm voice. "Draw your sword and stand behind the prisoner. If he takes a single step or if Commander Besenmut and his men take a step forward, you are to kill the prisoner at once. Do you understand?"

"Yes, sir." Huni drew his copper sword with a whisper of metal against leather and stepped behind Bay.

"Don't be a fool, Ament," Besenmut said. "Surrender now and you could still get out of this alive."

"And I repeat, stand aside, or Bay dies."

"You are bluffing. You would not dare kill the Chancellor."

"No longer Chancellor," Ament replied. "The arrest warrant strips him of all titles and allows me to kill him if he tries to escape. I would interpret an attempt to rescue him as an escape."

"I don't believe you. The king would never sanction the arrest of his uncle."

"Then come and see for yourself." When Besenmut stayed where he was, Ament laughed. "Don't you trust me, Besenmut? I swear by the gods you have safe passage to come and read the warrant."

"I'm not afraid of you," Besenmut growled. He stalked forward, pushing a couple of Ament's men aside. As he reached Bay, he stopped and spoke to the man. "You are well, my Lord? They have not ill-treated you?"

"I am well; Besenmut," Bay said, "but I have need of you and your men today."

"You may count on me, my Lord."

"I'm waiting," Ament said. "I gave you safe passage to read the warrant, not stand around gossiping with a traitor."

"You will pay for your insults," Besenmut replied. He nodded at Bay and stepped past him. "Show me this warrant."

Ament unrolled it and held it up for the Ptah commander to read.

"That is an obvious forgery."

"It has the king's seal on it," Ament pointed out. "A document with the king's seal attached can only be legal. You know that."

Besenmut looked closer at the seal and grunted. "Perhaps the king was unaware his seal was being used for this purpose."

"Then you may ask him when he returns." Ament rolled up the scroll and handed it to a soldier. "In the meantime, I will obey my orders."

The Ptah Commander scowled. "Where are you taking him?"

"As the warrant commands, to his estate at Per-Bast, there to await his majesty's pleasure. I have a barge standing by to transport him."

"Do not let him take me, Besenmut," Bay said in a low voice. "I fear for my life."

"I shall not desert you, my Lord." Besenmut fixed Ament with a determined stare. "I and my men will accompany you to Per-Bast to ensure the Chancellor's safe arrival."

"May I see your orders to that effect, Commander?" Ament asked.

"The Chancellor's command will suffice. Do you so command, my Lord?"

"Unfortunately," Ament murmured, smiling, "this man is no longer Chancellor. He was stripped of his titles the moment he was taken into custody. His words no longer carry any weight." He shrugged his shoulders. "You could seek the permission of the Regent, if you desire."

Besenmut ground his teeth as he looked about him at the determined men in the squad of Set soldiers. "I still outnumber you," he rasped. "If I give the word, you will all die."

"And if you give the word, Bay dies first. How will that serve your master?"

Besenmut swore under his breath. "You will not take Lord Bay out of the palace. My men will offer no violence, nor try to release Lord Bay, so there is no attempt to free him--note that, Ament. If you harm Lord Bay, you will answer for it to the king, I promise you that."

"So we just stand here?" Ament asked.

"All day and night, if that is what it takes."

"Oh, it won't take that long. Already I can hear the sound of my men approaching. The full Set legion, Besenmut, brought down from Iunu on the orders of the Regent. Now you are outnumbered."

The Set legion marched into the entrance of the palace with weapons drawn, scattering the servants, officials and palace guards. Parahotep, the Captain of the Guard put up a show of objecting to the legion's presence but backed down when he saw the arrest warrant. Besenmut and his fifty men had no option but to stand aside, and Ament marched Bay out into the street, surrounded by soldiers with their weapons at the ready. The people of Men-nefer looked on, amazed at the unexpected sight of a high official in custody, but made no move to interfere.

Bay was marched down to the waterfront, where Besenmut made one last attempt to rescue Bay. As soon as Ament had left the palace, he had sent runners to gather the Ptah legion, and his men now crowded the streets near the river.

Ament turned his men to face the Ptah legion, and had them beat their swords on their leather shields, raising a fearsome clamour. The Ptah legion, soft from city life, were reluctant to move forward, and Ament took advantage of their indecision to board the barge with his prisoner and Huni's squad.

The barge eased away from the dock, and the oarsmen guided the craft out into the current. Ament waved to his deputy Mose, who immediately stood his men down, offering no resistance to Besenmut. There was nothing the Ptah commander could do now, so he too dismissed his men, and stood staring after the receding barge carrying his Lord Bay.

Ament directed the barge into the branch of the river that flowed past Per-Bast, and then, out of sight of any habitation, he ordered the barge put in to shore, nosing up against the reed-lined bank where lush grassy meadows spread out before them.

"Why are we going ashore?" Bay asked. "Is this where you kill me?"

"Do you deny you deserve death? Seti-Merenptah died an agonising death in the name of your ambition. Well, that heinous act will be avenged today."

Bay shrugged. "Have you given any thought to what the king will say when he finds out you have killed me?"

"He put his seal on the order."

The barge nudged the grassy bank and swung gently alongside. Sailors leapt onto the shore with ropes and hammered in stakes to hold the barge in place. Others secured a gangplank between craft and land, bridging the small marshy gap on the water's edge.

"Perhaps he did," Bay commented, "and perhaps he did not really know what he was agreeing to. Either way, I am certain he will regret his action and order my return from exile. What will your excuse be when you tell him you killed me?"

"That you tried to escape. What else?"

"But these men know the truth." Bay raised his voice and called out so everyone on board could hear him. "Good people, come to my help. This man intends to kill me, against the wishes of the king. Help me and I will pay you much gold, ignore me and the wrath of Akhenre Siptah will descend on you."

"Won't do you any good," Ament said. "These soldiers are from my Set legion, and the sailors are all loyal to Queen Tausret, whose innocent son you so callously slaughtered. Now, if you would please go ashore, we'll do what must be done." He took Bay's arm and started moving him toward the gangplank.

Bay pulled back, and a note of desperation crept into his voice. "I can pay you gold, Ament. A lot of gold. I have the treasury of the Kingdoms at my disposal."

"No longer, Bay. Your offices were stripped from you, remember?"

"I have private resources..."

Ament swung Bay round to face him. He leaned close and spoke quietly. "There is not enough gold in the Two Lands to ransom your life, Bay. You lost all right to keep on living when you ordered Seti-Merenptah's death. Make your peace with the gods as best you may, because shortly you will be in the underworld facing their judgment. What do you think will happen when they weigh your heart against the Feather of Truth?"

Bay stumbled and almost fell when he came off the end of the gangplank, but he steadied himself and looked around. He tensed for a moment when he saw the open fields around him and gathered his strength, but the presence of alert soldiers convinced him escape was impossible. Instead, he shrugged and pretended a nonchalance he did not feel.

"Well, how is it to be?" he demanded of Ament. "Am I to be tortured or will you grant me a clean death?"

"You don't deserve a clean death, but I'll grant you one. Kneel and pray to your gods if you want."

"I have nothing to say to them that they don't already know," Bay replied. "I have lived my life in service of my king, and I die in the knowledge that I have secured a place for Akhenre Siptah on the throne of his father."

Ament nodded and gestured toward the grassy sward. "Enough, Bay. Kneel and let's get this over with."

216

"Is there nothing I can say to make you change your mind?" Bay waited, but when Ament gave no response, he sighed and sank to his knees in the grass. He looked up at Ament. "Who strikes the blow?" he asked. "You, Ament? You have always hated me."

"Hate should not strike the blow," Ament said after a few moments' thought. "Your death is a just punishment for your crimes against Kemet."

"I'll do it, sir," Huni said. "I'm a soldier and used to killing."

Ament nodded. "Do so then. Strike his head from his shoulders."

"It should be you, Ament. You command these..." Bay screamed in agony as Huni slashed at his neck with his copper sword. The blow hit a vertebra and failed to penetrate more than a finger width. Blood spurted and Bay collapsed onto his hands and knees, groaning loudly and shaking.

Huni swore and stepped to one side, slashing down again, but as Bay was moving, his blade missed its target and only opened up a great wound on the side of Bay's neck. He chopped down once more and caught the back of Bay's skull.

Bay screamed in agony again and Ament pushed Huni away, dragging out his own sword. He positioned himself, paused a moment, and then slashed downward, his own blade biting deep into Bay's neck and almost severing his head. The screams cut off abruptly.

"Sorry, sir," Huni muttered. He stooped and wiped his blade on the grass.

"He was an evil man, but I promised him a clean death," Ament said. "I broke my promise to him." He sighed and pointed to the corpse. "Finish cutting his head off."

Huni sawed at the tendons and vessels of Bay's neck and quickly cut through the flesh, severing the head completely. "What should we do with it, sir? Take it back to Men-nefer? It's usual to put the heads of traitors on a spike as a lesson for others."

"The man was uncle to the king, Huni. It would be an unnecessary cruelty to parade his uncle's head in front of him."

"Take him back for burial then?"

"No. Just throw the head and body into the river. Let the crocodiles bury him."

Chapter 36
Year 5 of Akhenre Siptah

King Akhenre Siptah returned from his hunting trip dispirited and nervous, unsure about what had happened in his absence. He avoided Queen Tausret and retired to his rooms after making desultory enquiries about Bay. Nobody was willing to tell him anything on that score except that the Chancellor had laid down his offices and duties and had vacated the palace under guard.

Then came a summons from the regent to attend a full Council meeting in the throne room. Siptah felt anger stir that he, the king, should be summoned, but he thrust the feeling away, not wanting to argue the point. Instead, he dressed in his royal finery and made sure he was in the throne room, seated on the gold and ebony throne, well before the appointed hour.

The Councillors entered, looked surprised to see the king already in attendance, and made their obeisance. Siptah greeted each one in turn, some more warmly than others and bade them take their seats while they waited for Tausret. As they sat in silence, Siptah looked them over, mentally sorting them as friend or foe, ally or enemy.

Tjaty Mentu--enemy; Commander Besenmut of the Ptah legion--friend; Commander Emsaf of the Heru legion--friend; General Iurudef of the Northern Army--possible friend; General Setnakhte of the Southern Army--enemy; Commander Ramesses of the Amun legion--enemy; Head Scribe Pepy--neither friend nor enemy; several assistant scribes that could be safely ignored; Captain of the Palace Guard Parahotep--possible friend; Assistant Treasurer Huy--unknown, possibly a friend. Siptah felt despair creeping over him. The Councillors were evenly split but if Huy was here, his uncle might not be appearing and the Queen and her dog had not yet put in an appearance. Their presence would surely tip the meeting against him.

Just why that would matter, Siptah did not know, but the balance of power had changed in the last few days. The young king shivered, but sat still, the Double Crown heavy on his head and the heka and nekhakha clammy in his sweating palms. His eyes looked toward the doors as he heard the tramp of feet outside, and then the doors were thrown open. Queen Tausret entered, with Commander Ament to her right side and a pace behind her. A score of soldiers spread out around the periphery of the room and stood at attention.

The Councillors rose to their feet as Tausret entered, and Siptah started to move with them until he caught himself and pressed back into the throne. He glowered at Tausret and Ament as they took their places in the circle of chairs and the throne room doors were closed. Tausret looked around at the other Councillors, nodding and smiling, whereas Ament stared hard, challenging each man.

"Thank you all for attending," Tausret said. "Despite this not being the appointed time for a Council meeting, I am grateful that so many of you could be here at such short notice. It is for an important reason..."

"Your pardon, Regent," Besenmut interrupted. "But I do not see Chancellor Bay here. Should we not wait until he arrives?"

"As you already know, Commander," Ament said. "Bay has been stripped of his titles and has been exiled from the palace."

"We heard the rumours when we arrived in the city," Setnakhte said. "It is true then?"

"True enough," Emsaf said, "but we have not been told the reason."

"I saw the arrest warrant," Besenmut said. "It talked of forfeiting the king's love and trust but was silent as to the actual charges."

"I cannot believe it," Parahotep said. "Bay loved the king, more than anyone, for he was kin to the god, and we know the king loved him in return. I can think of no deed he would commit that would make the king love him less."

"We, as King's Councillors, have a right to hear of what Bay is accused," Tjaty Mentu said.

"That is why we are gathered here," Tausret said. "A little patience and all will be revealed."

General Iurudef stood and faced the throne. "Son of Re, is it true that the one who was Chancellor Bay has sinned against you and forfeited your love and trust?"

Siptah shifted uncomfortably on his throne and let his symbols of kingly authority sag. He looked at Tausret but did not say anything.

"The king put his seal onto the arrest warrant," Tausret said. "There is no need to question the king further."

"Then will you answer, my Lady?"

Tausret bowed her head for a moment and then looked up. "Commander Ament will speak for me."

Ament rose to his feet and looked round the assembled Councillors. "This will be painful for Queen Tausret and, indeed, for any other person who loved the heir to the throne, Prince Seti-Merenptah. As you all know, the Prince was struck down and killed by a cobra while playing in the palace ground. What you may not know is that a man brought that cobra into the palace gardens and released it by the pond where the Prince liked to play. The facts are inescapable; the Prince was assassinated."

"And what has this to do with Chancellor Bay?" Emsaf asked.

"Bay was the man who ordered the cobra brought in."

Everyone started talking at once, asking questions, making statements, shouting the innocence of the king's uncle. Ament waited for silence to resume and then continued.

"The killing of the Prince followed hard on the heels of another attempt, this time by poisoning cakes sent to me, knowing I would share them with the Prince."

"You have proof of this?" Mentu asked.

Ament nodded. "As close as matters. Bay did not deny it when I confronted him."

"Why should he bother to deny it?" Besenmut protested. "It is arrant nonsense and I have no doubt Chancellor Bay thought the charge utterly contemptuous and beneath him."

"No longer Chancellor," Ramesses said.

Besenmut glared at the young commander. "A lot of accusations are being thrown around, blaming a man who has no chance of answering these charges."

"Then bring him in," Setnakhte said. "I would like to hear Bay deny these charges."

"He has been exiled from the city," Besenmut said. "False charges were laid against him--without proof--and now he cannot be questioned to get the truth of the matter. Ament knows. He was the one who took him out of the city to his Per-Bast estates."

"Then you must bring him back, Commander Ament," Setnakhte said. "We need to get to the bottom of this."

"I could bring him back if I could find him," Ament said, "but he would not be answering any questions."

"What do you mean you cannot find him?" Hori asked. "Is he not on his Per-Bast estate?"

Besenmut went pale. "By all the gods, he has killed him."

"Is this true, Commander Ament?" Setnakhte asked.

"Bay is dead," Ament confirmed.

Siptah leapt upright, throwing his regalia aside, his crown slipping and falling to the floor with a dull clunk. He took a step toward Ament and stumbled as his withered leg gave way. A scribe ran forward to support his king.

"You have killed my uncle?"

Ament bowed to his king. "Son of Re, I carried out the instructions on the warrant that was given me bearing the royal seal. I arrested Chancellor Bay, stripped him of his titles and conveyed him from the palace toward his estate at Per-Bast. On the way there, he attempted to escape and, as the warrant instructed, I executed him."

"You murdered him," Siptah cried, his face screwing up in grief. "I gave no permission for him to be killed. He is...he was my uncle...my family...and I love him. Where is this so-called warrant? Read it and you will see it said nothing about executing him."

"Show us the warrant," Besenmut demanded.

"You've already seen it," Ament countered. "Don't you remember what it said?"

"The rest of us need to see it," Mentu said. "Where is it?"

"The warrant was handed in to the Chief Scribe upon my return to the palace," Ament said.

"Pepy, do you have the warrant?" Setnakhte asked of the scribe.

"It has been filed, my lord," Pepy replied. "I could send someone for it." He dispatched a junior scribe to find the warrant.

"You have done this," Siptah accused, limping toward Tausret. "You could not stand it that I loved Bay and he had my ear. You were afraid of him, afraid that he was growing too powerful--so you had him killed."

Tausret watched the young king limping toward her and then stood, staring into his grief-reddened eyes. "You are overcome with regret and guilt, Son of Re, and for that I forgive you, but do not forget that my innocent son has also died, killed by this very man you claim to love. He admitted his guilt and was sentenced for it, by your order, Akhenre Siptah. If you now regret his death, do not think to blame others for it."

Siptah quailed in the face of the Queen's fury. "I...I didn't know that was in it," he muttered. He turned and retreated back to his throne where he sat with his face buried in his hands.

The scribe returned with the warrant, and the document was passed around so every man could see the instructions on the king's warrant.

"It does say he is to be executed if he attempts to escape," Ramesses said.

"And that is the king's seal," Mentu added. "I know, for I brought it into the king's presence myself and affixed it to that warrant. I gave it to the king for his mark to be made above it. It is genuine."

"You have reason to lie about it though, don't you?" Besenmut accused. "Ask yourself who stands to gain by this. It is the Queen and her cronies."

"Have a care, Commander," Setnakhte said. "Your accusations could be read as treasonous."

"But it is true, isn't it?" Besenmut insisted. "Bay was growing too powerful, so you had him removed."

Ament strode forward to stand before the throne. "Son of Re, does this man speak for you?"

Siptah looked up; his cheeks streaked with tears, and shook his head.

"This man has voiced treasonous accusations," Ament went on. "I demand his arrest."

"Son of Re..." Besenmut started, but was shouted down by Ament.

"Unless this is what you believe, Son of Re, you must order his arrest."

Siptah sighed and nodded. "I accuse no one," he whispered.

"You heard the king. Guards, arrest Commander Besenmut and confine him to await the king's pleasure."

The soldiers rushed forward and grabbed Besenmut, hustling him off toward the door while the other Councillors looked on with mixed reactions--some were horrified at what had just happened, others nodded their heads in agreement.

"Will you have me killed too, Ament?" Besenmut yelled as he was dragged away. "Am I to be executed because I oppose your ambitions?"

"What about you, Emsaf?" Ament asked as Besenmut's cries were cut off by the closing doors. "Everyone knows you were a confidant of the traitor Bay."

Commander Emsaf shook his head and seemed to shrink in his seat, as if to distance himself from his recent claims.

Ament looked around again. "Is there anyone else who believes Queen Tausret has acted improperly?"

"No one doubts the Queen," Setnakhte said. "I am satisfied she acted properly here."

"You all agree that Bay was executed under law? By order of the king?"

Siptah stared at Ament again, but said nothing. The Councillors looked at one another and slowly began to nod, offering their agreement.

"Then let a proclamation go out to all of Kemet, to every village, town and city between the southern borders of Kush and the borders with the Hittite, from the Ribu in the west to the desert tribes in the east. Let it be known that King Akhenre Siptah, Life! Prosperity! Health! issues this proclamation, dated in the royal palace of Men-nefer, on this twenty-seventh day of Shemu III, Year Five of the reign of Akhenre Siptah, Life! Prosperity! Health! that this day he has killed the Great Enemy Bay."

There was a profound silence in the throne room, broken only by the quiet sobbing of the king.

Chapter 37

Akhenre Siptah speaks:

It has come to pass as my Uncle Bay said it would. The Queen Regent and her dog have acted coldly and viciously to kill those closest to me and isolate me from the affections of my subjects and the protection of those whom I relied upon. My uncle Bay is dead, struck down by the Regent's dog himself, using a warrant that bore my seal but did not reflect my will. Yes, it has all the right phrases written upon it, but I know...I think...no, I know that the phrases that carried death were not there when I affixed my seal. They were added later, but how can I prove that? Even if I could prove it, to whom would I take my concerns? Bay is dead, Commander Besenmut is dead, and any others who had crowded around the throne in the hopes of favour or advancement have fled.

I am alone and afraid.

Yes, I know that it could be said I have brought this on myself. I could have refused to countenance the killing of Seti-Merenptah, but I was fighting for my life. The way Bay told it, the Regent was about to tip me off the throne and consecrate her own son in my place. A King of Kemet does not step down, and if he is removed from the throne his life span is reckoned in days. Look what happened to my father, Menmire Amenmesse. He was a legitimately anointed king, yet he was toppled and then killed. That would have been my fate too, if I had not acted. I had no choice; it was Seti-Merenptah's life or mine. It grieves me though that my Uncle Bay, my only close family member, had to pay the price, but he offered up his life for his king, sacrificed his own life for mine.

I honour him for it and would give him a royal burial if I could. He has a fine tomb in Ta-sekhet-ma'at that could swiftly be prepared for him, but his body is lost. Not content with murdering him, the Regent's dog threw his body in the river for the crocodiles and fish to eat. How can Bay possibly live again in the Field of Reeds without a body, without the necessary ceremonies and offerings. His shade will wander homeless and wailing for eternity.

I wake up in the night, tears streaming from my face, for he comes so often into my dreams, showing me his wounds and silently demanding justice. I would give him justice, but I don't know how. Before, I was a powerless king with a champion, someone to fight for me. Now I am just a powerless king.

Oh, the servants obey me readily enough--with the little things at least. If I command obedience on anything of note, though, they bow and hurry away to the Regent, and she gives me permission or not, as if I was a servant like them, and not a king. I am still required to lead the dawn services to the gods, for as king I am High Priest of every god, and I still sit in judgment in the law courts, but Tjaty Mentu relieves me of most of my duties there.

Queen Tausret came to see me unbidden the day after the Council meeting.

"You need to know what will now happen," she told me without preamble. She also did not use any of my titles or honorifics. "As you know, the agreement that you become king was a temporary affair that would last until my son Seti-Merenptah was old enough to assume the throne alongside you. He was your heir, and in due time would become sole king. Until the time of his ascension to the throne, I would act as Regent, making decisions for you and him. It was my intention that I would resign the regency at the end of this year and allow the two kings to rule in their own names.

"That has all changed," she went on. "I will not now resign the regency, but continue to rule Kemet in your name."

"If I was capable of ruling before, I am capable of ruling now," I pointed out.

"And I say not."

"I am nearly sixteen floods old," I said. "Old enough to be sole king. There is no reason for you to remain as regent."

"Except that I cannot trust you."

I stared at her, feeling righteous anger grow in me. "You doubt the word of your king?"

She smiled coldly. "I doubt the word of a boy who can be swayed by treasonous words. I doubt the word of a king who would sanction the slaughter of an innocent child."

"So what is to become of me?" I demanded.

"You will remain king for now, and I will continue to rule for you. You will carry out such priestly and kingly duties as I deem you are capable of performing. More than that, I will have to see."

She left me then, and I have been afraid ever since. I am to remain king 'for now', whatever that means. I fear it is what I think it is--that she means to raise up another to sit on the throne of Kemet in my place. But who is this incipient king? I can think of no one that has a claim to the throne, no one in the line of Baenre Merenptah. She must mean to look further afield then--among the numerous descendants of Usermaatre Ramesses. I cannot find out, for whom can I trust enough to ask?

What can I do? Queen Tausret plainly wants me to remain a figurehead, a king in name only while she rules Kemet and looks for my replacement. She wants me to remain a lonely and frightened boy; reliant on her servants and dogs, having no power of my own, but can I do anything else? I have few resources and no friends...yet, I am king. Surely even a figurehead king has some power? I can perform my duties to the best of my abilities, converse with the priests of every temple, show myself to be a man who holds the gods in high regard, and be as generous as I am able to every temple. I must show myself to be a good king, merciful and just in all my actions.

Such a plan is good, but it lacks one essential component--a king must be a fit and active man. During the festivals, a king is supposed to carry the paraphernalia of the god and run ahead of the god's barque during the holy processions through the city, but with my withered leg that is an impossibility. Up until now, I have had to forego that aspect of kingship or have another stand in for me. When the people see a weakling playing the part of king, they lose confidence in me, so I must do something to restore that confidence.

I cannot go to war, leading my armies into battle, for Tausret would not allow it--and Kemet is at peace right now--but there is something else. I can hunt, but not just any beast. I must hunt the royal lion, subdue it with an act of bravery that will raise my standing in the eyes of all men. My withered leg will mean nothing if I can show people that despite this infirmity I am a strong and capable huntsman, worthy of leading my people.

Perhaps then I can make a case for ruling alone.

Chapter 38
Year 6 of Akhenre Siptah

The inundation was late that year. Some eight days into the second month of Akhet, the Great River still flowed sluggishly with only a slight stain of discoloured water that was the harbinger for the flood that everyone looked for. Along with that stain came the news that Siptah was awaiting, a response to the word he had sent out to all the huntsmen of all the cities and towns within a three day barge trip from the capital. 'Search for lion' had been the command, and now word had come in from the Overseer of the Hunt in Henen-nesut on the eastern bank. Two male lions were wreaking havoc on the royal herds.

For a moment, Siptah toyed with the idea of sneaking out of the palace, but knew he risked humiliation if he tried and was caught. There was only one thing for it--he would have to try and convince the Regent to let him go. On past experience, it was unlikely she would let him hunt such dangerous beasts, but then again, he was older now and more accomplished. He set off to find the Queen and found her sitting with Ament under the shade of a blossoming tree in the palace gardens.

"Son of Re," Tausret said pleasantly as the king limped toward her. "It is good to see you outside. Will you sit with me?"

Ament rose to his feet and indicated the bench he had been sitting on. "Majesty."

Siptah sat down, not so much because he desired to sit next to the Queen, but because his leg pained him. Also, standing in the presence of the seated Regent lessened his status.

He came straight to the point. "Lady, I have received news that lions are plaguing the royal herds in Henen-nesut."

"Yes, we had heard the same," Tausret said. "I was just suggesting that Commander Ament should go there and kill them."

"They are royal beasts, Lady, and should be killed by a king."

"I daresay neither the cattle nor the herders will care who kills them," Ament said. "Majesty," he added as an afterthought.

"I would like to hunt them," Siptah declared.

Tausret looked at him for what seemed like a long time. "Have you come seeking my permission?"

Siptah clenched his jaw and looked away. "I should not have to seek permission from anyone to hunt in my own lands."

"I still rule Kemet in your name, and for your benefit. It does not hurt to ask."

"Lady, I have said I would like to hunt them. If you have little regard for the king of Kemet, you will refuse permission, but if you truly believe I am king, you will wish me good fortune."

"May the gods go with you," Tausret murmured.

Siptah's eyebrows rose. "You mean..."

"Providing you take due care, I have no objection if you go hunting li-on."

Siptah leapt up and almost fell as his leg lurched beneath him. Despite his determination to appear serious and calm, he grinned as he stammered his thanks.

"Do not thank me, Son of Re," Tausret said. "You are king and it is high time you hunted a lion."

The king's barge pulled out of the swift current and into a backwater in the lee of the eastern shore. Henen-nesut sprawled untidy from the low hills down to the water's edge, where a crowd was gathering by the city docks. The captain of the barge rapped out his orders and the rowers tugged once more on their oars and then raised them aloft, the water streaming from the red-painted wood. Perfectly timed, the barge surged forward and then lost way, drifting slowly in toward the dock. Sailors leapt ashore, carrying ropes, and secured the vessel as it delicately nudged the wooden dock. Woven linen ropes protected the paintwork on the royal barge, and now city men ran forward bearing lengths of brightly coloured cloth to drape over the sides of the barge to welcome their young king.

Siptah leaned on his cane and limped toward the gangplank. He hesitated for a moment and then plunged ahead down its short but narrow length, reaching the firmness of solid ground before he could lose his balance and risk humiliation. The city governor greeted him as did the High

Priest of Heryshef, the ram-headed Ruler of the Riverbanks, whose temple dominated the city.

"Greetings, Son of Re," said the Governor. "I was about to send out huntsmen to rid ourselves of the lions when I heard your Majesty was on the way here. We are honoured that you would attend to this matter yourself."

"I will need your huntsmen to guide me," Siptah said. He looked up at the sun to judge how much daylight was left. "Tomorrow morning at dawn."

"I am delighted that you will be able to sample our hospitality tonight, Son of Re."

"And perhaps you might offer at the temple of Heryshef?" asked the High Priest.

"Of course. I shall do that now."

Siptah limped, leaning on his cane, up the low hill to the temple of Heryshef and through the first pylon. The forecourt was small, and Siptah went further in with the High Priest beside him, through the second pylon and into the multi-columned hypostyle hall. Here, columns carved in the form of lotus stems topped with carved lotus blossoms supported the heavy stone ceiling, dimming the afternoon light to a dusky gloom. The public figure of the god awaited him here at the entrance to the shrine itself, a gigantic stone statue of a man, ram-headed and crowned. Siptah paused and then passed through into the torch-lit Holy of Holies where the priest presented him to the god, smaller and sheathed in gold. The king stood here in the presence of the god for some time, communing in silence--god to god--while the priest waited in silence. At last, Siptah finished and after bowing respectfully to the presence of Heryshef, limped out again into the late afternoon sunshine.

The Governor had ordered preparations to be made for a feast at his residence, where the officials and overseers of the city of Henen-nesut awaited the arrival of the king. The long drawn-out series of introductions was hurriedly brought to a close only when the king stifled a yawn. They moved on to the feast, with the city and surrounding farmland offering the finest produce the area could find.

Roasted beef, mutton and lamb was on the top of the menu, along with goose, duck, and a number of dishes that involved shredding the meat and cooking it with onions, leeks, garlic and a variety of spices. Siptah complimented the Governor on the cooks within his palace and arranged for the recipes of some that most took his fancy be sent to Men-nefer. Sweet dishes followed, tarts and puddings made from dates and figs mixed with honey and spices, pastes made from lentils and beans smeared on crusty bread fresh from the ovens, cheese and goose egg custard. Wine was in plentiful supply, as was beer, milk and fresh cool river water.

Siptah left the feast early, being tired after his day's activities, and wanting to be up early for the hunt. He was escorted to the Governor's own rooms, where the cool night breezes off the river provided a pleasant sleeping environment. The king slept without disturbance and awoke in the pre-dawn darkness. After bathing, dressing and being suitably perfumed and made-up by the Governor's servants, Siptah ate a light meal and was out in the palace courtyard, ready for the day, just as the first of the sun's rays tipped the tops of the palace in rosy and gold hues.

The king had arrived in Henen-nesut without hunting companions, as Siptah lacked friends, and in the aftermath of his uncle's demise, no longer felt he could fully trust the young men who hung about the court and offered up sycophantic platitudes. Some of the young men of Henen-nesut clamoured for the honour of joining the king on his hunt, and Siptah nodded his agreement, selecting Mentek, son of the Overseer of the City Granaries, and Raia, son of the Governor's Head Scribe. Both young men bowed deeply and then smirked at their companions who had not been selected.

Siptah led the hunting party out of the city, driving the royal hunting chariot which had been unloaded from the barge overnight. Mentek and Raia drove chariots of their own, and behind them trotted a detachment of soldiers, royal and local huntsmen, and a small procession of wagons containing everything the king could possibly need for a hunt likely to last for two or three days.

The huntsmen had informed the king that the lions had recently made a kill some three hours from the city, and such was Siptah's desire to get to grips with the beasts that he pushed his horses on and rapidly outdistanced his companions, with the exception of Mentek and Raia, and two huntsmen that had leapt onto their chariots when they saw them drawing away. Hours passed and the heat grew, but apart from one short stop to drink, they did not pause. Dust stuck to their sweat and caked their bodies, but Siptah revelled in it, welcoming the hardship. He felt the need to push himself, to make his mark once and for all.

I am sixteen now, he thought. *It is time I became the true king of all Kemet and these lions will be the perfect way to show them I am ready.*

One of the huntsmen now called ahead to the king and pointed off to one side. The king stopped and the huntsman bowed and pointed again.

"Over there, majesty. Where the pasture gives way to scrub. They made a kill two days ago."

They drove the chariots closer, then tied the horses to low scrub and walked over to an area of flattened and bloodstained grass and sand where the kill had taken place.

"See here, majesty, where one lion sprang onto the bull...and here where the bull ran, staggering under the weight of the lion. See his paw print, majesty? He is old and lame in the front left foot. And here..." the huntsmen ran a few paces, casting about and acting out the drama that had taken place. "Here the second lion waited and took the bull by the nose, bringing him down. He is younger and appears uninjured. They started to eat him here and then dragged the carcass this way...into the scrub and down here...toward that gully."

The huntsmen stopped and pointed toward an eroded gully choked with huge boulders. "We followed and saw the hindquarters of the bull poking out from behind a boulder, majesty, but when we moved closer, we heard this deep growl and knew the lions were laid up close to their kill and were watching us. So we came away and reported it."

"And this was how long ago?" Siptah asked.

"Day and an half, majesty."

"So they could have left already."

"I had a local herdsman keep an eye on it and he sent word this morning that they are still here, majesty. They won't move now, with the heat of the day coming on."

Siptah nodded and looked at the boulder-choked gully. "That is no place to hunt from a chariot," he said.

"We could wait until the other huntsmen arrive and have them beat toward us, driving the lions out into the open," Mentek said. "Then we could kill them from the chariots."

"Dangerous for the huntsmen," Raia commented.

"I agree," Siptah said. "And cowardly to drive such royal beasts as if they were cattle. No, we shall meet them on foot. Lead on," he told the huntsmen. "Find where they are lying up."

"Better to wait for the other huntsmen and soldiers, Son of Re," Mentek said. "There's only three of us with bows, and my spears. We might need some help."

"You can wait here if you like," Siptah replied, "but a king does not seek safety in the face of danger. Are you with me, Raia?"

"Of course, Son of Re. Where you lead, I will follow."

Siptah led, but slowly, limping along with his cane in one hand and the bow and sheaf of arrows in the other. Raia and the huntsmen followed close on his heels and after a moment, Mentek joined them, looking shamefaced. They approached the boulders and the huntsman who had seen the kill the day before lightly touched the king on his arm, dropping to one knee as Siptah turned to stare in disbelief at the man who had dared to touch him.

"Forgive me, majesty. I meant only that I should lead here as I know the way to where the bull's body lies."

Siptah frowned, and then nodded. "What is your name?" he asked.

"Bek, majesty."

"Well then, Bek, you are forgiven...this time. Lead on, and find me this lion."

"Majesty, remember there are two."

Bek moved ahead of the others, with the other huntsman, Nehi, creeping along some twenty paces to the side. They approached the boulders in almost complete silence, and Bek looked toward Nehi, who shook his head slightly before scrambling up onto one of the huge boulders. His naked feet gripped the rough stone, propelling him rapidly to the top. He peered over the edge and then slowly withdrew, turning carefully to face Bek and the royal party. Leaning back against the rock, he gesticulated with both hands, conveying his report to the other huntsman.

"He says the older lion is lying in the shade of a boulder about fifty paces beyond this one," Bek whispered. "He is awake but not alert."

"Which way is he facing?" Mentek asked.

More arm waving took place. "He faces the west."

"What about the younger lion?" Raia asked.

Bek waved his arms and Nehi answered in the same way.

"He says there is no sign of it."

"Good," Siptah whispered. "The lions have separated. We will kill the older one first and then pick up the track of the young one."

Bek signalled again to his companion on the rock. "Nehi will wait up there and distract the lion when we are in position. He will also shout if the second lion appears."

Siptah nodded his assent and limped off around the boulder field to the west, Mentek and Raia following close behind, Mentek with two flint-tipped spears and Raia with bow and arrows like the king. Bek carried nothing but the dagger at his belt. They rounded the large boulder and Siptah discarded his cane so he could shuffle bent double taking cover behind the lower boulders.

Bek raised his head slowly over the rim of the boulder they all crouched behind. Hardly moving, he eased his head over the edge, paused, and lowered it again.

"The lion faces us, Majesty," the old hunter whispered. "But his eyes open and close as if he would sleep in the heat of the day."

Siptah nodded and took an arrow from his sheath. "If I stand up, I will have a clear view of the beast?" he asked.

Bek hesitated. "Yes, Majesty, but it would be better if you moved to the end of this boulder and step out between it and the next one. You will have a clear view of the chest and flanks of the lion and can put an arrow into its chest, just behind its foreleg."

"What about us?" Mentek muttered. "Where should we be?"

"Raia can shoot over the top of the rock," Siptah said. "Mentek, stand with me and lend me your strength."

The king limped to the end of the boulder and eased his head around the end. He saw the lion lying half on its side with its head lowered on its forepaws. It faced the king's left and its eyes were closed. Siptah felt his breath coming faster as he contemplated the great tawny beast lying not twenty paces away. He nodded to Mentek and stepped out between the boulders, one hand on the other man's arm. The lion did not move, and Siptah fitted an arrow to the string of his bow with trembling hands. He raised the bow and sighted on the lion's flank, just behind its foreleg.

"Shoot, Majesty," Mentek breathed.

Siptah slowly lowered his bow. "He is asleep," he whispered. "It seems shameful to kill him while he sleeps."

He thought for a moment and then called softly, "Ho, Royal One, wake and meet your fate."

The lion was on its feet facing Siptah even before he had finished speaking. Siptah raised his bow and released his arrow at the beast now facing him, but the arrow, aimed at the lion's left eye missed, glancing off the bone of the skull. It roared with pain and crouched, ready to spring across the intervening space and crush this thing that had hurt it.

Then Raia loosed his arrow and missed, and Mentek fumbled his spear, taking several steps back. Bek yelled, and Nehi took up the cry, tossing pebbles from his vantage point on top of the first great boulder. The lion's head came round to search for this new threat and it half-turned, roaring its rage and defiance.

Siptah snatched another arrow from his sheath and raised the bow in a fluid movement, targeting the now exposed flank of the great lion. The arrow sped across the short distance and thwacked into the tawny hide just behind the foreleg, burying itself deep in the beast's side. Roaring, the lion rose up on its hind legs and then collapsed onto the sand. Its paws scrabbled for a few moments and then its great shaggy head fell back and it died.

Raia and Mentek cheered, the former leaping over the low boulder and racing across the hot sand toward the fallen beast, while Mentek strutted forward as if it had been his spear that brought down the lion instead of the king's arrow. Bek scrambled up on top of the rock but stopped when Nehi yelled. The huntsman looked toward his companion and saw his urgent gesticulations.

"Majesty, the second lion," Bek yelled.

The king and his two companions were in the open, in front of the slain lion, when the second, younger beast burst into view. It raced across the intervening space from where it had been lying up in the shade of another rock, and bore Raia down before the young man could even think of moving. Siptah clearly heard the man's skull crunch in the beast's jaws before it gathered itself again and leapt at him.

Siptah stumbled back and his withered leg gave way, spilling him to the ground. At once the lion was upon him and the relief and pride he had felt at the death of the older lion evaporated like water on hot desert sand. The jaws of the younger lion closed on his left shoulder, biting deeply as his hot blood spurted. He gagged as the hot stinking breath of the beast blew into his face and dimly he felt the great claws rip into him, but pain and even fear seemed to have fled along with his pride. It was as if the lion lay on another man, worrying at him like a tabby cat in the city granaries plays with the mouse it has caught. Siptah felt as if he was dreaming; that soon he would awaken and none of this would be real.

Voices cried out as if from a distance and a spear and then arrows flitted into view. He felt the lion's body shudder under the impact of these missiles, though the jaws only bit deeper, teeth grinding against bones. The lion growled deep in its throat, its shaggy mane brushed his face. His right hand came up and brushed the lion's flank, felt the muscles rippling beneath its hide and marvelled at it. Then the claws of the animal ripped his belly open and consciousness fled as pain belatedly washed over him.

"Is he dead?" Nehi whispered.

Bek knelt beside the torn and bloodied body of the king and laid a trembling hand on his chest, feeling for the faint movements of life within. "He lives, but I think not for long."

"What should we do?" Nehi asked. "The king will die and it is our fault. They will execute us."

"We cannot just leave him here." Bek looked up at Mentek. "You saw, sir. There was nothing we could have done."

"I tried," declared the young noble. "It was my spear that killed the lion."

"And my arrows," Bek said.

Nehi nodded his agreement to both claims, but addressed Mentek. "You are a nobleman, sir. Tell us what we must do."

Mentek stared at the body of his king and licked his lips, feeling resentment that such a decision should have been thrust upon him. "We...we must notify the court...and carry the body of the king back to Henen-nesut."

"The king still lives, sir, and we cannot easily carry him," Bek said. "His intestines will...will fall out, and that will surely kill him. Besides which, there is Raia lying dead over there."

"Forget Raia," Mentek said. "He is beyond help. We must get the king to the priests and physicians." He snapped his fingers at Nehi. "Run back and find the other huntsmen and soldiers. Tell them what has happened and bid them bring a litter." The hunter nodded and turned to go, but Mentek called him back. "The king lives, Nehi. Remember that. Do not even hint that he might die."

While they waited for help to arrive, Mentek crossed to his friend Raia and straightened his outflung limbs, hiding the crushed skull under a cloth. Bek made the king as comfortable as he could, using some water from his flask to wash the blood from Siptah's face, and gently eased the coils of bloody purplish intestine back through the ragged rents in the young man's abdomen. He could see the life of the king slipping away, but continued to minister to him as best he could.

The huntsmen and soldiers arrived and for several minutes the rocky space echoed with cries of grief. Mentek and Bek finally impressed on them the fact that the king was still alive and needed urgent help. Soldiers ran to prepare the physicians and priests of the city, while the huntsmen made litters out of spears and tunics and gently bore Siptah away to where the chariots waited. Mentek drove the chariot, with Bek bracing himself at his feet and holding the king's body in his arms as they sped as fast as the road would allow, back to Henen-nesut.

The Governor and High Priest of Heryshef were appalled at the fate that had overtaken the king and conferred together as physicians and lesser priests busied themselves with their patient there in the temple forecourt. There was little they could do, but the physicians stuffed the intestines back into the belly, and the priests wrote prayers out on paper and bound them to Siptah's pale body.

"We must send him back to Men-nefer immediately," the High Priest said.

"Is that wise?" asked the Governor. "He could die if he is moved again."

"Better he dies on his barge than here in Henen-nesut."

The Governor stared at the High Priest in silence.

"Have you any idea how inauspicious it is to have a king die within the city? Within the temple of Heryshef?"

"Kings die all the time..."

"Mostly from old age or sickness or from a wound inflicted by an enemy. The priests of all gods can deal with such ill luck, but to have a young king struck down in such a way...no, it is better he dies elsewhere."

"The gods will know he as good as died here."

The High Priest shrugged. "The gods will know we did what we could and sent him home to Men-nefer in the hopes of recovery."

The Governor stood and looked at the torn body for a few minutes longer and then sighed. "Perhaps it would be best. Put the king on his barge and have it set sail for Men-nefer immediately. Let the gods decide his fate."

Chapter 39

Tausret speaks:

I am appalled by the news, and those responsible will suffer the consequences of their negligence. It is what I thought might happen if the boy ever hunted a lion, but what could I do? He was growing into a man and a man will reach out for manly pursuits like war and hunting.

Terribly savaged on the hunt, he was brought to Henen-nesut barely alive, and instead of treating his wounds the Governor put him on the royal barge and sent him to me. Unmoving, but still breathing, he arrived in Men-nefer, but was dead by the time he was brought to the palace.

Yes, King Akhenre Siptah is dead on this twelfth day of the second month of Akhet in the sixth year of his reign. Once more, the land of Kemet is thrown into turmoil by the death of this last male scion of the House of Ramesses. What is to become of our beloved land? I called the King's Council immediately, and though some members could not attend-- General Iurudef and General Setnakhte notable among them--enough were there to lend the proceedings legitimacy.

"The king is dead," I told them.

After cries and groans from all assembled, I informed them of the facts of his passing and asked for their thoughts.

"Who is to blame?" one or two called out.

"The huntsmen were negligent and will be dealt with," I replied.

"Who is the heir?" Tjaty Mentu asked.

"There is none," I said. "At least no one obvious."

"Then we are doomed to renewed civil war," Mentu concluded.

"Worse," Scribe Pepy said. "Then we had too many men contending for the throne. Now we have none."

"You think we have none?" Captain of the Palace Guard Parahotep asked. "Anyone remotely related to the royal family will be eyeing their chances. There are countless grandsons and great-grandsons of Usermaatre who will now decide they have a right, if not a duty, to claim the throne.

We could have a hundred armies marching and countermarching across Kemet, rending the Two Lands until nothing is left."

"Then the answer is clear," Treasurer Huy said. "We must find a suitable candidate and present him to the people immediately."

"Yes, but who?" Mentu asked.

"Surely there is no great urgency," Ament said. "We have Queen Tausret as Regent already. She can continue her duties in the meantime."

"I cannot be regent without a king," I pointed out. "I stand in for the king during his minority, but I only have temporary authority."

"So make it permanent," Ament urged. "Rule in your own right."

"A woman can rule as Queen alongside her husband the King," Mentu pointed out. "She can also act as Regent during the minority of the legitimate heir, but she cannot rule alone as King."

"It has been done before," Pepy said softly. "Maatkare Hatshepsut ruled as King."

"I do not want to be king," I said. "I had already decided to stand down and retire to my estates."

"I fear that is no longer an option," Pepy said.

"There are other candidates if the Queen is adamant she does not want to rule," Huy said. "Men who are descendants of Usermaatre and who are skilled in warfare."

"I hope you are not talking about that Meryre, son of Meryatum," Tausret said with a smile.

"Or Ramses and Meryma'at, who rebelled late in Userkheperure's reign," Ament added. "I would see them dead rather than sitting on Kemet's throne."

"I was actually thinking of General Setnakhte," Huy said. "He's an old man, being a son of Usermaatre born late in his reign, and a proficient soldier. I don't think you could find a better candidate for the throne."

"He was always opposed to Menmire Amenmesse and disliked his son Akhenre Siptah," Mentu said.

"He thought of them as usurpers of the true line of kings. Would he accept the Kingdoms if offered them?" Parahotep asked.

"There is no need to ask him," Ament declared. "We have the best possible monarch right here. Queen Tausret is daughter of Baenre Merenptah, wife of Userkheperure Seti, and was regent for Akhenre Siptah. She is royal by birth and by marriage and has experience of ruling. Furthermore, she has taken the field against the enemies of Kemet and prevailed. I can think of no one more suited to guide the Kingdoms through the troubled days ahead and restore Ma'at."

"But would the people accept her?" Huy asked. "Regent is one thing as long as there is a proper king, but to accept a woman as king..."

"Fornicate the people," Ament interrupted. "The choice of a king has never been up to the common man. A king is chosen by his predecessor or by the Council. They'll accept who we choose and there's an end to it."

And so the Council declared that I should be king, though there were some dissenters. I was reluctant to take up the burden at first, but I accepted in the end because Kemet needs stability and as I have been all but ruling these last few years, the transition promises to be smooth.

In fact, I am minded to count my reign from the death of my husband Seti. I have effectively ruled Kemet while waiting for the legitimate heir, our son Seti-Merenptah, to reach his majority, so why should I not just continue my rule? The reign of Siptah will disappear, and this year, the sixth of that unhappy boy, will become my sixth regnal year. It is fitting that the troubles of the last few years are finally put to rest.

I will be king in my own right, and I must select a suitable coronation name. Titles have been showered upon me - Hereditary Princess, Great of Praises, Lady Sweet of Love, Mistress of Ta Mehu and Ta Shemau, King's Great Wife, Lady of the Two Lands, God's Wife of Amun--but I need strong throne names too, that tie me in to the gods I will need to hold the people. In particular, I need to take hold of the south where Amun is strong, but I can forego Ptah--he will understand--and Set is not for me.

I shall be Sitre Meryamun Tausret Setepenmut--Daughter of Re, beloved of Amun, Mighty Lady, chosen of Mut.

Chapter 40
Year 1 (6) Sitre Meryamun Tausret

Tausret, along with many of the nobles and court officials, made the journey upriver in the middle of the fourth month of Akhet. The flood was dying down by then and a stiff northerly breeze helped the barge on its way. The body of Siptah lay in state on the deck, shaded by an awning and encased in a richly worked gilded sarcophagus. Other shells were being prepared in the Mansion of Millions of Years dedicated to Tausret and would enclose the king's inner sarcophagus when the time came for the burial.

That day came on the twenty-second day of the fourth month of Akhet. Tausret led the procession into the valley of Ta-sekhet-ma'at, to the dark mouth of the rock-cut tomb that had been prepared for the king. It stood near Tausret's own tomb and opposite the one that had been prepared for his uncle Bay. The burial party studiously avoided looking at Bay's tomb, pretending it was not there. The man's body had been lost anyway, but nobody could think what to do with the tomb itself. No doubt some other king would claim it, chisel off all references to the son of Amenmesse and replace them with his own holy names.

The burial of Siptah was short and straightforward. Tausret opened the lips of the dead king's Ka statue, made the necessary offerings, and departed. The priests offered up their prayers and then sealed the tomb. As the party wound its dusty way back down the valley, few people gave a thought to the young boy now consigned to history, but all thought of the days to come.

Tausret met with the priests of Amun and Tjaty Hori to make the last arrangements for the coronation the next day. There were a lot of details to finalise, and there were several arguments over the phrasing of the prayers and priestly pronouncements.

"But those are the words I would use for crowning a king," said Hori, Hem-netjer of Amun. "You are a woman...a Queen."

"Exactly right," Tausret said. "I am a Queen, but tomorrow I become a king. Those are the words that must be used."

"It would not be proper."

"It has been done before," Tjaty Hori said. "Look up the temple scrolls for the forms used in the coronation of Maatkare Hatshepsut when she became king."

Hem-netjer Hori muttered some more but gave in, saying he could perhaps adapt the forms. Tjaty Hori had another matter that gave him some concern.

"When your father Baenre Merenptah was crowned, nobody among the people knew the correct forms as there was hardly anyone living who could remember the coronation of your illustrious grandfather Usermaatre Ramesses. It was a grand event and elicited much rejoicing. Then only a few years later there came the coronation of Userkheperure Seti, then quickly that of Menmire Amenmesse and his son Akhenre Siptah. Now there is to be another." Hori bowed his head. "Forgive me, Lady Tausret, but the people are tired of continued coronations. They desire stability above all else, and I fear they will not display much enthusiasm for tomorrow's events."

"Then I shall have to make sure this is the last coronation they see for a generation," Tausret said with a smile. "A period of stability will be good for everyone."

"And who will be your heir?" Hem-netjer Hori asked. "Continuity is very important."

"There is no one," Tjaty Hori said. "Unless you turn to a lesser relation of Usermaatre."

"I am old," Tausret admitted, "but not too old. I still have my monthly courses. I intend to marry and produce an heir of my own loins."

"With whom?" Hem-netjer Hori asked sharply. "A Queen...or a King...cannot choose just anyone. Your consort must be noble at the very least, preferably royal..." A horrified expression crossed the High Priest's face. "I hope Your Majesty is not contemplating a foreign marriage."

"Not foreign; no. As to whom, well, you will have to wait upon my decision. Nothing has been planned yet, nor the subject broached with the intended recipient." Tausret slashed the air with a hand, signifying an end to the discussion. "For now, concentrate on the coronation."

The next day dawned and, as in every coronation in recent years, Tausret waited outside the Great Temple of Amun dressed only in a plain linen dress, waiting for the priests to call her into the holy precinct. Most of the ceremonies would be the same, but some were different, as she was a woman. Though she had no difficulty with being naked in the right circumstances, she balked at the idea of stripping off in the Holy Lake and being bathed by men in the guise of gods. She would remain clothed during that aspect of the ceremony and change into dry clothing behind a screen of priestesses of Mut, Auset, and Tefnut. Then she would advance into Amun's House for the presentation to the god.

Everything went according to plan, and despite the priests' misgivings as ordaining a woman as King, the god Amun accepted her and the priests presented her to the people, calling out her royal names as they placed the varied crowns of Kemet on her head. They chose names that reflected her desire for peace and stability, but also her known attributes as a warrior against the enemies of Kemet.

"Let Heru empower you," called the first priest. "Your name in Heru shall be Kanakht Merymaat, Strong Bull, Beloved of Maat."

"Nekhabet and Wadjet name you also," the second priest said. "Your name of Nebty shall be Geregkemet Wafkhasut--Founder of Kemet, who vanquishes foreign lands."

"The gods recognise you as their daughter on earth," said the third. "Heru Nebu names you Kanakht Merymaat Nebanemnisutmiitum— Strong bull, beloved of Maat, Lord beautiful of kingship, like Atum."

"Nesut-byt--King of Ta Mehu and Ta Shemau, North and South," cried the fourth priest. "Sitre Meryamun--Daughter of Re, beloved of Amun."

"Sit-Re--Daughter of Re," the fifth priest said. "Tausret Setepenmut-- Mighty Lady, chosen of Mut."

The Tjaty of the South had used his influence in the city to encourage the crowds out with the promise of food and drink for everyone, and Tausret's formal procession through the streets of Waset to the old eastern palace was beset by cheering crowds. She had intended to take a ferry to the western shore and sleep in the western palace, but after seeing the enthusiasm of the populace, she decided to remain in the city.

Almost every noble in Ta Shemau, and a great many from Ta Mehu were there to kneel before their new king and swear allegiance in the sight of their peers, and those that could not make the sometimes arduous journey for reasons of health, sent a proxy to make the oath on their behalf. After the nobles came the officials, overseers, merchants of the city and army officers, each bowing to the throne and the female king who sat upon it. They hailed her as Hereditary Princess, Great of Praises, Lady Sweet of

Love, Mistress of Ta Mehu and Ta Shemau, King's Great Wife, Lady of the Two Lands, God's Wife of Amun.

There were, however, a few exceptions and these elicited much comment.

"Where is Ramesses, Commander of the Amun legion?" Tjaty Hori asked. "Let him step forth and offer his allegiance."

There was a pause, during which heads turned and people searched the crowded throne room for the young man.

"He is not here," the Captain of the Palace Guard reported.

"If he is sick, then let his proxy give the oath."

"He is not sick, and neither does he nominate a proxy."

The crowd muttered and several turned to stare at General Setnakhte, who stood to one side.

Hori followed the direction of the stares and beckoned Setnakhte. "Where is your son? Does he have good reason for not being here?"

"I ordered him not to attend," Setnakhte said.

"Why? It is his duty to swear allegiance to the new king."

Setnakhte took a deep breath and turned to regard Tausret on the throne. "Lady, I..."

"Address the king in the proper manner," Hori snapped.

Setnakhte frowned. "I recognise Queen Tausret, Great Wife of Userkheperure Seti and God's Wife of Amun, who was once Regent and mother of the legitimate heir, Seti-Merenptah, but I do not see a king."

"How dare you!" Ament came out from his position behind the throne and strode toward Setnakhte.

"Wait, Ament." Tausret waved him back and looked at the southern general with interest. "General Setnakhte, you stand high in my regard, as you were in my husband's regard, and for that I would hear you. Do I understand you right? You refuse to acknowledge me as king?"

"That is so, Lady Tausret."

"And your reason?"

"Lady, the line of succession is clear. Usermaatre Ramesses to Baenre Merenptah to Userkheperure Seti, to his young son Seti-Merenptah. I never recognised the legitimacy of the one called Menmire Amenmesse, nor his son Akhenre Siptah. I withheld my allegiance from the pretender and his son and I withhold it from you."

"But why, Setnakhte? I am daughter of Baenre and wife to Userkheperure. My son Seti-Merenptah was snatched from me, but they are all of my family. Why do you exclude me?"

"The line descends from father to son, not to daughter. I recognise and bend my knee to you as Great Wife, as God's Wife of Amun, and as Regent--even as Regent to the false king Akhenre--but a woman cannot be King of Kemet."

"Many would say she can. It has been done before."

"Times have changed, Lady. And anyway--I cannot."

Tausret looked calmly at Setnakhte, ignoring the hisses and angry stares of the nobles and courtiers. "What would you have me do, General Setnakhte?"

"Step down from the Regency, for there is no one to be regent over. Retire to your estates and leave Kemet to its legitimate male successor."

"That's just the point, you fool," Ament growled. "There is no male successor. No one to...by the gods, you are talking about yourself. You would aim so high?"

Setnakhte shrugged. "Kemet could do a lot worse. I am a son of Usermaatre and I have a grown son and heir."

Cries of 'Treason' and 'Arrest him' arose on all sides, but Setnakhte ignored them all.

"Well, Lady? Will you step down?"

Tausret shook her head gently. "I think not. I am already crowned and anointed and to step down and let others fight for the throne would be to consign Kemet to bloody warfare once more. I will not do it...I cannot do it."

"You must arrest him, Majesty," Tjaty Hori said. "You cannot allow this rebellion to go unpunished."

"Well, Setnakhte? Will you bow to me as king, or will you plunge the Kingdoms into civil war again?"

"I cannot bow to you as king, Lady Tausret."

"Then you do not leave me much choice. I must have you arrested. Ament..."

"Hold!"

Setnakhte turned to see his son Ramesses pushing through the crowd with a detachment of the Amun legion.

"You will not arrest my father," Ramesses declared.

"Will you also declare yourself a traitor?" Hori demanded.

"Never a traitor to Kemet or the true king," Ramesses said. "Come, father, there is nothing more to be said here."

"You should not have come," Setnakhte murmured. "Did I not order you to stay away?"

Ramesses smiled. "Indeed you did, father, and no doubt you will think up a suitable punishment for my disobedience, but for now I suggest we get ourselves far from here."

Setnakhte nodded and started toward the doors, the Amun soldiers forming a guard around him.

"You declare yourselves traitors, and your lives and lands are forfeit. Why do you insist on engendering another civil war?" Ament asked.

General Setnakhte turned back and Ramesses paused. "You mistake me, Ament," Setnakhte said. "I would give my life for Kemet, but not for a woman who should not be on its throne. I will not start a war, but if one is forced on me, I will finish it."

"You would be crushed..."

"Not in the south. Amun and Mut will follow me."

"Two legions. King Sitre Tausret can call on ten from the north."

Setnakhte nodded. "That is with the gods."

He turned to leave and Ament roared with rage. He grabbed a spear from one of the soldiers and threw his arm back to hurl it at Setnakhte's back.

"Stop, Ament!" Tausret cried. "Let them go."

With a great effort, Ament aborted his throw and the spear clattered harmlessly to the tiled floor. He snarled his rage and disappointment and turned, pushing through the crowds to leave through a side door.

"Call the Council," Tausret said to Hori. "We must decide what this means for Kemet."

Hori started issuing orders to clear the throne room and then sent out runners to call in those Council members who were not in attendance, including Northern Tjaty Mentu who, though having come down to Waset, had been indisposed for much of the time. After a few moments' consideration, he summoned Setnakhte and Ramesses as they were also on the Council, but they did not respond. Within the hour, the King's Council met in the lesser throne room to face the first crisis of the new reign.

"That was a mistake," Ament said bluntly by way of an opening statement. "If you had let me strike him down an hour ago, we would not need this meeting."

"Moderate your language, Commander," Hem-netjer Hori said. "This is the king you are speaking to."

"I speak as I see it," Ament replied. "The king knows I have only her good at heart. The biggest mistake was only bringing down a few men and putting ourselves in the hand of Amun..."

Hem-netjer Hori leapt to his feet. "How dare you? Amun favours the king."

"Your pardon, priest. What I meant to say was the Amun legion. If we had brought the Set legion down with us, that traitor would not have dared to do anything."

"What's done is done," Tausret said quietly. "For good or ill, I did not want blood shed on my coronation day, so now advise me. Where do we go from here?"

"With respect, Majesty," Tjaty Hori said. "We must act fast to prevent the south rising against you. Setnakhte is popular in Ta Shemau."

"Doesn't matter how popular he is down here," Tjaty Mentu said. "The north can raise enough legions to crush him."

"And that is exactly what I do not want," Tausret commented. "I want to restore the Ma'at of Kemet, not rip it asunder once more."

"If you will not spill blood today, you must be prepared to spill it tomorrow," General Iurudef said. "Setnakhte has already started to withdraw the Amun legion from Waset and the Mut legion is in Ta-senet. By tomorrow, he will be beyond the reach of your hand."

"Send me down to Ta-senet alone then," Ament said. "I will rid you of Setnakhte...and Ramesses too."

"I seem to remember your last foray into the south as an assassin was not too successful," Mentu commented. "Perhaps we should leave this to the legions."

"I agree," Tjaty Hori said. "How soon could you have say...four legions down here, General?"

"A month...maybe a month and a half."

"No. I will not take the path of violence until I am forced to it."

"Majesty, Setnakhte may force you to it sooner than you think."

"Perhaps not," Tausret said. "Setnakhte declared he would not start a war."

"You would trust him?" Ament growled.

"He could have ended it once and for all today, but he did not. He has command of the whole Amun legion and his son commands the Mut legion. If he had chosen to, he could have overwhelmed the small force I brought with me and ended my rule at one stroke. He refrained from violence, so I will do likewise."

"It is never a sign of strength to leave an enemy unscathed behind you," Hori said.

"Another mistake," Ament muttered.

"Enough. I have made my decision. I will return to Men-nefer and en-deavour to rule well so Setnakhte has no reason to openly take up arms against me. Meanwhile, Hori will allow the Amun legion back into Waset and will try and persuade Setnakhte to accept my rule. I do not want a civil war and I will not start one. Setnakhte has said he will not start one either, so if both parties keep to their words, we should have peace."

Chapter 41
Year 1 (6) Sitre Meryamun Tausret

Sitre Tausret returned to Men-nefer aboard the royal barge a few days after her coronation, and stopped at every city and temple on the way downriver to enact a copy of the ceremonies so that every person could see that she truly was the new king. Whenever a Governor had a Window of Appearances in his palace, she would speak to the assembled people and assure them that days of peace were there to stay. She stressed her reign was a continuation of the reign of her husband Userkheperure Seti, and that is why she dated her rule from his death. The listeners were reminded that she had effectively ruled the nation since then, though her title had been regent. That was now at an end, she said, and Kemet could look to prosperous and peaceful years ahead.

She ordered bread and meat be distributed in each city so the people could celebrate, but though they ate the food readily enough, the people were apprehensive and half-heartedly cheered Tausret as she left the city. By the time the barge reached Men-nefer, she was thoroughly despondent and wished more than ever that she had someone close in whom she could confide. There was Ament, of course, an old friend she had met as a girl and who had supported her readily enough over the years, but he was not the same as a husband. For the first time, she looked at him as a man rather than just as a friend and loyal servant.

Tjaty Mentu came to Tausret's private apartments in answer to her summons and every servant was dismissed. Tausret paced in silence for a while, watched by Mentu, who grew more worried as time passed. At last, she spoke, though hesitantly.

"You remember we spoke before my coronation, of who would be my heir?"

"I do, Majesty. Have you reached a decision?"

"There is no one truly acceptable but..." Tausret hesitated again. "There is another possibility. I could yet bear a son of my own body to inherit the throne."

Mentu nodded. "We spoke of this too, Majesty, and I asked you if you were considering a foreign prince. You denied it then--have you changed your mind?"

"No, not a foreign prince but rather a man born in Kemet, loyal to the House of Ramesses and who has served it for many years."

"Does this man have a name, Majesty?"

"Ament."

"Ament? Commander Ament of the Set legion?"

"Yes."

"Majesty, he is a commoner and...and the son of a mere fisherman."

"Even the great Usermaatre Ramesses had a commoner for a grandfather--Paramessu son of Judge Seti. He was a soldier, like Ament, yet he went on to become a great king."

"Majesty...you are surely not contemplating raising him to the throne? Such an action would certainly precipitate the civil war you seek to avoid. Your great-great-grandfather Menpehtyre Ramesses arose to power within a time of civil war and if there was another such time it would not be Ament who became king. General Setnakhte, for one, who barely tolerates your presence on the throne, would march on Men-nefer with his legions and...and I fear he would not be the only one to do so."

Tausret shrugged. "I had not thought to make Ament king, only a husband by whom to generate an heir."

"Even so, Majesty, it is out of the question."

Tausret sighed and faced her Tjaty. "Look upon me as a woman, Mentu, not as a king. Is there no way I can take Ament as my husband?"

"No, Majesty."

"I could ennoble him; give him rich estates and high titles."

"He would still be the son of a fisherman. Nobody would accept him and very soon you would have active rebellion on your hands." Mentu regarded his king with compassion. "If you are discreet, you could take him as a lover. No one would think the worse of you for that."

"And if I had a child?"

"It is unlikely they would accept it as an heir. I am sorry, Majesty, and of course you can do as you please--but there will be consequences for any action you might take."

"I suppose you would prefer I accepted the offer from Meryre, son of Ratep?"

"The man who rebelled against your husband? He has the advantage that he is a noble and descended from Usermaatre, but if you were asking my opinion, Majesty, I would not even deign to reply. It is absurd."

"So I am to live out my years without a husband?"

"There is only one real candidate, Majesty, and I fear he is not acceptable to you."

"If you mean General Setnakhte, then no. Not under any circumstances."

"I was thinking more in terms of his son Ramesses," Mentu said. "Setnakhte is too old, being of your father's generation, but Ramesses is young and virile and I'm sure quite capable of planting a son and heir in your Majesty's belly."

Tausret made a face. "He would expect to be king though, relegating me to Great Wife. I have been that but now I am king. I don't want to step backwards."

"I think Setnakhte would prefer to be king before him anyway, with you marrying his son and heir."

"That is not going to happen."

"But Ramesses...?"

"I will think on it."

Tausret had another problem on her hands when she brought the northern legion commanders together to talk about the defence of Kemet and the southern troubles. Each commander left their legion in the hands of their deputy and, together with the northern general Iurudef, made their way to the capital for talks. The king came straight to the point.

"General Setnakhte and Commander Ramesses have effectively withdrawn their support of my rule. What effect is this going to have on my ability to govern?"

The commanders and general looked at each other, each afraid to be the first one to show apprehension at the news. Ament said nothing, though of course he was aware of the problem already. In the end it was Iurudef as senior officer who broke the silence.

"When you say 'effectively withdrawn', Majesty, what exactly do you mean?"

"They do not acknowledge my right to rule as king. They withdrew their legions to Ta-senet until I left Waset and then returned to the city. As far as I am aware, they are not interfering in the government of Ta Shemau. Tjaty Hori continues to rule in my name."

"Have they indicated they will do more than just refuse to acknowledge you?"

"By all the gods, Iurudef, what do you mean by 'just refuse'?" Ament shouted. "That is treason and should be punished."

"Ament, please," Tausret said. "General, so far they have given no hint that they would do more."

"Then, Majesty, I do not see that you have a problem." Iurudef saw Ament snarl with rage and held up a hand to forestall his outburst. "I agree their actions could be interpreted as treasonous, but it could just be that they feel unsettled by recent events..."

"Do you feel unsettled, Iurudef?" Tausret asked.

The General considered his answer. "I would have to say I do, Majesty."

"In what way?"

"The male line of Usermaatre Ramesses has come to an end with the death of your son. I was prepared to support King Akhenre Siptah as this was the will of the Council, but now that he too has died, we are left without a male heir. I know the arguments for your assumption of the throne, Majesty, and in principle I accept them, but it is unsettling to have a female king." Iurudef remained on his feet, but paused as if in thought. "I am loyal to the duly anointed king of Kemet, of that you may be assured."

"I see. Is this how the rest of you feel? Disebek?"

Commander Disebek of the Re legion stood and bowed to the throne. "I am loyal, Majesty."

"And I," said Ahhotep of Ptah.

Merymose of Heru also bowed and spoke words of loyalty, while Ament bowed and remained silent. Ramose of Khent-abt, Djutep of Sept, Natsefamen of Shu likewise silently bowed, and Ankhu of Sobek loudly proclaimed his loyalty.

"So I have eight loyal legions in the north?" Tausret asked. "And a loyal general?"

The commanders and Iurudef once more affirmed their loyalty.

"Whereas only two legions are less than loyal, possibly three as the Kushite legion has sent no word. Should I be worried, Iurudef?"

"No, Daughter of Re...provided they do not actively oppose you. If they do, then we might have a problem."

"Two...or possibly three, against eight? How is this a problem?"

"General Setnakhte is a very able commander, and his son Ramesses has learned his lessons well. You may assume that the two southern legions are well trained though perhaps a little inexperienced in battle, though of course, the recent civil war proved a good training ground. The Kushite legion is an unknown quantity--no doubt full of fierce warriors but without discipline.

"Opposing them in the north are eight legions, four of whom--Ptah, Heru, Re and Set--are well trained and experienced. The other four less so, on both counts."

"Even so, four well trained legions against two?"

"Setnakhte has no border to guard. I need three legions to hold the northern border against the nations. Two at a pinch, if I can use two of the lesser legions. That leaves two against two with two lesser legions to balance the Kushites. It is an even battle, Majesty, and not one I relish."

"But you are a better general than Setnakhte, aren't you?"

"Yes, Majesty, but...he is very capable. As is his son Ramesses."

"So what exactly are you saying, Iurudef? That my position is hopeless?"

"Have a care how you answer," Ament growled.

Iurudef sneered at Ament. "Remember your place...Commander." He turned back to face Tausret. "Majesty, the two kingdoms are evenly matched. You may reign over both, but Setnakhte effectively rules in the south. My advice is to rule wisely in the north, while giving him no reason to be dissatisfied with your rule. When he sees that catastrophe does not fall on Kemet because a woman is king, he may come to the realisation that the gods do indeed support you."

"What say the rest of you?"

The Commanders murmured their agreement, but Ament went further.

"I have always said it would be better to remove two men for the good of Kemet. Let me take a few men south and rid you of this man and his son once and for all."

Tausret stood and everyone scrambled to their feet and bowed.

"Thank you all for your reasoned advice and considered opinions. I have taken note of every argument and will weigh your words carefully, even yours, Ament. I thank you all for your loyalty and bid you return to your legions. No precipitate action will be taken and you may be certain I will consult with you, my loyal commanders, before any move is made."

Tausret refused to allow Ament to put in place his plan to assassinate Setnakhte and Ramesses, but stopped short of forbidding him to even contemplate the thought. The future might necessitate some such action, but for now she decided to put such thoughts from her and concentrate on ruling well. Ament knew she was wrong but recognised she was not open to persuasion. He would have to act without her knowledge. In the meantime, Tausret met with Treasurer Huy, Tjaty Mentu and the High Priests of every god in Ta Mehu and the northern parts of Ta Shemau.

"I wish to make my mark on the land," Tausret said. "Make a list of every temple construction work that needs doing, and make an estimate of the cost. I want men to look at my reign as an age in which building flourished and the gods prospered."

"That will be very expensive, Majesty," Treasurer Huy said. "I am not sure the Treasury can pay for large scale building projects."

"Why not? There seemed to be ample gold under your predecessor."

"Chancellor Bay employed...shall we say, unorthodox methods, Majesty. He drew on taxes not yet paid and paid others in promises. I have had to dispose of a large part of the gold in the Treasury just paying promissory notes since his, er...demise."

"And what of building projects that are unfinished?" Tjaty Mentu asked. "A number of constructions were started during the days of Akhenre Siptah. Should those works be finished or not?"

Tausret thought for a moment and then nodded. "Yes, that fits in with my plans. Every temple, shrine or other work started under Siptah is to continue, because in reality, they were started during my reign." Huy opened his mouth, a puzzled expression on his face, and Tausret continued. "Remember, I date my accession to follow directly on from my husband Userkheperure. Every work of the last six years has been my work. You will finish them but put my name in place of Siptah's. Furthermore, all of Siptah's finished works, in both kingdoms, are to be modified. His name is to be chiselled out and replaced with mine where appropriate, or my husband's."

"It shall be done, Majesty," Mentu said. He checked what the scribe had recorded and appended his personal seal.

"Finally, the mines at Timna and the nearby temple of Het-hor. I know Siptah had an inscription placed there. You will add my name to the inscription. Now, the most important aspects--my tomb and my Mansion of Millions of Years--how are they progressing?"

Mentu consulted his notes. "I received a report from Tjaty Hori indicating that work on your tomb is progressing well, but that work on your Mansion has slowed. It seems there is a shortage of suitable stone. Er, Hori indicates he has told the builders to continue with mud brick."

"That is not acceptable," Tausret said. "Send word that stone is to be quarried and shaped and the mud brick torn down."

Treasurer Huy coughed, and Tausret flashed him an irritated glance.

"Find the gold, Huy. I don't care what you must do; this quarried stone takes priority."

Word came south to Tjaty Hori of Tausret's commands, and Hori issued the necessary orders for more stone to be quarried and for masons to chisel out Siptah's name on several inscriptions and substitute the present king's own name. The news spread quickly and, along with every other scrap of information brought into Waset, quickly found itself in the hands of General Setnakhte and Commander Ramesses.

Both the Amun legion and the Mut legion under the command of Panhesy were now housed within the city barracks, which had been enlarged for the purpose. Setnakhte studied the report and then passed it to his son for comment.

"She is determined to rule in the south, isn't she? Are you going to let her?"

Setnakhte took back the report and tapped the relevant passages. "Why should it concern me whether she commands her tomb and Mansion be built? She won't remain king long enough for it to matter. As for putting her name in the inscriptions--well, Siptah never was the real king, so his name should be removed."

"So you are going to act against her. When?"

"When the time is right. Look, we have two legions against what? Six? Eight? We need to get the Kushite legion behind us first. Panhesy, you were going to bring them over--how are you progressing with their commander?

"With Taharqa, General." Panhesy shrugged. "He doesn't like the idea of a female king, but he is uneasy about rebelling against an anointed one. He says that if he gods have accepted her, how can he not?"

"Keep working on him. Who's his deputy?"

"Shabalka, General."

"And what does he think about Tausret?"

"He is more inclined to oppose her."

"Perhaps we should just get rid of Taharqa and promote Shabalka," Ramesses said.

"It may come to that, but for now we do nothing that might bring the northern legions down on us. Continue to support Hori and keep the peace in Waset." Setnakhte say the disappointment on his son's face. "Do not be despondent, my son. I cannot believe that the woman will be able to rule effectively. Discontent within her own ranks is our sure ally. If the gods favour us, one or more of the legions will change sides and then we strike."

Chapter 42
Year 1 (6) Sitre Meryamun Tausret

L eader of Fifty Meryset had taken fifteen years to rise through the ranks of the Amun legion. He had joined in Baenre's day as a simple soldier, learning his basic skills against desert tribesmen and the occasional foray into northern Kush. By the time Menmire Amenmesse claimed the kingship in Waset, Meryset was a Leader of Five and was adding the lessons that leadership taught him. When Menmire's general led the southern army northward, Meryset went with it and learned the hard way that the northern legions were far more battle hardened and experienced than the southern ones. Fellow officers fell in battle And Meryset was promoted to Leader of Ten and then Fifty.

Menmire was captured and died, and his son Akhenre Siptah took the throne. General Setnakhte took over the southern army, and he recognised talent in young officers, promoting them. Meryset had been confidently expecting to be made Troop Commander but was passed over in favour of officers junior to him. The insult rankled and his bitterness against Setnakhte grew over the years as his career stagnated. Siptah had now died and Queen Tausret had been elevated to the throne, but still he remained in the lower middle rank of officers.

Meryset drank more than was wise and talked to strangers more than he should, complaining to anyone who would listen about the disservice that had been done him. On one such drunken ramble a man approached him and engaged him in conversation. The man plied him with strong barley beer, listened attentively to Meryset's complaints and fed them with provocative comments.

"Sounds to me like you've well and truly been raped, my friend. Anyone can see you're a man of worth and from what you've told me you're an experienced officer. Why, you should be a Troop Commander at the very least, maybe even legion commander."

"Jus' what I been saying, friend," Meryset agreed. "Gen'l Setnakhte's got it in fer me. Pass me over fer permotion fer no good reason..."

"You should complain to the proper authorities. Get them to overturn his decision."

"'Ow's I gonna do that? 'E's a gen'l an' I's just a Lead...Leader o' Fif'." Meryset belched loudly and the man refilled his mug.

"You could take your complaint to the king. Every man has the right to approach the king."

Meryset drank deeply from the foaming mug, wiped his upper lip and belched again. "King's a woman now."

"So? She's still king, isn't she?"

"What's a woman know 'bout solshurs an' war an' stuff?"

"Have you forgotten she fought the Ribu in Baenre's day? And quashed two rebellions in her husband's reign? I think you'll find she knows a lot about military matters and what is fair. If you put your case to her, I'm sure she'll find in your favour."

"'Gainst a gen'l?"

"Even against a general. You do know that Setnakhte insulted the king to her face here in Waset? He refused to swear allegiance to her. It was only that he led the legions out against her that kept his head on his shoulders."

"Sunnuva whore. Why 'asn't she led the legions 'gainst 'im?"

The man shrugged and refilled Meryset's mug. "Setnakhte is too strong down here. Talk is he's going to declare himself king and lead the kingdoms into civil war again."

"Set's bollocks. 'E can't do that! Can 'e?"

"I'm afraid he can--and will. Unless someone stops him."

Meryset nodded. "Yerss...sommun should."

"Whoever does will be hailed as a hero and saviour of Kemet. I would imagine the king would reward that person with gold, with land, rank, anything they wanted."

"Might make 'im Troop C'mander mebbe? What I...'e 'afta do?"

"Well, it would be useless just to bring charges against him. You'd have to remove him...permanently."

Meryset looked around the tavern to see if anyone was near enough to overhear them. He leaned closer to the man. "Yer mean kill 'im? That's dang'rous."

The man nodded and sighed. "Yes, it is. I thought perhaps you knew a brave man prepared to perform a loyal act for your king and for Kemet, but you're right. It would be too dangerous. You're only a Leader of Fifty. I need to find someone closer to Setnakhte, someone who hates him and loves the king."

"I love th' king."

"Yes, I'm sure you do."

The man started to get up and Meryset reached out a hand and grabbed his arm. "Yer sure the king'd reward me...'im? Make me Troop C'mander?"

"At least. Gold too. But why are you asking? You said it was too dangerous."

Meryset nodded. "'Tis...but I can do it. 'E passes our rooms ev'ry noon ter get 'is meal. I could kill the sunnuva whore easylike."

"What about the danger?"

Meryset screwed up his face as he tried to pin down his thoughts. "I gotta way out after," he said. "Nobody gonna catch me."

"When you get out of the barracks, make for the Tjaty's palace. I'll make sure he has guards waiting to take you in and hide you."

"An' my reward?"

"The moment he's dead, I'll send word to the king." The man took Meryset's half empty cup from his hand and poured the beer out on the ground. "Now, I think that's enough drinking for tonight. You've got to get yourself sober and ready. Sooner done, sooner rewarded, eh, Troop Commander?"

Meryset grinned and lurched to his feet. "Tha's Legion Commander to you, me frien'."

Meryset could scarcely move the next morning and by the time Setnakhte walked past the room where he lay groaning at noon, the only part of his body he could move were his eyes, which he rolled in their sockets to follow the course of the General. By nightfall, he had recovered and started giving serious thought to his plan to kill Setnakhte and reap the reward from a grateful king. He stood in the doorway of his barrack's room and looked at the path the General took each day, mentally measuring distances and wondering whether a sword or spear would be the better weapon. It might depend on whether Setnakhte walked alone or in the company of others--like his son Ramesses. Alone would be easier, Meryset decided, but it was possible either way.

The next day dawned, and Meryset prepared to change his fortune. He sharpened his curved copper sword and placed it just inside the door to his room, selected a spear from the legion armoury, looking along its length to make sure it would fly straight and true. This he propped against the wall in his room next to his sword. Then he paced out his escape route, making sure the passages and doorways were free of obstruction. From the barrack's back door to the Tjaty's palace was no more than five hundred paces, and Meryset believed he could cover that distance before his pursuit was properly organised.

His duties that morning called for him to drill his squad of fifty in the barrack's courtyard, but his mind was not on the job. The men knew it and took advantage of his obvious distraction. Meryset dismissed them early and went to his room where he sat, tapping his heels on the dirt floor, or lay on his cot, moving restlessly, or pacing up and down, glancing out of the door frequently. As the noon hour approached, he grew more agitated, and hovered in the doorway waiting for the approach of the General.

The aromas of the noon meal wafted in the air, and people started moving toward the kitchens. Senior officers ate apart from the men, but often collected their own food from the cooks before taking it to their dining room. Setnakhte made a point of collecting his own meals most days so as to display unity with his officers, and this day was no different. Setnakhte came into view, talking with his son Ramesses and Commander of the Mut legion, Panhesy. Their path took them close to the junior officers' rooms and as they passed, Panhesy looked up and saw Meryset watching them. He frowned and then nodded his head toward the Leader of Fifty, continuing on his way.

They passed by; the three senior officers. Meryset glanced around to make sure he was unobserved and reached for his spear. He stepped out of his room and drew back his arm, preparing to throw. Setnakhte walked alongside his son with Panhesy a pace or two to one side and behind, while ahead of the trio, Meryset could see other men hurrying toward the kitchens. No one was looking in his direction, so Meryset offered up a swift prayer and started his throw.

At that moment, Panhesy glanced back and saw Meryset release his spear toward them. He yelled an inchoate warning and stumbled toward his General, who was also turning. The spear, heading straight for Setnakhte's naked back, clipped Panhesy's arm and was deflected just enough to skim past the General. Ramesses uttered a roar of rage and hurled himself after

Meryset, who had turned tail and was racing for the doorway that would lead to safety.

Meryset's lead was such that he might have beaten even an instant pursuer like Ramesses, but a soldier who had been in the latrines, now hurried along, intent on getting his meal, and collided with Meryset. The would-be assassin threw aside the soldier, but the delay allowed Ramesses to throw himself onto the running man and bear him to the ground. Other men ran up and secured Meryset, beating him severely and throwing him into a cell.

Setnakhte was shaken by the assassination attempt, but put off the midday meal in an effort to find out how extensive was the plot against his life. Ramesses closed down the barracks and put an armed guard on his father, while a physician attended to Panhesy's wound. Then Setnakhte and Ramesses had Meryset hauled before them.

"Why?" was Setnakhte's first question.

Meryset shrugged. "What does it matter? I failed."

"It matters because you are a capable officer and I thought a loyal one. Why would you try to kill your commanding officer? I presume I was the target?"

"After fifteen years I am only a Leader of Fifty. I deserve more."

Setnakhte considered the bound and bleeding man kneeling before him. "As I said, you are capable, but in my judgment you are at the rank you deserve. I could see you rising to Leader of a Hundred in a few years, but no more. Would you kill for such a slight promotion?"

"If I had succeeded I would be Troop Commander, maybe even Legion Commander."

"Who would have made you that, Meryset? Would Commander Ramesses have promoted you? Or Commander Panhesy? Someone else?"

Meryset said nothing, just staring at the floor.

"Come, Meryset, tell me who promised you this. It will go better for you if you are honest."

Meryset kept silent.

Ramesses cuffed the bound man's head. "Give me an hour and I will drag the truth out of him," he growled.

"You hear that, Meryset? Must we put you to the question to get the truth? Better for you to spare yourself some pain."

Setnakhte waited for a reply, but when there was none, shrugged. "Take him away, Commander Ramesses. Make sure he doesn't die, but get the truth out of him."

Meryset was dragged away and Ramesses followed. Setnakhte went to find Panhesy and was relieved to find that his wound was not judged to be serious. The spear point had scored a deep wound across the man's upper arm, but the cut had bled freely and was even then responding to the physician's treatment.

"You saved my life, Panhesy."

"No more than my...ah...duty, General."

"You suspected something, didn't you? I saw you look at him and then you yelled a warning."

"It was such a small thing, General. Meryset likes his food and yet here he was, standing in the doorway watching you walk by instead of heading for the kitchens like everyone else. I wondered why and then looked back just in time."

"Lucky for me you did. I'll not forget your vigilance."

"Do you know why he did it, General?"

"It seems he was put up to it when he was passed over for promotion. Ramesses is..." Setnakhte was interrupted by a hoarse scream emanating from the cell area. "...interrogating Meryset as we speak. If I know my son, we'll have the answer quickly."

Meryset held out for a full day, but no man could hold out much longer when inventive minds explored the pain threshold. The Leader of Fifty screamed a lot, and wept, begging for mercy and for death but, broken and bleeding; he told everything that he knew. Ramesses had a scribe take down Meryset's confession and carried it to his father.

"It is as I suspected, father. An agent of the king bribed Meryset with promises of gold, land and advancement if only he would kill you."

"Who was the agent?"

"Meryset had no name, but he is sure he came from the king."

"You are certain of that? From Sitre Meryamun Tausret? There is no mistake?"

"None, father. Sitre wants you dead."

Setnakhte paced the floor, slapping his fist into his open hand. "Does she not realise I have done nothing to counter her? I would do nothing. I may not support her claim to the throne, but I do not support anyone else's either."

"Yours is the better claim, father, and it seems she now realises that. The only way she can safeguard her throne is to kill you, so she has ordered her assassin down to Waset."

"Doesn't she realise this will plunge the country into civil war again? I cannot ignore this attempt."

"She must believe she can win."

"So she will risk all. Well, if that is what she wants, that is what she will get. Prepare the legions and send word to Shabalko. If Taharqa is still undecided, have him relieved of his command, but I want the Kushite legion in Waset inside a month."

"What about Tjaty Hori?" Ramesses asked. "He's loyal to Sitre Tausret."

Setnakhte thought for a few moments. "He's a good man. Give him a choice. He can stand aside and remain at liberty, or he can be incarcerated."

"My guess is he'll send a warning northward that the plot has failed and that you have openly rebelled."

"Well, shut the city up tight then. Nobody leaves without my permission."

"Yes, father." Ramesses turned to go and then hesitated. "Will you claim the throne?"

Setnakhte nodded slowly. "When the time is right. First we must defeat the northern legions."

Chapter 43

A ment speaks:

A brief message from Hori saying only that an attempt had been made on General Setnakhte's life arrived in Men-nefer over a month ago. Since then, nothing. I have sent men south to find out what is happening, but they report back that Waset is locked up tighter than a cat's back passage. People are allowed in, but no one is allowed out. Something has happened, and I fear it is nothing good, for the Kushite legion has also marched north and is nearing Amun's City.

Who was it that made the attempt on Setnakhte's life, and why? I have been quite forthright in my opinion that the way out of our current troubles would be to assassinate the General, but if I had sanctioned it, I would have succeeded. All that seems to have happened is that he has been alerted and will be much harder to kill in the future. And who knows how he will react? That is why I need to know who did it. If it is an internal matter, a result of some slight whether real or imagined, Setnakhte would deal with it and that would be an end to it. But if the king is somehow implicated, the General may decide this is the first act in a battle for survival. He assured my Lady Sitre Tausret that he would not be the first to break the peace, but if he imagines she has broken it, he may attempt to grasp the throne.

All right, let us imagine that he now desires the Double Crown--can he succeed? On the face of it he has three legions against our eight and would be a fool to risk everything on a throw of the stones, but do we really have eight legions? It hinges on the four experienced legions--Re, Heru, Set and Ptah--and their General. Set is loyal to a man for I have made sure of that, but there is some doubt about the others. General Iurudef too. He has offered qualified support for the king, indicating that her path to success depends on her ability to rule well. He has a point, I suppose, but the gods have accepted her as king and who is any man to deny what the gods have allowed?

So, let us suppose that Setnakhte has decided to rebel openly. He marches north with three legions and we must send legions south to oppose him. Who do we send? Two of the experienced four are needed for the northern border, so if I was in command, I would send Set and Re south with two of the auxiliary legions, say Sept and Shu. It would be an even match and everything would depend on superior tactics on the day and the favour of the gods.

That it should come to this. The House of Ramesses is down to its last true king and the pretenders are out in force, seeking to wrest power away from a family that has ruled for a hundred and fifty years. Yes, I know Setnakhte is a scion of the great Usermaatre too, but he was never anywhere near the line of succession and has ideas far above his station. If only that unknown man had not attempted to kill him. I could have succeeded where he failed and the problem would have gone away. Well, it is no use weeping over a broken wine jar. It is done and we must make the best of it. A King's Council will be held later today to discuss the future and we will see what we will see.

The king has met with her Councillors and the decision is war. The latest report in from the south shows all three legions are armed and moving slowly northward. Unlike the army of Amenmesse, however, these men are not rapacious and are cheered on by the populace. The common man already calls Setnakhte king, though he has not, so far, claimed that title. Sitre Tausret will send three legions south to meet the rebel army--Re, Heru and Sobek. Set is to take its place in the north and I am to serve with it. Command of the army is given to Iurudef, at his request, and I cannot but feel apprehensive at this decision. Re is under the command of Disebek, a capable and loyal man, but Heru is commanded by Merymose who is relatively inexperienced and the Sobek legion under Ankhu is the least capable of the auxiliary legions. One has to ask why Iurudef would select these legions for his army.

In stark contrast to the cheering crowds in the south, our northern army set off today with the populace looking on in silence. Nobody wants war again, yet here we are tearing the fabric of the kingdoms apart and shattering Ma'at. The priests tell us the gods are on our side, but I am sure the priests in Waset have also told Setnakhte that the gods favour his enter-prise.

I look at King Sitre Tausret and I see a woman who has visibly aged in the last year or so. Her son died and sundered her spirit and then the cares of the kingdoms were heaped upon her, crushing her under their weight. I think that if she had a choice, she would hand over the throne to someone else and retire. She always meant to, but her sense of duty was too strong. There is nothing that would give me more pleasure than to retire with her and serve her on her estates while others shouldered the burdens of state. I have been with her now twenty-five years and it is time she was allowed to be just a woman and I was allowed to be just a man.

Speaking of a man and a woman, a spy told me of an interesting bit of conversation that recently took place between Sitre Tausret and Tjaty Men-tu. It had to do with the non-existent heir and Tausret's future plans. The spy said that the names of Setnakhte and Ramesses had been raised as pos-sibilities for a future consort for the king. I dismissed the spy immediately, of course, and told him he must be mistaken, but it set me thinking.

Both Setnakhte and Ramesses are descended from royalty, lesser mem-bers of the House of Ramesses, and if she was looking for a man to sit be-side her on the throne of Kemet, then either would be suitable. Setnakhte is old, but experienced and a ruler of men already; and his son Ramesses is younger and virile. If she seeks a husband to plant an heir in her belly, then the son is the logical choice.

Ah, but it hurts to consider the possibility. I loved Tausret when first I met her all those years ago, but of course my station in life was far too low for me to entertain any hope that she might reciprocate my feelings. I rose in rank to become Legion Commander, personal adviser and confidant, but no matter how high I rose I was always far below her. I loved her then, and I love her now, but I know better than to declare my love for her. I am a soldier and son of a fisherman and it is only under exceptional circum-stances that a common man such as I might seek greater advancement.

Maybe those times are upon us...The House of Ramesses stumbles, fal-ters and falls and the way opens up for a strong man to grasp the heka and nekhakha of authority, placing the crowns of the kingdoms upon his head, and ruling Kemet as the first of a new royal family. Will it be me? Could it be me?

Ha! Who do I seek to deceive if not myself? I am not a king, nor am I the stone of which a king might be carved. The only interest I have in the royalty of Kemet is the woman who sits upon the throne, and I am not for her. I will always love her and will die for her should the need arise, but I could never be king. Put that from your mind, Ament. Tausret is not for you.

Chapter 44
Year 1 (6) Sitre Meryamun Tausret

General Iurudef led the legions south, moving fast, knowing his opponent was heading north slowly and using the time to whip the Kushite legion into shape. His obvious thought was to face the northern legions with three disciplined legions of his own and inflict a decisive defeat. Iurudef knew that the longer Setnakhte went unchallenged and undefeated, the stronger his position would become, so the northern general meant to bring him to battle before he was ready and nip this rebellion in the bud. The continued kingship of Sitre Tausret depended on there being no credible challenges to her rule.

The land between Men-nefer and Waset was well known to all parties from the recent battles that had been fought upon it. Armies of Menmire Amenmesse and Userkheperure Seti had spilt blood in profusion upon the sand and rocky soil of the eastern desert, and there was every indication that more would soon be shed. The legions met some distance south of the all-but abandoned city of Akhetaten, on a battlefield that was haunted by the blood of thousands.

Iurudef was the first general to reach the rocky plain and he at once saw the possibilities for a chariot charge. His own legions had many chariots, whereas the southern legions relied more on conventional foot soldiers, leading him to believe that he could deliver a decisive defeat to Setnakhte. The plain itself was level but bore many scattered rocks and boulders that would interfere with a charge, so Iurudef had his men swarm out onto the field and pick up rocks, roll boulders away, casting the offending lithic fragments into the rocky desert to the east or down the cliffs to the river.

His right flank was secured by the river cliffs and his left by the boulder field of the stony desert, so Iurudef drew up his legions with the chariots of all three massed in the centre, facing the cleared plain. He stationed archers on the sides, with the massed foot soldiers to either side of the chariot squadrons, and settled down to wait for Setnakhte's forces. Scouts had told him the enemy legions were still a day away, but also that the land beyond was broken and uneven, unsuitable for his own battle plan.

The hours passed slowly. Iurudef had his men fed on cold meat and bread where they stood to arms, bedded them down in shifts without the benefit of tents and had cut forage and water brought to the horses. He was determined that the enemy was not going to take him by surprise, so he risked his men being uncomfortable for a day and night. Setnakhte's men would be marching to meet them and if the gods smiled, they would be tired and dispirited before the battle.

Dawn broke, and Iurudef led the praises to the gods and Re in particular who would look down on him as he defended the future of Kemet. Dust rose into the still morning air on the southern horizon and scouts came racing in to bring the news that the enemy was in sight.

"How many legions?" Iurudef demanded.

"Three, sir, but they appear to be undermanned, particularly the Kushites."

Iurudef nodded sagely and turned to Disebek of Re, his most senior commander. "I knew Setnakhte would struggle to hold the Kushites in order. They are undisciplined at best. It appears many have deserted him."

"Then let this be the death blow for his pretentions, sir," Disebek replied.

"Prepare the men. We will strike as soon as they arrive."

By noon, the southern legions appeared on the rim of the prepared battlefield and stopped as if to examine the ground ahead of them. Iurudef could recognise the banners of Amun and Mut, and an unknown banner that he reasoned was the identifying mark of the Kushite troops. They had only a handful of chariots, but drew these up in battle formation anyway. Rams' horns blew to the south and Setnakhte's legions moved forward onto the cleared ground.

"He's very confident to attack immediately," Disebek murmured.

"Overconfident," Iurudef opined. "He believes himself already king." He turned to the other commanders. "Be ready for my signal." They saluted and hurried to their legions, shouting commands to their junior officers.

Setnakhte's legions drew closer, moving steadily in their Troops and as they advanced completely onto the plain, Iurudef gave the signal for the chariot squadrons. Horns blew again, voices rose in cheers and battle cries and the horses leapt forward. Chariots bounced and bucked on the rough ground and then settled into a roaring advance that swept down upon the enemy like a desert storm. The legions followed, men breaking ranks as they ran, eager to get to grips with what they felt certain would be the shattered ranks of the enemy. The Amun and Mut legions did indeed break apart as the chariots crashed into their ranks, archers standing alongside the charioteers pouring volley after volley of arrows into the milling mass of humanity.

"We have them," Disebek cried out exultantly. "See how they..."

The Re legion commander frowned and stared at the unfolding battle, where the racing chariot squadrons had ripped through the opposing legions, but instead of a field of dead and dying men left in their wake, men were picking themselves up and hurling themselves at the onrushing foot soldiers. To the south, where the chariots were in disarray as they halted their charge and struggled to turn and reform their units, black men rose up around them, stabbing spears in hand and wrought great damage on men and horses.

The battle devolved into a great struggle of fighting men, a multitude of individuals striving to kill their single opponent rather than work with their fellows for overall victory. Iurudef's men had the initial advantage, but the chariot charge had not dealt the death blow he had hoped it would. Then Setnakhte's men gained the ascendancy, swarming over and decimating the chariot squadrons. Ankhu's Sobek legion, held in reserve, were thrown into the fray, stiffening the resolve of the northern men for a time before the superior number of archers in Amun and Mut cut swathes through them.

Sobek turned and fled, and with a roar, Amun was upon them. Ramesses led the pursuit in his war chariot, routing the fleeing legion, while Setnakhte directed Panhesy of Mut and Taharqa the Kushite against the remnants of Re and Heru. The northern legions gave way, but did not run. Instead, they drew upon their experience and determination to sell their lives dearly as they retreated northward, pursued by the victorious forces of Setnakhte.

When darkness fell, calling a halt to the killing, Iurudef pulled his forces back as quickly as he could, ordering Disebek to guard the retreat with his Re legion. He also sent a chariot racing northward to carry the news to Men-nefer and beg for reinforcements. Such was the disarray of the northern legions that if Setnakhte had pressed home his attack, he must certainly have destroyed the backbone of his enemy, but he was overly cautious, not wanting to risk the gains he had made. His son Ramesses pleaded to attack, but the southern General called a halt to the advance while his scouts were sent out to judge the strength of the enemy legions.

269

"Iurudef has been defeated," Tjaty Mentu said. "A messenger arrived not an hour past with the news."

Tausret said nothing, just looked at Ament.

"How badly?" the Set legion commander asked.

"Re is largely intact, but Heru and Sobek have suffered substantial losses. They have withdrawn north of Akhetaten, and continue to retreat, though no longer in disarray. Setnakhte stopped for a while but now presses forward slowly, with the Amun legion under his son Ramesses leading the attack."

Ament shook his head. "It is not like Setnakhte to be so cautious. Why did he not follow up his victory with a swift push to Men-nefer?"

Mentu shrugged. "I cannot know his mind, but perhaps he cannot believe he had so easy a victory. His cautious advance may be because he believes our other legions are about to fall on him."

"Then his spies are playing him false. We only have Sept and Shu available."

"Set is in the north," Mentu observed, "yet you are not with your legion, Commander Ament, despite being ordered there by the Council. May I know the reason for your disobedience?"

"I ordered him back," Tausret said. "I presume I can still overrule my own Council?"

"Of course, Majesty. It is just that...who commands in the north if Ament is down here?"

"My own deputy Mose," Ament said. "He is a competent officer and well capable of handling the Retenu."

"Then, Commander Ament, as you seem to be senior officer until Iurudef returns to the city, what are we to do?"

"I will lead Sept and Shu south to shore up the other legions and deny the rebels the northern cities."

"Sept and Shu have their own commanders already, whereas your command lies in the north," Mentu observed.

"Mose will lead the Set legion now," Tausret said. "I am making Ament a general. I will relieve Iurudef of command and return him to the north to guard the frontier."

"He will see that as a punishment, Majesty. Is that what you intend?"

"If he chooses to interpret it as such," Tausret said. "He had the men to defeat Setnakhte but squandered his chances. I have full confidence in Ament to turn the situation around."

"With respect, Majesty," Mentu said with a frown, "I don't think you can afford to offend anyone at the moment, least of all your senior army officers."

Tausret glared at her Tjaty. "You think I am not qualified to judge military matters, Mentu? I, the victor of Perire?"

Mentu could do nothing but bow to the inevitable and to his king. "No, Majesty, of course not, but...perhaps you could give Iurudef a bit more time to accomplish his mission? A demotion following swiftly on the heels of a defeat may unsettle the populace. Already, crime is rising within the city because men fear the privations of another war."

"Enough, Tjaty. Follow my instructions or hand over your office to one who can."

Mentu bowed again, averting his eyes from the anger of his king. "Yes, Majesty."

Ament marched the Sept and Shu legions south within days. He had meant to convey them swiftly on barges, so that they would arrive rested, but the first flood waters had swollen the river and all he could do was transport them over to the east bank. He marched them along the desert road as the farmlands along the river were already swampy. The inundation lapped the riverbanks and filled the irrigation channels, making swift movement all but impossible on the eastern shore.

Ramesses was moving faster than Ament had been led to believe and outriding chariots of the Amun legion, including many captured from the northern legions, clashed with the Shu legion. They had encircled Iurudef's men and pushed northward instead of finishing them off, and now fell upon Shu, sending them reeling back in disarray. Sept moved up in support and repulsed the attacking chariots, pushing southward to join up with the other northern legions.

"This is all that remains of your army?" Ament asked of Iurudef when the Generals met. "What has happened?"

Iurudef took Ament by the arm and drew him aside. "Re remains loyal, but desertions are high among the other two legions."

271

"What is the matter with them? Setnakhte won't stop here. He means to take over the north too. They may flee to their homes, but the war will follow them."

"They have not fled the war," Iurudef said grimly, "but have joined the enemy. We were outnumbered, but at least your two legions will have restored the balance. I will use them to wrest the initiative from Setnakhte."

"No." Ament handed over a scroll. "These are my orders direct from Sitre Tausret. You are relieved of your command and are to resume command of the border legions. I will take your place as General."

Iurudef went pale and stared at Ament. "I am relieved of my command? After all my good work in containing the enemy? Has the king lost her senses?"

"Careful, Iurudef, your words reek of treason. It is only because I hold you in high regard that I overlook them."

"Very good of you, I'm sure, Ament." Iurudef read the document carefully and checked the seals before handing it back. "I have no doubt your hand is in this, but what do you hope to gain by dividing the king's forces? Is this some plot to gain the throne for yourself?"

"That is quite enough, Iurudef. Stop now before you say something that I cannot ignore. I suggest you gather your personal staff together and leave."

"And what will you do?"

"That does not concern you. I am now the Commanding General and will act as I see fit."

Iurudef left within the hour, taking five chariots with him and speeding north. Ament sent out scouts to report on the enemy positions and then called an assembly of his five legions, inspecting them and conferring with their commanders. As Iurudef had indicated, Re was still at almost full strength and loyal, but Heru was at half strength and Sobek even worse. He transferred officers from Re into the under strength legions to stem the flood of desertions and executed some twenty men caught leaving the lines.

"We are here to oppose the traitor Setnakhte," he told the commanders. "I expect every man to offer up his very life for King Sitre Tausret if necessary."

When the reports from the scouts came in, Ament changed his orders. "We will continue the withdrawal," he said.

"We do not oppose the traitor?" Disebek enquired.

"He is too strong for us, and the flood has started."

"It does not affect the desert road," Merymose said. "Let us bring Setnakhte to battle once more."

"We have one and a half experienced legions and two and a half auxiliaries to confront three experienced and however many of our men who have deserted," Ament countered. "I will not waste men in a futile battle."

The northern army withdrew in good order, each legion covering the retreat of its fellows. Ramesses and the Amun legion harassed them all the way, descending upon them in lightning strikes and melting away in the face of firming resistance. Meanwhile, Setnakhte's army advanced behind them, still gaining strength from continued desertions.

By the time Ament had pulled back as far as Men-nefer, the river was in full flood and it was all he could do to pull as many men as he could back over the river into the city, while sending the Re legion northeast to rejoin the border defences. Setnakhte camped out on the plains to the east of the river and contemplated the seat of the king in the capital city across the waters.

Tausret was not pleased to see Ament back again so soon, or to look out upon the burgeoning camp of her enemy on the far side of the river. She ordered Ament into her presence and made her feelings known.

"I made you General so you could defeat the enemy, but instead you have brought him back with you. How are your actions any better than those of that incompetent general, Iurudef?"

"It would have been impossible to defeat him, Majesty," Ament said, bowing low before her anger. "We were outnumbered and desertions among our legions further weakened us."

"Instead, you brought the enemy to the gates of the city."

"The river in flood will prevent an attack, Majesty."

"And when the water goes down?"

"Then we will attack him with the full force of our northern army and destroy him utterly."

Tausret sat on her throne in all her kingly regalia and stared at her new General for a long time. "Let it be as you say," she said at last. "You are dear to my heart, Ament, but even I cannot put you before the Ma'at of

Kemet. You must succeed when the months of Akhet have passed or you too will pass."

Chapter 45
Year 2 (7) Sitre Meryamun Tausret

The flood waters receded at last and the two armies bestirred themselves. Ament had not sat idle in Men-nefer during the months of the inundation, but had completely refitted the legions with him and instituted training programs on the high ground to the west of the city. Nothing could make up for the lack of battle experience, but at least the Troops within each legion were now acting in unison and could be relied upon not to break and run when attacked. Artisans within the city had been hard at work building more chariots too, to replace the ones now gracing the legions under Setnakhte.

Ament ordered two legions south from the northern borders and, as they threatened Setnakhte's soldiers, threw the revitalised Heru and Sobek legions across the river to take him in the rear. Setnakhte's legions had suffered during the protracted inundation and were weaker than they had been when they first arrived. Although outnumbering the legions thrown at them, they pulled back in the face of a determined assault. The Sept and Shu legions joined the fray, and their added strength tipped the balance—Setnakhte withdrew southward, though in good order, while Ramesses guided his chariot squadrons against the northern legions, slowing their advance.

"I have done as I said I would," Ament reported. "I have driven the enemy from the gates of Men-nefer and he now retreats back whence he came."

"I knew you would do it, faithful friend," Tausret said. "Soon this time of trouble will be past and I can bring peace to the Two Kingdoms once more."

"I fear that might be somewhat optimistic, Majesty," Tjaty Mentu said. "Even here in Ta Mehu we are beset with problems, and there is no word from Paraemheb in Waset. I fear the worst for Ta Shemau."

"You see troubles where there are none, Mentu," Tausret responded, waving a hand dismissively. "Setnakhte retreats and will soon surrender. Ma'at will be restored."

Hori looked at Ament. "Why do you hide the true situation from the king?" he asked. "Setnakhte is no longer retreating but has formed a defensive line above Akhetaten. That is not what I would call going back whence he came; nor the action of a man who believes himself defeated."

"Is this true, General Ament?" Tausret asked.

Ament shrugged. "He has halted his retreat," he admitted, "but I have every reason to believe he will renew it. We can bring pressure to bear on him."

"And how long can you keep the northern legions from their duties?"

"Long enough, Mentu. Do not concern yourself with military matters and I will not concern myself with the ruinous situation in Ta Mehu. Fields lie fallow when they should be burgeoning with new life after the inundation, and armed bands spread terror and disaffection throughout the Kingdom. Why are you doing nothing about that?"

"You dare ask me that? One is the result of the other. How can men lead productive lives when their Ma'at is shattered by renewed civil war? Armed men are no longer just found in the army but can now wander with impunity, taking all they desire. Meanwhile, honest men must wait for a victory by the royal legions, but it seems they must wait in vain."

"Enough, Mentu," Tausret said. "The whole nation waits for peace and the restoration of Ma'at, but such things take time to accomplish. Ament, when may I expect reports of a final victory?"

"You have had reports of victory already, Majesty," Ament replied. "There will be more in the future, and one of them will be the final one."

"Before the year is out? I need to ensure that my tomb and Mansion of Millions of Years is finished and I cannot do that while Setnakhte controls the south."

Ament hesitated and then nodded. "If I can use all the legions."

Now that the eyes of the king were fixed upon him, Ament left a single legion, Set, on the northern borders and amassed an army to attack Setnakhte's position. Re, Heru and Ptah led the assault, with Sept, Shu, Sobek and Khent-abt in support. Setnakhte's men fought valiantly, and at one point a charge by Ramesses almost carried the day, but the numbers were too great and first the Kushites and then Mut and Amun were pushed back. By sunset on that first day, the southern army was streaming away, and only darkness prevented Ament from claiming a decisive victory.

Dawn saw the northern army pushing forward again, but messengers arrived from the north, fast chariots bearing the insignia of the Set legion. The Retenu had risen in revolt once more, and the single northern legion could not contain them. Ament cursed, but knew he could not ignore this summons. He sent Heru and Ptah north, with Sept and Sobek in support, ordering Disebek to take over the Ptah legion and command the legions until they arrived at the northern border. They were to report to Iurudef, crush the rebels and return as soon as possible. In the meantime, Ahhotep the commander of Ptah, took Disebek's place in command of the Re legion.

Ament pushed his three remaining legions hard, determined to carry the fight to Setnakhte while his men were still in retreat, but the unrest that Mentu had reported in Ta Mehu flared up and Tausret ordered him to send men to put down a revolt in the western sepats. Ament raged and swore, but he could not ignore a direct order from the king. He left Re and Shu to contain the southern army, now a few days below Akhetaten, and took Khent-abt to put down rebellion in the western sepats.

Ament pushed his men hard, rage consuming him, and ten days later arrived on the western bank downriver from Men-nefer, from where the reports of rebellion had originated. There he founds scenes of devastation--crops burned and livestock slaughtered, and dead and dying men. Interrogations of the survivors revealed that two nobles had rebelled, offering up themselves separately as suitable male heirs to Usermaatre. Both claimed descent from the great king though neither had any military background. Their armies consisted of peasants and robber bands who scented profits by throwing in their lots with a noble. One of the rebels was Meryre, son of Meryatum who had been the Hem-netjer of Re at Iunu and had rebelled in the days of Userkheperure Seti.

"Better for him had he died at the hands of Tausret," Ament snarled when he heard who it was. "I will have no mercy this time."

Tausret had dissuaded Meryre from his previous rebellion, but the man had apparently not learned his lesson. He would not have another chance. Ament thrust deep into Meryre's lands and surprised his ragged army of peasants while they slept. Many were slaughtered, more fled, and Meryre was hauled in chains before Ament.

"Why, Meryre?" Ament asked. "Tausret granted you your life and freedom before. Why spurn that gift now?"

"I am descended from Usermaatre like her," the noble replied proudly, "but unlike her, I am male and can legitimately rule as king. I offered to take her as wife and sit beside her on the throne, but she did not even deign to reply."

"How do you wish to die?"

Meryre went pale. "You cannot kill me. I am a noble and of the line of Usermaatre. You must send me to Men-nefer where I can stand before Lady Tausret. She knows my worth and I am sure will now reconsider my offer."

"You mean King Sitre Tausret."

Meryre shrugged. "I will discuss such matters only with your betters."

"You will have no opportunity to talk to anyone else. I have full powers in this matter. I would have granted you a clean death had I taken you in rebellion the first time," Ament said. "No mercy will be shown you this time." He beckoned Commander Ramose forward. "Impale this man."

Meryre was dragged out screaming and before his shrieks of agony had died away, the Khent-abt legion was on the move once more, seeking out the second rebel in the western sepats.

Amenmose son of Siamun was not hard to find. He was an elderly man who had relied too much on his ancestry and not enough on his talents. Fifty years of managing an estate had convinced him that running the Northern Kingdom could not be much harder, so when the opportunity presented itself, had raised five hundred retainers and mercenaries and declared himself the rightful king of Ta Mehu. It was his belief that the people of Kemet and even the legions would declare for him.

He marched his little army south toward Men-nefer, imagining that the disaffected peasants on the farms he encountered along the way would flock to his banner. They did not, so he halted his march at one of the better estates on his route, and sent out messengers to proclaim his new status and offer rewards for all who followed him. Two days later, one of the messengers arrived back with urgent news and was shown through to the chamber that Amenmose used as his throne room. The would-be king sat on an ebony and copper inlay chair, with Sa-Nekhamun his estate Chamberlain standing beside him, and received the messenger into his presence.

"My lord, I bring news..."

"Kneel when you address your king, and call him Son of Re," Sa-Nekhamun said sharply.

The messenger bowed and then dropped to his knees on the hard earthen floor of the room. "Son of Re, I bring news of Meryre, son of Meryatum, who rose in rebellion against the lady king Sitre..."

"Yes, I shall have to deal with that upstart," Amenmose mused. "But after I have got rid of that Tausret woman. Go on, man. What was your news?"

"Son of Re, Meryre is dead."

"Ah, excellent news, Majesty," Sa-Nekhamun said. "How did he die?"

"My lord, he was executed by impalement on the orders of General Ament three days ago and...Son of Re, General Ament and the Khent-abt legion are but half a day behind me. Their intention is to capture you too."

"What?" Amenmose lurched to his feet and stared wildly around the room. "Prepare for battle, Sa-Nekhamun. The enemy is upon us."

Sa-Nekhamun dismissed the messenger and dared lay hands on his king, demanding his attention. "It is too late for that, Lord Amenmose..."

"I am King Amenmose. Don't forget it."

Sa-Nekhamun shook his head. "You have declared yourself so, but you are not yet king and now I fear you never will be. Your hope lay in the common people rising for you, but they have not. And now General Ament is knocking on your door."

"I have men..."

"Four hundred farm workers and a hundred mercenaries, Lord Amenmose. Ament has a full legion of trained soldiers. They won't even notice your men."

"So what do I do?"

"Your choices are limited, Lord Ramose. You can attempt battle and be annihilated; you can surrender; or you can kill yourself."

Amenmose sat down again, sweating. "If...if I surrendered..."

"Then I imagine Ament will deal with you as he has dealt with Meryre. Impalement is not a pleasant death."

Amenmose swallowed, looking pale. "I could offer him gold."

Sa-Nekhamun laughed. "My Lord, he stands high in the regard of Lady Tausret. I imagine he has more gold than he knows what to do with."

Amenmose got to his feet again. "Then I must flee."

"Where to, my Lord?"

"I...I don't know. The Amorites perhaps? The Retenu? The Ribu?"

"No Kemetu ally would give you refuge, and no enemy would take you in unless you could offer them a huge bribe. What then would sustain you? No, my lord, your only options are to fight, to surrender, or to die." Sa-Nekhamun smiled, seeing the terror on the face of the man who had been his lord for over thirty years. "In fact, you have even less choice, my Lord, for death awaits you no matter what course you choose. You can only choose the manner of your death."

"I...I could not face Meryre's fate."

"Then your choice narrows further, my Lord. If you surrender to Ament he will likely impale you, and your body will be thrown on the midden heap. You will not live in the afterlife. Take up arms against him and you may die in battle by axe, spear or arrow or be captured and impaled. Again, your body will probably not be preserved." Sa-Nekhamun led his master to the chair once more and knelt before him. "My Lord, the choice before you is not one of life or death but whether you will live in the afterlife or not. Write a letter to Ament saying you were misled by false advisers and that you are loyal to Sitre Tausret..."

"And he will let me live?" Amenmose quavered.

"No, my Lord, but if he finds the letter on your dead body, he will likely not exact further retribution. Your family will be allowed to keep your estates and property and will be able to bury you properly. Thus you will live on in the Field of Reeds."

"I...I must think on this..."

"You have no time, Lord Amenmose. Ament is close by and any delay may result in your capture and humiliation."

"Then how?" Amenmose licked his lips. "Must I...must I plunge a dagger into my throat? I don't think I...I could."

"I have poison," Sa-Nekhamun admitted. "I had thought to take it myself should your venture fail but...your need is greater than mine."

Amenmose clasped Sa-Nekhamun's hands in his own and looked at him with tear-moistened eyes. "You would do that for me? May the gods bless you in the afterlife, my faithful servant."

Sa-Nekhamun sent for paper and ink and using his own skills as a scribe, set out the necessary phrases, putting the blame for the abortive rebellion on unnamed advisers. He included assurances that Amenmose's loyalty should not be questioned and that he had acted for what he thought was the benefit of Kemet. Amenmose added his seal, and Sa-Nekhamun passed over a tiny pottery phial with a tightly tied bark stopper.

Amenmose looked at the phial in his hand and licked his dry lips. "Will it hurt?" he whispered.

"I am told it is swift and relatively painless, my Lord, though I have never seen it in action."

Amenmose untied the stopper and removed it. A faint acrid smell assailed their nostrils. "Should we both drink from it? I do not like to think of you left to face Ament alone."

"Alas, my Lord, there is only a single dose. Drink and escape Ament's wrath. I will tend to your body and take my chances with the enemy. And if he should exact vengeance on me I will count it an honour to have served you."

"You are indeed a faithful servant, Sa-Nekhamun. I am minded to offer you a reward for your long years of service now that you can no longer attend upon my needs. My estates, of course, are left to my wife and children, but I have a small chest of gold, some jewels, an ingot or two of copper which I brought with me. It contains nearly a hundred deben of fine gold..."

"You are indeed generous, my Lord."

"...and I want you to deliver this and the jewels to my wife when I am dead, but you may keep the copper for yourself as a reward. Will you do that last thing for me?"

Sa-Nekhamun bowed deeply so his master could not see the expression on his face. "I am your faithful servant as always, Lord Amenmose."

Amenmose took a deep breath and let it out in a trembling rush. His hand shook as he held the phial of poison. "I am afraid," he murmured.

"Death is nothing to be afraid of, my Lord, for we live with it all our lives, preparing for it. A few moments and you face an eternity of comfort and luxury in the Field of Reeds."

"That is true. I have been a kind and generous man all my life, tending my vineyards, raising a family and providing for them, honouring the gods. There is no reason why my heart should weigh more than the Feather of Truth. The gods will welcome me to the afterlife as a worthy grandson of Usermaatre Ramesses."

Amenmose hesitated a moment longer and then tossed the contents of the phial into his mouth and swallowed convulsively. He stood for a moment, grimacing at the taste and the effect it was having on his body and then ventured a tentative smile.

"It has only a slightly bitter taste and there is no pain..."

His features twisted and he clutched his belly. "Ah, perhaps there is a bit. Should I sit or lie down, Sa-Nekhamun?"

"You will lie down for eternity soon enough. I would enjoy standing while you can."

Amenmose frowned, and sat down on his erstwhile throne. "Your tone is somewhat discourteous. I do not...ah!" He doubled over and clawed at his throat. "It...it burns," he rasped. "Bring me water to soothe my throat."

"Fetch it yourself," Sa-Nekhamun said. "I do not serve a dead man."

"What? You dare..." Amenmose cried out as agony bit deep into his gut and he slid off the chair and onto the ground. "Oh, gods...it hurts...you s...said it would...not."

Sa-Nekhamun stood and looked down at his master curled at his feet. "Perhaps I did not know, or perhaps I lied." He shrugged. "I have repaid your overwhelming generosity over the years, my Lord Amenmose."

Sweat broke out on the face of the dying man as he stared up at his servant. "I have...always...been good...to you..."

"I have been all but a slave these past twenty years, so poor that I have no wife or children. And now, having risked my life on your last foolhardy venture, you think to reward me with a pittance of copper." Sa-Nekhamun squatted beside Amenmose. "No more. I will take your gold as my reward and flee this place before Ament gets here. He will find your body and seek no one else."

"May the...the gods curse...y...you, but at...at least...I shall live...in eternity."

Sa-Nekhamun got to his feet and smiled. "Maybe, if Ament feels generous toward a known rebel."

"The...letter..."

Amenmose uttered a final groan and lapsed into unconsciousness. His sphincter gave way releasing a foetid stink into the room and Sa-Nekhamun stepped back with a look of distaste on his face. He picked up the letter pleading Amenmose's case and took it with him as he left the room.

Half a day later, Ament and the Khent-abt legion marched into the estate, by which time Amenmose's retainers and mercenaries had scattered. Ament entered the main chamber of the estate and stood over the body of the rebel. He nudged it with his foot.

"He has taken poison, I see. An admission of guilt if one was needed." Ament turned to the army scribe. "Let it be recorded that the rebel Amenmose son of Siamun sought to escape justice by taking his own life. As a punishment, his estates are to be confiscated."

"And the body, General Ament? Shall I tell the family to collect it for burial?"

"He does not deserve a burial. Have his corpse thrown in the river to feed the crocodiles."

Chapter 46
Year 2 (7) Sitre Meryamun Tausret

Coincidentally, on the day that Ament stood over the dead body of Amenmose, Setnakhte became aware that his pursuit had dwindled to only two legions. He turned at once and launched his own assault, halting the Re legion in its tracks and hurling the Shu legion back in disarray. The Kushites kept Re pinned down in one of the desert forts, while Amun and Mut broke free, racing north as fast as they could. They overwhelmed Shu and captured several hundred including their commander, Natsefamen. Though he expected death at the hands of the southern General, Natsefamen stood with his men and refused to bow down to his conqueror. Instead of immediately killing him, however, the Shu legion commander was brought before Setnakhte and Ramesses.

"Commander Natsefamen, you fought well but now it is time to lay down your arms. Bow your head to me and I will spare you and your men."

"Why would you do that, General Setnakhte?"

"I am not a barbarian who kills for pleasure, nor a fanatic who desires the death of all who oppose him. I seek only what is good for Kemet and is right in the eyes of the gods."

"And what is that, General?"

"To end this civil war and restore the Ma'at of Kemet."

"It seems to me that the easiest way to do that is for you to bow your head to the king and return to your duties in Waset."

"I would gladly bow my head to the king if there was a legitimate one. The House of Ramesses fell with the death of Prince Seti-Merenptah. The woman who now sits upon the throne has no right to it."

"And you do?"

"More right than Lady Tausret. I am from the loins of Usermaatre, and I have a grown heir already, here in my son Ramesses. The line that Usermaatre chose to succeed him has been broken and it is time to place another family over the Two Kingdoms--my family. I will destroy this woman who pretends to be king and mean to be king in her place. Join me, Natsefamen, and restore peace to our tired land."

Natsefamen sighed and closed his eyes, praying to the gods for guidance. Whether or not they answered he never spoke of it, but bowed low before Setnakhte and hailed him as king.

The Shu legion was strengthened and stiffened with loyal officers drawn from Amun and Mut, and Setnakhte resumed his northward march, now at the head of three legions. A fourth and fifth joined him half a month later when the Kushites caught up with him. They brought Ahhotep, newly appointed Commander of Re, captive with them, and most of the Re legion now marched under the banner of Setnakhte. Ahhotep followed the example of Natsefamen and bowed to Setnakhte. The General put other officers over the remnants of Re, and reached the plains to the east of Men-nefer at the head of an army almost as large as the northern one.

Tausret immediately dispatched messengers to the northern borders while Ament, who had returned to Men-nefer with the Khent-abt legion, set about preparing the city for a siege. He withdrew every boat from the river, determined to deny Setnakhte any means of crossing the river, and then had his troops scouring the neighbouring countryside for food, bringing it into the city and storing it. Other soldiers rounded up gangs of masons and unskilled labourers to go over every cubit of the city walls and make repairs as necessary.

"The city is prepared," Ament reported. "At least as much as it can be. We have the Khent-abt legion for defence and the palace guards, but most of all we have the city walls. They will keep out an army--for a while, anyway."

"Ah, the shining white walls of Men-nefer," Tausret said with a smile. "I do not want to see the city suffer, Ament. We must march out and face the enemy."

"That would not be a good idea, my Lady. Setnakhte has five legions under his command now, while we have only one. Wait until Iurudef arrives with the northern legions and then we can make plans."

"How is it that the king of Kemet must sit inside city walls while my enemies go where they please? What has happened, Ament?"

Ament regarded the worn woman on her throne with compassion. "It was not always so, my Lady, but the civil war that ripped the Kingdoms apart in the reign of your husband Userkheperure has left its scars on the people. They thought that the days of your regency heralded a time of healing and peace, but now they see renewed warfare staring them in the face. You are weighed against Setnakhte and I fear many see him as the hope for the future."

"I have ruled well this past year, haven't I? And when I ruled Kemet as regent? Why should people choose Setnakhte who has never ruled and has done nothing for the common people? At least when some chose the side of Menmire Amenmesse against my husband, they were choosing another king. Setnakhte's supporters have no such excuse."

"Some see him as king already--people in the south. Others see him as the likely victor in any civil war, so reason that supporting him now will shorten that war."

"And you Ament? What do you think?"

Ament pondered Tausret's question and his answer before speaking. "You know that I will follow you to the death, my Lady."

"I know, Ament, and I love and honour you for it, but I meant the war against General Setnakhte. Is it a war that I can win?"

"Ah, Lady, that depends on circumstances outside your control. A month ago, I would have said it was possible but today, if you look across the river, you can see the banners of the two legions I left to contain the enemy. Blame me for their loss, if you will, but the commanders of those legions are either dead or have changed their allegiance."

"I do not blame you, my friend," Tausret said. "There was little you could do but leave them to put down rebellion in Ta Mehu. We must do what we can with what we have left."

"That is little enough," Ament said. "Setnakhte has five legions; we have five on the border and one here, but with that we must defend against Kemet's external enemies as well as her internal ones."

"So you think it is hopeless? I refuse to admit there is nothing we can do."

"Not hopeless, my Lady, but everything depends on the loyalty of the remaining army commanders. If they stay loyal we may yet defeat Setnakhte; if they change sides..." Ament shrugged and left the thought unexpressed.

Another month passed, during which Tausret's kingdom shrank as she pulled her loyal forces into Men-nefer and Setnakhte spread his control over the east bank of the river. He still did not have enough boats to cross the river and carry the fight to his enemy, but he made sure that his army was well supplied and in good spirits. A messenger boat sped into the Men-nefer docks, bearing word from the north. General Iurudef had come south with three legions--Set, Sobek, and Sept--and had taken up a defensive position in Iunu.

"The legions are no use up there," Ament fumed. "Send orders that he march south, my Lady. With Khent-abt and the palace guard we may yet match the enemy."

Tausret send word immediately and five days later she had Iurudef's reply. She read it in silence and then handed it to Ament. "He says he cannot hope to defeat Setnakhte in open battle, so he awaits the will of the gods."

"Traitorous dog."

"One can hardly blame him, I suppose," Tausret said calmly. "But it does complicate matters. I cannot defeat Setnakhte without him, and so the will of the gods becomes manifest if he does not aid me. In other words, he believes Setnakhte will win and does not want to be seen fighting the man who will be Kemet's next king."

"Let me take some trusted men and I will kill this traitor," Ament said.

"No, I have had enough of killing. Rather, send Mentu to negotiate with him. There must be something that will induce him to come to my aid."

Tjaty Mentu sailed north to Iunu, bearing messages from Sitre Tausret that offered encouragements to Iurudef to remain loyal. He was to return within five days with the General's reply, but it was ten days before Mentu's message was delivered to the king. Tausret read it and then screwed up the scroll, tossing it aside. With a sweep of her linen dress, she turned and left the room, her cheeks flushed with anger.

Ament picked up the crumpled letter, smoothed it out and read it. 'Daughter of Re,' it read, 'I have completed my assignment and carried your words and offers of reward to General Iurudef. We entered into discussions of his loyalty to Kemet and to you, and of his duty. He is adamant that he will await the manifest will of the gods before venturing out of Iunu with his legions, and he has convinced me of the legitimacy of his decision. Therefore, I cannot return to Men-nefer, but will remain in Iunu pending resolution of the civil war that presently tears Kemet apart. I will pray to all the gods for a speedy end to the troubles.'

"I will have your heart for this act of treason, Mentu," Ament swore. "As soon as I can issue the orders, an assassin will pay you and Iurudef a visit. Without your poison, the legions will remember who is truly king."

Ament ordered his most trusted spies into his presence and told them of his desires regarding the man who called himself Tjaty of the North. They went to arrange passage to Iunu, but before they could sail, the situation changed. Sails by the tens and then by the hundreds dotted the wide green waters of the Great River; boats of all sizes sweeping down on the current toward Men-nefer and docking on the eastern shore. The means had arrived for Setnakhte to cross the water and lay siege to the city. While he had waited, he had sent word to Waset and the cities of Ta Shemau to send every available boat and they had responded enthusiastically.

Within five days, Setnakhte transferred three legions to the western bank and surrounded the city of Men-nefer, cutting off King Sitre Tausret from her kingdoms.

Chapter 47
Year 2 (7) Sitre Meryamun Tausret

For half a month, Setnakhte sat outside Men-nefer, slowly tightening his grip on the city. As well as preventing anyone entering or leaving the city via one of the land gates, he stationed archers on boats to ring the docks and hastily erected defences along the river. Nobody could enter or leave by water either, and the populace was also limited in the water they could scoop from the river.

Setnakhte waited until there was no doubt that he had complete control of the city before sending a herald to convey a message to Sitre Tausret. Guards at the northern gate brought the herald to General Ament, who read the message and told the herald to wait upon his return. Ament took the message to Tausret and handed her the scroll in silence, waiting for her to read it.

"I cannot accept this," she said quietly, handing it back to Ament.

"He offers to discuss a bloodless solution," Ament replied. "One that will end the war without further destruction or hardship. It might be worth at least hearing what he has to say."

"He addresses me as Lady Tausret, Great Wife, as if I was no more than the wife of my husband the king. How can I receive him if he will not recognise me as king?"

Ament looked at the scroll again and frowned. "I did not see that, hurrying as I was to get to the meat of his message. Forgive me, my Lady; of course you cannot speak with him. I will tell the herald that."

The herald returned to the camp of the besiegers and delivered Ament's reply on behalf of his king. Setnakhte shook his head and dismissed the herald. He waited another half month and sent the herald back with another message. Again, Ament took delivery of the scroll and this time scanned it carefully before taking it to Tausret.

"At least he addresses you as king, even if he leaves out almost all your honorifics."

"The same message though?"

Ament nodded, handing over the scroll. Tausret glanced at it and put it aside.

"I suppose I will have to meet with him."

"At least to hear his proposal, my Lady. The problem is the meeting place. You cannot go out to his camp, and I dare say he will not trust you enough to put himself in your hands by coming into the city."

"I will go to him."

"You will do no such thing..." Ament shut his mouth with an almost audible snap, and bowed, blushing with embarrassment. "Forgive my presumption, my Lady, but I cannot let you offer yourself up to the enemy. I...I speak as your military adviser."

"I would rather you spoke as my friend, Ament, for I have many who would advise me though mostly for their own ends." Tausret sighed. "I must go out to him, if for no other reason than I am an anointed king of Kemet. No one will harm me, for to do so would call down the wrath of the gods. I also cannot show fear, Ament, for then all is lost."

"I see your point, my Lady, but because you are king you cannot go to Setnakhte as if you were a petitioner. Any support you still have would vanish at a stroke."

"I must do something though. The city is restless as food runs low and soon people will start dying. They should not die because I am too stubborn or too proud to meet with my enemy."

Ament considered while Tausret sat in silence, observing him. "You should remain in the city, my Lady. Let Setnakhte come to you."

"He will not do that, and if he will not, then I must go to him."

"I advise against it--both as a friend and as your General."

"I know, but I must."

"Then let me seek a compromise. You leave the city, but he comes to you."

Tausret tilted her head to one side and regarded Ament. "I don't understand."

"I set up a throne under a canopy just outside the gates. You sit there in regal dignity and receive Setnakhte as a formal petitioner. All the official niceties are observed, and both can claim the upper hand."

"Do you think he will agree?"

"I can ask him."

Ament put the suggestion to Setnakhte and he agreed, saying that he was prepared to give up a little dignity if it would result in an end to the war. Ament replied, asking for a short truce so that he might set up the meeting place. This was granted, but Setnakhte made the stipulation that the site must not be within bowshot of the city walls. Ament then insisted that Setnakhte withdraw his army back at least a bowshot beyond that. Negotiations continued, gradually sorting out the details. Tausret entered into the discussion, requesting that Setnakhte allow food into the city during this time of negotiation, but here he refused, saying that Tausret had it within her power to alleviate the suffering of her people. The longer the negotiations were drawn out, the longer it would take to resolve the issues and bring peace to the Kingdoms.

The day of the meeting dawned, and before the heat of the day increased too much, Ament led a group of servants out of the northern gate, pacing out the agreed-upon distance, while Setnakhte's encircling army drew back, allowing a great open space to appear. Tausret's servants levelled the ground with mattocks and hoes, laid down rush mats and linen cloth on top, erected a large canopy to banish the sun's heat and linen walls to channel the breezes, and set up the royal throne amid much splendour.

Rams' horns blew and a small procession wound its way out of the city, Tausret held aloft on a cushioned chair with fan-bearers shading her with ostrich feather plumes. Priests chanted songs of praise to the god-on-earth King of Kemet, and the people cheered. The enthusiasm of the people was somewhat subdued, but Ament made sure Tausret remained unaware by making a big show of banging drums and shaking sistra. In this way, the procession made its slow way to the open air pavilion where Tausret mounted the throne and sat in full regalia, heka and nekhakha of kingly authority crossed on her chest.

"Let General Setnakhte approach," called the royal herald.

After a brief pause, Setnakhte walked out from his camp with a small entourage of army officers and marched toward the royal pavilion. He stopped some fifty paces away and, telling his officers to wait, approached with only his son Ramesses as companion. The two men looked wary as they strode into the shade of the pavilion, but unafraid of Ament and the soldiers of the palace guard. Neither rebel bowed low or knelt as was customary in the presence of the king, but instead offered up a courteous inclination of the head and hailed Tausret as Lady and Great Wife of Userkheperure Seti. Ament sucked in his breath at the studied insult, but kept his temper, offering Setnakhte and Ramesses chairs and wine. They accepted the first but not the second.

"So, Lady Tausret," Setnakhte said. "Do I speak directly to you or through your servant Ament, who all know has your ear at all times?"

"And other parts too, by all accounts," Ramesses murmured.

Anger swept across Tausret's face. "If your son cannot keep a civil tongue in his head, then this meeting is over. General Ament is a dear friend and adviser and he speaks for me often. Today, though, I speak for myself."

Setnakhte inclined his head once more. "Forgive my son's impetuous words, Lady Tausret. He meant no disrespect, merely repeating common gossip. However, such speech has no place here, so consider his words withdrawn and unspoken."

"I can readily forgive the impetuousness of youth, though your son is a grown man and should know better. However, in this instance I forgive him. Now, General Setnakhte, you have left your station without the permission of your king and threaten the peace of the Kingdoms. These actions must be explained and I presume it is for this purpose that you seek audience with me. Say what you will now that you have my ear."

"Lady Tausret," Setnakhte said after a few moments. "We must come to an agreement for the good of Kemet. I do not seek to threaten the peace of the kingdoms, and I have left my station in the south without permission because there is no one to give or withhold that permission. You refer to the king but Lady, there is no king, and has not been since the death of Userkheperure these seven years past."

"If you deny Sitre Tausret is king then you are a fool or a traitor," Ament growled.

"Lady Tausret, I have come here to talk to you, not to listen to your dog yapping."

"Then speak," Tausret replied. "Ament, let us hear what he has to say without undue interruption."

"As I was saying," Setnakhte continued, "Kemet is without a legitimate king and consequently suffers because of it."

"You have always claimed that, General Setnakhte, even in Waset after I had been crowned, but your claim is without foundation. Amun himself accepted me as King of Kemet. Must I send for the god's Hem-netjer to explain matters to you?"

"Lady Tausret, I am quite capable of understanding that men claiming to speak in Amun's name have accepted you as king, but I hold that is exactly what it is. Men have named you king for their own purposes, not the gods."

"That could be said of any king," Tausret observed. "Men--priests--speak for the gods. Do you dispute also that Usermaatre was king? Or Baenre? Or Userkheperure? Or Akhenre?"

"Except for the last, they were all true kings, as every man accepts."

"Even Akhenre," Tausret said, "though I had no cause to love the boy who supplanted my son. Yet the gods accepted him too, so who was I to defy them?"

"Siptah, for I will not acknowledge the throne name he was given, and his father Amenmesse before him are all the evidence you need that men can place kings on the throne, claiming it was the gods who put them there. Why, it was even that Amorite Bay who claimed to have put his nephew on his father's throne."

"Can we ever be sure that the gods have not put a king in his place though?" Tausret asked. "We may say that men put them there, but maybe it really was the gods acting through men. Once we start to question the decisions of the gods, where do we stop? Must we call into doubt every facet of Kemetu society?"

Setnakhte looked uncomfortable and shifted on his chair. "I have not come to argue about everyday matters, Lady Tausret. Only to dispute the most important aspect of our lives--that Kemet has no king."

"And I would say that you are mistaken, General Setnakhte. Kemet does have a king. I have been duly anointed and crowned, accepted by every god--King Sitre Meryamun Tausret Setepenmut."

"Then we are at an impasse, for I will never accept you as king."

Tausret sighed. "Not even for the sake of peace and Kemet's wellbeing?"

"How is Kemet served by allowing a false king to sit on the throne?"

"If it stops the fighting, the shedding of innocent blood, then it is worth it."

Setnakhte shook his head. "There is another solution, Lady Tausret. One that would restore peace and Ma'at. Step down from the throne and allow another to rule in your place."

Tausret smiled wryly. "Now we come to it. By another, I suppose you mean you?"

"I am the best qualified," Setnakhte admitted.

"Qualified how? By men's standards or by gods'? You are perhaps the choice of men, but I am the choice of the gods."

"How did the gods choose you, Lady Tausret? To the best of my knowledge you seized power when Siptah died, there being no natural heir to the line of Usermaatre."

"I ruled Kemet in all but name during Akhenre's reign, and when he died my son Seti-Merenptah should have succeeded him. There was no one else, so of course I put myself forward. Someone has to sit on the throne of Kemet and I was the logical choice. My grandfather was king, my adoptive father was king, my husband was king, and my son would have been king. I was Great Wife and God's wife of Amun, royal by birth and marriage, and Chosen of Amun. Who are you to dispute my right?"

"I am Setnakhte, son of Usermaatre, and my blood is as royal as yours."

"Your mother was a concubine, whereas I descend from Queen Isetnofret, mother of both Baenre and my natural father Sethi."

Setnakhte scowled and made a chopping motion with his hand. "This all signifies little," he said. "You are a woman, Lady Tausret, and whatever your antecedents, you are unsuited to reign as king."

"Women have reigned as king before. Check your histories."

"Never for long, and never successfully. Kemet needs a man who can lead armies against the Nine Bows."

"I have successfully led an army against the Ribu and against rebels."

"I am talking about serious foes, Lady Tausret."

"I have Generals and Commanders for such occasions."

"And yet none of them can succeed against me," Setnakhte pointed out. "Here I am outside Men-nefer with an army five legions strong and none dare oppose me. I am king already, in all but name."

"And I am king in name."

"Queen maybe, Regent, Great Wife, God's Wife--but not king."

"I am all of those things, General."

"You could be."

Tausret looked puzzled. "What do you mean?"

"You need a husband to rule beside you; one who is also royal."

Puzzlement turned to humour. "I think you are too old for me, Setnakhte; even if I was so inclined."

"Not me, Lady Tausret, but my son Ramesses. I will reign as king, but in five or ten years--whatever the gods grant me--Ramesses will succeed me with you as Queen beside him. He is strong and manly. A son of yours may yet rule Kemet."

"You put this forward as a serious proposition?"

"Yes."

"I am not looking for a husband, nor do I need one."

"I am giving you a way out, Lady Tausret. Refuse me and I will sit outside the walls of Men-nefer until everyone inside is dead of hunger, if need be. Nobody is coming to save you."

"Then why make your offer. Wouldn't it be easier to pluck the crown from a dead woman than to make her your son's wife and share the crown?"

Setnakhte shrugged. "You have played your part in the affairs of Kemet, Lady, guarding the throne as best you could, and I honour you for that, but times have changed. The old House of Ramesses has all but vanished and it is time for a new family to rule. I have the power to make it happen whatever you do, but it pleases me to be generous. Join your family to mine and continue to rule Kemet; refuse and go down into death."

Tausret sat and contemplated Setnakhte's words for several minutes. At last she stirred. "I thank you for your words, General Setnakhte, and will consider them carefully."

Setnakhte stood, and Ramesses joined him as he looked bleakly down on the seated woman. "Don't take too long," he said softly.

Chapter 48

Setnakhte speaks:

I am committed. Before this moment I could have made my excuses and retired to my estates, even having shed Kemetu blood. As General of the South I could have argued that I fought the enemies of Kemet in the guise of loyal forces, but once I faced Lady Tausret I had no excuse. Not that I wanted one. She is a royal lady but no king, and she has had shocking advice from her councillors.

I have the military might to take the throne--five legions of my own, five waiting to see the outcome of my bid for power, and only one actively opposing me. The throne is mine, and I only have to stretch out my hand to take it. Yet I would rather not spill any more Kemetu blood to take what is mine, which is why I made the offer to Tausret. Bind her family to mine in bonds of marriage and there is nothing left to fight for. I did not think she would leap at the opportunity, so was not surprised when she temporised. She may or may not accept my offer, but it does not matter if she rejects me--it just means that the blame for further bloodshed falls on her head.

Tausret is comely enough and the sight of her stirs my aged loins, but I am happy enough with my Tiy-Merenese, mother of my son Ramesses. The Queen is older than my son, but their marriage would not be for the sake of an heir, despite what I intimated to Tausret. Ramesses has a wife already, and a young son to succeed him, and while a king may have many wives, he does not need a son by that one. I shudder to think of it--that a son of Tausret should one day sit on the Double Throne. No, her purpose is solely to lend legitimacy to my family. The marriage is to merge two families--the present rulers and the future rulers. After a few years, when the people can appreciate that Ma'at has been restored, she can quietly disappear into the Women's Quarters along with a host of other wives and concubines, or into death. I care not which. She will be granted a simple tomb somewhere--certainly not the grand one excavated for her in the valley which houses the kings. I will find another use for it.

Ament is another matter. He hates me, and I him. When I become king, one of my first acts must be to eliminate him, otherwise he will always cause trouble. Ramesses spoke the truth when he mocked Ament's intimacy with Tausret. Rumours are rife, and seeing them together, it is obvious they are lovers, though he is a commoner. That is another reason not to let the woman breed. How could my son trust that a child he planted in her was his, when her field had been ploughed by a common man? And if he was allowed to live, would he then claim the child was his and attempt to disrupt the new ruling family? It is not to be countenanced, and so Ament must die.

What then of the other men of note within the kingdoms? I am prepared to let Tjaty Paraemheb and Tjaty Hori live and continue on in their positions. Whether they will do so after me is a matter for my son to decide. The army commanders are, for the most part, capable of loyalty to me, so I will let them live too. Exceptions might be Ramose, Commander of Khent-abt, as he is altogether too close to Ament; and Mose, acting Commander of the Set legion. I think I will remove them as a precaution. Iurudef I shall leave for now as General of the North, for he is an experienced army officer. He has shown he knows I will succeed, by keeping his legions in Iunu and not attempting a rescue of Lady Tausret.

So, I await Lady Tausret's decision. If she agrees to the marriage, then I will stay in Men-nefer long enough to see her wed to my son and then go immediately to Waset to be crowned as king. If she does not agree, then my task is a little harder, and my coronation must be delayed. I will have to stay until the city is taken. I could leave Ramesses in charge, but he is headstrong and I do not want him to be deceived by Ament. Furthermore, I want him with me to name him Crown Prince publicly in Waset. Our strength lies in Waset and Ta shemau, and the people of that southern kingdom deserve to know all their woes have been rewarded by a king from among them.

It is no great thing whether my coronation is delayed a few months or not--I am effectively king already and when the scribes start the accounts of my reign, they will date my accession to the death of Seti-Merenptah. In the eyes of the gods, the child succeeded his father Userkheperure, who was the last legitimately crowned king of Kemet, and I succeeded the child when he died. It is two years since Seti-Merenptah died, so I have been king for two years already. What gods shall I choose to honour above all others in my throne name? Re of course, and Amun, but also Ma'at, I think, for I shall be restoring all good things to Kemet. I shall reign with Truth and Justice; Order and Balance shall rule the kingdoms; Harmony and Law will govern the people's lives, while Morality and Generosity bathe their hearts.

Chapter 49
Year 2 (7) Sitre Meryamun Tausret

Tausret said very little when she returned to the palace after the meeting with Setnakhte and Ament took this to mean she was seriously considering the marriage proposal made by the southern General on behalf of his son. It angered him, and a measure of his anger had its roots in jealousy.

"Well, you won't have a better offer than that, will you?"

Tausret said nothing; just looked at him.

"He already has a wife and an heir too, but I don't suppose that matters to you. He's young enough still to pleasure you."

One of the ubiquitous servants entered the room with a wine jug and cups. He hurriedly set the tray on a low table and as he turned to go, bumped the table and some wine slopped over the edge of the jug.

Ament strode over and clipped the servant across the head. "Clumsy oaf!" he roared. "Get out before I batter you senseless." He pushed the servant and the man scurried from the room.

"Don't take your frustrations out on the servants," Tausret said mildly. "It ill becomes you."

"What do you care? I'm just another one of your swarming servants-- useful for a time and then cast aside." Ament poured himself a cup of wine and downed it, spilling the rich liquid down his chin and spattering his tunic.

"Where is this coming from?" Tausret asked. "What have I done to offend you?"

"Offend me? You? As if you didn't know." Ament poured more wine and drank more slowly this time, wiping his mouth with his forearm. "I suppose that show out there pleased you? One moment a king in your own right about to lose your throne, the next a queen of a revitalised family with a virile young man to plough your field."

"Pour me some wine, Ament."

Ament scowled but did as he was told, handing Tausret the cup.

299

"Thank you, Ament." She sipped. "When did you hear me say I accepted Setnakhte's offer?"

"You said you'd consider it. How could you even contemplate it? Just because he's descended from Usermaatre..."

"Is that important?" Tausret asked.

"Well, of course it is. Even I know that a royal lady cannot bed just anyone if she hopes to produce an heir."

"And there is the good of Kemet to consider." A faint smile lit Tausret's face and she sipped from her cup again. "If I did not lie with Ramesses, who should I lie with?"

Ament mumbled something and examined his own cup closely.

"What was that you said, Ament?"

"I said, 'exactly'." He shrugged. "You are the king, you will lie with whomever you choose."

"I'm glad you understand that."

Ament sighed and put down his cup. "My apologies, Sitre Tausret. I don't know what I was thinking, making utterances like that."

"I do," Tausret said softly. Louder, she asked, "You will really help me take the man of my choice to my bed?"

Ament went pale but he nodded. "Whomever you choose, my Lady."

Tausret regarded Ament for a minute, but he stood a few paces away, staring at the floor. "Do you really not know the man I want, Ament?"

Something in her tone made Ament look up and he saw a smile on Tausret's face.

"Don't you know I love you?" she asked.

Ament's jaw dropped open. "Wh...wh...what?" he stuttered.

"Will you hold me, Ament? I am greatly in need of comfort."

Ament did not say anything but stepped forward hesitantly and awkwardly embraced her. After a few moments, she pressed herself against him and laughed.

"You hold me with a show of reluctance, Ament, but your body tells another story."

Ament blushed and held her tightly. "I cannot help it, my Lady, for I have always loved you."

Tausret turned her face up and stood on her toes, kissing Ament gently. A second or two passed and he returned it, hesitantly at first, and then with passion.

"My bedchamber lies through that door," Tausret said. "Will you not take me there?"

Ament held her at arm's length and searched her face. "Are you sure, my Lady? You are...the king, and I am just a commoner."

"You are not 'just' anything, and as for being sure, I have wanted it almost as long as I have known you."

"Then..."

"Yes."

Ament took Tausret to her bedchamber and together they slaked the love they had felt for so many years. After, they lay together naked on the bed and talked, remembering.

"You are the first...and probably the only man I have truly loved," Tausret said.

"But my Lady, what of the king your husband? Userkheperure?"

"You can use his personal name when we are alone, dear Ament, just as you can call me Tausret or any other term of endearment you choose. None of this 'Lady' nonsense." She snuggled closer. "You have to understand that my marriage to my brother Seti was arranged from an early age. It is standard practice within royal families, and a woman is considered fortunate if she loves the man she must marry. I was very fond of Seti, and I honoured him, but I didn't really love him. Instead I fell in love with a dashing young Leader of Five when he escorted us to Waset so many years ago."

"Even then, my La...Tausret? I fell in love with you too, before I ever knew who you were. I imagined all sorts of things happening between us on that journey."

"Oh? What sorts of things? Tell me."

Ament's hands moved. "I'd rather show you."

He did, and for another long while nothing was said. They slept and woke and made love again. Nobody disturbed them, though servants came and went in the outer rooms. Knowledge of Ament's revised status spread rapidly through the palace but few were surprised by it, having assumed something must already have taken place between a man and a woman who so plainly loved each other.

Toward evening they rose, bathed and sat down to a light meal in the privacy of the royal chambers. Not much was said as they ate, but they looked in each other's eyes and fed each other morsels of food.

"What do we do now?" Ament asked, wiping his lips with a linen napkin.

"Do? We enjoy each other's company for as long a time as the gods allow us."

"There might be a way we can increase that time. I have been thinking."

"What about?"

"About our situation here in Men-nefer and Setnakhte outside."

Tausret sighed and stretched her limbs like a cat. "How like a man to be thinking of what comes next even as he sows his seed. A woman thinks only of the present, of being in her man's arms, but a man always seeks something more."

"That is not true, my love...well, not completely true. We cannot remain in your chambers all our lives...much as I would like to," he added quickly. "Events outside these walls won't wait for us, so we must prepare ourselves."

"I suppose you are right. What is your plan?"

"We can do nothing if we wait behind these walls until the food runs out. The people will most likely throw open the gates and surrender. However, we do not have the strength to fight Setnakhte--he has five legions to our one--unless we can use the northern legions."

"That won't work. Iurudef remains in Iunu, just waiting for the city to fall so he can kneel before Setnakhte. He will never come to our rescue."

"Not if we only send messages," Ament said. "But what if I appeared before him with the royal warrant giving me supreme command of the army? He, or more likely the legion commanders, might see sense then."

"But we're surrounded. The city is effectively walled off from the rest of Ta Mehu. How can you possibly appear before them?"

"A man might be able to slip past the legions unseen."

Tausret shook her head. "It is too dangerous. I won't lose you having just found you."

"I won't get caught. I go and come back to you unharmed; I promise."

"How can you possibly promise that?" Tausret demanded. "This is just another one of the games you men delight in playing. I'm bigger than you, tougher than you, smarter than you. Well, I won't have it. Send somebody else if you must but I won't risk you."

"The legion commanders won't obey anyone else," Ament said gently. "Believe me, there's nothing I want more than to stay here in your arms, but I have to go. If I don't, there's no future for us."

Tausret argued some more but Ament knew he had won, though he wondered why it felt like a loss. It was agreed that Ament would slip out of the city in the middle of the night, so he left the royal suite to make his preparations. He returned late in the evening, dressed in coarse servant's clothing.

"I hardly recognise you," Tausret said.

"As long as the legion commanders do," Ament replied with a grin.

"Here is your letter of authority." Tausret handed over a scroll.

Ament opened it and scanned the contents. He then rolled it back up and slipped it into a small waxed bag, drawing the strings tight. Tausret's gaze was upon him, asking the question she could not bring herself to ask, so he told her.

"The river. It's the only way. I've arranged a diversion and I'll slip into the water at the northern end of the docks, allowing the current to carry me past the blockading boats."

"You can't swim to Iunu."

"Just past the blockade. Then I'll steal a boat."

"Crocodiles?"

"I'll drift for the most part and only swim when I must. If I don't splash around they won't know I'm there."

"If they...if they catch you?"

"I'll bluff it out. I'm just a poor fisherman caught up in the war and looking to get home."

"They won't believe you if you have that document on you."

"I'll get rid of it." Ament stepped closer and took Tausret in his arms. "Stop looking for excuses," he said. "I have to go and I've planned for every eventuality."

"I can't help it. I've only just found you and I can't bear the thought of losing you."

"You won't. I've waited all my life for you and I'm coming back with the legions to rescue you so we can spend the rest of our lives together."

Ramose, the Commander of Khent-abt, accompanied Ament to the docks. Earlier, his men had thrown a cordon round the area, limiting the access the people had to the darkened streets and wharfs, and others were now waiting at the opposite end of the city to start a diversion. The two men slipped past the barricades and fortifications and crouched in the darkness near the water's edge. Men-nefer lay silent behind them, and aside from a chorus of frogs in a distant reed bed, the only sound that intruded was the lap of tiny waves against the mud bank.

"Are you sure you know what you're doing, sir?" Ramose asked. "Let me get a couple of men to sail a boat through the blockade for you. It's risky swimming."

"A boat would make too much noise," Ament replied. "A lone swimmer, drifting with the current, will pass unnoticed." He rummaged in the bag he held and took out a jar of goose grease, smearing it all over his body.

"What's that for? Is it to make you too slippery to catch or as a tasty treat for the crocodiles?" Ramose stifled laughter.

"It keeps out the cold."

Ramose swirled one hand in the water. "It doesn't feel cold."

"It will after I've been in it an hour or so. I know, I've swum at night before." Ament finished smearing the fat on his body and slung his pouch and a larger waxed bag around his neck. Ramose was just a dark mass beside him but he felt an unspoken question. "Some decent clothes, my insignia of office and a weapon," he murmured. "Wish me good fortune, Ramose."

"Oh, I do sir. I will din the ears of the gods to keep you safe."

"Start the diversion."

Ramose clapped his General on a greasy shoulder and slipped away into the night. Time passed, measured only by the slow creep of the stars across the body of Nut. Just when he thought something must have happened to prevent the diversion, he saw a faint orange glow to the south. The glow grew, and suddenly there were thin streaks of fire arcing out from the city walls and plunging into the river. Then a fire arrow hit a boat anchored offshore and flames leapt high. Shouts of alarm came from the blockading boats and a lot of splashing as the sailors tried to extinguish first one and then several fires.

Ament slipped into the water, stroking slowly to carry himself away from the shore. Darkness swallowed him and he stopped swimming, allowing the current to take him. The shouting died away behind him as the fire arrows stopped and the fires on the blockading boats were put out. Ament found that the waterproof bag containing his effects was more buoyant than he had anticipated, and he found himself being pushed up in the water, riding higher than he wanted. There was only starlight to see by, but he needed to slip past the guard boats unseen, and the lower he was in the water, the better. He unslung the bag from around him and paddled one-handed while keeping a tight grip on the waxed goatskin.

He heard low voices, murmuring, somewhere ahead of him and stopped swimming, just letting the river's current carry him. A shape loomed in the darkness, and a dim light cast by a small oil lamp flickering in the night breeze. Ament could just make out two shapes of men, and then the current carried him past. No alarm call was given, and Ament grinned with the relief, lying on his back and letting the cool water carry him away.

The chill of the water bit into his limbs after a while, so he righted himself and started swimming toward what he thought must be the east bank. He was less careful about keeping quiet now that he was past the cordon of boats, knowing that he would have to be ashore and hidden before the dawn. Then a voice called out from very close by, and he immediately ceased swimming, sinking lower in the water.

"There's something out there," the voice said.

"Where?" asked another.

"There. See? Ah...it's a crocodile."

"Huge brute...it's gone..."

Ament was sure they had caught a glimpse of him and misidentified him, but then he felt a swirl in the water and something scaly touched his leg. He almost screamed, and for a few moments seriously considered calling out to the men in the boat for help. Captivity and humiliation was better than death in the jaws of a crocodile. His heart hammering, Ament lay still, waiting for the beast to take him but time passed and nothing happened. He started swimming again, slowly, trying not to disturb the water, and became aware that the current was moving more slowly. This was just as well, as exhaustion and cold sapped the strength from his limbs. It would have been so easy to just lie on his back and let the river take him where it wanted, but he clung to his mission. He thought of Tausret and what his new-found love would mean for the future, and the thoughts warmed his heart, sustaining him through the darkness.

The first flush of dawn found him drifting close to the eastern shore, tired and stiff, but a little extra effort brought him staggering onto a muddy bank, dragging his waterproof bag behind him. No one was in sight, so after a few minutes spent shivering on the grass, he stumbled into the cover of a reed bed and collapsed.

Hot sun woke him. He rolled over, groaning at the stiffness in his muscles and peered out over the riverside pasture. A few cattle were in sight, but nothing else, so he rose to his feet and stretched, wincing at the twinges of pain in his back.

Getting old, he thought. His stomach gurgled. *And hungry.*

305

He had carried no food with him so he grubbed up a few roots of rushes and reeds and chewed them while he searched for duck eggs. A nest provided a bit more sustenance, though the eggs were not new laid. Ament shrugged; it was not the first time he had dined on immature duckling. He broke the eggs one after another into his mouth, swallowing the more or less liquid contents quickly, crunching on the thin bones of the developed embryos. Washing his mouth out with river water, he spat and looked at the sun to estimate the time.

Midmorning. I'd better get started.

Ament picked up his bag and shouldered it, setting off across the fields toward the road which ran to the northeast and the city of Iunu. Three legions, including his beloved Set, waited there, and he was determined to lead them against the foe outside Men-nefer.

Chapter 50
Year 2 (7) Sitre Meryamun Tausret

Ament arrived in Iunu five days later, tired and dusty, but would have taken much longer had he not been found by scouting light chariots of the Set legion. He showed his identifying insignia to the young charioteer in charge who had never actually seen his commanding officer close up, and ordered him to convey him swiftly to Commander Mose. This was done, and the chariot officer contrived to avoid the camps of the other legions, sweeping around the city to deliver him to the command tent near the river.

Mose stared at the dishevelled man clutching a stinking goatskin bag suddenly deposited at his tent and then, as his gaze delved below the dirt and unshaven face, his eyes widened in shock. He dropped to his knees on the packed earth floor.

"General Ament, by all the gods. What are you doing here? I'd heard that you were locked up in Men-nefer with the king."

"So I was. I had to break out to find out what was keeping you. You were supposed to come to our aid months ago. Come on, get up and talk to me."

Mose got to his feet. "Weren't able to, sir, though we all wanted to. We were under orders from General Iurudef not to move from Iunu."

"I am senior to him, you realise?"

"I know that, sir, but...well, he was on the spot and saying 'no' while you were out of touch. I didn't want to disobey orders, but I thought Iurudef must have more up-to-date orders. Was I wrong, sir?"

"Yes and no," Ament said. "You were wrong to ignore my orders, but right to obey Iurudef in the absence of a specific command from me. However, that changes now." He opened the small waterproof bag and took out the scroll. "You can read this well enough, or should you get the army scribe to read it to you?"

Mose glanced at it and grinned when he saw the common cursive symbols. "Well enough, I think, sir." He opened the scroll out and read it, muttering the words to himself as he did so.

"You recognise the seal on it?"

"Yes, sir. It's that of King Sitre Tausret."

"And you see that she gives me total control of all matters civil and military?"

"Yes, sir."

"I can commandeer anybody or anything?"

"Yes, sir."

"And I have authority over any person in the kingdoms save the king herself?"

Mose brought himself to attention and saluted the grimy figure before him. "Command me, sir," he said.

Ament nodded. "A bath first, I think, and some decent food. Then I'll need a squad of your most trusted men..."

"You can trust any of them, sir. We'd all die for you."

"Let's hope it won't come to that, Mose. But I do need to confront Iurudef and the traitor Mentu. I don't know how they'll react."

"Well, if it comes to a fight, your Sets will see you right, sir."

Ament grinned, his teeth pale in his weather-beaten and dirty face. "Good man. Now, have your cooks prepare a light meal and point me toward the river, then we'll see what we'll see."

The two Troops of the Set legion made a fine sight as they marched through the camp of the Sept legion, and the hubbub brought Sobek's soldiers out as well. Ament and Mose led their men to General Iurudef's command tent and halted them outside, ordering them to surround the site.

"Offer up no violence," Ament ordered, "but also strike back if violence is offered to you. And men of Set," he added with a smile, "you are named for the god of warfare and destruction. I would take it amiss if your two Troops could not hold your own again the whole Sept and Sobek legions."

The men cheered, beating their spear heads against their leather shields, and the noise brought Iurudef from his tent with Tjaty Mentu at his heels.

"What is the meaning of this, Mose?" Iurudef demanded. "Why are your men...?" He caught sight of Ament and he frowned. "Commander Ament. By what right do you enter my camp unannounced?"

"I'm announcing myself now, Iurudef," Ament replied, "and you will address me properly. I am General of all the Armies of Kemet, and I speak in the King's Name." He held out the scroll of his appointment. "Here is my authority."

Iurudef took the scroll and read it carefully before passing it to Mentu.

"It's a forgery," Mentu said.

"I would not take any notice of a known traitor," Ament commented. "Mentu has been removed from his post and holds no office. You can see the King's seal on the document, and you know the powers it gives me. Disobey me at your peril."

"It seems you have risen high very quickly, Ament," Iurudef said. "One wonders what talents brought you such exalted office."

Mentu sniggered and one of the junior officers on Iurudef's staff made a crude gesture.

Ament controlled his temper with difficulty. "Believe what you will, but obey me. You are ordered to strike camp and march the legions down to Men-nefer, where you..."

"No."

Ament stared at Iurudef in silence for a long minute. "You refuse?"

"Under the circumstances, I must."

"Despite the king's direct order, through me?"

"Perhaps Lady Tausret..."

"You will address the king properly," Ament snapped.

Iurudef inclined his head. "Perhaps she is unaware of the situation. Setnakhte invests the city of Men-nefer with five battle hardened legions and all I have is one experienced and two auxiliary legions. It would be fool-hardy to risk them against such odds."

"You refuse to come to the aid of the king?"

Iurudef shrugged. "She is safe enough as long as she stays inside the city."

"Then, General Iurudef, you are relieved of your command. You will place yourself under arrest and hold yourself ready to answer the king's summons to answer a charge of disobedience and treason."

"You do not have the authority or the power, Ament. Go back to your woman and enjoy what time remains to you." Iurudef took the scroll from Mentu, crumpled it and threw it to the ground.

"Commander Mose," Ament said. "Arrest Iurudef and put him in chains. If he resists, cut him down."

"Sir?"

"That is a direct order."

Mose saluted, signalled to four of his men and stepped close to Iurudef. "You will accompany me, sir."

Iurudef twisted away. "Ankhu, Djutep, to me," he yelled. "Kill these men!"

"Cut him down, Mose."

Mose drew his sword. "Please, General..."

Iurudef seized a dagger and slashed at Mose, all the while yelling to the Sobek and Sept legions to come to his aid. Mose knocked the dagger aside and slashed at Iurudef, forcing him backward. Mentu scurried out of the way, and from all around came angry voices and shouted orders from the officers of the auxiliary legions.

"End it," Ament growled, and pushed Mose to one side. He stabbed at Iurudef, forcing him back, and then as the former General thrust back, knocked the blade aside and plunged his bronze sword into Iurudef's chest. The man groaned, dropped his dagger and sank to his knees. Ament pulled the blade out and pushed Iurudef's body over with his foot. Then he turned to where the auxiliary legions were massing and shouted aloud.

"Sept legion! Sobek legion! Attention! Officers to the front, now!"

The shouting died away and the Commanders and Troop Leaders pushed through to face Ament with drawn weapons.

"Ankhu of Sobek, Djutep of Sept," Ament said, loud enough to be heard by several ranks of soldiers. "You know who I am. I bear here..." he picked up the crumpled scroll and smoothed it out. "...direct orders from King Sitre Tausret to bring your three legions down to Men-nefer to raise the siege on the city by the rebel Setnakhte. I have been made General of all the Armies of Kemet and as such, command your obedience. This man..." he pointed at Iurudef's body, "...refused to obey and paid the price of his disobedience. What will you do?" He walked up to each officer and looked him in the eyes until they dropped their gaze. "Djutep? Ankhu?"

Ankhu held out his hand. "May I see the orders, sir." He perused them at length and then nodded. "Looks to be in order, sir." He saluted. "Sobek legion stands ready to obey."

"And you, Djutep?"

"I don't read so well, sir. I'll take Ankhu's word for it. Sept legion ready for your orders, sir."

"Good. Prepare your men. We march at daybreak tomorrow for Men-nefer."

Ankhu and Djutep saluted and drew their men away, shouting orders to their junior officers. Mose told his Troops to make ready and then turned back to Ament.

"What about Tjaty...ex-Tjaty Mentu, sir? Do you want me to find him and arrest him?"

Ament shook his head. "Leave him for now. There is little he can do."

The three legions marched after dawn prayers the next day, though not all in the same direction. Set and Sobek made their way south toward Mennefer, while Sept was given the task of finding a multitude of boats with which to cross the river. They could have waited in Iunu for the boats, but enforced inactivity was not good for morale, and it would not hurt to be further south when the boats caught up. All the supply wagons were left behind with orders to follow on at their own pace as Ament was determined to make good time.

They were close to the point where the Great River split in two before making its run to the sea, and almost within sight of the capital city when the small fleet of boats commandeered by the Sept legion caught up with the marching legions. They put ashore, while the legions set up camp and the commanders came to Ament's camp to learn of his plans.

"We must cross to the western bank before the enemy knows we are near," Ament said. "It would be an impossible task to cross in the face of hostilities, so it is my intention to ferry the legions across to the 'land between the waters', and march them across to the next part of the river. In the meantime, our fleet of boats will sail to the split and come down the western arm ready to ferry us across again."

"We don't have many boats, sir," said Djutep of Sept. "It was all we could find but only enough for five hundred men at most. I had to send most of my legion south by road."

"Well, unless we can build more boats, it'll have to do."

"Would it be worth risking a single crossing nearer the city?" Ankhu of Sobek asked. "It would be quicker."

"And more likely to be discovered," Mose observed. "I don't know about you, but I'd rather not be the lead legion if the enemy find us out. Five against one isn't my kind of odds."

"Five against three is still risky," Ankhu said. "Perhaps there's something else we could do?"

"It'll be five against four," Ament said. "The Khent-abt will break out of the city and help us once battle is joined." He looked around at his commanders, wishing he had more experienced legions. His Set legion was the only one of four that was truly battle hardened. "Don't forget that we have one other thing in our favour. Sitre Tausret is the true, consecrated King of Kemet, while Setnakhte is but a rebel. The gods themselves will be fighting for us."

The commanders looked more cheerful and nodded sagely. Ament gave them all specific instructions and then sent them off, though one order did not please Mose. He snorted when Ament told him and then shrugged as if to say he expected nothing less.

"The Set legion will be first across the river, Mose--both times. There is no other legion I would trust more to guard our landing should we be discovered."

The first crossing of the eastern arm of the river took place without major mishap, though three boats sank or came apart, spilling their passengers. Most struggled ashore though. Once the three legions were across, the rest of the Sept legion having caught up by the end, they set off across the grassy pastures while the crews of the fishing boats and ferries sailed south to the split between the river arms and thence down the western arm.

The second crossing took longer as the river was wider and the banks lower and more marshy. As before, the Set legion went first, and Mose was among the first to set foot on the western shore. Ament would like to have been there, but he had to learn that as commanding General he had to leave the individual legions to their commanders. Thus Ament stayed behind and oversaw the embarkation of the auxiliary legions.

Shouting attracted his attention, and he looked to the west. Soldiers of Set were scrambling to form ranks, facing inland, and it was a few moments before Ament could see what the matter was. Beyond the landing stage, on the higher, drier ground, chariots were approaching. There were at least twenty, and Ament cursed, knowing they had been discovered at the most critical moment. He called to Ankhu and Djutep to hurry with their men and leapt aboard a small fishing boat, casting off the mooring rope and poling out into the current. Anxious minutes followed as Ament watched the chariots--more than forty now--sweep down on the rough ranks of soldiers. Arrows rose and fell in the blue sky of morning and men started dying.

More Set soldiers hurried ashore and junior officers pushed them into the line, stiffening the ranks that were being driven back under the chariot assault. Ament splashed ashore and ran to where Mose was conducting the defence.

"Fall back toward the river," Ament commanded.

"But sir, we'll be spread thinly without back up."

"And the chariot wheels will get stuck in the mud. Fall the men back and prepare to charge again."

Mose did as instructed and ordered his men retreat toward the muddy river bank, spreading out as they did so. The charioteers, sensing victory, drove after them, their own tightly knit formation breaking apart as they did so. Then horses' hooves slipped and wheels become mired. The chariots slowed and faltered and with a roar, the Set soldiers turned and wrought havoc, slaughtering the floundering horses, pulling the men from the chariots and hacking them to death. It was none too soon, as the soldiers from the same legion as the chariots came into view, running toward the battle.

"They're from the Mut legion," Ament said. "But are they here because they knew we were coming or is this just coincidence? They might have been foraging."

Mose shrugged and started shouting orders, pulling men away from where they were mopping up the last of the chariots, and countering the new threat. The Sept legion was now landing and hurried to join the fight, overwhelming the disorganised Mut legion and routing them. Sept started to pursue the enemy, but Ament called them back.

"We can't hope to catch them all and anyway, they've probably reported our presence already. Concentrate on getting the rest of our men across."

There were a few prisoners, and Ament interviewed the most senior officer among them--a Troop Commander. He learned that the Mut legion had not been foraging for food but had been looking for them.

"You knew we were coming? To this spot? How?"

"Well, not exactly here, sir, but somewhere. The Mut legion were assigned this section of shore."

"But how did you know we were coming at all?"

The officer was a little bit reluctant to say, but when Ament pointed out that it hardly mattered now, that Mut had already made contact and were likely even now reporting their presence, he relented.

"It was Tjaty Mentu, sir. There was quite a to-do when he turned up in camp saying you'd killed General Iurudef--begging your pardon, sir, but that's what he said. Anyway, the Tjaty said you'd be coming to Men-nefer and we should be ready for you."

The prisoner was led away, and Ament conferred with his commanders. "We've lost the element of surprise, but that was always going to be a chancy thing. The important thing is to press on to Men-nefer as quickly as possible."

"We should have killed Mentu when we had the chance," Mose said.

"True, but there's nothing we can do about it now."

"We're still going to be three legions against five, sir," Ankhu pointed out. "Not that I'm complaining, sir, but er...just saying."

"A little less than five now," Ament said. "Mut won't be so keen to meet us again."

Ament took his legions south toward Men-nefer, and three days later the gleaming white walls of the beautiful city came in sight, its pristine splendour marred by the tents of the legions encamped around it.

"What now, sir?" Mose asked.

"Draw up a defensive line, with earthworks. We're not going to attack them, but if they attack us I want us to have the advantage."

And so it was. The loyal legions dug in across the western road north, digging chariot traps and earthen barricades, but not offering battle. Setnakhte's legions looked discomforted by the presence of Ament's army but also made no effort to attack. Their only response was to move the Amun and Re legions to face the dug in legions, and then sit and wait them out.

Chapter 51
Year 3 (8) Sitre Meryamun Tausret

Months passed with the war in Ta Mehu unresolved. Neither side felt itself strong enough to push for a resolution to the impasse, and each seemed content to wait upon the will of the gods. Ament's legions effectively cut off the northern road and the farmland in those sepats, while Setnakhte's army still controlled the city of Men-nefer and the southern farms. Both armies had enough to eat, though the peasant farmers suffered as a result; and the population of the city slowly starved. Grain stores ran low, every animal down to the rats and mice that pillaged those stores and every available scrap of greenery had been eaten, and the supply of river fish that could be brought into the city was limited by the blockading fleet.

Then the flood came, marked by a slow but steady creep of water up over the banks of the river, spreading out over the flat farmland and bringing with it discomfort and disease. The blockading fleet found it harder to maintain station in the swifter, muddier current, and a few brave souls put out from the city in fishing boats and brought in masses of fish to alleviate the hunger of the population.

Ament took advantage of the creeping sheet of water spreading over the land to make an unseen visit to the city. The water along the former shore moved slowly and sometimes eddies moved counter to the direction of the river's flow, so by night he slipped into the water and made it back to the city wharves unchallenged.

Tausret was overjoyed to see Ament again, and forgetting all protocol and dignity, threw herself at him with cries of joy. She dismissed her attendants and poured wine for him, feeding him morsels with her own hand, before embracing him once more and leading him to her bed.

"You are back to stay, beloved?" Tausret asked afterward, her head on Ament's chest.

"I wish I was, but there is still an army to defeat out there, and I can't leave my legions for long."

"I am the king. I command you to stay."

Ament smiled and stroked her hair. "Not even for the king," he whispered.

"I cannot do without you."

"You must; for a little longer at least."

"Your legions have commanders. Let them earn their bread."

"Yes, they have commanders, but I fully trust only Mose. Ankhu and Djutep are weak and need constant supervision."

"Then replace them with officers from the Set legion."

"Perhaps." Ament sighed. "It requires balance. If I remove them from office, I risk the men of their legions deserting. I cannot be too harsh on deserters, because then the whole legion might refuse to fight. They are afraid of Setnakhte already and only the bravado of my loyal Sets keeps them in place."

Conversation turned to more intimate matters for a while, but thoughts of their situation nagged at both of them.

"What is the mood in the city?" Ament asked. "I come and go by night, so I haven't been able to judge for myself."

"Not good," Tausret admitted. "I get booed if I go outside."

"They dare?"

"One can hardly blame them, beloved. I have brought nothing but sorrow and privation to my people. Many of them think they would be better off under Setnakhte, and they are no longer afraid to tell me so."

"Let me but hear them and I will lop a few heads to teach them respect."

"My fierce warrior. Find me a way to break the siege instead."

"Nothing can be done until the waters fall. The ground is boggy and soft, completely unsuited to warfare. Chariots are useless and any charge by foot soldiers falls apart within twenty paces."

They lay in silence for a time, enjoying each other's company.

"Setnakhte's men would find it as hard to fight as yours?" Tausret asked.

"Of course. Why?"

"If you could devise some effective means of attack, they would be unable to use their superior numbers to any great effect."

"Ah, love, it is not so easy."

"Will you think on it?"

Ament spent four days in the city, talking to the officers of the Khent-abt legion and the palace guards, touring the defences, and talking with the people in the streets. He refrained from lopping any heads off, but instead eavesdropped on conversations, noting the hungry and dejected looks on everyone's faces. On the fourth night, he took his leave of Tausret once more and slipped naked into the floodwaters and swam back to his own lines. Back in his own command tent, he dried off in front of Mose and sipped spiced wine to banish the chill in his bones.

"I'm getting too old for this," Ament grumbled.

"A man will do anything for love," Mose observed.

Ament looked sharply at his legion Commander, debating whether the man had been disrespectful. He decide to let it go and merely muttered, "Indeed." When he had dressed and partaken of a light meal, he raised the subject of the war with his trusted officer.

"Something has to be done, and quickly. The people of Men-nefer are stretched thin. It wouldn't surprise me if they threw open the gates and surrendered."

"Not much we can do until the waters fall and the land dries out, sir. A few raids maybe, but no general action."

"That is certainly the conventional wisdom, Mose." Ament was silent for a while, sipping his wine and nibbling on some dried figs. "What if we broke with convention?" he asked.

"I don't understand, sir. How?"

"What is it that prevents warfare during the flood?"

"Er, the water everywhere, sir? I mean, chariots are useless and the mud is slippery. Nobody wants to be splashing around trying to fight somebody and stay upright at the same time."

"So we could just stand back and use archers?"

Mose grimaced. "Why are you asking me, sir? I'm no archer."

"You should be conversant with every weapon at your disposal. The reason bowmen are not much use is that the damp warps the arrows and affects the bowstrings."

Mose shrugged. "So it's as I said--not much point in fighting until after the water falls."

Ament frowned. "What if we could move about without slipping on the mud?"

"How we going to do that, sir?"

"I'm not sure. You've seen camels?"

"Once or twice. Ugly mean-tempered brutes. I hope you're not asking me to ride one."

Ament laughed out loud. "That would be something to see. No, what I meant is, they can walk over soft sand by having feet that spread out. If we could wear something on our feet that spread out, we could do the same."

Mose scratched his head. "That's as maybe, sir, but sand isn't water. A camel would just flounder in flood waters, same as us."

"That's true, but it is an example of what I mean. We can't walk across soft sand easily but a camel can. If we had spread out feet perhaps we could too. So what animal walks across slippery mud without ending up on their backs?"

"I don't know, sir. Frogs?"

"What about a heron...or an ibis? They walk along muddy banks and I've never seen one slip. How do they do it?"

Mose grimaced. "Sorry, sir, I've never really looked at birds. Beyond eating them, that is."

"Their feet, Mose. They've got claws on their feet and they grip the mud. That's what we need."

Mose looked down at his feet and wiggled his toes. "I've got nails, but nothing like enough to grip mud."

"So we'll have to make some. Any ideas?"

Mose scratched his head again. "I don't like the idea of cutting off birds' feet to get their claws, begging your pardon, sir."

"There wouldn't be enough birds around here for even a hundred men, let alone a legion or three. We need to find something else." Ament yawned. "I'm too tired to go on. Think about it, Mose. We'll talk later."

Mose woke Ament a few hours later, bubbling with excitement. He waited impatiently while his General scratched himself, yawned and used the midden.

"All right," Ament said. "What's so important it couldn't wait another few hours?"

"Sorry, sir, but I've found the bird claws we need. Look." Mose ducked out and came back in with a thorn branch. It was one of a number that had been cut from thorn scrub on the edge of the desert and woven amongst the palisades used in the defensive wall. The branch sported several wicked looking thorns, some as long as a man's thumb. "If we cut off the thorns we could poke them through the soles of reed sandals and they'd dig in and grip."

Ament tested the point of one of the long thorns with his finger. "Well, you'd better get a pair of sandals and try them out."

"I have, sir," Mose said proudly. He lifted one foot and showed the sole of one of his sandals. Several thorns stuck out from the bottom, two of them broken off short.

"Some of them have broken."

Mose nodded and lowered his foot. "They do that, but they grip the ground well."

"Have you tried them on mud?"

"Not yet, sir."

Ament insisted on trying them out immediately, so they walked over to a muddy section of river bank out of sight of the camp. He pointed to a nearby tree.

"I'll race you to the tree."

Mose set off, lifting his legs high, his sandals making sucking noises as they lifted from the mud at each pace. Ament ran alongside, gingerly at first and then more confidently as his ordinary sandals showed no signs of slipping. He drew ahead of Mose and half turned with a grin.

"I'd say your thorn sandals are a waste of time, Mose. I can run faster without them and..." Ament yelped as his feet went out from under him and he slid several paces down the bank.

Mose laughed and stepped past him. "Sorry, sir, I'd stop and help you but I have a race to win."

Ament scrambled to his feet. "We'll see about..." He went down again, onto his face this time.

By the time Ament made it to the tree, Mose was sitting down and examining his sandals. "Another few thorns broke off, sir, and worse than that, mud clogged between them. By the time I got here I was carrying half the riverbank."

"It was still impressively fast across a muddy bank though," Ament said, squatting down to pick at the mud between the thorns on one of the sandals. "Do you think you could fight with these weights on your feet?"

"I think so, sir, but I wouldn't be as agile as a man without them. Better than a man sliding around in the mud, though."

"Worth trying on a larger scale?" When Mose nodded, he clapped him on the shoulder and helped him to his feet. "I think so too."

Back at camp, Ament brought Ankhu and Djutep in on the planning and Mose demonstrated his thorny sandals for them. Both commanders wanted to try them out and voiced their enthusiasm for the modification.

"When are we going to use them, sir?" Ankhu asked.

"We need to equip every man first," Ament explained. "There aren't enough thorns in the palisade, and I don't want to strip our defences anyway. We'll have to go into the desert and cut fresh branches."

"Perhaps we could just cut the thorns off the trees," Mose suggested. "It would be an awful lot easier carrying baskets of thorns back than hundreds of prickly branches."

"Good idea. I want you to head up the expedition to the desert, Mose. Take as many men as..."

"I'd like to volunteer, sir," Djutep interrupted. "I'll take the whole Sept legion and collect enough for everybody in a day."

"That's going to leave us shorthanded," Mose said. "Only two legions to face the enemy."

"Fewer men will take longer," Djutep answered. "Besides, isn't that the whole point? Nobody can attack through mud unless they have the thorns on their feet."

"It's only for a day," Ankhu added.

Ament nodded. "The Sept legion it is then. Go after sunset today, day one, so nobody sees you leaving and be back by the following day at the latest, no matter how many thorns you've cut. Mose, you're in charge of getting the thorns into the sandals, and Ankhu, you make sure every soldier has rush sandals. Make more if you have to. I want to attack the enemy at dawn on day four. If we leave it any longer, the falling river and the hot sun will allow the land to dry out and we'll lose any advantage this ruse will give us."

"Where will you be, sir, while we're doing all this?" Mose asked.

"I'm going into Men-nefer again. I want to arrange for Khent-abt to attack the rear of Setnakhte's legions as we attack the front."

Ament slipped uneventfully into Men-nefer the next night and after a pleasurable hour or two spent in the arms of his royal lover, went in search of Ramose, Commander of the Khent-abt legion. Because of the lateness of the hour, he had to rouse him from his bed to question him.

"Is your legion ready for action, Commander?"

Ramose looked at his General in some confusion. "Setnakhte has retreated from Men-nefer?" he asked.

"No, but our days of sitting around on our backsides are over. Is your legion ready?"

"Er, yes...sort of, sir. This enforced inactivity has lowered morale, sir. There are a lot of malingerers, but...I suppose about two-thirds strength."

"Not good enough. Unless a man has broken bones or is vomiting up blood, I want him clutching his spear and ready to go by dawn the day after tomorrow. Have your officers use whips if they have to, but I want nine out of ten men ready."

Tausret listened to Ament's plan soberly. "Is it going to work?" she asked.

"That's with the gods, but it's our last best chance. I think the thorns will help our legions, but Khent-abt will be handicapped not having them. They'll just have to help as much as they can."

"When?"

"Day after tomorrow, at dawn."

"I will lead Khent-abt."

"No, my love. This is going to be savage fighting and I would not have you in danger."

Tausret frowned. "And will you be sitting in your tent while your men fight?"

"Of course not..."

"Then neither will I." She gestured imperiously as Ament opened his mouth to protest further. "I am King of Kemet and sound of body; I must lead my troops into battle. I would not be deserving of the throne if I hid while my people died."

Ament nodded. "Of course you must. I was blinded by my love for you and sought only to protect you. Forgive me, Tausret."

"You are forgiven," Tausret said with a smile. "I look forward to fighting beside you against our enemies."

"Wait for Set's battle standards to be raised and then have Khent-abt head west toward the high ground when you break out of the city. You will be less affected by the mud that way. I will have my men come to join up with you and bring you safely to my side."

"I suppose you must leave me soon."

"I thought to stay a day and make my way back the night before the attack."

"I am most glad of it, beloved."

Tausret embraced her man and led him through to her bedchamber, and they spoke of nothing more consequential than love for the rest of the night.

Chapter 52
Year 3 (8) Sitre Meryamun Tausret

The sound of rams' horns woke the city in the early morning hours and servants rushed into the royal chambers to rouse the king and her partner. Ament raced for the city walls with Tausret only moments behind him, and as the first golden rays of the new sun touched the city, they saw all their plans disintegrate before them. They stared at the water-soaked plain outside Men-nefer, and watched as Setnakhte's legions stirred themselves, formed up into as good an order as the muddy ground allowed and marched toward the palisades of the loyal legions.

"Too soon," Ament groaned. "Pray that Mose can rally the legions. Curse it; I should be down there with them."

"Your men will have the new sandals though, won't they? That will still give them an advantage, even if surprise is lost."

"They've only had yesterday and...where is Sept legion?" Ament muttered. "They must have returned yesterday and should be back on station, but I don't see their banners. Ah...there's Set's...and Sobek's...they're responding to the threat, but look," he pointed, "Ramesses leads the Amun legion round our flank where Sept should be..."

Ament went pale as Sept's banners now flew in the morning breeze, but mixed in with Amun's banners. "They've changed sides," he whispered. "Oh gods curse them for the traitors they are, they've gone over to Setnakhte."

"What can we do?" Tausret asked.

"Nothing if we stay in the city. Setnakhte will destroy Set and Sobek and turn back to starve us out. Our only chance is to break out now, while their attention is elsewhere, and flee for the desert."

"I'm not leaving my loyal soldiers to die."

"They'll surrender quickly enough to save their lives," Ament said roughly. "But you'll lose any chance of rallying men to your support again if you get trapped in Men-nefer."

323

Tausret chewed her lip, thinking. "Very well, we leave the city, but only to go to the high ground with our men. I won't leave my people unless all is lost."

"Then gird yourself, Sitre Tausret, and let us go out to meet your enemies."

An hour later, and Tausret stood by the western gate as Ament spoke with Ramose of Khent-abt. He was angry that only eight in ten soldiers had turned up and that few of them were enthusiastic about actually fighting the king's enemies.

"You can hardly blame them," Ramose said. "We've all seen what's happening outside. It's two against six now and it's suicide at those odds." He saw the expression on his General's face. "Oh, I'll still lead my men out, sir. I know my duty to King and Kemet, but I can't answer for the fighting abilities of my under strength legion."

"Just get the king to the high ground and defend her long enough to allow my men to rally to her. Can you do that?"

They opened the gates and the depleted Khent-abt legion poured through, with Tausret, Ament and Ramose in the lead. The main conflict was to the north, where Set and Sobek were fighting for survival against overwhelming odds, so Khent-abt plodded away to the west, crossing a short muddy stretch of plain and then, as the ground became drier, increased their speed and climbed the low ridge that lay to the west. As they reached the top, Ament saw men break away from the battle in the north and head back in their direction. He called to Ramose to ready the men, but the enemy soldiers, who bore the banners of Mut legion, seemed content to block any escape to the city.

"What now?" Tausret asked.

"I would ask you again to flee into the west. As long as you remain at liberty, we can rally loyal men to your cause. If you fall or are captured, all is lost."

"I am King of Kemet; I cannot run from my enemies. Better to die on the battlefield."

"Then let us make our way north and see if we cannot join up with Set and Sobek. At least we will die in brave company."

They followed the ridge north, and the enemy sent to block them from returning to the city marched with them, though more slowly on the muddy plain. As they neared the battle, more men detached from Setnakhte's army and the Re legion advanced toward them.

"It's the traitor Ahhotep of Re," Ament muttered. "He'll wish he'd remained loyal by the time I'm done with him."

Ament called to Ramose and together they organised the Khent-abt legion into a semblance of readiness. The only real advantage they had was that the approaching Re legion had to climb the low ridge to get to them. They waited, axes and spears at the ready, and just before the ranks of the enemy reached them, the Khent-abt soldiers knelt and archers poured a withering volley of arrows into the Re soldiers. The enemy fell in droves, and now Khent-abt charged downhill, the shock of their assault shattering the Re legion.

Ament saw Ahhotep rallying his men and pointed. He leapt forward, sword swinging, and he and a double handful of men carved their way through the mass of struggling men and engaged the legion commander. It did not take long; Ament fought with a cold fury, while all Ahhotep could call on was a desire to live. The Re commander failed, and went down into death at the hands of Ament.

Despite the attack of Khent-abt and the loss of their commander, Re rallied and, still outnumbering Khent-abt, pushed back, forcing the King's men onto the ridge once more. Ament retreated and found Tausret near the legion standards. She had taken up a sword and fought alongside a group of young officers who vied for her respect and approval. When her General approached, she drew back and wiped the sweat from her eyes with the back of one bloodied hand.

"They are better fighters than the Ribu," she said.

"And now they lack a commander," Ament replied grimly. "It will not stop them though."

Khent-abt fought their way north, their numbers decreasing with every step they took, and Re harried them all the way. The ridge became lower, leading toward the main battle, and now both sides saw the royal banners flying and turned toward them, though with different intents. The lines of battle bent and broke, with the Set legion hurrying to defend their king, and Amun and Shu charging to the attack. With the strength of Set gone, Sobek went under, overwhelmed by the other rebel legions. Ankhu fought bravely to the last, but was cut down along with most of his men.

Mose fought his way to Ament's side and in a break from the fighting, grinned at him. "Thought you were never going to make it, sir."

"Nearly didn't. How is your command?"

"Down to three-quarter strength, and most of us are exhausted."

"Gods curse Djutep and his men. I saw them change sides."

Mose nodded. "Volunteering to get the thorns was just an excuse to leave the camp. He went straight to Setnakhte and surrendered."

Ramesses led a charge against the knot of soldiers around Tausret, and talking was put aside until they had thrown the Amun legion back.

"Have you got a plan, sir?" Mose asked. "Just asking, you understand. If you haven't, well..." He slashed at an Amun soldier who stumbled within range, "...there's always more of this."

"The only plan I have involves getting the king to safety, but she won't go. Says she won't leave her men."

"Bless her," Mose muttered, "but you've got to make her see sense. She's all we're fighting for, and it'd be for nothing if she died."

Ament broached the subject with Tausret once more, this time backed up by Ramose and Mose, as Ramesses launched another attack on her position. As they watched, the remnants of the Khent-abt legion disintegrated, some throwing down their weapons and others fleeing for their lives.

"It's come to this, Majesty," Mose yelled above the clamour of battle. "You die here and now and all these lives have been wasted, or you live to give hope to every loyal person in the kingdoms."

"Don't let my men have died in vain," Ramose added.

"Live," Ament urged.

The line of Set soldiers shivered under renewed attacks, and now others were swarming toward them.

"Quickly, Majesty. Before we are cut off. Save some lives out of this mess."

Tausret stared around at the bloody battlefield, tears streaming from her eyes. She nodded. "Very well; if it will save lives."

Mose whirled and looked around, picking out his officers among the throng of struggling men. "Men of Set, to me! First Troop, strike to the left, Third troop to centre, Fifth to the right. Second, Fourth and Sixth to the standard. Move!"

Ramose similarly called to his few remaining men and officers, concentrating them around the person of the king, and then Ament led the way, breaking away to the west, retreating from the battle into the stony wastes of the western desert where chariots could not easily go. The three Troops of Set fought on, slowly giving ground and guarding the retreat of their king. They fell back, running to catch up with the rest of their legion and then forming up again in a protective cordon. Their discipline was in contrast to the mob of soldiers that pursued them and despite being outnumbered, successfully fought their way through the day to the relative safety of the night.

As the pursuit fell away, the Set legion pushed on into the west, slowing and stumbling with exhaustion until all sights and sounds of the other legions faded from the senses. Eventually, Ament called a halt and the few hundred survivors of Set just collapsed where they stood. Tausret called Ament, Mose and Ramose together, and insisted the Troop Commanders join them.

"I'd have every man here if I could," she said. "Every man has given their all today and deserves to know what we decide."

"Our options are rapidly narrowing," Ament said. "We have no food, no water, and the men are exhausted. When the sun rises tomorrow, the following legions will be upon us and then we surrender or die."

"My men will give a good account of themselves before they do," Mose said grimly. His Troop Commanders nodded, vague shadows in the starlight, and one or two murmured their assent.

"And what's left of Khent-abt," Ramose added. "I have only a handful left, but there is fight in them still."

"No," Tausret said softly. "I will not have another man die for me. We will surrender and ask for mercy. Setnakhte is a reasonable man and if he truly hopes to heal our land, he will show mercy."

"Never, Majesty," Mose declared.

"Do not disobey me in this, Commander Mose," Tausret said. "The time for fighting is over, and Setnakhte has won. Make your peace with him."

"You cannot surrender, my love," Ament said. "Setnakhte will humble you before the Kingdoms and then marry you off to his son Ramesses, and that I could not bear. I will die first, and take them with me if I can."

"You are right, beloved, I cannot surrender, for to do so would be worse than death."

The Commanders looked at each other and drew back at Tausret's words, obviously embarrassed to be listening in to sentiments of love between their king and their General.

"I will kill myself before I let myself be humiliated," Tausret added.

"And I with you," Ament said. Ignoring the presence of the Commanders, he took Tausret in his arms and kissed her. "But not here, not now. I would not have our lifeless bodies paraded through the streets of Mennefer and held up to ridicule."

"Then where? When?"

"We will walk into the desert and lose ourselves in the wilderness. Nobody will find our bodies."

They took leave of their faithful commanders and of the men, amid much wailing and protestations of undying loyalty. Each man was thanked for their contribution and sorrow expressed for every injury suffered by them. At last they finished their farewells, urged on by Mose, who said the night was wearing on and if they did not leave soon, their efforts to escape unseen would be futile.

Hand in hand, Ament and Tausret walked into the western desert, carrying no more than a crust of bread and a flask of water. Tausret had not wanted to take anything, but as Ament explained, they had to keep their strength up long enough to elude any pursuit. As dawn broke, they were far to the west and north, skirting a large area of loose sand that would have impeded their progress. They sat on a rock and contemplated the first rays of the sun and the warmth it brought.

"I'm sorry I brought you to this, beloved," Tausret said. "I should have left you as a plain army officer. Then you'd be safe."

"I don't regret any of it, my love," Ament said, squeezing her hand.

They sat in silence for a time watching the sun rise above the red desert.

"Is that dark smudge on the horizon Ta Mehu?" Tausret asked. "That's the only thing I regret. I'd like to have died in my lovely green and well-watered land."

"And my only regret is that I never said goodbye to my sister and my adopted sons Jerem and Ephrim."

Tausret shaded her eyes and stared into the east. "They're just over there, you know. Do you think we could elude Setnakhte's patrols long enough to see them? Perhaps we could do away with both our regrets."

Ament smiled through cracked lips. "Entirely possible, my love."

Chapter 53

Tausret speaks:

We nearly did not make it back from the western desert. The small amount of bread and water we had lasted no more than that morning, and despite the apparent nearness of that dark smudge of well-watered land, it took us two days to traverse the intervening rock and sand. I will say little of the privations we suffered for I am well aware that others have suffered far more, but when our strength failed, Ament found a scrap of shade and a scorpion. Deprived of its sting and crushed with a rock, its juices sustained us, and nearer to Ta Mehu he found us grasshoppers and the fruits of some desert plant. He told me the name of it but I have forgotten, being more concerned with extracting a little bit of juice from its slightly bitter flesh.

I almost wept when we came to pasture and a little further on a tiny farming community of no more than a handful of huts. The people were poor and had so little in the way of food, that they could spare no more than a cup of milk and a handful of grain. They apologised for their lack of hospitality, saying that foraging soldiers had long since stripped them of their meagre possessions. One of my copper bracelets was worth far more than the food they gave us, but I pressed it on them, feeling guilty that my people should have suffered so.

The villages along the banks of the river were better off, for they at least had a never-ending supply of fish. Another bracelet bought us fish, a little bread, and passage across the westernmost arm of the river. We were not recognised--hardly surprising, for who would look to find a king and a general walking a muddy road or eating fish and bread beside a small fire on the riverbank? Not that I was a king any longer, nor Ament a general. Setnakhte had seen to that. Now we were only a man and a woman, anonymous commoners amongst ten thousand others.

Several more days brought us to the next arm of the river, the one on which Per-Bast sat. I was down to my last piece of jewellery by then, having had to buy food on our journey, but Ament bought us passage across the river by means of his own skills. He had been a fisherman in his youth, before he became a soldier, and he hired himself out for a few days. The young men of the surrounding villages had been taken off to be soldiers, so his skills with a boat and net were in much demand.

Two more days saw us nearing Per-Bast and the vineyards that were the property of Ament's sister Ti-ament and her Kaftor husband Zeben. Ament's two adopted sons, Jerem and Ephrim lived there too, and Ament assured me we would be warmly welcomed. Well, he was partially right-- they were glad to see us, but our welcome was less than warm.

"Thank the gods you are safe," Ti-Ament said, "but you can't stay here."

"Forgive my wife," Zeben added. "She is concerned that your presence will bring the soldiers down on us again. You are welcome...er, how do I address you?"

"Just plain Ament will do, and..."

"And Tau," I interposed. "I am no one special now."

"Except to me," Ament said with a smile.

"And to us," Jerem and Ephrim added together.

Ti-ament sighed and embraced her brother, but looked warily at me. "Come inside. You must be hungry and tired. You can stay a while, but..." she shook her head and hurried off to the kitchen.

I followed, and helped her clean platters and prepare food and drink. "We don't intend staying," I assured her. "Ament only came to say his farewells."

"It's not that I'm not glad to see him...or you, Majesty..."

"Just Tau, remember."

Ti-ament nodded. "We had soldiers here a few days ago. From the Amun legion, I think, and they searched the place for my brother. They knew I was his sister and questioned us all at length about his whereabouts. They may come back."

"Then we won't stay. Perhaps you could give us some food and blankets and we can sleep out somewhere. I don't have anything to pay you with...a single bracelet and a ring, but..."

"What do you take me for?" Ti-ament said indignantly. "Hospitality is not paid for. We owe everything to you anyway, so what we have is yours. I'm only afraid for my children." She had tears in her eyes, and I felt ashamed.

It was something new for me, but I thought I owed it to her, so I knelt on the hard-packed earth of the floor and embraced her knees. "Forgive me, Ti-ament. I spoke without thinking."

Now she became flustered and all but dragged me to my feet and we embraced like sisters. We carried food and wine into the other room and spread out the meal for everyone. We ate quickly and then leaned back in our chairs.

"What are your plans?" Zeben asked.

"We had none beyond coming here to see you," Ament said. "I could not die without bidding you all farewell."

"Dying?" Ephrim exclaimed. "What do you mean?"

"Only that if I am caught, I will die painfully. I would rather die at my own hand."

"And I," I added. "Setnakhte wants to shame me and I'd rather die."

Zeben frowned. "There must be somewhere you can live. I'd welcome you here, but I think anywhere in Kemet would be unsafe."

"What about among the Retenu?" Jerem asked. "No one would think to look for you there. And we'd come with you." He pointed at his brother.

"You are our father, after all," Ephrim said. "It is our duty to look after our parents."

"At least our father, seeing as he has no wife."

"Yet," I said softly.

"What?" Ament stared at me. "Did I hear you right? You'd consider it?"

"Marrying you? Of course. Were you waiting for me to ask you?"

"Men," Ti-ament said. "Leave it up to them and nothing would get done."

Zeben smiled and squeezed his wife's hand. "I wouldn't call our five children nothing."

Ament had blushed deeply. "I...I can understand taking a lover, but marrying me? I am only a humble soldier...not even that."

"And I am no longer a king, or even a member of the royal family," I said. "So what impediment is there to getting married?"

"None, I suppose, but...well, marriage implies a commitment to home and family, and we're homeless..."

"But not without a family," declared Ephrim. "Jerem and I are your sons."

"And another child is due," I whispered. I must have blushed myself, for while the men just stared, Ti-Ament broke into a delighted smile and embraced me once more.

"When?" she asked.

"I don't know." I thought back over recent events. "Another six months, I think."

"Then we have time. We must find a place for you to stay well before the birth, though, as you should not travel close to your time."

Ament wore a foolish grin. "I'm going to be a father?"

"You're a father already," I said, nodding toward Jerem and Ephrim.

"Uh, yes, of course, but..." He shook his head.

Zeben took charge. "You cannot stay in Kemet; it's too dangerous. Nor can you reasonably exist in the western desert, Kush, or the Land of Sin. That only leaves the north. I think that your sons have suggested the perfect solution--you must seek refuge among the Retenu."

"Would they take us though?" I asked. "Being who we are."

"It would be safer not to tell them. You will be the aging parents of two fine young men. You have skills, Ament, as a soldier, a fisherman, and I dare say you can turn your hand to farming. I don't think you'll have any trouble fitting in."

"But we're Kemetu," Ament said. "That will count against us."

Zeben grinned. "How can you be? You have two Retenu sons. You have obviously lived many years in Kemet, which is why you have a strange accent, but others have done that too. Change your names and don't ever reveal who you were."

We talked it over some more, but our future was effectively settled. In a few days time, Ament and I would travel northeast with our sons, on two donkeys, until we reached the lands of the Retenu. Here we would seek refuge, submerging our identities beneath those of two ordinary people. We would change our names and live in anonymity for the rest of our lives.

I am content. I have been as high in Kemetu society as it is possible to go. I have been king, queen, regent, princess, mother, and God's Wife. Now I will be a peasant and scratch a living from the soil and from a flock of goats. I shall raise my child to be honourable in the sight of the gods--of whatever nation he or she chooses. I am content, for though I lack worldly goods I have two strong sons, another child on the way, and above all a kind and gentle man I can love and who loves me. What more could a woman want?

Chapter 54
Year 2 (5) Userkhaure-setepenre Setnakhte Meryamunre

"I want them found," Setnakhte said. He regarded the remnants of the Set and Khent-abt legion huddled on the desert sand under the guard of his son's men and reached a decision. He strode forward and mounted a boulder so that he could look out on all the captives and be seen by them.

"Men of Set and Khent-abt, you fought well but the fight is now over and the Kingdoms can be restored to peace and security. No blame attaches to you, for you were misled by a woman who falsely claimed the throne, and a man who loved power more than what is right. That man and woman should be made to pay for their crimes, for all your dead comrades who paid the price of their treachery, for disturbing the very Ma'at of Kemet.

"But those traitors have fled from justice and cannot be brought to account--unless you give them up. Tell me where they went and I shall restore your legions to their former glory. Hide them, and remain outcasts from decent Kemetu society. Your choice, soldiers of Set and Khent-abt."

There was silence for a time, and then Mose stepped forward. "You are too late, General Setnakhte," he said. "King Sitre Tausret and General Ament walked into the western desert alone two days ago, without food or water. They are either dead already or will die before you can find them. Give up your search for them. You have won and the throne is yours. Let the dead lie in peace."

Setnakhte turned away without replying, and called his son Ramesses to him. "Send out chariots and men in all directions. I want them found, dead or alive. I must be able to show their bodies in every city and town."

"They are dead, father, or soon will be. Why bother? There are more important things to be done."

"If they are alive...or if people even think they are alive...they will become a focal point for discontent. All opposition to me--to us--must be shown to be gone. Find them."

"And the captives?"

"They are no longer any danger. Disband their legions and send them home."

Ramesses sent out a hundred chariots and half a legion of men, scouring the sand and rock to the west, north, and south, but found nothing. Setnakhte insisted they keep looking and though the desert was searched for several days travel in every direction, they had disappeared as if vanished into the air or underworld. He only called off the search when he found out some of his men were starting to believe the gods had saved them from death.

Months passed. Setnakhte and Ramesses smashed any further opposition to their rule, and eliminated the numerous robber bands that had sprung up in those disturbed times. Once the Kingdoms had been settled, Setnakhte appeared with his legions at every city in Ta Mehu and Ta Shemau, before presenting himself at the Great Temple of Amun in Waset.

He was crowned Userkhaure-setepenre Setnakhte Meryamunre, Powerful are the forms of Re, Chosen of Re, Set is Victorious, Beloved of Amun-Re; and his son Ramesses was made Crown Prince the next day amid great jubilation. Work started immediately on their tombs in Ta-sekhet-ma'at.

Setnakhte was in ill health. Racked by coughing fits that sometimes brought up flecks of blood, he retreated to his palace in Waset and left the running of the Kingdoms to his Tjaties and his son. Hori remained Tjaty of the South as he had not been overtly critical of the new regime and Setnakhte saw the value in continuity. The whole country had been ripped apart by civil war and uncertainty in recent years and a few familiar things would help settle the populace. The king made very few changes to the officials in either Ta Shemau or Ta Mehu, removing only a few individuals to make way for men who had done him a service in the past. Similarly, Mentu had been raised to become Tjaty once more in the north, though Setnakhte had his reservations about the man. In his view, a man who would betray one master would betray another, but until he found a better candidate for the post, Mentu would do.

Ramesses was made Crown Prince in a great ceremony following Setnakhte's own coronation. The king had swiftly realised his own days on the throne were numbered, and recognised the signs of his own death in his weakening body. The country was still unsettled, so in the knowledge that he needed to ensure a smooth transition to the next king, he raised his son to the throne as co-ruler soon after. Ramesses was crowned as Usermaatre Meryamun Ramesse-Hekaiunu, Strong is the Ma'at of Re, Beloved of Amun, Re has fashioned him, Ruler of Iunu. During his coronation, four doves were released to the four cardinal directions--north, east, south and west--to confirm to all that the living Heru, Usermaatre Meryamun Ramesses was in possession of his throne and that Ma'at prevailed in the heavens and upon earth.

The new king went north, seeking out the last of men who opposed the new family who now reigned in Kemet, and stamping his own and his father's authority on every aspect of daily life. His father had now reigned as king for just over a year, but as he dated his accession to the death of Seti-Merenptah, it could be said that he was nearing the end of his second or fifth year, and it was imperative that the nation settled down to a period of prosperity as quickly as possible. Ramesses was in the old Usermaatre's capital city of Per-Ramesses, hearing cases in the Law Courts, when news reached him that his father was ill, so he handed over his work to Tjaty Hori and set off upriver for Waset. The gods favoured him with a strong northerly wind and he was in the southern capital only thirteen days later.

"Welcome, my son," Setnakhte said, opening his arms to embrace Ramesses.

Ramesses was appalled to see how decrepit his father had become in a few short months, but hid his feelings, warmly greeting his father.

"Come walk with me in the gardens," Setnakhte said. "The air seems fresher and makes breathing easier." As if to underline his point, he coughed, doubling over and holding a stained linen cloth to his lips. A servant rushed to hand the king a clean cloth, and removed the soiled one.

Ramesses went to take his father by the arm to lend him support, but the old man shook him off. "I am not dead yet, so do not make me look weaker than I am."

"Of course not, father. May you live a thousand years and rival your own father Usermaatre."

"A thousand years?" Setnakhte wiped a fleck of blood from his lips. "I won't last another year. And speaking of names, I see you have taken your grandfather's throne name for your own. You would emulate him, would you?"

"He was Kemet's greatest king, so yes; I would be like him in every way. You named me Ramesses after him, so naturally I would take his other name. I will raise the fame and glory of Kemet to new heights."

They walked slowly out to the gardens, and Setnakhte was gasping for air by the time they got there. Servants ran ahead of them and dusted off a stone bench in the shade of a flowering tree, and the two kings sat down together, one old and dying, the other still young and virile.

"I had a bit of news from Hori, son of Kama, in Kush the other day," Setnakhte said. "It seems our old foe Sethi turned up. You remember him?"

"Refresh my memory. One hears so many names."

"The General in charge of Amenmesse's army. I fought him and beat him, destroying his army, but he escaped. After all these years, he has turned up in Kush. He was drunk in a tavern in Napata, trying to get support for a new army."

"By the Hidden God, what will you do? Haul him up to Waset and put him on trial or just quietly execute him?"

"Turns out Hori was a bit overzealous. As soon as he heard the report, he arrested him and killed him."

Ramesses considered the news. "Saves you the trouble, I suppose, but was it really him or just some drunk bragging to get another pot of beer?"

Setnakhte shrugged tiredly. "Hardly matters either way. People have forgotten Amenmesse and who his general was." He looked at his hands, now prominently veined and covered in finely wrinkled skin. They trembled slightly, and a wry smile crossed the old man's face. "The years pass more rapidly now, but I am glad I lived long enough to set my family on the throne. I never thought the day would come, yet here we are."

"Indeed, father. Long may the House of Setnakhte rule over Kemet. A thousand years at least."

"That's what they said of the House of Ramesses, yet it has crumbled and fallen, the stone of its edifice turned to dust and blown away."

"Weak men and boys took over when Usermaatre died. I will not make that same mistake, but instead leave the throne to a strong king who will follow me."

Setnakhte nodded slowly, and patted his son's knee. "There are no more rebels?"

"A few," Ramesses admitted, "but none of them serious. Their armies are of peasants and scatter when confronted by soldiers."

"And the Ribu? The Sea Peoples?"

"They have been quiet since Baenre's day, but my spies tell me they are restless. I will have to smash them soon, before they grow much stronger."

"Of more immediate concern is our predecessor. How is your search for Tausret going?"

"I called off the formal search months ago, father. You know that. I still hear rumours from time to time and follow them up..."

"Such as?"

"Oh, let me see...there was a rumour that she had become the chief of a tribe of Ribu and was leading an army toward Ta Mehu. Totally unfounded. Then a woman appeared in Men-nefer, declaring herself King. An imposter whom I put to death for impiety. A man led a revolt in the north, calling himself Ament. He was a peasant leading a hundred other peasants. I executed the lot. A handful of other sightings, but nothing definite. No, those two are dead, I'm sure of it."

"Ament had family in...where was it? Per-Bast? Have you tried there?"

Ramesses bit back an impatient retort. "Ament's sister and her husband own a small vineyard there. I sent soldiers there as soon as they disappeared and regularly since, but there's been no sign. As I said, they're dead and gone."

"Yet the rumours of their existence still abound."

"Fewer with every passing month," Ramesses said. "Oh, I just remembered, here's a story you'll enjoy. One of the border forts reported a man and woman with two grown sons riding north into the land of the Retenu. They were on donkeys, and the fool of an officer wondered if they were Tausret and Ament. Can you imagine a woman who claimed to be a king wearing peasant's clothing and riding a mangy donkey? And away from Kemet?"

Setnakhte laughed so hard he choked and almost stopped breathing. He struggled for breath and coughed up phlegm streaked with blood, eventually calming enough to wave his solicitous servants away.

"That, my son, is ridiculous. It is as you say, Tausret is dead and our family is secure on the throne."

Chapter 55

Ament speaks:

My old life is over, and a new life begins. I am old to be starting something new, but not too old, I think. I have left behind a life of honours, of glory, and of privilege, and taken up one of hardship and want. It is not all bad, however, as I have a wife whom I love more than life itself, two grown sons who honour me, and a delightful new daughter to bring joy to my dotage.

Yes, Tausret married me and gave birth to a daughter whom we named Adara, which in the local tongue means 'noble'. It is a fitting name, for she comes from the most noble in the land, and indeed from royalty--but all that must be forgotten if we are to remain forgotten and safe.

Jerem and Ephrim brought us safely to their tribal lands. For many days, months even, we travelled slowly north through the cultivated lands of Ta Mehu to the Great Sea, where we followed the military road along the coast, passing forts and marching legions on the way. I hid my face at such times in case I was recognised, for I knew some of the men and officers up there. Tausret did the same, though who would have recognised her? She was big with child by then, dressed in coarse peasant clothing and dusty from the road. Beautiful though she is to me, nobody would look at her twice, and we passed through this most dangerous of places unrecognised. We turned to the east, away from the coast and journeyed into the low hills of the land of Retenu.

Jethanah, leader of the Hashimite tribe, and cousin to my boys, welcomed us warily, though he recognised me immediately. Since the days of the rebellion, when we negotiated a peace, Jethanah has been careful to give no offence to the local Governor, and now I could see that our presence worried him. This concern for the safety of his tribe did not get in the way of hospitality, though, and we were hidden away from prying eyes, fed and rested well before he called us into his presence.

"You cannot stay here," Jethanah said bluntly. "I am sorry, but I cannot risk my people. We are too close to the seat of the Kemetu Governor and if he was to learn that I harbour two fugitives, he would show us no mercy."

I spoke for us all, for though Tausret outranked me (in our old life anyway), among these people a woman did not speak for men. I thanked him for his hospitality and told him we would move on the next day, seeking a place where we might find permanent refuge. His cousins Jerem and Ephrim muttered reproachfully, but I quieted them.

"I might be able to aid you further," Jethanah said. "We trade with the Khabiru, who live to the north of us, and are fiercely independent of their Kemetu overseers. They might give you refuge. If you agree to try there, I will send a man with you who knows their tongue, though a number of them speak Kemetu. Many of them resided in your land not so long ago."

I thanked him again and took him up on his offer. Two days later we left for the north, freshly provisioned, and with a guide from the Hashimite tribe called Nathanah. He spoke little, plodding along in front of us and eating alone on his side of the campfire at night before rolling up in a blanket. Ephrim told me he was one of their cousins too, but a more distant one than Jethanah. We travelled slowly as Tausret was now big with child and the bony back of the donkey she rode caused her some distress. She would get off and walk, but could not manage much of that either. To her credit, she seldom complained, though this pregnancy must have been very different from her previous ones as a pampered queen.

And so we came to the land of the Khabiru, not far from the city of Kadesh which most definitely was not a Khabiru city. As we came closer, the number of people on the road increased, and chariots and soldiers, both of Kemetu and Amurru were seen. On those occasions, Nathanah quickly took us off the road to avoid the scrutiny of curious eyes.

The particular family of Khabiru we were taken to had, we learned, affinities with Kemet, having come out of the south only a few generations before. They made us welcome once Nathanah explained our circumstances, and spoke to us in a mixture of Khabiru and Kemetu, though their accents made their speech almost unintelligible. I could not fault their hospitality, though. Tausret was whisked off by the women, and my sons and I were immediately helped to select a building site for our new home, and shown where we could obtain good wood and stone for the construction.

There are rivers in this new land, though none compare with the Great River of Kemet. I became a fisherman once more, and could provide for my family. Jerem and Ephrim took up goat herding and Tausret found hidden skills in preparing wool for garments and cheese making, aided by our daughter Adara. Far cries indeed from our days in the palaces of Kemet, but satisfying nonetheless.

Ah, where do I cease from writing, from recounting the days of my life? Do you want to hear about how many fish I catch or how many goats we own? Are you interested in how Tausret turns wool into fine garments? I think not. Perhaps you might be interested in hearing how Jerem and Ephrim found women of their own, or Adara a husband, but those tales are not for me to tell. Perhaps one day my children or my children's children will talk to you, but that must be their decision.

Tausret is calling to me, telling me that supper is ready, so I must go...

Places, People, Gods & Things in Fall of the House of Ramesses

Abdju
city of Abydos, near modern day el-'Araba el Madfuna

Abu
(1)   city of Elephantine, near modern day Aswan
(2)   elephant

Ahhotep
(1) Captain of the Guard in Waset
(2) Commander of Ptah legion, later of Re legion

Ahtep
Guard Captain

Akh
magical non-physical counterpart of the physical body or Khat

Akhet
the first of three seasons of the ancient calendar, the Season of the Inundation or Flood

Akhet-aten
the city built by the Heretic, Akhenaten

Amenmesse
born Messuwy, eldest son of Merenptah, later king Menmire Amenmesse

Amenmose
son of Siamun, grandson of Ramesses II, a rebel

Ament
Commander of Set Legion, Overseer of Vineyards in Per-Bast, General of the Armies of Kemet; Adviser and friend to the Queen

Amorite
a person from the land of Amurru, a Syrian

Amun
creator deity, local god of Thebes (Waset), often worshipped as Amun-Re (Amun-Ra)

Amurri
an Amorite, an inhabitant of Amurru

Amurru
roughly equivalent to modern day Syria

Anapa
the god Anubis

Anapepy
Chief Scribe of Merenptah and Seti II; father of Pepy

Aniba
administrative capital of Wawat (Northern Kush)

Ankhu
Commander of Sobek legion

Asar
Osiris, god of the underworld and resurrection

Ashkelon
a Philistine city

Atum
the Creator god

Auset
the goddess Isis. Sometimes called Aset or Iset

Ba
the self

Baenre
throne name of Merenptah

Bakenkhons
Hem-netjer of Amun in Waset after Roma-Rui

Bay
Chancellor, also uncle and adviser of Akhenre Siptah

Behdet
city south of Waset, modern day Edfu

Bek
a huntsman of Henen-nesut

Ben-ben
the sacred mound of creation; also the capstone on a pyramids and by extension the whole pyramid

Bes
god worshipped as protector of mothers, children, childbirth

Besenmut
Commander of the Ptah legion under Merenptah and Seti II

Deben
a unit of weight that in the New Kingdom was about 91 grams. Divided into ten kite.

Disebek
Commander of the Re legion; later Commander of Ptah legion

Djanet
city in the north-east of Ta Mehu, Tanis

Djehuti
the god Thoth

Djetmose
Overseer of the King's Table

Djutep
Commander of Sept legion

Duamutef
a protection god of the Canopic jars, son of Heru

Eilah
a coastal town on the east side of the Land of Sin; modern day Eilat

Emsaf
Commander of the Heru Legion

Ephrim
a Canaanite slave boy rescued and adopted by Ament

Geb
god of the earth

Gebti
or Gebtu, Coptos, modern day town of Qift

Gezer
a Philistine city

Ghazzat
modern day Gaza

Great Field
Ta-sekhet-ma'at, Valley of the Kings

Hapi
a protection god of the Canopic jars, son of Heru; the river god

Hashimite
a tribe of the Retenu to which Jerem and Ephrim belong

Hatti
the Hittites

Heka
the Crook, a symbol of kingly authority

Hem-netjer
High Priest

Henen-nesut
Herakleopolis, city near modern day Beni Suef

Henet
the nurse of Seti-Merenptah

Heq-at
the sepat or province of which Iunu is the capital

Heru
the god Horus

Heryshef
a creator and fertility god, Ruler of the Riverbanks

House of Purification
The House of Embalming

Horemheb
last king of the 18th dynasty

Hori
(1) son of Khaemwaset, later Hem-netjer of Ptah and Governor of Men-nefer
(2) son of Hori (1), Tjaty of the North, later Tjaty of the South
(3) son of Kama; King's Son of Kush after Setuy
(4) Hem-netjer of Amun under Siptah

Huni
Squad Leader of the Set legion

Hut-hor
the goddess Hathor

Hut-Repyt
city in Ta Shemau, near modern day village of Wannina

Hut-waret
city of Avaris in Ta Mehu that was absorbed into the city of Per-Ramesses;
centre of worship of the god Set

Huy
Assistant Treasurer

Ib
the heart
Iteru
the Great River; the River Nile

Iunet
city of Dendera

Iunmutef
the pillar; a priest representing Horus in the ceremonies of coronation

Iunu
a northern city, Heliopolis, now north-east edge of Cairo

Iurudef
General of the North

Jerem
a Canaanite slave boy rescued and adopted by Ament

Jethanah
leader of the Hashimite tribe; cousin of Jerem and Ephrim

Ka
the vital essence, the soul

Kadesh
town in southern Amurru or Syria, site of a battle between the Hittites and Egyptians under Ramesses II

Kaftor
one of the Sea Peoples, later became the Philistines

Kemet
the land of Egypt

Kemetu
Egyptian, the people of Egypt

Khat
the physical body

Khent-Min
city north of Waset, modern day Akhmim

Khepresh Crown
the Blue Crown commonly worn in battle; it was made of cloth or leather

Khepre
Khepri, an aspect of the sun god Re

Khmun
Hermopolis, city in Ta Shemau near modern day El Ashmunein

Khonsu
god of the moon; son of Amun and Mut

Khopesh Sword
curved sword evolved from a battle axe; later had more of a ceremonial function

Khor
a region in the south of Syria; Egypt's northernmost province

Khufu's Horizon
the Great Pyramid of Giza built by Khufu c.2560 BCE

King's Son of Kush
Viceroy of Nubia

Kush
Nubia; Egypt's southernmost province

Kushite
people of Kush

Ma'at
Goddess of Truth and Justice; also the concept of truth, order, law and balance

Maatkare
throne name of Hatshepsut

Mahuhy
Royal Secretary under Seti II, later Hem-netjer of Amun

Medjay
an elite paramilitary police force

Menkheperre
throne name of Thutmose III

Menmaatre
throne name of Seti I

Menmire
throne name of Amenmesse

Men-nefer
ancient capital of Lower Egypt, Memphis

Menpehtyre
throne name of Ramesses I

Mentek
a young nobleman of Henen-nesut

Mentu
Tjaty of the North after Hori (2) is made Tjaty of the South

Merenptah
thirteenth son of Ramesses II, King of Egypt, father of Seti and Messuwy

Meryma'at
a grandson of Pareherwenemef, a rebel

Merymose
Commander of Heru legion

Meryre
son of Meryatum, priest of Iunu; a rebel

Meryset
a Leader of Fifty in the Amun legion

Messuwy
eldest son of Merenptah, later King Menmire Amenmesse

Min
god of fertility

Mose
(1) Deputy Commander, later Commander of Set legion
(2) a servant within the palace at Men-nefer

Mut
the mother goddess; consort of Amun

Nakhtu-aa
close-combat troops

Napata
capital of Kush

Natsefamen
Commander of Shu legion

Nebkheperure
throne name of Tutankhamen

Nebmaatre
throne name of Amenhotep III

Nebmaktef
Governor of Perire

Nebt-het
the goddess Nephthys

Nefertem
Hem-netjer of Atum in Iunu

Nehi
a huntsman of Henen-nesut

Neith
goddess of war and hunting

Nekhakha
the Flail, a symbol of kingly authority

Nekhen
Hierakonpolis, city of Hawks, south of Waset, opposite modern day El Kab

Nine Bows
the traditional enemies of Egypt

Nine of Iunu
The Ennead of Iunu; the nine gods associated with creation--Atum, Shu, Tefnut, Geb, Nut, Asar, Auset, Set, Heru & Nebt-Het

Nubt
city in Ta Shemau, modern day town of Kom Ombo

Nut
goddess of the night

Opet Festival
a celebration held annually in Waset in the second month of the Inundation

Panhesy
Commander of the Mut Legion

Paraemheb
Tjaty of the South under Seti II after the fall of Amenmesse

Parahotep
Captain of the Palace Guard in Men-nefer

Pehe-mau
hippopotamus

Pepy
Chief Scribe after his father Anapepy

Per-Asar
a city in Ta Mehu

Per-Banebdjedet
city of Mendes in the eastern delta, known today as Tell El-Ruba

Per-Bast
Bubastis, a city in Ta Mehu

Peret
second season of the Egyptian calendar, the Season of the Emergence

Perire
a city on the western border of Ta Mehu

Per-Ramesses
the capital city of Ramesses II

Per-Wadjet
city in Ta Mehu near modern day Desouk

Pesheskef
a spooned blade of rose quartz used in the ceremony of the Opening of the Mouth

Place of Purification
the House of Embalming

Place of Truth
the village where the workers in the Valley of the Kings resided

Ptah
god of craftsmen and architects, associated with the city of Men-nefer (Memphis)

Puyemra
Governor of the Heq-at province or nome

Qebehsenuef
a protection god of the Canopic jars, son of Heru

Qenna
a Troop Commander in the Kushite army

Raia
a young nobleman of Henen-nesut

Ramesse Kha'amen-teru
chosen names of Bay

Ramesses
(1) King of Egypt (Ramesses II)
(2) son of Setnakhte, Commander of the Amun legion, later Ramesses III

Ramose
Commander of the Khent-abt legion

Ramses
a grandson of Pareherwenemef, a rebel

Re
(Ra) sun god, often worshipped as Amun-Re or Atum-Re

Remaktef
a scribe of the Place of Truth, grandson of Kenhirkhopeshef
Retenu
Canaan, present-day Israel, Jordan, and Lebanon

Ribu
a tribe in eastern Libya

Royal Butler
a high-ranking official in the Royal Court
Samut
Commander of the Amun Legion under Amenmesse

Sa-Nekhamun
Chamberlain to Amenmose the rebel

Sea Peoples
a loose amalgamation of sea-faring tribes from around the Mediterranean.
Included the Phoenicians, Greeks, and Philistines. Other tribes include the
Ekwesh, Denyen, teresh, Peleset, Shekelesh and Sherden.

Seb-Ur
an instrument made of meteoric iron used in the ceremony of the Opening of the Mouth

Sekhaienre
the initial throne name of Siptah

Sekhet Hetepet
the Field of Peace

Sekhet Iaru
the Field of Reeds

Sekhmet
warrior goddess and goddess of healing

Senefer
Overseer of the Hunt

Senet
a popular game involving a board and pieces

Senkare
a court physician

Senmut
Architect of the temple of Amun in Waset

Sensek
an Amorite servant of Bay

Sepat
a nome, or administrative district

Serket
goddess of healing venomous stings and bites

Set
Seth, god of desert, storms, disorder and violence, Lord of the Red Land (desert)

Setat
a unit of area, 10,000 square cubits or 0.276 hectares

Sethi
(1) ninth son of Ramesses II, father of Tausret
(2) son of Horire, military adviser to Messuwy, later General under Menmire Amenmesse

Seti
(1) Seti I, father of Ramesses II
(2) son of Merenptah, later Seti II

Seti-Merenptah
only living son of Seti II and Tausret

Set-ma'at
the Place of Truth; the workmen's village near the Valley of the Kings

Setnakhte
a younger son of Ramesses II by one of his concubines, General of the South, later King and founder of the 20th Dynasty; father of Ramesses III

Setuy
King's Son of Kush under Siptah

Shemu
third season of the Egyptian calendar, the Season of the Harvest

Shenu
the rope-like protective surround of the Royal Name; the cartouche

Sheut
the shadow self

Shu
god of the air

Sin
Land of Sin; Sinai Peninsula

Siptah
son of Menmire Amenmesse; King of Kemet after Seti II

Sitre
throne name of Tausret

Sobek
a god associated with the Nile crocodile

Sopdu
god of the sky and eastern borders

Stela
(plural: stelae) a stone commemorative slab, often with an inscription

Suterere
sister of Bay, wife of Messuwy, mother of Siptah

Ta-Bitjet
a scorpion goddess

Taharqa
Commander of the Kushite legion

Ta Mehu
Lower Egypt (in the north)

Taremu
Leontopolis, city in Ta Mehu, modern day Tell al Muqdam

Ta-sekhet-ma'at
The Great Field, Valley of the Kings

Ta-senet
a city south of Waset, modern day Esna

Ta Shemau
Upper Egypt (in the south)

Tausret
daughter of Sethi (1), adopted daughter of Merenptah, wife of Seti (2); Regent during reign of Akhenre Siptah; later King

Tawaret
goddess of childbirth and fertility

Ta-ynt-netert
Dendera, a city north of Waset, near modern day Qena

Tiaamet
daughter of Ahmose the Controller of the City Granaries in Men-nefer

Ti-ament
sister of Ament

Timna
a valley north of Eilah in the east of the Land of Sin; a site of ancient copper mining

Tiy-merenese
wife of Setnakhte

Tjaty
Vizier, the highest official to serve the king

Tjenu
Thinis, a city north of Waset, possibly near modern day Girga

Ur Hekau
an instrument pf polished wood used in the ceremony of the Opening of the Mouth

Userkheperure
throne name of Seti II

Usermaatre
throne name of Ramesses II

Ushabti
(plural: ushabtiu) a funerary figurine placed within a tomb that is intended to act as a servant for the deceased in the afterlife

Wadjet
goddess, patron and protector of Ta Mehu, protector of kings and women in childbirth

Waset
capital city of Ta Shemau, Amun's holy city, Thebes

Wawat
province of Northern Kush

Wenemef
temporary Commander of Set legion

Zawty
a city north of Waset, modern day Asyut

Zeben
husband of Ti-ament

You can find ALL our books up at Amazon at:
https://www.amazon.com/shop/writers_exchange

or on our website at:
http://www.writers-exchange.com

All our Historical Novels
http://www.writers-exchange.com/category/genres/historical/

About the Author

Max Overton has travelled extensively and lived in many places around the world-- including Malaysia, India, Germany, England, Jamaica, New Zealand, USA and Australia. Trained in the biological sciences in New Zealand and Australia, he has worked within the scientific field for many years, but now concentrates on writing. While predominantly a writer of historical fiction (Scarab: Books 1 - 6 of the Amarnan Kings; the Scythian Trilogy; the Demon Series; Ascension), he also writes in other genres (A Cry of Shadows, the Glass Trilogy, Haunted Trail, Sequestered) and draws on true life (Adventures of a Small Game Hunter in Jamaica, We Came From Königsberg). Max also maintains an interest in butterflies, photography, the paranormal and other aspects of Fortean Studies.

Most of his other published books are available at Writers Exchange Ebooks, http://www.writers-exchange.com/Max-Overton.html and all his books may be viewed on his website: http://www.maxovertonauthor.com/

Max's book covers are all designed and created by Julie Napier, and other examples of her art and photography may be viewed at www.julienapier.com

If you want to read more about other books by this author, they are listed on the following pages...

A Cry of Shadows
{Paranormal Murder Mystery}

Australian Professor Ian Delaney is single-minded in his determination to prove his theory that one can discover the moment that the life force leaves the body. After succumbing to the temptation to kill a girl under scientifically controlled conditions, he takes an offer of work in St Louis, hoping to leave the undiscovered crime behind him.

In America, Wayne Richardson seeks revenge by killing his ex-girlfriend, believing it will give him the upper hand, a means to seize control following their breakup. Wayne quickly discovers that he enjoys killing and begins to seek out young women who resemble his dead ex-girlfriend.

Ian and Wayne meet and, when Ian recognizes the symptoms of violent delusion, he employs Wayne to help him further his research. Despite the police closing in, the two killers manage to evade identification time and time again as the death toll rises in their wake.

The detective in charge of the case, John Barnes, is frantic, willing to try anything to catch his killer. With time running out, he searches desperately for answers before another body is found...or the culprit slips into the woodwork for good.

Publisher: http://www.writers-exchange.com/A-Cry-of-Shadows/
Amazon: http://mybook.to/ACryOfShadows

Adventures of a Small Game Hunter in Jamaica
{Biography}

An eleven-year-old boy is plucked from boarding school in England and transported to the tropical paradise of Jamaica where he's free to study his one great love--butterflies. He discovers that Jamaica has a wealth of these wonderful insects and sets about making a collection of as many as he can find. Along the way, he has adventures with other creatures, from hummingbirds to vultures, from iguanas to black widow spiders. Through it all runs the promise of the legendary Homerus swallowtail, Jamaica's national butterfly.

Other activities intrude, like school, boxing and swimming lessons, but he manages to inveigle his parents into taking him to strange and sometimes dangerous places, all in the name of butterfly collecting. He meets scientists and Rastafarians, teachers, small boys and the ordinary people living on the tropical isle, and even discovers butterflies that shouldn't exist in Jamaica.

Author Max Overton was that young boy. He counted himself fortunate to have lived in Jamaica in an age very different from the present one. Max still has some of the butterflies he collected half a century or more ago, and each one releases a flood of memories whenever he opens the box and gazes at their tattered and fading wings. These memories have become stories--stories of the Adventures of a Small Game Hunter in Jamaica.
Publisher: http://www.writers-exchange.com/Adventures-of-a-Small-Game-Hunter/
Amazon: http://myBook.to/AdventuresGameHunter

Ascension Series, A Novel of Nazi Germany
{Historical: Holocaust}

Before he fully realized the diabolical cruelties of the National Socialist German Worker's Party, Konrad Wengler had committed atrocities against his own people, the Jews, out of fear of both his faith and his heritage. But after he witnesses firsthand the concentration camps, the corruption, the inhuman malevolence of the Nazi war machine and the propaganda aimed at annihilating an entire race, he knows he must find a way to turn the tide and become the savior his people desperately need.

Book 1: Ascension
Being a Jew in Germany can be a dangerous thing...

Fear prompts Konrad Wengler to put his faith aside and try desperately to forget his heritage. After fighting in the Great War, he's wounded and turns instead to law enforcement in his tiny Bavarian hometown. There, he falls under the spell of the fledgling Nazi Party. He joins the Party in patriotic fervour and becomes a Lieutenant of Police and Schutzstaffel (SS).

In the course of his duties as policeman, Konrad offends a powerful Nazi official who starts an SS investigation. War breaks out. When he joins the Police Battalions, he's sent to Poland and witnesses there firsthand the atrocities being committed upon his fellow Jews.

Unknown to Konrad, the SS investigators have discovered his origins and follow him into Poland. Arrested and sent to Mauthausen Concentration Camp, Konrad is forced to face what it means to be a Jew and fight for survival. Will his friends on the outside, his wife and lawyer, be enough to counter the might of the Nazi machine?
Publisher: http://www.writers-exchange.com/Ascension/
Amazon: http://mybook.to/Ascension1

Book 2: Maelstrom
Never underestimate the enemy...

Konrad Wengler survived his brush with the death camps of Nazi Germany. Now, reinstated as a police officer in his Bavarian hometown despite being a Jew, he throws himself back into his work, seeking to uncover evidence that will remove a corrupt Nazi party official.

The Gestapo have their own agenda and, despite orders from above to eliminate this troublesome Jewish policeman, they hide Konrad in the

Totenkopf (Death's Head) Division of the Waffen-SS. In a fight to survive in the snowy wastes of Russia while the tide of war turns against Germany, Konrad experiences tank battles, ghetto clearances, partisans, and death camps (this time as a guard), as well as the fierce battles where his Division is badly outnumbered and on the defence.

Through it all, Konrad strives to live by his conscience and resist taking part in the atrocities happening all around him. He still thinks of himself as a policeman, but his desire to bring the corrupt Nazi official to justice seems far removed from his present reality. If he is to find the necessary evidence against his enemy, he must first *survive*...

Publisher: http://www.writers-exchange.com/Maelstrom/

Amazon: http://mybook.to/Ascension2

Book 3: Dämmerung

Konrad Wengler is captured and sent from one Soviet prison camp to another. Even hearing the war has come to an end makes no difference until he's arrested as a Nazi Party member. In jail, Konrad refuses to defend himself for things he's guilty and should be punished for. Will his be an eye-for-an-eye life sentence, or leniency in regard of the good he tried to do once he learned the truth?

Publisher: http://www.writers-exchange.com/dammerung/

Amazon: http://mybook.to/Ascension3

Fall of the House of Ramesses Series,
A Novel of Ancient Egypt
{Historical: Ancient Egypt}

Egypt was at the height of its powers in the days of Ramesses the Great, a young king who confidently predicted his House would last for a Thousand Years. Sixty years later, he was still on the throne. One by one, his heirs had died and the survivors had become old men. When Ramesses at last died, he left a stagnant kingdom and his throne to an old man--Merenptah. What followed laid the groundwork for a nation ripped apart by civil war.

Book 1: Merenptah

The House of Ramesses is in the hands of an old man. King Merenptah wants to leave the kingdom to his younger son, Seti, but northern tribes in Egypt rebel and join forces with the Sea Peoples, invading from the north. In the south, the king's eldest son Messuwy is angered at being passed over in favour of the younger son...and plots to rid himself of his father and brother.

Publisher: http://www.writers-exchange.com/Merenptah/
Amazon: http://mybook.to/FOTHR1

Book 2: Seti

After only nine years on the throne, Merenptah is dead and his son Seti is king in his place. He rules from the northern city of Men-nefer, while his elder brother Messuwy, convinced the throne is his by right, plots rebellion in the south.

The kingdoms are tipped into bloody civil war, with brother fighting against brother for the throne of a united Egypt. On one side is Messuwy, now crowned as King Amenmesse and his ruthless General Sethi; on the other, young King Seti and his wife Tausret. But other men are weighing up the chances of wresting the throne from both brothers and becoming king in their place. Under the onslaught of conflict, the House of Ramesses begins to crumble...

Publisher: http://www.writers-exchange.com/Seti/
Amazon: http://mybook.to/FOTHR2

Book 3: Tausret

The House of Ramesses falters as Tausret relinquishes the throne upon the death of her husband, King Seti. Amenmesse's young son Siptah will become king until her infant son is old enough to rule. Tausret, as Regent, and the king's uncle, Chancellor Bay, hold tight to the reins of power and vie for complete control of the kingdoms. Assassination changes the balance of power, and, seeing his chance, Chancellor Bay attempts a coup...

Tausret's troubles mount as she also faces a challenge from Setnakhte, an aging son of the Great Ramesses who believes Seti was the last legitimate king. If Setnakhte gets his way, he will destroy the House of Ramesses and set up his own dynasty of kings.

Publisher: http://www.writers-exchange.com/Tausret/
Amazon: http://mybook.to/FOTHR3

Haunted Trail A Tale of Wickedness & Moral Turpitude
{Western: Paranormal}

Ned Abernathy is a hot-tempered young cowboy in the small town of Hammond's Bluff in 1876. In a drunken argument with his best friend Billy over a girl, he guns him down. Ned flees and wanders the plains, forests and hills of the Dakota Territories, certain that every man's hand is against him.

Horse rustlers, marauding Indians, killers, gold prospectors and French trappers cross his path and lead to complications, as do persistent apparitions of what Ned believes is the ghost of his friend Billy, come to accuse him of murder. He finds love and loses it. Determined not to do the same when he discovers gold in the Black Hills, he ruthlessly defends his new-found wealth against greedy men. In the process, he comes to terms with who he is and what he's done. But there are other ghosts in his past that he needs to confront. Returning to Hammond's Bluff, Ned stumbles into a shocking surprise awaiting him at the end of his haunted trail.

Publisher: http://www.writers-exchange.com/Haunted-Trail/
Amazon: http://mybook.to/HauntedTrail

Glass Trilogy
{Paranormal Thriller}

Delve deep into the mysteries of Aboriginal mythology, present day UFO activity and pure science that surround the continent of Australia, from its barren deserts to the depths of its rainforest and even deeper into its mysterious mountains. Along the way, love, greed, murder, and mystery abound while the secrets of mankind and the ultimate answer to 'what happens now?' just might be answered.

GLASS HOUSE, Book 1: The mysteries of Australia may just hold the answers mankind has been searching for millennium to find. When Doctor James Hay, a university scientist who studies the paranormal mysteries in Australia, finds an obelisk of carved volcanic rock on sacred Aboriginal land in northern Queensland, he realizes it may hold the answers he's been seeking. A respected elder of the Aboriginal people instructs James to take up the gauntlet and follow his heart. Along with his old friend and award-winning writer Spencer, Samantha Louis, her cameraman, and two of James' Aboriginal students, James embarks on a life-changing quest for the truth.
Publisher: http://www.writers-exchange.com/Glass-House/
Amazon: http://mybook.to/Glass1

A GLASS DARKLY, Book 2: A dead volcano called Glass Mountain in Northern California seems harmless...but is it really?

Andromeda Jones, a physicist, knows her missing sister Samantha is somehow tied up with the new job Andromeda herself has been offered to work with a team in constructing Vox Dei, a machine that's been ostensibly built to eliminate wars. But what is its true nature, and who's pulling the strings?

When the experiment spins out of control, dark powers are unleashed and the danger to mankind unfolds relentlessly. Strange, evil shadows are using the Vox Dei and Andromeda's sister Samantha to get through to our world, knowing the time is near when Earth's final destiny will be decided.

Federal forces are aware of something amiss, so, to rescue her sibling, Andromeda agrees to go on a dangerous mission and soon finds herself entangled in a web of professional jealousy, political betrayal, and flat-out greed.

Publisher: http://www.writers-exchange.com/A-Glass-Darkly/
Amazon: http://mybook.to/Glass2

LOOKING GLASS, Book 3: Samantha and James Hay have been advised that their missing daughter Gaia have been located in ancient Australia. Dr. Xanatuo, an alien scientist who, along with a lost tribe of Neanderthals and other beings working to help mankind, has discovered a way to send them back in time to be reunited with Gaia. Ernie, the old Aboriginal tracker and leader of the Neanderthals, along with friends Ratana and Nathan and characters from the first two books of the trilogy, will accompany them. This team of intrepid adventurers have another mission for the journey, along with aiding the Hayes' quest, which is paramount to changing a terrible wrong which exists in the present time.
Publisher: http://www.writers-exchange.com/Looking-Glass/
Amazon: http://mybook.to/Glass3

Kadesh, A Novel of Ancient Egypt

Holding the key to strategic military advantage, Kadesh is a jewel city that distant lands covet. Ramesses II of Egypt and Muwatalli II of Hatti believe they're chosen by the gods to claim ascendancy to Kadesh. When the two meet in the largest chariot battle ever fought, not just the fate of empires will be decided but also the lives of citizens helplessly caught up in the greedy ambition of kings.
Publisher: http://www.writers-exchange.com/Kadesh/
Amazon: http://mybook.to/Kadesh

Hyksos Series, A Novel of Ancient Egypt

The power of the kings of the Middle Kingdom have been failing for some time, having lost control of the Nile Delta to a series of Canaanite kings who ruled from the northern city of Avaris.
Into this mix came the Kings of Amurru, Lebanon and Syria bent on subduing the whole of Egypt. These kings were known as the Hyksos, and they dealt a devastating blow to the peoples of the Nile Delta and Valley.

Book 1: Avaris

When Arimawat and his son Harrubaal fled from Urubek, the king of Hattush, to the court of the King of Avaris, King Sheshi welcomed the refugees. One of Arimawat's first tasks for King Shesi is to sail south to the Land of Kush and fetch Princess Tati, who will become Sheshi's queen. Arimawat and Harrubaal perform creditably, but their actions have far-reaching consequences.

On the return journey, Harrubaal falls in love with Kemi, the daughter of the Southern Egyptian king. As a reward for Harrubaal's work, Sheshi secures the hand of the princess for the young Canaanite prince. Unfortunately for the peace of the realm, Sheshi lusts after Princess Kemi too, and his actions threaten the stability of his kingdom...
Publisher: http://www.writers-exchange.com/Avaris/
Amazon: http://mybook.to/avaris

Book 2: Conquest

The Hyksos invade the Delta using the new weapons of bronze and chariots, things of which the Egyptians have no knowledge. They rout the Delta forces, and in the south, the unconquered kings ready their armies to defend their lands. Meanwhile in Avaris, Merybaal, the son of Harrubaal and Kemi, strives to defend his family in a city conquered by the Hyksos.

Elements of the Delta army that refuse to surrender continue the fight for their homeland, and new kings proclaim themselves as the inheritors of the failed kings of Avaris. One of these is Amenre, grandson of Merybaal, but he is forced into hiding as the Hyksos sweep all before them, bringing their terror to the kingdom of the Nile valley. Driven south in disarray, the survivors of the Egyptian army seek leaders who can resist the enemy...
Publisher: http://www.writers-exchange.com/conquest/

Amazon: http://mybook.to/conquest

Book 3: Two Cities

The Hyksos drive south into the Nile Valley, sweeping all resistance aside. Bebi and Sobekhotep, grandsons of Harrubaal, assume command of the loyal Egyptian army and strive to stem the flood of Hyksos conquest. But even the cities of the south are divided against themselves.

Abdju, an old capital city of Egypt reasserts itself, putting forward a line of kings of its own, and soon the city is at war with Waset, the southern capital of the Nile Valley, as the two cities fight for supremacy in the face of the advancing northern enemy. Caught up in the turmoil of warring nations, the ordinary people of Egypt must fight for their own survival as well as that of their kingdom.

Publisher: http://www.writers-exchange.com/Two-Cities/
Amazon: http://mybook.to/TwoCities

Book 4: Possessor of All

The Hyksos, themselves beset by intrigue and division, push down into southern Egypt. The short-lived kingdom of Abdju collapses, leaving Nebiryraw the undisputed king of the south ruling from the city of Waset. An uneasy truce between north and south enables both sides to strengthen their positions.

Khayan seizes power over the Hyksos kingdom and turns his gaze toward Waset, determined to conquer Egypt finally. Meanwhile, the family of King Nebiryraw looks to the future and starts securing their own advantage, weakening the southern kingdom. In the face of renewed tensions, the delicate peace cannot last...

Publisher: http://www.writers-exchange.com/Possessor-of-All/
Amazon: http://mybook.to/Possessor-of-All

Book 5: War in the South

Intrigue and rebellion rule in Egypt's southern kingdom as the house of King Nebiryraw tears itself apart. King succeeds king, but none of them look capable of defending the south, let alone reclaiming the north. Taking advantage of this, King Khayan of the Hyksos launches his assault on Waset, but rebellions in the north delay his victory.

The fall of Waset brings about a change of leadership. Apophis takes command of the Hyksos forces, and Rahotep brings together a small army to challenge the might of the Hyksos, knowing that the fate of Egypt hangs on the coming battle.

Publisher: http://www.writers-exchange.com/War-in-the-South/
Amazon: http://mybook.to/WarInTheSouth

Book 6: Between the Wars

Rahotep leads his Egyptian army to victory, and Apophis withdraws the Hyksos army northward. An uneasy peace settles over the Nile valley. Rebellions in the north keep the Hyksos king from striking back at Rahotep, while internal strife between the Hyksos nobility and generals threatens to rip their empire apart.

War is coming to Egypt once more, and the successors of Rahotep start preparing for it, using the very weapons that the Hyksos introduced-- bronze weapons and the war chariot. King Ahmose repudiates the peace treaty, and Apophis of the Hyksos prepares to destroy his enemies at last. Bloody warfare returns to Egypt...

Publisher: http://www.writers-exchange.com/Between-the-Wars/
Amazon: http://mybook.to/BetweenTheWars

Book 7: Sons of Tao

War breaks out between the Hyksos invaders and native Egyptians determined to rid themselves of their presence. King Seqenenre Tao launches an attack on King Apophis but the Hyksos strike back savagely. It is only when his sons Kamose and Ahmose carry the war to the Hyksos that the Egyptians really start to hope they can succeed.

Kamose battles fiercely, but only when his younger brother Ahmose assumes the throne is there real success. Faced with an ignominious defeat, a Hyksos general overthrows Apophis and becomes king, but then he faces a resurgent Egyptian king determined to rid his land of the Hyksos invader...

Publisher: http://www.writers-exchange.com/sons-of-tao/

Amazon: http://mybook.to/SonsOfTao

TULPA
{Paranormal Thriller}

From the rainforests of tropical Australia to the cane fields and communities of the North Queensland coastal strip, a horror is unleashed by those foolishly playing with unknown forces...

A fairy story to amuse small children leads four bored teenagers and a young university student in a North Queensland town to becoming interested in an ancient Tibetan technique for creating a life form. When their seemingly harmless experiment sets free terror and death, the teenagers are soon fighting to contain a menace that reproduces exponentially.

The police are helpless to end the horror. Aided by two old game hunters, a student of the paranormal and a few small children, the teenagers must find a way of destroying what they unintentionally released. But how can they stop beings that can escape into an alternate reality when threatened?

Publisher: http://www.writers-exchange.com/TULPA/
Amazon: http://mybook.to/TULPA

Scythian Trilogy
{Historical}

Captured by the warlike, tribal Scythians who bicker amongst themselves and bitterly resent outside interference, a fiercely loyal captain in Alexander the Great's Companion Cavalry Nikometros and his men are to be sacrificed to the Mother Goddess. Lucky chance--and the timely intervention of Tomyra, priestess and daughter of the Massegetae chieftain--allows him to defeat the Champion. With their immediate survival secured, acceptance into the tribe...and escape...is complicated by the captain's growing feelings for Tomyra--death to any who touch her--and the chief's son Areipithes who not only detests Nikometros and wants to have him killed or banished but intends to murder his own father and take over the tribe.

LION OF SCYTHIA, Book 1: Alexander the Great has conquered the Persian Empire and is marching eastward to India. In his wake he leaves small groups of soldiers to govern great tracts of land and diverse peoples. Nikometros is one young cavalry captain left behind in the lands of the fierce, nomadic Scythian horsemen. Captured after an ambush, Nikometros must fight for his life and the lives of his surviving men. Even as he seeks an opportunity to escape, he finds himself bound by a debt of loyalty to the chief...and his own developing love for the young priestess.
Publisher: http://www.writers-exchange.com/Lion-of-Scythia/
Amazon: http://mybook.to/Scythian1

THE GOLDEN KING, Book 2: The chief of the tribe of nomadic Scythian horsemen is dead, killed by his son's treachery. The priestess, lover of the young cavalry officer, Nikometros, is carried off into the mountains. Nikometros and his friends set off in hard pursuit.
Death rides with them. By the time they return, the tribes are at war. Nikometros must choose between attempting to become chief himself or leaving the people he's come to love and respect to return to his duty as an army officer in the Empire of Alexander.
Winner of the 2005 EPIC Ebook Awards.
Publisher: http://www.writers-exchange.com/The-Golden-King/
Amazon: http://mybook.to/Scythian2

FUNERAL IN BABYLON, Book 3: Alexander the Great has returned from India and set up his court in Babylon. Nikometros and a band of loyal Scythians journey deep into the heart of Persia to join the Royal court. Nikometros finds himself embroiled in the intrigues and wars of kings, generals, and merchant adventurers as he strives to provide a safe haven for his lover and friends. With the fate of an Empire hanging in the balance, Death walks beside Nikometros as events precipitate a Funeral in Babylon...

Winner of the 2006 EPIC Ebook Awards.

Publisher: http://www.writers-exchange.com/Funeral-in-Babylon/

Amazon: http://mybook.to/Scythian3

We Came From Konigsberg
{Historical: Holocaust}

Based on a true story gleaned from the memories of family members sixty years after the events, from photographs and documents, and from published works of nonfiction describing the times and events described in the narrative, *We Came From Konigsberg* is set in January 1945.

The Soviet Army is poised for the final push through East Prussia and Poland to Berlin. Elisabet Daeker and her five young sons are in Königsberg, East Prussia and have heard the shocking stories of Russian atrocities. They're desperate to escape to the perceived safety of Germany. To survive, Elisabet faces hardships endured at the hands of Nazi hardliners, of Soviet troops bent on rape, pillage and murder, and of Allied cruelty in the Occupied Zones of post-war Germany.

Winner of the 2014 EPIC Ebook Awards.

Publisher: http://www.writers-exchange.com/We-Came-From-Konigsberg/

Amazon: http://mybook.to/Konigsberg

Sequestered
By Max Overton and Jim Darley
{Action/Thriller}

Storing carbon dioxide underground as a means of removing a greenhouse gas responsible for global warming has made James Matternicht a fabulously wealthy man. For 15 years, the Carbon Capture and Sequestration Facility at Rushing River in Oregon's hinterland has been operating without a problem...or has it?

When mysterious documents arrive on her desk that purport to show the Facility is leaking, reporter Annaliese Winton investigates. Together with a government geologist, Matt Morrison, she uncovers a morass of corruption and deceit that now threatens the safety of her community and the entire northwest coast of America.

Liquid carbon dioxide, stored at the critical point under great pressure, is a tremendously dangerous substance, and millions of tonnes of it are sequestered in the rock strata below Rushing River. All it would take is a crack in the overlying rock and the whole pressurized mass could erupt with disastrous consequences. And that crack has always existed there...

Recipient of the Life Award (Literature for the Environment):

"There are only two kinds of people: conservationists and suicides. To qualify for this Award, your book needs to value the wonderful world of nature, to recognize that we are merely one species out of millions, and that we have a responsibility to cherish and maintain our small planet."

Awarded from http://bobswriting.com/life/

Publisher: http://www.writers-exchange.com/Sequestered/
Amazon: http://mybook.to/Sequestered

Strong is the Ma'at of Re, A Novel of Ancient Egypt
{Historical: Ancient Egypt}

In Ancient Egypt, C1200 BCE, bitter contention and resentment, secret coups and assassination attempts may decide the fate of those who would become legends...by any means necessary.

Book 1: The King

That *he* is descended from Ramesses the Great fills Ramesses III with obscene pride. Elevated to the throne following a coup led by his father Setnakhte during the troubled days of Queen Tausret, Ramesses III sets about creating an Egypt that reflects the glory days of Ramesses the Great. He takes on his predecessor's throne name, names his sons after the sons of Ramesses and pushes them toward similar duties. Most of all, he thirsts after conquests like those of his hero grandfather.

Ramesses III assumes the throne name of Usermaatre, translated as "Strong is the Ma'at of Re" and endeavours to live up to the sentiment. He fights foreign foes, as had Ramesses the Great; he builds temples through-out the Two Lands, as had Ramesses the Great, and he looks forward to a long, illustrious life on the throne of Egypt, as had Ramesses the Great.

Alas, his reign is not meant to be. Ramesses III faces troubles at home--troubles that threaten the stability of Egypt and his own throne. The struggles for power between his wives, his sons, and even the priests of Amun, together with a treasury drained of its wealth, all force Ramesses III to question his success as the scion of a legend.

Publisher: http://www.writers-exchange.com/The-King/
Amazon: http://mybook.to/StrongIsTheMaatOfRe1

Book 2: The Heirs

Tiye, the first wife of Ramesses III, has grown so used to being the mother of the Heir she can no longer bear to see that prized title pass to the son of a rival wife. Her eldest sons have died and the one left wants to step down and devote his life to the priesthood. Then the son of the king's sister/wife, also named Ramesses, will become Crown Prince and all Tiye's ambitions will lie in ruins.

Ramesses III struggles to enrich Egypt by seeking the wealth of the Land of Punt. He dispatches an expedition to the fabled southern land but years pass before the expedition returns. In the meantime, Tiye has a new hope: A last son she dotes on. Plague sweeps through Egypt, killing princes and princesses alike and lessening her options, and now Tiye must undergo the added indignity of having her daughter married off to the hated Crown Prince.

All Tiye's hopes are pinned on this last son of hers, but Ramesses III refuses to consider him as a potential successor, despite the Crown Prince's failing health. Unless Tiye can change the king's mind through charm or coercion, her sons will forever be excluded from the throne of Egypt.

Publisher: http://www.writers-exchange.com/The-Heirs/

Amazon: http://mybook.to/StrongIsTheMaatOfRe1

Book 3: Taweret

The reign of Ramesses III is failing and even the gods seem to be turning their eyes away from Egypt. When the sun hides its face, crops suffer, throwing the country into famine. Tomb workers go on strike. To avert further disaster, Crown Prince Ramesses acts on his father's behalf.

The rivalry between Ramesses III's wives--commoner Tiye and sister/wife Queen Tyti--also comes to a head. Tiye resents not being made queen and can't abide that her sons have been passed over. She plots to put her own spoiled son Pentaweret on the throne.

The eventual strength of the Ma'at of Re hangs in the balance. Will the rule of Egypt be decided by fate, gods...or treason?

Publisher: http://www.writers-exchange.com/The-One-of-Taweret/

Amazon: http://mybook.to/SITMOR3

The Amarnan Kings Series, A Novel of Ancient Egypt
{Historical: Ancient Egypt}

Set in Egypt of the 14th century B.C.E. and piecing together a mosaic of the reigns of the five Amarnan kings, threaded through by the memories of princess Beketaten-Scarab, a tapestry unfolds of the royal figures lost in the mists of antiquity.

SCARAB - AKHENATEN, Book 1: A chance discovery in Syria reveals answers to the mystery of the ancient Egyptian sun-king, the heretic Akhenaten and his beautiful wife Nefertiti. Inscriptions in the tomb of his sister Beketaten, otherwise known as Scarab, tell a story of life and death, intrigue and warfare, in and around the golden court of the kings of the glorious 18th dynasty.

The narrative of a young girl growing up at the centre of momentous events--the abolition of the gods, foreign invasion, and the fall of a once-great family--reveals who Tutankhamen's parents really were, what happened to Nefertiti, and other events lost to history in the great destruction that followed the fall of the Aten heresy.

Publisher: http://www.writers-exchange.com/Scarab/
Amazon: http://mybook.to/ScarabBook1

SCARAB- SMENKHKARE, Book 2: King Akhenaten, distraught at the rebellion and exile of his beloved wife Nefertiti, withdraws from public life, content to leave the affairs of Egypt in the hands of his younger half-brother Smenkhkare. When Smenkhkare disappears on a hunting expedition, his sister Beketaten, known as Scarab, is forced to flee for her life.

Finding refuge among her mother's people, the Khabiru, Scarab has resigned herself to a life in exile...until she hears that her brother Smenkhkare is still alive. He is raising an army in Nubia to overthrow Ay and reclaim his throne. Scarab hurries south to join him as he confronts Ay and General Horemheb outside the gates of Thebes.

Publisher: http://www.writers-exchange.com/Scarab2/
Amazon: http://mybook.to/ScarabBook2

SCARAB - TUTANKHAMEN, Book 3: Scarab and her brother Smenkhkare are in exile in Nubia but are gathering an army to wrest control of

Egypt from the boy king Tutankhamen and his controlling uncle, Ay. Meanwhile, the kingdoms are beset by internal troubles while the Amorites are pressing hard against the northern borders. Generals Horemheb and Paramessu must fight a war on two fronts while deciding where their loyalties lie--with the former king Smenkhkare or with the new young king in Thebes.

Smenkhkare and Scarab march on Thebes with their native army to meet the legions of Tutankhamen on the plains outside the city gates. As two brothers battle for supremacy and the throne of the Two Kingdoms, the fate of Egypt and the 18th dynasty hangs in the balance. Finalist in 2013's Eppie Awards.
Publisher: http://www.writers-exchange.com/Scarab3/
Amazon: http://mybook.to/ScarabBook3

SCARAB - AY, Book 4: Tutankhamen is dead and his grieving widow tries to rule alone, but her grandfather Ay has not destroyed the former kings just so he can be pushed aside. Presenting the Queen and General Horemheb with a fait accompli, the old Vizier assumes the throne of Egypt and rules with a hand of hardened bronze. His adopted son, Nakhtmin, will rule after him and stamp out the last remnants of loyalty to the former kings.

Scarab was sister to three kings and will not give in to the usurper and his son. She battles against Ay and his legions under the command of General Horemheb and aided by desert tribesmen and the gods of Egypt themselves. The final confrontation will come in the rich lands of the Nile delta where the future of Egypt will at last be decided.
Publisher: http://www.writers-exchange.com/Scarab4/
Amazon: http://mybook.to/ScarabBook4

SCARAB - HOREMHEB, Book 5: General Horemheb has taken control after the death of Ay and Nakhtmin. Forcing Scarab to marry him, he ascends the throne of Egypt. The Two Kingdoms settle into an uneasy peace as Horemheb proceeds to stamp out all traces of the former kings. He also persecutes the Khabiru tribesmen who were reluctant to help him seize power. Scarab escapes into the desert, where she is content to wait until Egypt needs her.

A holy man emerges from the desert and demands that Horemheb release the Khabiru so they may worship his god. Scarab recognises the holy

man and supports him in his efforts to free his people. The gods of Egypt and of the Khabiru are invoked and disaster sweeps down on the Two Kingdoms as the Khabiru flee with Scarab and the holy man. Horemheb and his army pursue them to the shores of the Great Sea, where a natural event...or the very hand of God...alters the course of Egyptian history.
Publisher: http://www.writers-exchange.com/Scarab5/
Amazon: http://mybook.to/ScarabBook5

SCARAB - DESCENDANT, Book 6: Three thousand years after the reigns of the Amarnan Kings, the archaeologists who discovered the inscriptions in Syria journey to Egypt to find the tomb of Smenkhkare and his sister Scarab and the fabulous treasure they believe is there. Unscrupulous men and religious fanatics also seek the tomb, either to plunder it or to destroy it. Can the gods of Egypt protect their own, or will the ancients rely on modern day men and women of science?
Publisher: http://www.writers-exchange.com/Scarab6/
Amazon: http://mybook.to/ScarabBook6

Made in United States
North Haven, CT
13 October 2022

25403633R00212